The Moons of Earth

The Moons of Earth

Chad T. Lewis

Authors Choice Press
San Jose New York Lincoln Shanghai

The Moons of Earth

Authors Choice Press
an imprint of iUniverse, Inc.

For information address:
iUniverse, Inc.
5220 S. 16th St., Suite 200
Lincoln, NE 68512
www.iuniverse.com

ISBN: 0-595-19329-3

Printed in the United States of America

To Patty, David, and Kevin

EPIGRAPH

"If seed in the black earth
can turn into such beautiful roses
what might not the heart of man become
in its long journey toward the stars?"

G. K. Chesterton

PREFACE

I really mean it when I say that this book is a work of fiction. Names, characters, and many places are fictional. For the most part, any resemblance to actual events or locales or people, whether living or dead, is entirely coincidental. For those who know me it will be tempting to try and identify who's who in the story. I want to thank those of you who got into the story enough to do that. However, the characters in this book, though influenced by my experiences, are constructions created to serve the purposes of the story.

I hope you like the story.

Chad Lewis
Everett, 2001

ACKNOWLEDGEMENTS

It's a relief to finally be done with this book. Having co-authored a number of textbooks I thought fiction would be easy. Was I ever mistaken!

Key elements in the story were first expressed in an essay I wrote 34 years ago in a sophomore English class at Edmonds High School. Then, about 13 years ago my friend Grant Mitchell suggested that we work on a book. I ended up writing the book, but the inspiration for doing so came from this conversation and also from a poster on the wall of Grant's living room.

Others have been involved over the years. I owe a lot of thanks to Kathie Anderson who worked with me on an early draft. Special thanks also go to members of my writing group, Mary Smith and Mike Clyburn, and to Chris Kane, a friend who proofed the final manuscript and tried to teach me that "writing is thinking."

I owe particular and special thanks to my wife and best friend, Patty. She read millions of rough drafts and was, as with all things, a gentle guide and loving critique.

PROLOGUE: 1958

The Peacemaker sighed.

He gazed out at the Hive Sea, its surface broken by the twinkle of the lamps and island lumps scattered across a purple-gray sheen. Life-support machinery chugged incessantly and sounded like the view, "Hive Sea, Hive Sea, Hive Sea, Hive Sea." Behind him, a bug crackled against electrobars. As with two hundred generations of Arkadians before him, the Peacemaker had known only life in the Hive, a deteriorating interstellar ark lost in space. Rain splattered against the portal. The raindrums pulsed in response, counterpoint to the chugging machinery.

The Peacemaker turned from the portal and floated back into the scummy, shallow pond lapping at the walls of the cell. He throttled consciousness, moved his claws together until they touched and willed the flame to appear. Mesmerized by the bluish flicker, the Peacemaker spiraled into meditation. A blue planet had to be found. Soon.

Electrobars powered down as a worker zeromaster rippled in with the Peacemaker's meal, a monotonous paste of blue-green algaes suitable for a wawren.

* * * * * * * * * * * * * *

Shadows deepened the desert canyons from pink to purple. A hawk screamed down at Mickie as she wandered away from the evening campfire. The tow-headed, obstinate five-year old wasn't in danger. But she would soon be missed. Mickie crawled over a boulder searching restlessly for something, anything to slake her curiosity.

Last light caught Mickie in its curl before splashing against a sandstone wall. She turned to follow the light and gasped, then giggled, at her shadow. It loomed large like a monster against the face of cliff. She danced, the monster danced. The little girl laughed out loud. A sparkle set low within the dirt and scrabble at the base of the wall caught her attention. She moved toward the glitter, crouched, and dug with stubby fingers to find a half-buried crystal. The youngster stood with the bauble squeezed tightly in her fist and turned to watch the sun slide quickly below the horizon. The day's heat of the desert quickly faded with it. The little girl shivered. But she hardly noticed the cold. The sparkly crystal warmed to her touch. And it whispered.

"Mickie. Mickie! Michelle Jane Cole! Young lady, you get here this instant!" Shirley Cole bellowed out from the light of a campfire some fifty paces from where the little girl stood lost in dreams. Shirley nudged her eldest. "Johnny, go find Mickie." But the boy didn't move. *What's with these kids? Didn't God give them ears?* The woman raised her hand as though to cuff the boy, thought better of it, and let her flabby arm fall. As though he truly had "snapped out it," John Cole jumped up to find his sister. He scurried away from the campfire as though burned by its flame. He soon found her.

"Mickie, Mom wants you back. Now."

The little girl jumped at the sound of her brother's voice, whirling to face him. Squinting through the twilight, with wisdom beyond her years, she glimpsed his sadness.

Michelle Jane Cole stuffed the crystal into a pocket and followed her brother back to punishment.

     ✶   ✶   ✶   ✶   ✶   ✶   ✶   ✶   ✶   ✶   ✶   ✶   ✶   ✶

Connor heard his mom yell something about a straw, a last straw. A last, goddamn straw.

"Get the hell out, you lush."

"Yoush should talk. Bitsh!"

The screaming, along with a thump against the wall and the sound of glass breaking, trailed down the hallway, passed through a closed bedroom door, and snaked its tendrils around a skinny child who sat forlornly on his bed, elbows on his knees, hands pressed hard against his ears, eyes cast down. Connor cranked up the radio on the bedside table. Elvis Presley singing about a hound dog blasted out of tinny RCA speakers. The boy stretched out on his back, hands clasped behind his head, and stared at the ceiling's sparkly texture.

Connor belonged to a mommy and daddy that hated each other as much as they liked to get drunk.

It hadn't been bedtime when he went to bed. Howdy Doody and Robby the Robot watched him from his dresser top in the half light of a bedroom decorated in high 1950s style: salmon pink walls, hardwood floors, a red and brown plaid flannel bed cover, and Roy Rogers cowboy sheets.

The front door slammed hard and adult footsteps clumped away. Connor turned over on his stomach, shut his eyes against bitter tears, and waited.

His bedroom door abruptly opened spilling hallway light into the room. His mother staggered over and kneeled clumsily next to the bed. She turned down the radio, patted Connor on the back as though to soothe him, and smiled down at the little boy through her tears.

"Daddy'll come back, Honey Bun. Jus' a little mad at Mommy. I'll take care of you no matter what. Don' fret.

"You know, Honey Bun. You're goin' to be special. There's a special job for you in this life. You'll see. Mommy loves you. She loves you no matter what." When Connor didn't respond, she continued, "Kay, now.

Night-night Honey Bun. Sleep tight, don' let the bed bugs bite." She rubbed her son's back, stood unsteadily and wobbled out of the room.

Connor wasn't sure what happened next. Maybe he fell asleep. One moment, his mom was there, the next moment he saw the face of an old man. The old man asked Connor why his folks fought so much. At least that's what it seemed like the old man had asked. The next morning, Connor thought of Eldon Moss's first visit as a dream.

✳ ✳ ✳ ✳ ✳ ✳ ✳ ✳ ✳ ✳ ✳ ✳ ✳ ✳ ✳

The hyperdimensional beings became concerned about activities within a universe they knew as 7844491222333. The beings assigned an ethnographer and ordered a study. The first part follows.

Greetings,

As you know, about 15 billion years ago reality was a singularity of infinite density. All that was, that is, and that ever will be across all the heavens and dimensions fit into a single geometric point of perfect symmetry. This point, the size of the smallest molecule, exploded and bubbled into an infinite number of expanding bits—each the beginning of a universe. Space and time began.

In each universe, a plasma maelstrom a hundred times hotter than a class G sun began to cool. Five hundred thousand years passed before this plasma cooled enough for atoms to form and to survive. Galaxies, stars, planets, moons, asteroids, comets, quasars, pulsars, nebulae, what humans refer to as Einstein-Rosen bridges, and black holes followed. The third planet in one system, known by humans as "Earth" and a reference point for time's passage in this paragraph was not even a twinkle in the cosmic creator's eye. Billions more years passed.

About five billion years ago, gravity collapsed a solar nebula into a spinning disk. Ninety-nine percent of this stardust formed a star. The other one-percent evolved into a solar system of nine planets, fifty-five moons and assorted asteroids, meteors and debris. As such, most of this solar system is empty space buffeted by a solar wind.

Within this infant system, swirling collisions of hydrogen molecules and dust grew into larger and larger clumps that coalesced into overheated globes. Fissures split the hardening crust across the breadth of one such globe, allowing lava and gases to escape. Over eons, this release formed a primitive atmosphere that included water vapor. The vapor cooled and condensed, falling as rain to the sizzling surface, creating steam and still more vapor. The cycle continued for millions of centuries until the cooling planet accepted its watery gift and the first seas appeared.

In time, the seas begat life.

1968: Days of Rage

CHAPTER 1

Connor Alexander dodged the baton. The cop cursed under his breath and swung again, but his target ducked under his arm and wiggled back into the mob. Less fortunate others writhed on the ground, arms wrapped around their heads to blunt the rain of blows. Connor glanced back as he ran, grimly satisfied at his escape, then slammed into a girl. Her surprised cry was muffled in the last wave of a chant that echoed throughout Seattle's University District: "Hey, hey, JFK, how many boys did you kill today?"

Thousands of demonstrators had marched down the 45th Avenue ramp onto the freeway during the dinner hour commute. Traffic was stopped. The sound of engines, horns, and the banshee sound of sirens tangled with the cries of the mob.

Connor paused and sized her up. Looking hard at the girl's vulnerable beauty, he noticed she bled from a small cut under her left eye. He grabbed her arm and said, "We gotta split." The girl let herself be led.

On a humid March day, 1968, the Age of Aquarius lay upon a troubled world. Shortly after the New Year, a B-52 carrying four hydrogen bombs crashed and burned through Greenland's ice. North Korean patrol boats seized the American intelligence ship Pueblo a few days later. Bobby Kennedy and Martin Luther King Jr. soon would be dead. Russian tanks soon would smash Alexander Dubcek's Prague spring and restore a worker's paradise to Czechoslovakia. John F. Kennedy had survived an assassin's bullet in Texas only to be buried by the war in Vietnam.

In March 1968, Connor Alexander and Annie Simpson didn't know that the Hive was lost.

Riot police worked the fleeing mob. Banners, Vietcong flags and picket signs fell to the ground beneath clouds of tear gas drifting east, carried by afternoon winds off Puget Sound. A phalanx of police in riot gear smashed into the heart of the crowd immune to the crack of rocks and bottles that bounced off gas masks and shields.

"We gotta keep moving," Connor urged the girl as she sagged beside him. Tear gas tore at their eyes as they struggled, gagging, through the center of the melee. Annie still said nothing. Her eyes watered from the acrid bite of the tear gas. Her straight, red hair streamed down her back as she ran alongside Connor.

✷ ✷ ✷ ✷ ✷ ✷ ✷ ✷ ✷ ✷ ✷ ✷ ✷ ✷

At 37, Shirley Cole was already gray. And obese. Fat quivered from her arms as she leaned forward squeezing the steering wheel as though to exorcise the demonstrators. She rustled and sweated uncomfortably in the muggy coolness. *Serves 'em right,* she thought. Shirley had been stranded on the freeway for the past 50 minutes. *Damn hippies.* Shirley gasped at the unclean thought and mentally begged God's forgiveness. Still, she had cause for anger, aside from the inconvenience of sitting in a stalled car for what seemed like hours. Johnny, her eldest, was fighting in Vietnam.

As an accountant, Shirley liked numbers. She couldn't control her craving for food, but she could control her figures. Numbers, straight and clean on a ledger, stayed where they belonged. They followed the rules, marched neatly into bottom-line totals. They didn't clog traffic in the middle of rush hour and didn't scream obscenities at the country's

President. Numbers didn't peg rocks at police to protest a war Johnny was willing to die for. Numbers didn't commit treason.

"Dear Lord, give me strength," she muttered as she searched for the bag of chocolate-covered peanuts she had stashed in the glove box. "What is wrong with these children? How could the Devil himself have reached so far into their hearts?"

Clutching the candy, Shirley looked with disgust at the demonstrators streaming up the freeway ramp alongside her. She glimpsed a young woman with long red hair being swept along by the mob. *Annie? At a demonstration?* With a shake of her chins, Shirley popped candy into her mouth and dismissed the thought. That couldn't be Annie. Johnny's girlfriend had long red hair, but would never be involved in a demonstration. "Dear Annie," she said out loud. "Such a good girl."

The clouds drifting in from over Puget Sound unzipped. The smell of spring rain mixed with the heavy stink of exhaust fumes and lingering bite of tear gas. Engines roared as the traffic picked its way through the dissipating mob like a centipede oozing through sludge.

Shirley restarted her engine. Her thoughts flickered from the demonstration to the meatloaf that waited in the refrigerator at home. Perhaps she'd add green chilies to the Cole family staple. The chilies added a zip that only Shirley and her eldest, Johnny, seemed to enjoy. Her thoughts drifted to Johnny. A good boy. She remembered rocky times when he had been young. That family vacation to the Grand Canyon for example. But things smoothed out right after she found the saving grace of the Lord.

* * * * * * * * * * * * * *

PFC John Cole wiped warm rain out of his eyes and looked up from the rattling burst of the M-60. *Hootch is still holding up. But not for long.* He sunk his skinny six-foot, two-inch frame down into the muck. Water streamed off the jungle hat covering his shaved head. He had angular, sharp features, a stark contrast to his mother's shaking flab.

The thick mud clawed at him. The monsoon cloudburst had soaked every fiber of his fatigues and his body. *God's pissing on us.* Cole smiled at the thought. Then, wiggling to stretch his cramped arm without giving away his position, he reconsidered his blasphemy. *What would Mom think?* He chuckled silently, with just an edge of bitterness.

He had finished high school graduation requirements early. Rather than sit in study halls, he got his mom's okay and joined up at 17. His dad had really fought her on that one. John couldn't remember another time when the old man had seriously stood up to him or to his mom.

At first, being in the army seemed a lot like playing high school football. Boot camp at Ft. Benning and Special Forces training had been like 'two a days' in the heat of early September. He experienced familiar chants, drills, sweat, teamwork, and sergeants as overzealous coaches. The experience in country changed his view of this particular game, however. And Annie wasn't on the sidelines. Only memories of her cheered him on now.

He unaccountably thought of the crystal Michelle had found as a little girl. *Now, why am I thinking of that?* Mickie was all right. If he ever got out of this mess he vowed to actually talk to his sibling, even to call her "Michelle" rather than use the family nickname she despised. Cole now viewed Michelle's rebelliousness in a different light. Vietnam had been a great teacher.

The reconnaissance team had tramped for three days through steaming, soaked elephant grass and brush in Quang Ngai Province. The enemy was nowhere, yet everywhere. A booby trap, a sniper's bullet, an ambush all offered their grim potential to the men during every minute, of every hour, of every day, of every night, on patrol. Tension never stopped circulating from Cole's guts to his palpating heart and back down again to his bowels. Not that he thought much about his bowels while on patrol. The men hardly ever dropped their drawers when in the bush. Quang Ngai Province was one place you just didn't want to get caught with your pants down.

The squad had reached a landing zone for extraction when the distinctive cranking of an AK-47 sounded from a hootch on the edge of the LZ. The patrol returned fire. M-60 and M-16 slugs started to sting and tumble through the hootch like a stream of hysterical wasps.

                    ✳ ✳ ✳ ✳ ✳ ✳ ✳ ✳ ✳ ✳ ✳ ✳ ✳ ✳

Annie smiled at the van. The blue Volkswagen microbus had dented sides and a porthole in the back door. A blue, green, and gold American flag had been painted just below the windshield. The tires were frayed.

Connor put his arm around her waist, happy when she didn't shake him off. The chick was absolutely gorgeous. Great body. He feasted on the perfect curve of her unencumbered smallish breasts under a thin white blouse. She wore a blue corduroy coat and a brown cotton granny dress that hung down to her ankles. With her beautiful smile, perfect white teeth, and flowing red hair, she was a picture of erotic perfection to Connor's testosterone-influenced sensibilities.

"Whose van?" Annie asked, still a bit out of breath.

"Mine. His name's 'Renny.'"

"What's your name?"

"Connor."

"Do you have a last name, Connor?"

"Yeah. Alexander."

"That's a first name." Annie smiled, then added, "I'm Annie Simpson. Nice to meet you, Connor." She gently took his hand.

Classy, Connor thought.

"So that's your van, huh?" Annie wasn't sure just how old Connor was, but he didn't look much older than 17 or 18.

"Yeah, Renny's really mine."

"Where's your place? Do you live with your folks?"

"No. I live by myself. Well, actually, with people in a house on Boylston."

"Over by Lake Union?"

"Yeah. We got a great view of the lake and Space Needle from the top-story balcony."

"What do you do?"

Connor looked uncomfortable. "I'm a stocker at a Safeway on Capitol Hill."

"You finished high school already?" Annie was capping off her senior year, then faced four more years of business school at the University of Washington. She planned to major in finance.

"Not exactly. I sort of quit last year." Connor added, "You know, we really should split."

"Your parents let you quit school? They sound mellow."

"Yeah. They pretty much let me do what I want. Hey, do you want to make it over to my place?" He fidgeted.

Annie looked at Connor. His long curly brown hair, wire rim glasses, and purple, collarless Joe Cocker shirt fit the times. He had an old look in his hazel eyes that she could just see through the distortion of his heavy glass lenses. He had a wiry, muscular frame. A large, unusually shaped strawberry-colored birthmark peeked out of Connor's hairline just above his right eye.

She flipped the coppery length of her hair back over her shoulder and laughed, as much in relief at the strange turn of events as anything else, and paused before responding. Her studies were important, and a pile of books waited at home. She was tired of guys hitting on her all the time, as this guy seemed to be doing. Her status as a high school cheerleader wouldn't score points with this flower child. Then, there was John.

Annie giggled nervously again. Who would have ever thought? A phone call from a friend enticed her away from her books. She had thought it'd be cool to experience a demonstration, but sure hadn't planned on being in the middle of a riot. She had lost track of the friend in the crush. Thoughts of studies faded as Connor's nearness caught her breath. *What would John say? Yet, his letters seemed from so far way.*

"What's so funny?" Connor looked perplexed.

"Nothing. Sure, I'll come over. But I need a ride home when *I* say it's time."

"Yeah, sure, no problem." An ambulance howling down the avenue in the direction of the freeway almost drowned out his Connor's words.

Connor walked over, yanked open the driver's side door and beckoned Annie into the cab with an exaggerated flourish. She delicately stepped up and slid across the bench seat to the passenger side. She looked out the window at a group of demonstrators laughing as they ran down the avenue. *What am I doing?*

Connor slid in beside her and said, "You know, you're still bleeding. I can put a Band-Aid on that at the house."

"Thanks, Connor. I'm sure I'll be all right. The blood's not exactly running into my eyes."

Connor started Renny and gently shifted the van's cranky gears. Renny puttered through the heart of Seattle's University District. Connor drove cautiously. Karma protected him because Fate offered the only insurance rates he could afford.

The squeaking wipers, put-put of the engine, and gasoline smell of the heater blowing hot air directly from the engine had a comforting feel, but Annie still felt shaky. *Did this guy just pick me up?*

Though Connor did most of the talking on the way to the house, he still found out Annie had never been to a demonstration. He realized, as he pulled up to the curb of the Boylston house, how scary and out-of-character it had been for Annie to leave with him, a stranger, to a strange place.

The house was a strange place. The beat-up Victorian mansion had eight bedrooms. Spreading the rent among ten people with food stamps shared equally among all meant the living was cheap and easy, though no one called the living arrangement a commune. That would have been too brown-ricey.

Oblio and Arrow, the house dogs, hardly stirred from their positions on a Salvation Army davenport as Annie followed Connor warily into the living room. Binky meowed in greeting and rubbed up against Connor's legs.

"You okay, Annie?" Connor moved closer to the girl. Her jasmine perfume mixed with the warmth of her breath. To Connor, she smelled like spring flowers on a beautiful day. He looked into her eyes and whispered, "I'd better get some peroxide and a Band-Aid for that cut."

"No, that's okay. I'm cool." Annie stared down at the floor.

Connor smiled, then walked over to sit on the couch. He looked up at the girl. She stood awkwardly in the middle of the room.

"I'm really all right. I don't need anything for the cut. It's stopped bleeding. The air does it good." Her voice had a husky edge. "Look, Connor, maybe it wasn't such a good idea for me to come over. Maybe I should go. I freaked out at the demonstration. Thanks for your help, but...well, if I could use your phone I'll call for a ride."

"We don't have a phone."

"No phone?"

"Yeah. Hey, stay for awhile. I'll drop you off when you want to go. It'll be okay. I won't hit on you. Really."

He looks sincere. Annie smoothed her dress, rumpled her hair, and finally said, "Okay, that's cool. But I can't stay long." She continued to stand.

Connor lit a candle, settled back on the dusty old couch, and reached over to switch on the stereo. Neil Young singing "Down by the River" whined from speakers in the corners of the room. He began to fiddle around with a pouch he had pulled from his pocket.

Annie looked around, unaccustomed to the disorder but drawn to the warmth and the earth colors of the room as the fading afternoon sun and candlelight danced off cheap East Indian tapestries on the walls. She smelled incense. Connor leaned over the battered coffee table and offered her a pipe. She froze.

"What's that?"

"Weed."

"Weed?"

"Yeah, grass. You know."

Annie looked toward the front door.

"You don't get high?" Connor asked, his voice laced with disbelief.

"No. Look, Connor, I really should go."

He put the pipe down. "I'll put it away. It's not a big deal. Really, everything's cool. Why don't you sit down? I won't bite."

She nodded, not entirely convinced, but sat on the couch a safe distance from Connor anyway.

"Connor, what were you doing out there today?"

What was I doing? Nothing in particular. I was bored. Marching in the street looked to be more fun than watching the tube, or dropping acid and watching the wallpaper melt. He stiffly replied, "I was making a statement about the war. It's not right. It was corrupt leadership, not the Vietnamese people who got us to invade their country."

"No…really, Connor. What were you really doing out there?" Annie laughed. "Why should I believe you?"

Connor returned the laugh. "I told the truth. I really am committed to ending the war." *And to getting into your pants.*

The two settled into a comfortable rhythm. Periodically, Connor switched tunes on the stereo. Annie moved closer. Shared middle-class values had created a common bond despite surface differences. They were members of the same tribe after all, though Annie's polish disconcerted Connor and aroused him. The spring rain returned and thumped the poorly insulated roof as the two murmured about nothing in particular. Jimmy Hendrix gazed down on them—a voyeur from his place in a black light poster.

Connor looked at Annie. She smiled back.

He held out his hand. "Come here…"

"Why?" She said coyly. "I thought you weren't going to hit on me."

"Uh…well, you know. I thought. You know, it just feels like I've known you all my life."

The oldest line in the book.

She looked softly at Connor with knowing eyes and smiled again. "You know, Connor, I have a boyfriend in Vietnam."

Crap.

She leaned over and kissed him gently on the lips. "But we weren't getting along all that well."

"Sorry to hear that." *Hee hee.*

"Anyway, I have to get home. I will see you again."

Connor dropped her off shortly after dark. He thought about Annie on the way home. They had talked about a lot of things, but he hadn't told her about his parents getting a divorce, leaving him and the Seattle area behind. He'd been lucky to find a job and a place to stay. He lived out of Renny for a while, crashing on couches, eating peanut butter and jelly sandwiches, and washing a knapsack of clothes at Laundromats before finally landing the job and finding the room at the Boylston house. The grind of working full-time and staying awake in class had been too much, so he quit school. He couldn't very well quit working.

Upon returning to the house, Connor stepped out on the dining room balcony. City lights reflected off Lake Union. Stars twinkled high above Queen Anne Hill in the distance.

CHAPTER 2

Shirley pulled into the garage next to Ralph's Ford Fairlane. She carried groceries into the house, dropping the sacks onto the kitchen table with a gasp. Ralph, sloth-like from his favorite chair in the living room, called out, "Hello, dear."

"Hi, honey," she wheezed back. "Where're the kids?"

"Mickie went for a walk and Chuck's over at Frank's," he said. "They'll be back in time for dinner. Why're you late?"

"Honey, you never would have believed what happened on the way home," Shirley's voice quivered with indignation as she started to put away cans of vegetables. "A mob of hippies blocked the freeway near the 45th Street exit. I was stuck forever in the rain. I thank the good Lord every day that our children have avoided that garbage. I stopped by to pick up those chilies you like so much in the meat loaf."

Ralph grimaced and said, "A mob of what?"

"Hippies," she said, walking into the living room to confront Ralph, hands on hips. "I told you, hippies blocked traffic. You wouldn't have believed it. It took the police an hour to remove the vermin. You know, I thought I saw Annie in the street. I haven't heard from her since the week after Johnny left. We should give the girl a call. See if she'd like to come to dinner. We did promise Johnny we'd keep an eye on her."

"Sure, sure," Ralph said, his attention swiveling between Shirley and a rerun of *The Outer Limits*. In silky tones, the commentator lamented the plight of a human transformed by scientists into an alien. The scientists wanted the arrival of the ersatz alien by "space ship" to scare humans into working together and cooperating. They wanted their scheme to make a difference. It didn't. Ralph returned his attention to his wife just in time to catch Shirley's backside as she waddled back to the kitchen.

Shirley went on about her day as she prepared dinner in the kitchen, calling out to Ralph, "I finished reconciling payroll. What a mess! I don't now— know what they were thinking, moving payroll to Maggie. It takes me twice as long at the end of the the month to fix her mistakes. She and I got into it today. I'm sorry she thinks I'm second-guessing her, but my books need to be right. You know I think Maggie's troubled. She should listen to the Lord. I think I'll introduce her to the Reverend Stringer. He would do her some good. Lord knows that would be a personal offering to have to spend Sunday mornings with that woman. It's bad enough that I have to put up with her all week long. You know…" Shirley rattled on like a stone-filled can swinging on a pendulum. She paused momentarily from her work, opening a new package of Oreos and devouring a few.

Mickie and Chuck pushed into the house through the back door at the same time. Chuck really had been at Frank's house. Mickie, who preferred being addressed by her given name of "Michelle," had been smoking a cigarette under the Madrona tree in the backyard.

"Wipe your feet, kids," Shirley called at the slam of the back door. The twins weren't really kids. They were mature 15 year-olds and very different. It was hard to believe they came out of the same womb.

Shirley refused to see that Michelle looked like the freeway marchers. Michelle was as petite as her mother was large though she was buxom for a female of any age. She still had on school clothes: a tie-dyed T-shirt and a leather skirt. The crystal, found by Michelle that a Grand Canyon family vacation so long ago, sparkled from its place outside her T-shirt where it hung from a gold chain—the chain, a gift from Ralph when

Michelle had turned 13. Michelle battled her mom daily over her long, blond ironed hair and, so far, had won. Shirley's pleas to "put some curl into it" went unheeded.

Chuck's looks mirrored his interests. He had actually enjoyed learning to use a slide rule. He favored white short sleeve shirts with pocket protectors, baggy slacks, white socks, and oxfords. He wore thick glasses and was fat like his mother. All the Cole children had high IQs, but only Chuck looked it.

"Mickie, honey, come help finish supper," her mother called as the girl attempted a quick, and quiet, getaway to her room upstairs. Michelle groaned inwardly and muttered "Don't call me 'Mickie'" and sat down on the stairs with her head in her hands.

Chuck tossed the evening paper to his father and plopped into the chair beside the sofa. Ralph unfolded the paper and made a half-hearted attempt to read the headlines, but his attention ping-ponged between the paper, the news that had just come on television, and Shirley's yammering that flowed in a steady stream from the kitchen. The newscaster started to talk about Vietnam and about body counts. Ralph stood up and gently clicked off the television. He collected the newspaper and headed for the dining room. Chuck joined him.

"Chuck, call your sister," Shirley said as she carried steaming dishes to the table.

"Mickie, get your ass down here!" Chuck shouted on his way to the dinner table, beating his father there by a step. He hunkered down with a playful smirk and waited for the fallout. Ralph glared at Chuck for a moment, then quickly retreated behind his paper.

Michelle came in. She and Shirley both jumped on Chuck.

"Don't call me Mickie! My name is Michelle!"

"Charles," Shirley spat out, rumbling into the room with a pan of meatloaf in one hand. "That is enough! We do not speak to one another like that and you know it. The Lord has asked that we honor one another. He asks precious little of us in return for His sacrifice. The least we can do is follow His commands. He is, after all, protecting Johnny in Vietnam." She returned to the kitchen with a shake of her head.

Michelle leaned back in her chair restlessly.

"Thank the good Lord this day is almost over," proclaimed Shirley from her place at the head of the table.

Michelle smartly replied "Amen" and feigned eating.

Shirley frowned, first at Michelle, then at Ralph.

On cue, Ralph meekly muttered a frozen blessing over the meatloaf that had survived Shirley's traffic delay. Chuck and Ralph grabbed for the mashed potatoes, but Shirley got there first.

"Nothing like a good meal," she said. "I'm starved. Maggie and I had an early lunch. Ralph, after dinner, I think I'll make up a batch of those brownies Johnny likes so much. Remember that time over on Green Lake when he snuck a whole batch by himself? He was a sorry little boy that day."

"Dad, when's John coming home?" Michelle asked, frowning at the green chilies she was picking out of her meatloaf.

"When we're done with the job we started over there, Mickie." Ralph took another bite of meatloaf and chewed distractedly. He tried not to think about Vietnam. He doubted what the politicians said about a "quick victory." He remembered the same breezy confidence about having the boys home for Christmas from Korea. Then the Chinese counterattacked across the Yalu River. The quick retreat across the frozen waste of the Chosin Reservoir had been frustrating and horrifying. Still, Ralph and his comrades-at-arms at "frozen Chosin" had felt pride when they returned home. He doubted John would feel the same upon his return.

Under the surface, drowning in dark waters that had defined him since his return sixteen years before, he remembered bracing a crew-served weapon—that had lost crew members and a bipod along the way—with the frozen corpse of a Chinese soldier. He remembered firing into waves of screaming, grenade-throwing, brown-quilted enemy. He remembered the chattering of the burp guns. The bugles. Bugles used by the enemy to signal an attack. How could he forget the wailing of the bugles? Twenty below zero in the days before they ever talked about "wind chill factor." Screaming shadows leaping over his foxhole. How could marines be overrun? He hid in his hole all night afraid to look up, afraid to peer over the edge under the frozen, headless torso of his buddy; death's reek and hopelessness his only companions. At daybreak, Marine Corsairs scorched the battlefield with flames that boomed and rolled over the hills and over the enemy.

Then, the long retreat south. Wounded from shell fragments, hungry, thirsty, burning from frostbite, soiling himself with diarrhea from eating dirty snow, Ralph returned with a Silver Star he never wore. The true heroes had already died. The most important part of Ralph died with them.

"Dad, please don't call me 'Mickie,'" Michelle stabbed Ralph's thoughts with that icy edge to her voice that is a particular specialty of teenage girls. "I really don't understand what John is doing over there."

"Oh, I'm sorry, honey. John is…"

"Michelle, that will be enough," warned Shirley. She had wanted Johnny to fight Godless Communism, but struggled with fear for his safety every day. She kept this fear behind a Great Wall of patriotism, religion and order. She felt any chipping away at that wall threatened Johnny's safety.

"Your brother's helping us stop Communism," Ralph finished. "Your brother is fighting Communists right now, as we eat." He took another bite. "Good meatloaf, dear," he added.

Michelle wrinkled her brow for a moment and continued. "My history teacher says the Vietcong are nationalists, that Ho Chi Minh fought the Japanese, the French and now us, that we backed the wrong side, that…"

"Shut up." Shirley's voice was cold and quiet. "How can you talk like that with Johnny over there? Do I pay tax dollars for you to learn that garbage? That teacher should be fired."

"God, Mom," Michelle sputtered. "Maybe there is another side to all this. I want John home, too. I want the war over. Give peace a chance."

"Yeah…You and John Lennon." Chuck cut in.

"Mellow out, Chuck."

Shirley glared down the table. What was this world coming to? First, those hippies this afternoon. Now her own home was being infected. Her voice rose. "Michelle, do *not* use the Lord's name in vain. And what is this 'mellow out?' And what about your *hair*! God, give me strength!"

✶ ✶ ✶ ✶ ✶ ✶ ✶ ✶ ✶ ✶ ✶ ✶ ✶ ✶

The patrol slithered away from the burning hootch. No one could have survived that inferno, but the enemy might still be lurking in the tree line. Contingency called for an alternate LZ two klicks south. If that failed, it would be a three-day walkout for the team. Link-up with friendlies wouldn't be easy at the end of the trail.

Damn, Cole thought to himself. He wanted to load up and get out. It was late afternoon, one hour before dusk. The rain had stopped. The dripping jungle smelled like low tide.

The Lieutenant gave the signal to advance. Lurps rose up and splashed forward in the direction of the alternative LZ. LRRPs ("lurps," long range reconnaissance and patrol) were two to six-man elite forces that operated deep in enemy territory. Lurps were the eyes and ears of the army units they served.

Advance? Cole thought, as he moved slowly, feeling the fear of the other men. He muttered out loud, "How's he know it's clear?"

"*INCOMING!*"

The team dove into elephant grass at the side of the trail and crawled back toward the double-canopy protection of the jungle. Mortars and heavy machine gun fire tracked their position. The team had stumbled across a company-size force of Vietcong, probably elements of the VC 48th Local Force Battalion. A tree line 200 yards distant across a clearing had cloaked the enemy.

The sniper fire had come from the tree line, not the hut. Blasting the hootch gave away their position. *Damn!* Cole, face down in the muck, cursed silently. He wondered again about the people that might have lived in the hut.

"We need help! Call in fast movers now. Call it in. Now. Now!" Lt. Rogers whispered urgently to the communications officer. Support could sometimes be called in from napalm-bearing jets or Cobra gunships. Often, no help was available. This time, it was. Calling in a strike on a position two hundred yards away was risky, but the team had no choice. If they retreated, they would be run to ground and die, or be captured. If they stood their ground they would just die.

"The Lieutenant shouted down the line, "Five minutes. Keep down and be awake," buzzed Cole's radio. Cole didn't need to be reminded.

Battle smoke encouraged the deepening dusk. The enemy added green tracers to the barrage. The lurps stretched out in the brush, each mortar blast lifted them off the ground.

Cole willed his body still deeper into the muck.

The rattling, freight-train scream of rocket propelled grenades joined the barrage. Cole sensed and felt the grenade that blew his lieutenant to pieces twenty paces away. Foliage cut by whizzing bullets drifted down like a perverse snowfall.

A brace of F-100 Super Sabre jet fighters boomed over the battlefield. The barrage stopped. Cole lifted his face out of the mud. The jets blasted over the target and circled back, this time just above the treetops. A cluster of shiny canisters tumbled out of their bellies as if in slow motion. The whoomp and heat of the napalm rolled over the team as the men lay on their stomachs in the warm muck. *Just like openin' an oven when the broiler's on,* Cole thought. The distance and roaring blaze cushioned the team from the screams of dying men but the oily, purple-black smoke that boiled from the jellied gasoline looked, and smelled, like death.

The team waited, motionless, another hour. One hundred percent humidity and 90-degree heat, dripping vegetation, smoke, dust and stinging insects tortured them. Cole wanted to sneeze, and then to scratch, then to sneeze, and then to wipe the sweat funneling off his brow. To kill time now that the enemy was dead, he looked at patterns in the clumps of smoke that rose from the pockets of fire across the clearing. He watched mesmerized as a death's head grinned in the smoke and then disintegrated as a Huey assault transport clattered through the illusion. The doorgunner shredded the opposing charred, smoldering treeline with his M-60 as the helicopter gently swirled onto the LZ. The men ran toward safety.

On the trip back to Firebase Alice, Cole sat on his helmet in the transport bay. He knew sitting on the helmet was nuts but didn't want to lose his to a lucky round from below. *Only 170 days and 12 hours until I return to the World,* he thought. He thought about an upcoming two-week R&R, rest and relaxation perverted by the troops to "I&I," intercourse and intoxication. He thought he might go to Saigon. Thoughts of intercourse made him think of Annie.

"Hey, amigo, got a light?" Parsons shouted above the clatter. Cole handed him a lighter. "Nice barbecue, huh?" Parsons flicked the lighter and expertly cupped it to start a cigarette. He looked up and said, "Too bad about the lieutenant. At least there wasn't much to scrape up."

But Cole didn't think he meant it so didn't reply. He had been well inclined toward Parsons but now, after his time in country, Parsons struck Cole as a typical gung-ho, blood-and-guts type. But then wasn't that what he was? What's the point? He despised being around morons like Parsons while the enemy, like jungle mud, oozed back into every hole punched in their ranks. He wasn't even sure anymore who the enemy even *was.*

* * * * * * * * * * * * * *

Two weeks after the lieutenant's death, Annie sprawled next to Connor on a blanket at the Woodland Park Zoo. The place swarmed with families, children, frisbees, and the napalm smell of lighter fluid on charcoal briquettes. Every now and then, an elephant trumpeted from the distant elephant house, or a toddler squealed at monkey house antics. Final exams beckoned. Annie had to get back to schoolwork. What had happened to throw her so completely into hanging out with a guy she hardly knew? Her friends disapproved. And John. She hadn't been away from him for any length of time since the sixth grade. Now, she lay in the sun next to Connor.

With her folks out of town, she had spent last night at Connor's. The two made love the first time the previous evening, then again in the morning. She liked being with Connor. She treasured memories of John. She didn't like feeling guilty.

"Connor, what about John?" she said.

Connor rolled over, smiled sleepily and replied, "What about him?" Not expecting an answer, he asked another question. "Tell me again. What's he do over there?" The March sunshine, sandwiched between Pacific Northwest storm fronts, was unseasonably bright and warm.

"He's a lurp," Annie said. "I'm not sure what that is, but I think he's some kind of green beret. I know it's dangerous. John and I have been together a long time."

Connor smiled. *Yeah, but not last night.* He considered his adversary's bad luck to be crawling around in the jungle risking his life, and for what? Meanwhile this gorgeous chick had moved on. Or had she? He looked into Annie's soft, green eyes and thought about the night before. He smiled again. *Whatever. She's with me now.*

Though Connor felt sorry for John, he sure didn't feel guilty. War is hell for a lot of reasons. It always changes lives. They'd all be dust in 100 years anyway no matter what happened. Maybe even dust much sooner from getting nuked.

Be here now. That was the thing.

CHAPTER 3

Lurp recons kept failing. More often than not ambush teams were ambushed and search and destroy missions found little to destroy. Top brass screamed. Command decided to take the fight to the enemy during the third week of March.

The captain scowled down at Parsons and Cole.

"Okay, listen up. You guys have sat on your butts long enough. You're going out as forward-observers. Cole, you're team leader."

Cole looked up. The steamy humidity in the briefing room felt like the locker room after football practice. Cole missed football practice.

"Yes sir. What's the target?"

"A hamlet north of here."

"What's up?"

"You'll be scouting the ground for Charlie Company, 1st Battalion. G-2 has F1 intel that figures 250 to 280 well-equipped and motivated enemy to be in the area. You'll need to blend in on this one. Now, keep your mouths shut until I'm finished."

The briefing droned on for a half-hour. Heat pounded down through the corrugated metal roof of the hooch. Bluebottle flies buzzed everywhere. They could have run the rapids in the sweat pouring off the men.

Cole and Parsons prepared for insertion the next day.

Cole gathered his pistol belt, web-carrying harness, first aid pouch, knife, strobe light, grenades—six frag, three smoke, two white phosphorous and two claymore mines, flares, compass, canteens, map, rations, ten loaded M-16 magazines and his rifle. He taped all parts of the gear that might reflect light or rattle. He cleaned and lubricated his M-16, oiled the bolt, and slammed in a magazine. He jumped up and down and rolled on the packed dirt floor to make sure he didn't make noise. He covered his face and hands with black and green greasepaint that matched the tiger-striped camouflage of his fatigues and took a deep breath.

"Hey Cole, ready to rock and roll?" Parsons chuckled. A real poet. Cole sighed.

✳ ✳ ✳ ✳ ✳ ✳ ✳ ✳ ✳ ✳ ✳ ✳ ✳ ✳

"Carry out on three!" Connor winced. He'd been breaking down cardboard boxes in the back, fantasizing about Annie.

His job stocking groceries at the Safeway on Seattle's Capitol Hill didn't pay much, but it helped make ends meet. Occasionally, he had to do scut work, like carrying out groceries during the day when the boxboys were in school. Still, the job paid union scale of $3.35 an hour, $1.60 an hour more than the part-timers, and his boss, Larry, let him keep his hair, even if he had to wear a hair net.

Connor walked to the front. He felt dizzy as he hoisted a lady's groceries from a check stand into a cart. He followed her out the automatic doors into a downpour, her screaming kids in tow. He carefully placed the bags into the trunk of the harried woman's car. She smiled. He smiled back. Another wave of dizziness rolled over him. He started to sweat.

"Thanks, ma'am. Have a good day." *I feel awful.*

Connor turned toward the store entrance. Through sheets of rain he saw an old man trying, without much success, to stuff loaded sacks into the back seat of a huge, strange-looking maroon station wagon. Odds and ends, clothing, and just plain junk kept getting in the way. It looked like the gnome lived out of his car. *Now, why did I think of him as a 'gnome'?*

Connor trotted over. "Here, let me give you a hand."

"Why thanks, son. Good of you to give a feller some help."

The sight of the customer unsettled Connor. It wasn't just the old man's peculiarity. Something tickled at his memory. He'd seen the little old man somewhere before. He unaccountably thought of the times he had spent in his bedroom listening to his parents' fight. He helped the old man get his groceries piled on top the bird's nest chaos of the back seat, and slammed the car door several times before it stayed put. The effort exhausted Connor.

"Name's Moss. Eldon Moss. I'm pleased to make your acquaintance." With that the little man reached out and seemed to shake Connor's hand.

What the hell is going on here? Gawd, I feel awful!

"You don't look so good, son." When Connor didn't reply, Moss continued. "Why ain't you in school?" Eldon Moss rasped as he grabbed his benefactor's arm and moved toward the driver's door. He barely stood level with Connor's armpit. Connor stumbled after him as both stepped through an ankle-high puddle.

The question surprised Connor. He answered without thinking. "Don't know exactly. Have to make a living and can't do that sitting in class."

"Did ya like high school, Connor?" Moss stopped moving, and looked up at Connor.

"It was okay. I got some good grades. Hey, how'd you know my name? I didn't tell you my name."

Moss didn't reply. He shuffled to the door and waited for Connor to open it. Once settled in his seat, he rolled down the creaky window. He smiled, reached into his pocket and offered Connor a handful of change. Connor returned the smile and said, "Sorry, you know we can't take tips. How'd you know my name?"

"You're a good kid. How about if I jus' leave you with a bit of advice? How's that grab you?"

"Well sure, Mr. Moss." *Advice. Just the thing I need. Why's this fossil so nosey? How does he know me?*

"Important things gonna happen in your life. Gotta get involved. Times a changing, boy. You'll get passed by if you don't get your shoot together, and you can dot the 'i' on that! By the way, I ain't a fossil, son. Matter a fact, I'm pretty special myself." He winked at a surprised Connor, started the engine and, dwarfed by the steering wheel, turned to wave back at Connor as the car chugged out of the parking lot, spewing blue smoke that swirled into the leaden sky.

It kept raining. There was more rain than normal that spring in 1968. Connor walked back into the store shaking his head. The old guy gave him the creeps. Larry, his boss, met him as the automatic door swished open.

"Hey, what were you doin' out there?"

"What do you mean? Helping out. I carried out for a lady and then helped an old guy."

"I saw the lady. Then I saw you talking to yourself. Making like you were putting away invisible groceries."

"What? C'mon Larry, give me a break."

"No. Really, it was weird. You all right, Connor?"

Larry's having fun. "Look, I'm not feeling so hot. If it's okay, I'll take my break now. Maybe even split a little early. I'm just about finished in back."

"Sure. We don't want you gettin' sick."

Connor went over to the closed snack bar, walked behind the counter, poured some coffee, and settled on a stool. He thought about Annie and her old boyfriend, John. *She likes that army guy a lot more than she lets on. Maybe it's because he's older than me.* His mind wandered. Maybe he had a fever.

The store door swished open to his left. Eldon Moss tottered in and walked up to Connor.

Connor stood. "Forget something? Everything okay?"

"I'm okay. How in the Sam scratch are ya, son?" Wispy gray hair peeked out from under the New York Yankees baseball cap Eldon Moss favored. He wore old Levis, with an old-fashioned white dress shirt and a brown bow tie. A red hanky jutted out a back pocket. His tennis shoes were scuffed. Robin egg-blue eyes, set back in the craggy recesses of a weathered face, twinkled.

"Well, actually I think I'm sick. Why're you back?"

"Been thinking about what we was talking about?"

"What? You mean about getting involved?"

"Yup. What did you think I was talking about? Get the wax out of your ears, son."

"I'm doing the best I can." *Yeah, sure I'm doing the best I can. Actually, it's tough enough just getting through the day and night.* Thinking about the night reminded him of Annie.

"Who's Annie?"

"What? How'd you know about Annie? And how do you know my name?"

"I know about a lot of things, son. Like, for instance, I know you're gonna end up cleaning that grill." Moss pointed to the snack bar grill. "Is cleaning grills and packing groceries any way to make a difference? Didn't your ma used to say you were goin' to be someone special?"

"Give me a break. I need a job. Hey, how did you…"

"You're close to being dead meat, son. You'll get drafted unless you get through high school and into college. You realize boys just wet behind the ears—boys like you—is being blown to bits over there? Where's your brains, son? You ain't got the judgment the good Creator gave a grasshopper. Why do you humans always have to fight things?"

"I've thought about that. I've thought about going to school. How'd you know about my mom? And about Annie? And what's this about humans? What are you?"

Eldon Moss turned and abruptly swished back out through the automatic door. Connor followed. The rain had stopped; the sun fought through the gray. He jogged through mist rising from the pavement only to be surprised by the sight of the old guy starting his odd-looking maroon station wagon on the other side of the parking lot.

How'd he move so fast? The station wagon picked up speed. Suddenly, the front doors became wings, back panel transformed into the rear exhaust of a rocket ship, and the station wagon shot straight off the ground. It hovered ever so briefly, then blasted off billowing fire and steam. Connor looked up at a rainbow. The rainbow talked.

"Connor? Connor. Come on, Connor! Wake up."

Connor jerked out of sleep. The muggy heat of the day struck him even in the air-conditioned womb of the store. The snack bar counter—greasy sheen and all—had beckoned and had become his pillow.

Larry patted his shoulder. "Get on home, pal. It don't look good to the customers to see you sawing logs when you should be working."

"Sorry, man. Let me finish up first and then I'll go."

"Naw, that's okay. Go home."

A cloudburst raged outside.

✳ ✳ ✳ ✳ ✳ ✳ ✳ ✳ ✳ ✳ ✳ ✳ ✳ ✳

Connor shivered with fever by the time he dragged home and to his room. He crawled under the quilt on the waterbed, fell asleep, and awoke by early evening. The sound of stereo rock and roll, giggles, and muted shouts from the party below filtered up the stairs to where he lay sweating. Rain rattled the roof. He looked up at the Jefferson Airplane poster on the far wall. Its effect, under the spell of the black light in the bedside lamp, now on, and the high 1968 decoration of the closet where he slept usually entertained him. Now it just made him dizzy. He returned to sleep, fitfully.

Who is that? Oh...it's Moss. The little old man approached Connor across a sun-splashed meadow. He wavered in the sunlight like a poorly focused film. Connor stood transfixed. *Something's wrong here. I don't like this...*

"Tell me, son. Is this a nightmare or is this a sweet dream? You choose." Moss chuckled. His breath fluttered across Connor's face. Then, his face rippled and changed.

What's going on?

The Moss-thing cackled. It had grown three feet. A horn, topped by a glittering crystal, jutted from its forehead, and sharp horns stood along the sides of its head. It had gray, rough scaly skin and claws. It wore a long, dirty, white robe.

A demon... Got to get away!

Connor woke. The room was pitch black. *Who turned off the light? Must've been Annie.* The party downstairs continued. He wished away its sounds without success. He reached up and flicked the black light back on, then stretched, kicked Oblio off the waterbed, and sat up. He stunk from sweat born of fever and strange dreams. The clock radio he'd had since he was a kid said midnight. He wrapped up in the quilt, and walked downstairs, wincing in the light. He didn't want any part of the party, so turned away and walked out onto the dining room balcony.

Connor tottered to the balcony rail and watched night lights bounce off Lake Union. The rain had stepped down to a fine mist. With a start, he realized sick people shouldn't be out in the middle of bad weather.

"Connor. Connor Alexander."

Conor startled.

"What's important to you, son?" The whispery rasp sounded familiar.

"What? Who are you? I can't see a thing! Wait a sec..." Connor twisted his head side-to-side squinting into the dim light. He gasped.

Dripping, Eldon Moss smiled like a mischievous elf from his place in an old rattan chair. His baseball cap sat askew on his head. He was dressed the same as before.

"What's really important to you, son?" Moss' blue eyes glittered.

"To be left alone." Connor shook his head. *Am I dreaming again? No, can't be. Actually, wish I was asleep. What's he doing here?*

Moss continued. "You're wonderin' what I'm doing here. Well, son, I'm here cause I got things to say and you got things to learn…beginning with why're you wandering about in the rain with a fever? You ain't too bright."

"Huh? How'd you know what I was thinking?"

"I know lots a things, son. I know there's a big difference between what you do and what you think. Like, what's this marching in the streets all 'bout? You and I know you just been trolling for a good time. You're a phony, son."

Where was Annie? She could talk him down. Talk him down? From what?

"You gotta chance to make things better, but you gotta get with the program. Got to stop spinning your wheels if you're gonna make your mark. And you do have a mark to make, son."

"My mom used to tell me I was going to be special. Wait. Who are you? Really."

Moss ignored his questions. "Need to treat gals with more respect. Annie's a nice gal. But you treat her like a plaything. Right, ain't I?"

"Connor, where are you?" Annie's voice coming from the house sounded like chimes under water. Connor heard approaching steps. Eldon Moss dissolved when the balcony door creaked opened.

She stared, hands on hips. "You look awful, even worse than when I checked before. Why are you out here?"

Connor slumped against the balcony. "Leave me alone."

"Who were you talking to?"

He mumbled again.

She gave up. "I've got a ride and got to get going. My folks will kill me for being late. I just wanted to check on you one more time before I leave."

She pushed Connor up, and supported him through the door into the house and up the stairs. "Come on. To bed."

Connor stumbled into his bedroom nook. Something flitted from the far-left corner. He looked. Nothing there. He looked again.

The face of Eldon Moss grinned, then receded into darkness to the sound of faint laughter.

CHAPTER 4

The Huey clattered along just above the treetops. Combat conditions meant no lights. Inky darkness enveloped the crew chief, gunner, pilot, co-pilot, Cole, and Parsons as well as the Huey. Cole wanted to check the bowline knot that held 120 feet of nylon rope to the anchor point, but he couldn't see it. He hated to rappel, but there were no LZs close to the objective. Of course the knots were secure. The crew chief knew his stuff.

The chief yelled out, "Time!"

The transport rose up like a bucking horse, then hovered, buffeted by the wind. Cole and Parsons climbed out opposite sides. Cole hung on, weighted down by fifty pounds of gear and his M-16. His feet searched for landing skids. He found them and stood. He leaned forward and verified the connection point. A last check.

The crew chief screamed again, "Go, go, go!"

Cole pushed out, spiraling down into a hot, wet black well. A gust kicked the transport up ten feet and Cole with it. He sensed Parsons coming down the other side.

He slowed his descent, sensing the end of the rope. *Why do they always cut it so damn close?* He thought of training, an incident involving a short rope, and a new recruit who got off with just a broken ankle. He slammed through trees, vegetation, and into the soft jungle turf, then fell backwards. He heard a muffled crash to his right. Cole stood cautiously, backed out of the rope, and then grabbed it with both hands and yanked twice. It shot away and the Huey with it.

The men waited for the jungle to start breathing again. It did with a natural, dripping rhythm. A monkey chattered; a bird squawked, "re-up, re-up, re-up," like an overzealous army recruiter. The rangers stepped slowly, carefully moving brush aside rather than crashing through. They walked two klicks to the village, then began a loop around its perimeter. They listened. They moved. Listened and moved again. Three hours passed before Cole and Parsons completed the circle.

The lurps scooped out a rough trench on a bluff overlooking the village and prepared to wait until morning. There was no moonlight, but that wasn't a problem because both men carried starlite scopes. Cole thought of words from a Moody Blues tune, "Cold hearted orb that rules the night, removes the colors from our sight…" Cole then considered, as he stared into darkness without the scope, that he could just as well be at a campsite in the rain forest in Washington state's Olympic Peninsula on a particularly hot, muggy, wet, cloudy night. Then the monsoon rain increased. The men wrapped up in their ponchos and waited the long, lonely hours until dawn.

The rising sun dashed any illusions Cole had about where he was. He remembered scoring the winning touchdown on the last play of homecoming against Meadowdale High. He thought of Annie on the sidelines with pom-poms, a short skirt, and a smile. Smoke rose from hootches in the village. A water buffalo lowed and re-up birds chirped. Cole unaccountably thought about his mom's meat loaf. He hated the chilies she always stuck in the stuff. The rain stopped, but heavy clouds overhead held the promise of more.

The village began to stir. A water buffalo lowed again. Another buffalo answered. Cole checked his watch.

"Parsons," he whispered, "I'd say mission accomplished. There's no enemy on the perimeter or in the village. Give the 'all clear.'"

Parsons toggled the radio and passed the news on to Charlie Company.

The heat and humidity rose. The men had khaki-colored bandannas tied around their foreheads, but this technology did a poor job of stopping the sweat streaming and burning into their eyes.

At 1030 the first wave of transport Hueys whooped overhead and fluttered down 150 yards from their position. Dozens of grunts leaped out of the bays with M-16s in hand and started to shoot anything that moved. Cole saw a soldier shout something to his buddies, then cut down an old man with a three shot burst. A high, almost female scream signaled a water buffalo torn apart in the barrage that collapsed and thrashed next to the old man.

Cole was stunned. The landing had been unopposed. Maybe killing the old man made some sense. You could never tell about an enemy. But why the water buffalo? He whispered urgently to Parsons, "Tell 'em to hold fire. This isn't right."

Parsons couldn't get through. But then he didn't seem to care one way or the other.

Soldiers pushed through the high bamboo grass and hedgerows that surrounded the village. Several villagers made a break for it. A woman and her two children catapulted through the grass in grim cadence to the slugs that tumbled through them.

Cole hissed, "Hold tight."

Parsons nodded and smiled.

Cole watched a soldier chase a duck with a knife. Another grunt speared a water buffalo with his bayonet. Cole watched a mama-san try to get two soldiers off a pretty girl about Annie's age; he watched an infant bayoneted and tossed like a sack of flour. A group of villagers were led to a drainage ditch just in front of his position. He motioned Parsons down. The men peeked through the elephant grass.

A lieutenant talked brusquely to the squad guarding the prisoners and walked away. The village quieted. Screams and loud groans, punctuated by an occasional M-16 report, were all Cole now heard. Clouds of dust boiled up obscuring his vision of the village behind the prisoners.

The lieutenant returned. Cole heard his angry shout ring out, "I want them dead!" A cry went up from the villagers, "No. No. Not VC. Not VC!"

The lieutenant unholstered his 45-caliber pistol. He stroked the barrel. Cole held his breath. The lieutenant abruptly squared his shoulders; pointed the pistol in a two-handed grip at a middle-aged man's stomach, and squeezed off a round. The weapon boomed and a body flew backwards into the ditch.

Other soldiers joined in, switching to single shot to conserve ammunition. Children cowered behind their mothers. The drainage ditch filled. Miraculously, a toddler survived. A blood-drenched little girl clambered away from the twitching, groaning bodies, climbed up over the edge of the ditch, and toddled away. Catlike, a pistol-wielding soldier scooped her up, like an uncle who hadn't seen his favorite niece in a long time, catapulted the little girl backwards toward the ditch, and fired. The youngster blossomed into a fine pink mist. Her torso dropped off the pile.

Cole glanced over at Parsons. He was still grinning. Cole shook his head in disgust and signaled to move out.

The rangers rolled back into a bamboo grove and worked around Charlie Company. They had to get through to the LZ without getting shot. Finally, they made it.

On the trip back Cole learned Charlie Company had suffered one casualty. A grunt had shot himself in the foot.

Officially, the My Lai action netted 128 enemy killed in action and three weapons captured.

Unofficially, the truth of five hundred and sixty dead Vietnamese men, women, and children would haunt John Cole for the rest of his life.

CHAPTER 5

Two weeks after the My Lai massacre, Annie and Connor hung out in the living room of the Boylston house. Though it was a beautiful and mellow morning, Connor's mood was anything but. Even a Crosby, Stills, and Nash tune playing on the stereo couldn't dent his mood.

"Connor."

"Huh?"

"You've been acting weird since the party a few weeks ago. What happened to you out on the balcony?"

"I've had things on my mind." Connor didn't answer the question.

"Like what?"

"Let's talk about something else."

"I want to talk about this," Annie whispered. "You've been real moody. You've been real uptight, ever since I pulled you off the balcony at the party. I mean you were talking to yourself. What happened?"

"Like I said, I've had a lot on my mind."

"Why not talk to me about it?" Annie sniffed.

"Sure you want to talk?"

"Well, it's a lot better than *not* talking about it, whatever *it* is."

Connor paused, then asked, "What're you and me doing?"

"I don't understand. What do you mean? You mean physically what are we doing? Spiritually? You mean right now, at this moment in time, or at this time in our lives? What do you mean?"

"I mean right now."

"We're talking."

"I don't mean now in terms of this conversation, I mean now in terms of our lives. Where's it all heading?"

"I don't get what you mean. Where's what heading? Do you mean you and me? Our relationship?"

"No, Annie. I am talking about us, but I'm also talking about things in general."

Annie got up and walked into the dining room. She looked out at the sailboats on Lake Union as she leaned against the back window. Connor joined her.

"Annie, I'm not trying to bum you out. It's not your fault I'm confused. I like you. I could even love you—and I didn't think I could love anyone or anything. I just need to figure out what to do. With my life. There's been too much difference between what I think and what I do. I'm sick of it."

She didn't respond.

Connor continued. "I need to find out something. The day we first met, you asked me what I had been doing at the demonstration. I gave a half-assed answer. The question now is what were *you* doing? You're not exactly the demonstrating type."

"That should be obvious. I was demonstrating against the war. Just like you."

"You didn't answer the question."

"I don't get it. I was there for the same reason you were."

Connor thought for a moment. "Annie, I wasn't there because I wanted peace. Neither were you. I was being hip and you were just being curious. I'm right, aren't I?

"A while back, a weird little guy I met said I was a phony. I didn't agree with him. I do know, though, I've got to get my act together. The guy got me thinking I've been placed on this earth for a reason. That

I've got a special purpose. My mom used to say the same thing when I was little."

Annie's smile returned. "Special purpose? I think you're pretty special. But you're still not clear. What little guy? What're you talking about? What about going to school?" Connor confessed his lack of a high school diploma to Annie the night before. She still hadn't told him about being a cheerleader.

"I'm not sure what I want. I haven't nailed it down yet."

Annie persisted. "Want to get married and have kids?"

Connor frowned.

Annie laughed. "God, you're really serious, Connor. What's got into you?"

Connor told her about Eldon Moss.

* * * * * * * * * * * * * *

Two hundred generations of Arkadians had lived in the Hive.

Computer-controlled fans sucked the increasingly foul oxygen out of the Hive's atmosphere and recycled it through the increasingly polluted Hive Sea and atmosphere. Radiation from the lamps was hardly sufficient to photosynthesize the hardy green and purple broad-leafed vegetation that covered the islands, the algae, seaweed, kelp, and microscopic life that floated on, and under, the sea. There was no wind except just a suggestion of a breeze from the climate controllers.

Glass and metal structures built long ago from asteroidal materials and from Tirlol, the moon of Arkadia, spiraled in toward the inner center. The name Tirlol no longer held real meaning for Hive dwellers. They had a foggy notion that Tirlol and harmony were related, but the moon and its true significance as a totem of Wa on Arkadia had long since been forgotten, except through oral tradition carried on within the wawren caste.

Arkadians moved through tubes by conveyor to and from Hive structures, or traveled through the Hive Sea by transfer pod. Glow globes lit the increasingly murky waters; ceiling lamps brightened the atmosphere. Periodic brightening and dimming of the lamps defined the Arkadian day and night. Some lamps had burned out, casting shadows upon the waters. There were no replacements.

Clouds generated from the climate controllers no longer dissipated after dumping warm rain. The clouds persisted, blending into the gray of the Hive ceiling periodically dropping lower to dump moisture, activating the raindrums in the process, then rising to begin the cycle anew. Fog that streamed across the Hive Sea made it difficult to see more than a few body lengths away, though the mist occasionally cleared revealing a bland aquatic environment that, to a human, would have seemed more like a huge fish tank than a place where intelligent life lived.

✶ ✶ ✶ ✶ ✶ ✶ ✶ ✶ ✶ ✶ ✶ ✶ ✶ ✶

"We'll help you, Connor. A tuition waiver will be just the thing until you finish high school courses. After that, a financial aid package will get you started on college."

Mrs. Mosney and Connor had walked over to the food service where the kindly counselor had treated Connor to a cup of coffee. She had listened patiently for over an hour while he told his story. Though it wasn't her way to make quick decisions, she decided to help the young man.

"No. The counselor at the high school you attended should confirm your situation. Doesn't sound like your parents would cooperate anyway. Am I correct?"

"Yeah. I'm not even sure where they are."

She looked Connor Alexander over. He seemed like so many angry, lost, idealistic, and frightened young people she had encountered. A draft deferment might save his life. She didn't want to help Connor just for that reason, though. It was a good reason, but the young man also had potential.

"Like I said, we'll certainly help you, Connor. You'll have to complete at least 12 credits every quarter and keep your grades up. Think you can do that?"

"Yeah, I sure can. I really didn't expect this much help this quick. Thanks, Mrs. Mosney. You won't be sorry."

Jo Mosney looked evenly at Connor. "I know that."

Even Connor's adroit double clutching couldn't keep Rennie from spewing clouds of blue smoke as he drove the van out of the community college parking lot. Besides Mrs. Mosney's help, he had appreciated her advice. At least she was real. Eldon Moss had left him alone lately, but the old guy kept popping into his thoughts like a disapproving jack-in-the-box. It felt like being watched.

Connor pulled in front of the administration building at Edmonds High School and looked for Annie. He spotted her standing with a group of straight-looking football hero and student government-types. She saw Connor and waved. He coolly nodded back. Connor thought, *Man, I wouldn't be caught dead hanging out with those geeks.* He pushed the thought aside as Annie stepped up into the cab and slid over to him. Her perfume flooded his senses. She playfully kissed him on the mouth, and said, "Where to?"

"Out to the house?"

"I've got to be back by six. My parents will freak out otherwise."

"That's cool."

"How'd things go at the college?"

Connor gave her the good news as they drove toward Seattle. Annie was delighted. They talked about going to college in the fall though to different institutions, she to the University of Washington and Connor to the community college.

Connor changed the subject. "I've been thinking about quitting my job this August and going on a trip. I'd like to go to the convention in Chicago. About getting involved with the campaign before school."

"What campaign?" Annie asked absentmindedly. A stick of sandalwood incense burned in Renny's cab. The van was in fine shape. The microbus had just been tuned and burned fresh 30-weight. Annie tugged at the leather ring she wore. That and the peace symbol that dangled between her breasts were Connor's doings. She'd never be a real hippie. She often thought Connor wasn't either, despite what he might think.

"McCarthy's campaign." The upcoming Democratic Party convention might lead to nomination of a Joseph McCarthy as a peace candidate for president of the United States.

"McCarthy? I don't know, Connor. My dad say's there's not much to him. I want the war to end too, but that's all McCarthy's about. He's a one-trick pony. Besides, we're too young to vote."

"People too young to vote are dying in rice patties right now. I've got to get involved. Besides, you got anything better to do in August?" Connor turned onto the I-5 ramp heading south toward Seattle.

"I don't know. What about your job and school in the fall?"

Talking out of the corner of his mouth, eyes on the road, Connor replied, "I can quit my job. We'll go before school and get back in plenty time. Where's your commitment?"

Annie snapped back. "I am committed, but I've got other things on my mind. I feel awful about that letter I sent to John. I'm still thinking about that. *And about John.* You're being unfair."

A mile rolled by.

You're right," Connor said. "It's my life, not yours. Just trying to stop being a phony."

"I don't think you're a phony."

"You don't think I'm a phony?"

"No." She looked away.

More silence.

"Okay, Connor, maybe I'll go. But how would we work it?"

"No, it's not right." Connor cut her off. Don't do this for me. You don't have to get caught up in my trip." Connor smiled at the pun.

"We'll be back by the first week of September? That'd give us three weeks before school starts." She paused. "Connor, my life's been crazy since I met you. There's a lot about me you don't know. Did you know I'm a cheerleader?"

"What?"

"We can talk about it later." She grinned. "For now, tell me how we're getting to Chicago, and how long we'll be gone."

Connor scratched a wispy sideburn and replied. "We'll pack light. We'll sleep in Renny and stay in a park when we get to Chicago. We'll only be gone a couple of weeks." Connor looked to his right. The Northwest sun streaked through the clouds and painted Seattle's Queen Anne Hill. He took the Boylston exit.

"What'll I say to my folks? They're not going to like me cross-country with a guy. Plus, they'll know the convention might be dangerous. They're not stupid." She jerked in her seat as Connor swerved to avoid a dog.

"Tell them you're going as part of a car caravan as kind of a post-graduation vacation. Don't mention Chicago or me. You'll still be telling the truth. Tell your folks you're going with your cheerleader buddies and the captain of the football team."

Annie smiled in agreement thinking *John was captain of the football team.* "Very funny. I'll give it some thought, Connor. If I go, I sure hope I don't regret it."

"You won't." Connor smiled impishly.

Connor parked in front of the Boylston house. He excused himself after they walked in and went upstairs. Annie relaxed on the couch with a coke. Twenty long minutes passed by. Where was he? She got up, walked upstairs and down a hallway, and took a look through the open bathroom door. She gasped.

Connor hacked away at his hair with the aid of a hand mirror and a dull pair of scissors. He appeared to be half done.

"What are you doing? Have you flipped?"

"I'm just getting "clean for Gene." People at McCarthy's campaign headquarters downtown said I should do this to show I'm really serious."

Annie smiled.

Chapter 6

Cole and Parsons didn't talk much at the post-action debriefing. Parsons bound by a rudiment of military code and a spiritual bankruptcy; Cole by a horror that cut through to his soul. Four long months passed. Card games, cleaning gear, guard duty, an occasional patrol, and an occasional drunk. Cole didn't smile much. And he didn't sleep much. Sleep wasn't worth the dreams. Hollows under Cole's eyes deepened as the nights stretched by. Peace of mind was a fairy tale in the ruin of the present and the horror of the past.

Cole had smiled bitterly at the "Dear John" letter Annie sent him. After all, his name *was* John. The letter had hammered him with the full force of a mortar round. He wrote an abrupt letter to his folks, telling Ralph and Shirley of Annie's decision.

He got up from his bunk, splashed water on his face, and looked in the mirror. Had My Lai aged him? His hair had streaked with white after that day. His father had always had streaks of white in otherwise jet black hair. Cole never wondered why. Shirley always kept her graying, brown hair bleached blonde.

He shuffled back to his bunk and sat down, head in hands. What to do? Where to go?

The next day, Cole requested a change of R&R venue from Saigon to Tokyo. He began a two-week leave at end of July.

Cole spent the first day in Tokyo finding a cheap place to sleep. By the middle of August he was AWOL. That line of demarcation passed just like any other day he'd spent wandering the crowded streets of Tokyo. He dropped another letter off to Shirley and Ralph telling them of his decision to leave the military.

As was his habit, in the evening of the day he went officially absent without leave, Cole ate dinner at a window seat of a favorite noodle shop in the Ginza District. He interrupted the flow of soba into his mouth with frequent gulps of sake. A smiling hostess refilled the decanter whenever Cole looked up; the rice wine soothed him as did the welcome he felt from Tokyo citizens. Japanese are polite to *gaijin*, to strangers.

The city never slept. Cole also had trouble sleeping, but not by choice. His resting-place was a *kyapuseru hoteru*, a capsule room, where dozens of men lay stacked in closets barely large enough to hold a body. Cole slept with his army issue duffle bag as company.

Cole stumbled out of the noodle shop, fought through a wave of students dressed in navy blue skirts and sailor tops and headed uptown, drunker than usual. He jumped when a friendly shout from behind stopped him on the street. Pocketing the returned change, he slurred, "*Domo arigato*." Cole had forgotten that Japanese don't take tips.

He usually had a nightcap at a tavern close to his sleeping place. The night blazed with thousands of neon displays, some so big they covered the sides of skyscrapers. The air was muggy. He found the subway kiosk, and shuffled down the steps to a ticket machine. After gaining passage, he pushed up to the subway platform through masses of short, dark clothed travelers. Messengers, shoppers, students, and salarymen—the soldiers of corporate Japan—were everywhere. The train arrived and hissed to a stop, the on/off bell dinging incessantly as waves of people moved on and off.

Cole stepped into the human flood, a large salmon swimming upstream against the human current. By now, he didn't notice stares much. But stationary in a packed subway or subway station, it was impossible for the Japanese not to notice him. His *gaijin* height, more than a foot taller than those around him, white-streaked hair, and scruffy beard stuck out in the land of the rising sun. Standing on the train, Cole slung his arm over the bar from which dangled the hooks that shorter Japanese travelers grabbed for support. He looked over a sea of bobbing black hair to the end of the subway car.

Without thinking, Cole patted his waist. He carried $3,000 in a money belt. The U.S. cash could be exchanged for a lot of yen. He could go on indefinitely. But go on doing what? He couldn't go back to Vietnam. The car jumped as it pulled away. Fifteen minutes later it rocked to a stop. The dinging began.

Cole followed the crowd off and realized he missed his stop. He was still in the Shinjuku District. No panic. He'd have a few drinks and think about what to do. He entered a small bar, of the type on every street in some districts in the city. "The Blue Dot" was home away from home for many, for Cole the bar was just temporary sanctuary. But one drink led to another, and still another. He finally stumbled out the door, cutting a wide swath through still-crowded Tokyo streets. A drunk *gaijin* was scary even to an early morning Japanese night flyer. Cole became thoroughly and utterly lost and just couldn't seem to get close enough to anyone to ask directions. Just as well. His Japanese was only a few weeks old.

"Where am I?" he muttered. Where was a cop when you needed one? Whoops. "*Suimasen*, excuse me," he said as he bumped into a salaryman in front of him. The man quickly shrugged and moved away.

Pink mist. Pink mist. Thumps of bullets whacking flesh. Why? *Whoops. Something's coming up.* He lurched into an alley searching for privacy, his stomach roiling toward an explosion. Pink mist…*God, feel sick. That's better.* Ah. Back to the street. Need a cab. There! Better signal. *It stopped!* The door's opening. The address, the address. What is the address?

Cole slowly spoke the address in broken Japanese to the cabby, then in English he asked, "You know the place?" Stumbling forward, he belched in the cabby's face.

The cab roared off. Cole staggered back onto the sidewalk, then decided his bladder needed immediate attention. He moved into the darkness of an alley and unzipped his fly. He didn't see the shadow that rose up out of the night like a ninja in a low budget martial arts movie. But, sensing the whir of the sap, Cole ducked. Special forces training was a lot like riding a bike. Of course, one shouldn't attempt bike riding—and one definitely shouldn't attempt a sidekick—when falling down drunk. Cole fell over. Another shadow dove over him at the attacker.

"What?" Cole tried to get up, but couldn't. He heard yelling, staccato Japanese and running feet. The world spun. From his knees, he fell headlong into the side of a brick building and collapsed in a sodden heap like a basket load of damp laundry.

Where am I? The bright morning light assaulted him. The futon felt as hard as outdoor carpeting without a pad. He shivered. *Nothing's broken. My head is killing me. Too much whiskey, sake, beer, whatever.* He looked up quickly, reeled from the pain in his head, and dry heaved a couple of times. He spotted the full money belt on the floor next to his neatly folded cleaned clothes and a *yukata*. Someone had washed his clothes. He stood up gingerly and put on the *yukata*. The starched cleanliness of the bright red, flowered cotton garment—often mistaken for a kimono by *gaijin*—felt good against his salty, grimy body.

The small brightly whitewashed room was sparsely furnished. Besides the futon, there were a couple of chests, a straight-backed chair, and wood prints on the wall opposite a shoji screen. He slid open the screen, walked into a cramped hallway, and noticed a small room directly ahead, and stairs going down to the left. Cole was suddenly glad to see the Japanese-style toilet in the small room. Cole finished nature's call, splashed water on his hands, wrung them dry and stepped downstairs.

A Japanese man about his own age, maybe a few years older, sat peacefully in a small living room. Furniture in the living room and small kitchen breathed a zen simplicity, much like the room in which he'd slept. Japanese pop music fluttered in the background.

"Cole-*san*, you look tired." The stranger smiled. He cracked open a pack of Mild Sevens and offered one to Cole.

"No, thanks. I don't smoke. How'd you know my name?"

The man inhaled and blew a smoke ring, smiled, and said, "I looked in your wallet. I hope you do not mind. My name is Hiroshi Akai." He stood, faced Cole, and bowed deeply. Cole clumsily returned the bow and stuck out his hand. Akai transferred his cigarette to the other hand, and shook Cole's hand limply with an exaggerated up and down motion.

"What happened?" Cole checked Akai out more closely. His benefactor stood a muscular five foot-six with short black hair and even features. He dressed informally, wearing blue jeans and a New York Jets sweatshirt. His brown eyes sparkled with intelligence and empathy.

"I stopped a man from attacking you last night. I brought you here afterwards. You are welcome to my home."

"Thank you, Akai-*san*. Uh...where are we?"

"I live in the Harajuku District. Please sit. Would you like tea?" Akai walked into the galley kitchen off the living room.

"Yeah. Sure. Thanks." Cole sat and watched Akai bustle a few steps away. His host returned with green tea, two cups, and a variety of rice balls on a decorative plate.

Cole accepted tea from Akai, holding out his cup clumsily with two hands to show respect. He poured tea for Akai who also held his cup with two hands, but in a more elegant fashion. Suddenly hungry, Cole picked up and munched on a rice ball. He savored the flavor of rice vinegar, scrambled egg, and radish bits folded into the gooey rice.

With his mouth full he said, "Thanks, man. I don't know what would have happened if you hadn't come along." But he did know. He'd be in military custody right now, $3000 poorer, and nursing the results of a beating. He might even be dead. "I really appreciate your help."

Akai nodded.

"How'd I get here?"

"I called cab. Driver and I got you in the car and up the stairs to my place. We got you to bed. It was no trouble."

"How did you learn to speak English so good?"

"It is a long story I can tell later. For now, let us just visit and get to know each other. I also have friends who are coming over that I want you to meet. Do not worry. They will not betray you to the American military police."

"What? What about the MPs? You know about me?"

"You are carrying too much money for a soldier who is just visiting. You are hiding?"

Cole paused. *Guess there's nothing to lose.* "Yeah. I'm kinda hiding out." He took a bite of rice ball and looked at the ceiling. Akai waited patiently. "I went AWOL yesterday. I guess I started to celebrate my new freedom too much."

"You went AWOL?"

"Yeah. Absent without leave. Anyway, I'm not going back to 'Nam." Abruptly shifting gears Cole asked, "How was it you were near me when I got jumped?"

"Jumped?"

"Yeah. Attacked, beaten up, hurt. You know."

Akai paused before responding. "I saw you in the bar, in the Blue Dot. You looked lost so I followed you after you left."

"Followed me? Why?"

The doorbell chimed. Hiroshi Akai got up and opened the front door. A beautiful Japanese woman stepped into the room. She slipped off her shoes and smiled at Cole. An American man trailed behind her.

The American talked while trying to shake off his shoes. "Hi guys. Hey, Hiroshi-*san* you're looking good. This the guy you told us about?" The American nodded in Cole's direction. He was almost as tall and thin as Cole. He had slicked back brown hair, icy blue eyes, but a warm smile. He hopped around on one foot yanking off his last shoe. Cole stood and offered the American his hand. He shook it firmly. Cole smiled and bowed slightly to the woman. She returned the bow. Both visitors dressed casually in blue jeans and t-shirts; the woman wore a jean jacket, the American's jacket was leather.

"Cole-*san*, please meet my sister Fumiko and her husband, Alan Pool."

"Pleased to meet both of you. Sorry, I'm a mess."

"Hey, we're glad to meet you anyway, John." Alan seemed amused. He looked Cole up and down ferret-like. The group stood awkwardly.

Hiroshi Akai turned toward Cole and spoke up. "Why don't we go out for food and talk? I'll visit with Fumiko and Alan while you have a bath and get dressed. The bath chamber is upstairs next to the toilet. Feel free to take aspirin in the medicine cabinet. You look like you may need them." Akai chuckled.

"Sure, I'd like that. By the way, thanks for washing my clothes. Man, you were busy this morning."

"No problem, Cole-*san*."

Cole went upstairs. He stopped before the bath chamber opened the medicine cabinet over the toilet, and dry swallowed four aspirin from the bottle he found. He slid open a pocket door, walking into a small tiled chamber that held a tub filled to the brim with steaming water. This was, literally, the bathroom. He recalled polite laughter the first few days in Japan when he had asked for directions to the bathroom instead of the toilet. A shower nozzle poked out of a wall. He took off the *yukata*, blasted open the shower, and moved under its needles. Layers of dirt swirled away down the floor drain. Time for a soak in the tub? Nah. Better get dressed and back downstairs to learn more about his new friends. Japanese were hospitable, but washing his clothes? Inviting friends and family over? The woman looked vaguely familiar.

Later, Cole, Hiroshi, Fumiko, and Alan laughed across a table at a local restaurant. "It feels great to eat food with nice folks." Cole's comment reflected the warmth and concern that radiated from the others. Things didn't add up. But his new friends seemed to have good intentions.

"How did you all get to know one another? And what exactly is it you do?"

The three looked at each other. Fumiko responded mischievously, "You already know Hiroshi and I are brother and sister."

"Hey, stop pulling my leg. Tell me something I don't know."

Fumiko reached over as though to pull Cole's leg, then backed off and giggled, holding her hand over her mouth. She said, "Hiroshi is a teacher. He teaches English to Japanese. Alan and I run the Blue Dot, a small tavern just a few blocks from here."

"*That's* where I saw you before." Cole looked intently at Fumiko. "Why aren't we meeting there, instead of here?"

"Today is Sunday, John-*san*. Alan and I like to get away from the Blue Dot on Sundays."

"How did you and Hiroshi-*san* learn English?"

Hiroshi gently interjected. "Our parents died in an automobile accident when Fumiko and I were very young. Our uncle Matsuura raised us. He served as a Fullbright Scholar in the United States. Fumiko and I attended high school in Cleveland during that time. That is where Fumiko and Alan met."

"How'd you get into the tavern business?"

Fumiko replied, "Our parents left us the Blue Dot. Uncle Matsuura rented it to others, on our behalf, for many years. It was originally a sushi bar, but we remodeled it after returning to Japan three years ago. We now have soba, beer, and sake as well as sushi."

The party quieted. Hiroshi slurped his green tea and eyed Yumiko. She and Alan looked at each other, then at Cole.

"Look, you guys have been great to me," Cole blurted. "I'd be hurting if it hadn't been for Hiroshi-*san*. I guess he told you about me."

Alan and Fumiko nodded.

"Question is what should I do?"

Fumiko responded without hesitation. "John-*san*, why not stay with us at the Blue Dot? Alan and I will give you a job. It will not pay well, but your pay will be…" She turned to Alan and spoke rapidly in Japanese.

Pool replied, "Ah, you mean under the table, honey." She pretended to look under the table and giggled again at Cole, with one hand covering her mouth, then said, "What do you say, John-*san*?"

"I'd like that." It was too good to be true. He flashed on his dad telling him if something was too good to be true, then it probably was. Ralph might have been right. Still, hanging out with these people sure beat wandering around Tokyo waiting to be nabbed.

CHAPTER 7

"Ralph dear, please pass the syrup." Shirley grinned at the hotcakes, fried eggs, and brown-and-serve link sausages spread before her. The late August morning sun was bright and warm as it streamed through the dining room window.

Ralph passed the syrup. With a rattle of the newspaper, he spoke softly, "This Martin Luther King business sure angered the Negroes. Paper says rioting is going on in 170 cities. Forty people have died so far. Wonder why this King fellow won the Nobel Peace Prize?"

Michelle looked up from her breakfast, "Dad, black people prefer to be called Afro-Americans."

"Mickie, don't correct your father."

"Mom, please *don't* call me Mickie.

Chuck burped. Shirley scowled at him and started to speak but was cut off by Michelle.

"Mom, have you heard from John?" The Cole family had just learned that John was AWOL.

"No. First he and Annie break up and now this. A deserter. I can't believe it. He had so much promise. I've never known Johnny to be a quitter. Sounds like he gave up on life, though. Gave up on doing his duty." Shirley swallowed another bite of sausage, pancake, and egg dripping in butter and syrup.

"What was his duty, Mom? Looks to me like he finally came to his senses."

Ralph cut in. "Michelle, leave your mother alone. Can't we ever eat in peace?"

"Okay, Dad. But since you mentioned it, what do you mean by 'peace?'"

The doorbell rang, saving Ralph from having to reply.

Shirley snorted, hauled herself up, and shuffled to the front door. Two young men stood on the porch. They had short hair, white shirts, slacks, and dark ties. Shirley noticed a couple of bicycles parked at the end of the walk.

"Good day Ma'am. My name's Al, this is Ken. We represent the Church of Jesus Christ of Latter Day Saints. Are you worried about events in the world today? If so, we'd like to talk with you and other family members. That is, if you have a few moments to spare."

Shirley turned purple with rage and bellowed. "Heretics! The Lord Jesus Christ said in Luke 10:7: Go ye *not* house-to-house! How dare you violate this command of the Lord! Get off my property and don't come back. I won't have you in my presence, neither would He!" She slammed the front door.

Shirley's reaction caught Al by surprise. He tumbled backwards off the porch, grabbing Ken for support, and tripped him as well. The two missionaries ended up in a pile at the base of the steps. Intent on returning to the table, Shirley didn't know about hurting the boys. But Michelle, who had followed her mother out of curiosity, observed their shocked faces through a corner of the front window. She hurried back to the dining room.

"Jesus, Mom. You hurt those guys!"

"Do *not* use the Lord's name in vain! God give me strength!"

Michelle smiled at her mother and quietly replied, "Mom, how can a guy who makes you behave like that truly be called the Prince of Peace?"

"Go to your room this instant!"

Michelle did, sat sullenly on the bed for a few minutes, then packed a knapsack, emptied her piggy bank, grabbed her cigarettes, and crawled out the window. She made it to the interstate and hitched east.

She knew nothing of the Arkadians. Yet, like them, she needed a new home. And like them, she wasn't quite sure where to find it.

A kindly trucker transported her through Colorado at about the same time the Hive approached a straddlepoint inside the star constellation humans either call "Cygnus," the Swan, or the "Northern Cross" based on the five brightest stars in the constellation. It was as though the sideways "X" of the constellation marked the spot.

✳   ✳   ✳   ✳   ✳   ✳   ✳   ✳   ✳   ✳   ✳   ✳   ✳   ✳

"Man, what a drag: Eastern Washington, then Idaho, now this. Where is everybody?" Connor said as he and Annie drove across the empty reaches of eastern Montana on their way to the Chicago convention. They had been on the road for three days and had switched to night travel to beat the 100-degree plus late August heat. It was mid-morning.

"Just because no one's here now doesn't mean there wasn't in the past. You're looking at a lot of history, Connor. A lot of ghosts."

"Ghosts? What do you mean?"

"Custer's last stand was just southwest of here. He got wiped out, but that didn't stop the white man. The Indians really got totaled. Imagine what it was like living peacefully within your culture only to have technologically-advanced aliens arrive and to take *your* home."

"It'd be a bummer. Be weird at first dealing with the aliens. It'd *really* be a bummer getting toasted by death rays."

"I'm serious, Connor. Put yourself in their shoes."

"Whose shoes? Are we talking alien shoes or moccasins?" When Annie ignored his questions, Connor tried a different tack. "How did you know about Custer's last stand? I didn't see any signs."

"I got an 'A' in American history."

"Figures. I'm going to have to get better at school or I'll still be stocking groceries when I'm an old man." Thinking of an old man made him recall Eldon Moss. He shuddered.

"What's wrong? You can't possibly be cold."

"I'm fine."

"Ready for a break? I'm getting hot." Annie coyly pulled up the bottom of her t-shirt and knotted it below her breasts.

"Hot? Right on," Connor smiled.

"You know what I mean. I'm beat. Let's stop and get some sleep."

"Okay."

Connor handed a map over to Annie. After a cursory glance she replied, "There's a place just ahead, about ten miles down the road."

Connor and Annie were pushing it. They wanted to arrive in Chicago early to find a good camping spot. So far, the trip had been uneventful. Renny grumbled a bit, but the van kept put-putting along.

Connor pulled into a campground near the Yellowstone River. Annie broke out the tent while Connor walked around the campground. The tent had provided scant protection the previous day against a summer thunderstorm that had hit with little warning and swamped them in warm liquid and electricity, but having the canvas overhead was comforting, nevertheless. The big sky—azure to the horizon—now held no hint of a thunderstorm. The color green dominated, from the pine forests to the drifting turbulence of the mighty Yellowstone River that roared just beyond their campsite.

"Far out. Looks like there's fishable water here," Connor said upon his return. He had learned to bait a hook as a five-year old at the knee of a kindly grandpa who had always been there to comfort him when his parents were not. His grandpa had virtually raised him, as the Alexander parents spent more time screaming at each other than attending to their only child. Connor always traveled with his fishing gear. He loved to wet a line even when the fish weren't biting. His grandpa had liked to say to young Connor if "catching fish was what it

was about, then we'd have to call it 'catching' instead of 'fishing.'"
Grandpa had passed on two years ago.

"Don't know what challenge you see in fishing. Fish have a brain pan
the size of a pea. Brings 'em to your level I guess." Annie nudged Connor
in the ribs. "Have fun. I'm going to take a nap." She stretched from her
place at the picnic table and climbed into the tent.

Connor yawned. The idea of nap and Annie's soft curves pulled him
to the tent. But fishable water couldn't be ignored. *Plus, she'll still be
there for me later.* Connor still couldn't believe his good luck in snagging
Annie. But he knew John Cole also still had a claim, even if Annie didn't
acknowledge it. He grabbed his spinning gear and started down the
path to the river. He didn't have a Montana fishing license but figured
the local gendarmes wouldn't mind if he poached a few.

A worn path took Connor through a tunnel of tall evergreens, the
roar of the river background to the journey. He heard something
rustling in the bush. A woodpecker tapped somewhere beyond the
rustle. The river boulders appeared first, then the river. He moved along
the Yellowstone traveling on enormous ice age boulders, mute sentries
to the river's life. The great river poured through its channel in starts
and stops like an impatient traveler.

Connor found the pool after a short search. It looked like a fish
hotel—a deep emerald hole with just enough current to bring food to
big lazy western cutthroat trout. Connor covered a treble hook with fish
eggs and fired six-pound test monofilament into the middle of the
pool. He found shade under a boulder and settled in as the late morning
heat continued to build. The breeze kept the mosquitoes away. He
sighed and dozed.

"Connor. Connor! Wake up, son. We gotta talk."

"Huh?" Connor looked up from his nap. No fish. No Annie.

"Look behind you."

Connor pegged the soft voice and twisted around to see Eldon Moss
sitting on top of the shade boulder. His baseball cap was off and he

wiped his face with a red handkerchief. He wore the same bow tie and blue jeans he had worn the last time the two had talked.

"Why did you sneak up on me? What're you doing here? Who are you?"

"Where's your imagination? Mebbe you should be askin' *what* are you?"

"All right. What are you?"

Instead of answering, Moss gruffly replied, "I ain't a sneak, son. Jesus, it's hotter'n the hubs a hell out here."

"Why don't you answer my question?"

"Who or what I am ain't important."

"I want to know."

"You don't git to know everthing in life, son. That's the way it is. Mebbe I'll tell you later. Right now, you tell me something. Where're you and that pretty gal goin'?"

"Going?"

"You're gonna demonstrate for this McCarthy fella at some convention. Right?"

"Yeah. So?"

"Real reason you're goin' on this trip is cause you like demonstrations. Still after that ole excitement, ain't you Connor. Same dog, just different fleas. Right, ain't I?"

Moss continued when Connor didn't disagree. "Where's your head at, son?"

"I'm fishing! Why are you hassling me?"

Eldon Moss shimmered in the heat and smiled.

"Keep in mind you shouldn't bring yourself to the level of the one's you're fighting. To believe in peace people gotta act peacefully. Don't fight unless you're trying to break up a fight. People gotta be what they believe in. Get my drift, son?"

"You're a preachy old guy."

"Getting to you, ain't I?" Moss said gleefully. "Remember, son, it takes two folks to speak truth. One to speak, the other to listen. Think on it. By the way, congratulations on going back to school."

"How'd you know about that?"

Eldon Moss dissolved into the egg-frying heat.

Connor shook his head like a dog shedding water after a swim. He looked around. "Who is this guy?" he said out loud.

The boulder didn't answer.

       ✶   ✶   ✶   ✶   ✶   ✶   ✶   ✶   ✶   ✶   ✶   ✶   ✶   ✶

The waters were dying and the Hive with them. The Peacemaker sat in his cell. He rubbed the nub of his forehorn and pondered the fate of Arkadians. He shuffled through the tepid puddles in his cell and again gazed out the portal at the Hive Sea.

       ✶   ✶   ✶   ✶   ✶   ✶   ✶   ✶   ✶   ✶   ✶   ✶   ✶   ✶

The creature protected its territory. Peacemakers were unknown in the blue/green gauze and currents of the waters. Only overwhelming strength prevailed. Only force counted. The creature had killed and fed. But it wanted more.

A tantalizing waft drifted on the current. The creature moved out from shadow. Heavy muscles rippled as it torpedoed toward its objective. The cannibal closed razor-sharp teeth on eggs of its kind, a favorite food…

       ✶   ✶   ✶   ✶   ✶   ✶   ✶   ✶   ✶   ✶   ✶   ✶   ✶   ✶

A strike! Connor woke with a start. The drag on his reel screamed as a big cutthroat yanked at the light fishing tackle, trying to break it with brute strength or to wrap it around a rock or snag. The battle went back and forth. Connor expertly turned the power of the trout's rushes. Though nip and tuck, the trout soon lost out to the spinning reel's six-to-one gear ratio, and lay helpless on its side. Connor wiped the sweat out of his eyes and leaned over to lift the trout out by its gills.

The echo of a recently familiar whisper stopped him.

"You really need that fish? You and that gal brought along plenty of grub, didn't you?

"Yeah, so?"

"Then you're gonna kill another livin' creature for sport?"

"Well, yeah. I guess so."

"Killing for sport whilst on your way to demonstrate for peace! Geez Louise, you ain't got the moral backbone of a worm."

The whisper stopped. Connor looked down at the trout in the pool at his feet. A trophy. But he gently unhooked the panting fish and set it free.

Connor walked back to the campsite. A warm wind blew music through the trees. He felt sunlogged, sleepy, and not a little bit confused.

* * * * * * * * * * * * * *

"Hey, amigo. How's it hangin'?"

"John Cole turned around from wiping a back counter at the Blue Dot. *Parsons!* My God! Where did you come from?" A few patrons glanced up at the shout, then quickly looked away.

Cole moved closer to at his patrol-mate. The man studied him with shark eyes. Parson's civvies fit poorly.

"What in the hell you doing here?" Cole whispered. "How'd you find me?"

"The captain knows people in the MPs. He got a list of places you might be. This is the third place I been."

"A list of where I might be? How's that?"

"Get me a beer and I'll tell you." Parson's licked his lips.

"I've only been here a few weeks. How'd you find me?"

"Hey, lighten up, pal. Captain and me are doing you a favor. Put that rag down, take off the apron, and come back with me now. You won't be busted. Captain says he's covered for you. Transport's arranged."

"Transport? Others know about me?"

"Of course, Cole. What'd you expect? Look…"

"Excuse me. I am sorry to interrupt." Fumiko Pool appeared suddenly at Cole's shoulder. Parsons leered at her beauty.

"Fumiko-*san*. I'm in the middle of something here."

"Yes, John-*san*. I am very sorry. But we need you in the back just for a moment."

"Okay. Hey, man, I'll be back."

Parsons shrugged.

Cole followed her to the kitchen. She closed the door and looked at him squarely. "I heard you shout and listened to your conversation. I am sorry for this rudeness, but there is much we did not tell you. There is no time now to talk. Go to Hiroshi-*san's* place. I will phone and tell him you are coming. You and he must leave Tokyo immediately. You must go to Shinjuku Station now."

"Leave? I don't get it."

"Hiroshi-*san* will explain everything on the train. It is dangerous here. They have come for you. You must go. Go to Yokosuka." Fumiko whispered urgently.

"Hey, Cole. Where you gone to buddy?" Cole heard approaching footsteps.

Parsons wasn't his buddy. Never had been. He'd only left him sitting at the bar for a moment. Why the big rush? Fumiko also had a secret. *Who to trust?*

"Go. Go now." Fumiko pleaded.

Cole rushed out the back door, surprising the two MPs standing next to a government-green Ford sedan. He wiggled past one and stiffed-armed the other. It was just like returning punts in high school. He sprinted down the alley through the roaring crowd on the street. The throaty rumble of another sedan opened up behind him.

"*Halt!*"

Cole didn't look back as he wove his way through familiar Harajuku streets toward Hiroshi's apartment.

* * * * * * * * * * * * * *

"Blazing like a torch, a great star will fall from the heavens to the sea. It will be an evil star. After its falling, one-third of the water of Earth will run with the blood of Man. An evil horned beast will be birthed by the star and will rise from the sea. The beast will rule the water and men will fall down in worship of its power. The beast lives and rules by the sword. It will perish by the sword, the sword of salvation wielded by our Lord and Savior, Jesus Christ!"

The Reverend Isaiah Marcus Stringer of the First Church of Jesus Christ Washed in the Blood of the Lamb was in fine early August Sunday form. Shirley Cole quivered in agreement. Ralph and Chuck rustled beside her. Ralph disliked Stringer and his church. But as with most things it wasn't worth the trouble to fight Shirley about it.

"Sinners! The Hammer of Satan—the star Wormwood and the beast—will come from the sky to fool Man. The Great Deceiver will have his deception. Only believers will stand before him!"

"Amen," Shirley agreed.

Ralph jerked himself awake before his chin hit his chest. He tried to see through a stained glass pictorial of the virgin birth that ringed the small sanctuary. *A fried ham and cheese sandwich and a bottle of beer sure'd taste good about now. When's this guy going to shut up so we can get out of here and eat?*

Thoughts buried deep inside, however, spoke of a different hunger and thirst Ralph had felt on the hasty retreat south. Couldn't thaw the

C-rations. Stopping to build a fire attracted fire from the Chinese on the hills. Had to keep moving or die.

Like John, Ralph Cole had been a strong, supremely confident young man. Like his son, he took naturally to being a warrior, but that was before 120,000 Chinese overran the First Marine Division on the Chosin Reservoir. Outnumbered 10 to 1 some marines, like Ralph, escaped to become like shiny wind-up toys used hard by a malevolent child and then forgotten. He never talked about it. Guys from his generation never did, but the shakes, the dreams, and their screams betrayed them. He came back a man easily bent to Shirley's will. She never understood why.

Chuck's thoughts were even further away—in the fifth dimension. He had just learned the Kaluza-Klein theory that integrated Einstein's theory of gravity with Maxwell's theory of light. The geometric reconciliation was elegant and exciting; he wanted to be home with his beloved books and slide rule instead of sitting on a hard, uncomfortable church pew next to his mother.

As her father salivated uncomfortably and her twin brother savored dimensional geometries, Michelle stood next to a highway that sliced through a cornfield outside Iowa City. She took a last hit on a Marlborough and flicked the butt to the pavement.

Her stomach rumbled. Heat and humidity plastered her tie-dye shirt to her braless torso. The crystal found on that family vacation so long ago hung between her ample breasts. Her breasts were always a hassle, particularly when she hitched, and always when she met new guys. Still, wearing a bra was against her principles. Besides, she needed a ride.

An old Chevy pickup with "flower power" and "love is peace" painted in bright red over its yellow body rattled to a stop. "Going our way?" The sweet aroma of marijuana wafted out the truck's cab. A cute longhaired guy—about 20 years old—smiled pleasantly at her. Another long hair sat next to him.

"Where you headed?"

"Chicago. We're going to the convention."

She paused.

"Come on and get in. You got something better to do?"

The other guy leaned over, checked out Michelle, smiled, held up a joint, and said, "Hop in."

Michelle smiled back and moved toward the truck.

The Democratic convention was five days away.

The Peacemaker meditated. The raindrums pounded.

CHAPTER 8

Arkadia hadn't spun as fast as Earth, nor had it twirled as rapidly about its star. Yet, the differences in an Arkadian and Earth "year" and "day" had been remarkably slight. Arkadians thought in terms of 24-hour days and 365-day years.

Arkadia once had Tirlol, a single moon that also pulled the tides and beautified the night sky. Like Earth, Arkadia had also been a water planet. Erosion and slowed-down tectonic plate activity, typical of an aging planet, kept much of Arkadia's surface under salt water oceans, fresh water rivers and lakes, and seas. Arkadians live much of their lives either in, under, or around water, preferring fresh or brackish water, though prior to life in the Hive Arkadian gills easily handled the heavy salt of the oceans of Arkadia.

Arkadia *had* a single moon and was a water planet because the planet is no more. Arkadia was vaporized when its class G star moved into the red giant stage of the main cycle. Only descendants of Arkadia remained, the 200th generation of aspiring colonists surviving badly within the confines of the Hive, a broken-down, Tirlol-sized starship lost in space.

To a human, the Arkadian forehorn, sidehorns, gray scaly skin, height, and webbed claws would appear monstrous, even devil-like. A fundamentalist preacher like the Reverend Stringer would have a hard time telling the difference between an Arkadian and a demon.

Arkadians have genitals and reproduce sexually but don't have sex. Romantic love is unknown to them, as is the eager passion typical of newly matched human lovers. Arkadian egg and sperm are joined anonymously in mating pools, the identity of parents as random as the mingling of genetic material. About every 30 days, Arkadians periodically and ritualistically visit a mating pool to deposit sperm or eggs during a brief swim. The call to mate is precipitated by unpleasant cramps, the only relief gained by swimming within a few body lengths of a ripe member of the opposite sex. No pleasure is derived from this act, only relief from pain.

Caste distinctions are discarded with robes in the changing room. In a mating pool the genetic material of all Arkadians, from the lowly workers to the ruling caste of wyruls, is equal, thereby maintaining variety in the gene pool.

Worker quartermasters collect fertilized eggs for transport to a birthing tank. After a short incubation, Arkadian tads wiggle free, leaving behind the residue of egg sacs. Tads are raised in broods by worker nannies of halfmaster rank until they grow limbs and lungs and become bipedal, at which time they are assigned to a caste.

Arkadian robes have a unique weave and syntheofabric construction that repels water. The robes are worn to denote caste and rank, not to cover nakedness. Nakedness and bodily functions are never a source of embarrassment or concern to an Arkadian.

To varying degrees, Arkadians possess the powers of telepathy and telekinetic manipulation, though it is much easier for an Arkadian to send a message telepathically than it is to receive one. Besides, mind reading is bad manners; by custom, Arkadians use telepathy only when communicating under water. Telekinesis is *never* okay. Mentally manipulating physical objects is the epitome of rudeness. On the planet Arkadia heavy fines were levied against those who violated this social norm. In the Hive, telekinetic manipulation is just not done.

Arkadians also have the ability to store and to discharge electricity. Ravans are chosen in the Hive's replacement allotment, in part by their ability to vent deadly levels of power. A fully-charged ravan zeromaster can fry an opponent with a well-placed bolt. Ravans like to kill.

*   *   *   *   *   *   *   *   *   *   *   *   *   *   *

Life on the planet Arkadia should have been paradise for its sentient life, but it wasn't; their history reeked of conflict, including nuclear conflict.

The ravans used nuclear weapons shortly after a wizard halfmaster developed her theory of relativity. Three city-level atomic confrontations preceded the first global holocaust that slaughtered billions and left no victor. After recovery, Arkadians were left with a healthy, even hysterical, fear of war. They developed elaborate offensive weapons and equally elaborate defenses for protection. Offense always won. Over thousands of centuries, drawn like moths to a nuclear flame, Arkadians continued to blast away, with each holocaust occurring about as soon as technological advances allowed.

The nuclear fire was again being stoked when a final peace came unexpectedly. This peace, like many good things, carried a steep price tag.

Physicist members of the wizard caste discovered that Arkadia's star had become unstable and that life-threatening change in climate within two thousand years was a certainty. Cooperation became necessary to develop the technology to leave the planet. Escaping to the stars became a superordinate goal for the Arkadians—a goal that transcended all individual differences.

CHAPTER 9

"So, Hiroshi-san, what's the deal?"

"The deal? What do you mean? Do you wish to play cards?"

"No, I mean what's happening? Why are we running?"

John Cole and Hiroshi Akai sat in the backseat of a cab on the way to Shinjuku Station. From there, the red line subway would carry them to Tokyo Station where they would catch the train to Yokosuka.

Hiroshi replied instead to the cabby, "Excuse me, sir, do you have a cigarette I might have?" The cabby's confusion and subsequent reply in Japanese satisfied Hiroshi. He shifted in the seat and faced Cole. "I am sorry, John. We planned to talk to you soon. You had earned our trust." Akai's dropping of the usual Japanese honorific of *san* signaled that he was genuinely upset. "You and I will travel to Yokosuka. The Beheiren has a language school there that we use, how do you say it…as cover. We planned to switch operations away from Tokyo anyway. It had become too dangerous to operate in the city."

"Dangerous? What're you talking about? What's the Beheiren? What's so dangerous about a language school?"

"The Beheiren is not really a language school. It helps American soldiers find alternatives. We help soldiers find sanctuary. We…"

"I don't get it. What are you saying?"

"We help soldiers leave the American military. We help Americans who are tired of fighting. My uncle Matsuura founded the organization.

For the past three years, Yumiko and I have helped soldiers who want out..."

"What?"

"We provide help with new papers. We get people out of Japan to Canada usually by regular passenger line..."

John interrupted again. "I'll be damned. I wondered why you people were so friendly. Why didn't you just tell me all this up front?"

"John, we genuinely wished to help you. But we have contacts in Saigon we use to check out people for our help. You and I met by accident. Alan, Fumiko, and I needed to learn more about you. Please, you must understand. We were going to speak with you."

John paused, then softened, "I'm sorry, Hiroshi-*san*. It's just this whole thing's so unexpected. You guys should have trusted me up front."

The cab stopped. Out the windows ribbons of hurrying Japanese and an occasional *gaijin* streamed through Shinjuku Station.

Later, on the subway to Tokyo Station, Cole whispered to his protector. "What am I doing in Yokosuka?"

Under the roar of the subway, Akai quietly replied. "You can help with our English school and Beheiren business until we get you out of the country. It may be some time before it will be safe. Travel is okay for the next six hours or so. After that, the word will be out. Japanese authorities will report you to the Americans if you are discovered. You must trust me, John-*san*." Akai looked nervously about. "Let us now talk of other things."

The transfer to the Yokosuka train went smoothly. Cole realized he was no longer clenching his fists; perspiration that had soaked his shirt began to cool in the air conditioning of the train. He and Hiroshi found good seats on the Yokosuka train and settled in for a game of gin rummy. The two men shared a passion for minor stakes gambling.

Cole and Akai ate while they played, salted fish chips and cheap vegetable sushi that Akai had purchased from vending machines on the boarding platform. Cole took a big bite of sushi spread liberally with *wasabi* and washed the mix down with a swig of Kirin beer.

"This is *oishi*."

"It is just station food, John-*san*. I will take you to a good restaurant when we arrive in Yokosuka. It is your deal." Akai handed the cards over to Cole.

"Why do you suppose they put Parsons up to catching me?"

"I am not sure, but I suspect the Americans wanted to take you quietly. The war is unpopular in Japan. The authorities did not want a loud confrontation with an American soldier in the middle of Tokyo."

"Yeah. Makes sense. Sure pisses me off." Cole shuffled and dealt the dog-eared cards. "Tell me more about Yokosuka." The sprawl of an industrial section of Tokyo rattled by. The brown/gray sides of buildings and gray shingled roofs slide by in the foreground of a yellow, gray sky and the suggestion of hills behind the pollution and mists of the Japanese countryside.

Akai replied, "Yokosuka is a small town by Japanese standards. It was a naval base during World War II. The American First Marine Division was expected to invade there."

"My dad was in the First Marine Division in Korea...God, invading Japan would have been a real bloodbath. I'm glad it didn't happen."

"Bloodbath?' What does that mean?"

"I guess the term is gross. Means there'd be a lot of blood from killing. So much blood people could take a bath in it."

"I understand. It is an apt term. If soldiers had invaded Japan, well over a million Americans might have died and many, many more Japanese. My mother told me as a child that she had trained to kill white devils with a sharpened bamboo stick. Every Japanese citizen was prepared to die for the Showa Emperor."

"Didn't dropping the bomb on Hiroshima and Nagasaki make invading Japan unnecessary? The bombs stopped the war, didn't they?"

Cole knew the answer, but wanted to see how his friend had been taught. Akai's reply surprised him.

"Yes and no, John-*san*. The war did stop, but it would have soon stopped anyway. It is said after the Potsdam Declaration our government wished to hold to a policy of *mokusatsu*. This term does not exist in English. Depending on context, it can mean either to not to comment or to ignore. Unfortunately, the world thought the Japanese government planned to ignore the allied request for surrender. Shortly thereafter, the Americans dropped atomic bombs on Hiroshima and Nagasaki." Akai shook his head sadly. "Humans often kill because of poor communication. Yet, we all have more in common than they realize."

John nodded thoughtfully.

The men continued to play cards and washed down travel dust with Kirin beer as the city clicked by. Cole's hair had continued to come in white. It had grown enough that he now passed for civilian.

"Gin." Akai won another hand, putting Cole down 900 yen. Cole looked from his cards to a Japanese mother in a pink, western-style jumpsuit leading a little girl toward the toilets at the end of the car. Suddenly, the child broke away and ran down the aisle away from her mother and toward Cole. Cold sweat beaded Cole's brow as he watched the toddler's escape and remembered the unsuccessful escape of another toddler. The mother moved catlike; quickly caught up, and swung the child up into her arms. The toddler squealed with delight. Cole was swept with a wave of nausea.

"Are you all right, John-*san*?"

"Yeah, sure. Sorry."

⁎ ⁎ ⁎ ⁎ ⁎ ⁎ ⁎ ⁎ ⁎ ⁎ ⁎ ⁎ ⁎ ⁎

Connor and Annie set up camp in Chicago's Lincoln Park. The park was about two miles north of the convention site, the old International Amphitheater near the shore of Lake Michigan.

The 1968 Democratic National Convention led to a military call-up that rivaled a major troop movement in Vietnam. Hundreds of secret service agents, National Guardsmen, federal narcotic investigators and police swarmed throughout the city. Helicopters whirred over the 2,000 police patrolling on the ground. Hundreds of firefighters waited on standby in anticipation of fire bombings; 5,500 Illinois National Guardsmen waited in armories or in machine gun emplacements along Michigan Avenue; 7,500 regular army troops stood ready at Fort Hood, Texas to be airlifted on 24-hour notice to Chicago.

Tension between the security forces and the rag-tag army of war protestors had escalated as the convention neared. Minor clashes and name-calling had turned ugly by the time Connor and Annie wheezed into town aboard a worn-out Renny.

Connor and Annie joined a communal cookout in Lincoln Park shortly after arriving. Connor had saved his draft card thinking about just such an occasion. To the cheers of the crowd, he dramatically ripped it up and tossed it on the bonfire. At that moment, as though in response, the Chicago police poured into the park swinging their batons. Annie and Connor had just enough time to throw their knapsacks into Renny and escape down North Avenue. A mile down the road they parked, climbed out, and at Connor's insistence hiked back on foot to join the gathering storm.

"Connor, let's not go," Annie pleaded, racing two steps to his one in her attempt to keep up with him. "Come on, someone's going to get hurt. Let's get back to the van."

Chants of "Oink, oink. Kill the pigs. Oink, oink. Kill the pigs!" and "Hey, hey, JFK, how many boys did you kill today!" merged as the protestors taunted the security forces trying to clear the park. The sting and stench of tear gas hung in the air triggering Annie's memory of the day she met Connor.

The crowd surrounded a patrol car and began to rock it back and forth.

"This is wrong. Don't drop to their level!" Connor yelled at the top of his lungs, but only Annie heard Connor's plea over the roar of the crowd. A squad of police charged to liberate the patrol car and to gain revenge. Connor swerved from the patrol car and pushed through the mob to the front ranks.

"Connor, stop! let's get out of here!" Annie screamed.

"No. We came to make a difference," Connor yelled over his shoulder. He was within minutes of making it to the front. The chanting had merged into a dull and continuous roar punctuated by screams and howls of anger and the thwack of police and Guardsmen batons.

In desperation Annie leaped and grabbed the shoulder of Connor's shirt.

As Connor turned to look back at the insistent tug on his shirt, a gas canister fired moments before exploded against the back of his head. He rocked forward into Annie's arms. She staggered. A man and woman materialized out of the melee and helped Annie drag Connor to refuge.

But there was no refuge. The panicked crowd blocked their escape, as did an alien vision of glimmering shields, bug-like masks in a gray-brown dust mist, cold blue uniforms, and flailing, prodding batons. In an unexpected flash, the man let go of Connor, turned, and launched himself at a cop. He pushed the cop to the ground, took his baton, and began to pound with maniacal rage. The element of surprise, adrenaline energy, and muscle gave the aggressor a temporary advantage.

The cop rolled away bleeding, gagging from gas seeping through his shattered mask. Annie and the woman took advantage of the moment to skid Connor away from rampaging police and demonstrators.

Connor roused.

"You all right?" Annie asked, bending close as she supported his head and stroked his short, blood-matted hair. Blood trickled down Connor's forehead over his birthmark. His wire-rim glasses hung off a bloody ear. Annie set them back on his nose.

"Yeah, I think so."

Annie looked up at the young woman and held out her free hand in a gesture of thanks. She stopped.

"Mickie? Uh...I mean Michelle? *Michele*! Is that you?"

"Hi," Michelle replied, a little nervously. "I was hoping you wouldn't recognize me. It's been a while, Annie. What are you doing here? I mean it's really far out to see you doing something like this. Wow... what a way to meet. I can't believe we connected."

"What are you doing here! Do Ralph and Shirley know where you are? God, I wonder what John would think!"

The women had to huddle closer together to be heard over the roar

"No, they don't know where I am. I couldn't stand it anymore at home. Is this John's replacement? I heard Mom tell Dad you two broke up. This guy looks like an improvement over my blood-and-guts brother. God, I hope Norm's okay. He gave me a ride here. He sure was trashing that cop."

Norm probably wasn't okay. Michelle looked in her friend's direction and saw him drowning in a vat of angry blue uniforms and flashing batons. The crowd never stopped moving. It again threatened to swallow them.

"We better split, Annie."

"Renny's just down the street," Annie said, helping Connor to wobble to his feet.

"Renny?"

A gas canister blossomed at their feet. Annie choked out, "Connor's van. Let's split!"

The women and Connor backtracked to away from the mob to the van. The women poured Connor in the back. Annie took the wheel and headed west down North Street.

"Where to?"

"Double back," Michelle replied. "Take a left at Halsted, then a left on Roosevelt. The cops won't bother anyone near the Amphitheater."

Annie hesitated. But she didn't know anything better to do in a strange town that Michelle already seemed to know well. She turned left on Halsted.

"Michelle, really, what are you doing here? How did you get here?"

"I just hitched. Nobody has any idea where I am," Michelle said. "I couldn't stay. They couldn't see who I was. All I ever heard about was John, John, John. John and his country. John and his 'yes sir' haircut. I doubt they know I'm gone. If they do, it'll only be because Chuck finked on me. Mom wouldn't know I was alive unless she tripped over me on her way to the pantry. All she ever does is eat and yell. Get this, get that, sit down, shut up, curl your hair. Curl your hair! The only thing my mother says to me besides 'praise the Lord' is 'curl your hair.'"

Annie ground down into second gear and turned into a side parking lot at Grant Park. It was dark. The glare of floodlights circled the convention site. Hot and muggy, it was a typical late summer evening in Chicago. Thunderclouds boiled in the sky. Fireflies flickered. Connor groaned and turned over on the pile of rugs in the back. Michelle turned to pull a blanket back over him.

Annie peeked a glance at Connor, then back at Michelle. "I know what you mean. Shirley can be hard to talk to. When she called to tell me about John going AWOL, I tried to talk with her about John and me breaking up, but it was like… like she didn't hear me. Of course she was frantic with worry. I worry about him, too. We were together a long time."

Michelle answered, "John was so straight. Bad enough he didn't go to Canada or at least wait to get drafted, but he actually joined some kind of killer elite. Then he deserted! I wonder what got into him. It must've been real heavy whatever it was."

"He's supposed to be hiding out somewhere in Japan."

"Hope he's okay." Michelle sounded like she really meant it as she gazed out Renny's open window. The rain started to fall.

* * * * * * * * * * * * * *

Cole watched Hiroshi Akai teach English his first few days in Yokosuka. By the third day, Hiroshi had him involved with Beheiren business. The Beheiren's front in Yokosuka had 30 students. Most were real English students. Four were AWOL 'teachers' like Cole. During those first days, long dinner conversations stretched into the early morning as the men and Cole shared the type of stories that only those who had been there could understand.

Late one night, during the second week in Yokosuka, Cole and Hiroshi had just finished talking with a lonely marine at a corner tavern. Akai walked the marine back to his room leaving Cole alone at the bar. The clock above the bar ticked toward midnight. A blue haze hung below a wheezing ceiling fan. A couple of drunks slouched in red-felt veneer booths. At the bar itself, a few stools to Cole's left, a sleazy blonde Japanese barfly eyed the white-haired, stringy American. Oriental pop music twanged as a backdrop. Cole finished his beer chasing it with a final slug of whiskey.

Cole didn't know he was being watched.

A second lieutenant looked at Cole through a brightly-lit window of the bar from his place behind the wheel of a Ford sedan. He whispered into a short-band radio to reinforcements standing behind the tavern's exit doors.

"He's alone at the bar. Let's take him. All units check in."

"Mitchell, ready," crackled a reply.

"Knight, ready."

"Woslowitz, ready."

"This scumbag got away before. Don't let it happen again. I want him down, secured, and out the door ASAP."

The lieutenant paused.

"Go, now!"

Doors exploded in as MPs converged on the bar. Cole instinctively spun sideways and broke the nose of the first MP with the flat of his left hand. He turned, kicking out, and disabled another attacker whose momentum carried him into the blonde. Screaming, she flipped over backwards with a flash of stocking and garters. Whirling again, Cole took a stream of mace in the face from the third MP. A second blast missed and nailed the MP with the broken nose as he came up behind Cole, adding to his misery and anger. He howled. The lieutenant leapt from his car on the street to join the fray. Cole was wrestled to the floor. His arms and legs cuffed.

The brawl made the evening news on NHK, the national public television station in Japan. A follow-up story aired when it was discovered Cole had been a member of Special Forces. As part of the second story, Hiroshi Akai told the TV reporter and the Japanese people the story of My Lai.

Before the month was out, a military tribunal sentenced Cole to six years for desertion in the face of the enemy. Another two years was added for resisting arrest and assaulting military police. Cole would be in the cold gray embrace of the military stockade in Leavenworth, Kansas until 1976.

Military police rounded up the rest of the Beheiren cell. Alan and Fumiko Pool, and Hiroshi Akai, were released after questioning by American and Japanese authorities. Only circumstantial evidence tied Alan and Fumiko to the real purpose of the language school in Yokosuka. Hiroshi Akai's samurai lineage and Japanese society's tacit opposition to the war in Vietnam helped him escape unscathed. Other American servicemen waiting in Yokosuka received dishonorable discharges, an outcome that met their needs. Cole was to be the example.

Chapter 10

Connor woke up with a bad headache. He, Annie, and Michelle spent the next three days on the move. By night, they camped in a shopping center parking lot or side street. One time, cops in the middle of the night rousted them.

The day before final balloting at the convention, Annie pleaded with Connor to help her pack up Renny so they could all go home. By early evening of the same day, after an uneventful day of hanging out in the crowd where ever it could be found, the three returned to Lincoln Park and sat in front of the van screened by birch trees from the cops that circled the park. The setting sun fell as tension in the park rose.

"Connor, you don't even know for sure that you don't have a concussion," Annie said. "This is nuts. Demonstrations aren't doing any good. You're going to get really hurt, if not killed. Let's get out while we can. At the very least, we need to get Michelle home."

"No way, Annie. I've got to stay. It'd be too easy to pack up and leave." Connor said this as he sank back on Renny's still sun warm side.

Michelle nodded in agreement.

Annie rolled her eyes. Connor had become quite the philosopher. "I've tried really hard to understand what you're doing. I know you're doing what you think you need to do. But nobody's going to find peace here. The best thing we can do is to split. So, I'm leaving. Tomorrow. It's fine with me if you don't want to go. But you can at least take me and

Michelle to the bus station." Annie stalked away angrily and flounced down under a nearby tree. John was missing somewhere in Japan. Connor had turned peace evangelist. She jumped at a loud scream, then realized it came from a party close by. She got up, walked over to the van, leaned against a door, and muttered. "I'm leaving, I've to get ready for school. We should never have come. This whole thing is crazy..."

"Why, Annie?" Michelle materialized out of the dark.

"You scared me," Annie sputtered.

"Who're you talking to?"

"I guess you could say I'm having a conversation with myself. A conversation I should've had long before coming on this trip."

"I don't think it is wrong for you to be here. In fact, I'm going to stay. I'm staying with Connor. I hate for you to go back alone, but that's the way it's got to be."

Annie looked over at John's sister. Mickie wasn't the little girl in pigtails she had met six years before. "This is serious," Annie said with quiet determination. "The cops are going to kick ass tomorrow. People are going to get hurt. You're just a kid. We all are, really. You should come back with me."

"No," Michelle said stubbornly. "You sound like Shirley. She's always after me to do the sensible thing. This time I'm going to do what I want to do. I'll be careful. But I've got to be here. Just don't tell my parents you saw me."

"I have to. Think how they must feel. Your folks must be freaking out. I wouldn't be surprised if they called the cops."

"Okay. Okay, tell 'em. But let them know that if they come after me, or send the cops after me, I'll lose myself again. Permanently."

Annie sighed. "Okay, but take care, Mickie."

The young women embraced awkwardly. Michelle then grabbed her sleeping bag and pillow, the binoculars she used for stargazing and backed out of the van. She walked over to a soft spot on the grass some distance from the van and Annie. She lay down and put the glasses to her eyes. A short moment later Connor joined her as though he'd been waiting for this opportunity.

"What're you looking at?" Connor floated a blanket out next to Michelle and settled in. "Annie says you're a genius." Connor pointed quickly. "Prove it. What's that fuzz over there?"

"That's a star cluster, Connor. And no, I'm not a genius. Chuck got most of the brains."

"How can that be? Annie told me he's your twin."

"He is, but we're fraternal, not identical, so he could be a lot smarter than me."

"Somehow I find that hard to believe," Connor replied. "What's that?" he asked, stifling a yawn as he again flailed his right arm upward.

"What's what?"

"Those stars over there." Connor pointed more precisely.

"Might be the Cygnus cluster. It has about 30 stars. You see a cross made up by the brighter stars? That's called the Northern Cross."

"Uh…no, not really. What does 'Cygnus' mean?"

"The swan. Quick. Look," she pointed.

A shooting star. Connor missed the streak of light. He took the binoculars from Michelle. "What're those stars over there?" He pointed again with his unencumbered hand.

Michelle followed Connor's gesture. "I think that's Sagittarius." She took back the binoculars. "Yeah, that's it. It's hard to pick out from here because of city lights."

"How far away are those stars?"

"I'm not sure. Probably several thousand light years, though. Plenty far enough. But at least Sagittarius is in the Milky Way. The next closest galaxy is two million light years away. Galaxies billions of light years away have been found. There's billions of galaxies, trillions of stars. The size of the universe blows me away."

"Far out." Connor chuckled at his pun. Michelle didn't. "How'd you learn all this stuff?"

"Chuck and I got into astronomy when we were little. Ralph bought us a telescope from K-Mart. We got star maps and tracked constellations. Chuck's still really into that stuff."

"Who's Ralph?"

"My dad."

Connor paused before responding. He didn't think of dads as having first names. "What's that star over there that's not twinkling?"

"That's a planet, Connor. Mars, I think. Planets don't twinkle."

Connor looked at the precocious 15-year old, then sat up to look through the binoculars. "Wow, there's another shooting star." He pointed in the direction of the Northern Cross constellation he had just learned about.

"Good eyes. But you can't be sure that that was a shooting star."

"Well, what was it then?"

"I'm not sure."

Connor yawned again and laid the binoculars down. "Why'd you leave home?"

Michelle rolled over on her side and looked at Connor. His gaze was drawn like a magnet to her cleavage.

Michelle looked up at Connor and said, "What're you looking at?"

"That jewel you're wearing around your neck. What is it?"

"The crystal? It's something I found on vacation when I was little…is there something else about that part of my body that interests you?"

Flustered, Connor paused, then said, "Yeah, well, no. I mean, yes I do want an answer to my question. Why'd you leave home?"

"Problems with Shirley, mostly. She's always been a real bitch. Everything has to be her way. Ralph just ignores her and sits in front of the TV. Chuck is a bookworm. He has his nose buried in a book when he isn't solving math problems for fun. Shirley's a Jesus freak. I think she thinks Jesus Christ somehow protects John. John and Jesus. That's all she ever talks about. Doesn't care about anything else, including me."

Connor noted that Michelle also referred to her mother as "Shirley" rather than "Mom" in framing her reply. He thought back to his own mother. She had promised him that he was destined for something special in life. As bad as things got between her and his dad, and between his parents and him, he still never thought of her and his dad as anything else but "Mom and Dad."

Michelle turned over on her stomach and picked at blades of grass beside the blanket. Sirens wailed in the distance. "She's a Reverend Isaiah Marcus Stringer fanatic. She goes to this nut's church. It's called the First Church of Jesus Christ Washed in the Blood of the Lamb."

Connor laughed.

"Mom started out listening to his late night radio broadcasts on KRRO, then she met Stringer in person and got hooked. He has, like, this end of the world obsession. He thinks we're going to be invaded by the Antichrist. Anyway, the whole thing was driving me nuts, so I left. I would have split anyway. It was just a matter of time. Better sooner than later."

Connor glanced up at the stars, as though trying to find the right response. "I've had…had problems with my folks too. I don't know. It's like they have problems too, but when we're little we can't see them."

Michelle didn't reply.

"Like you said, the Universe is a big place. Must have taken some kind of God to create it. Maybe Shirley's right." Connor said this sardonically, as though not believing his own words. He turned over on his side, propped his head in his hand and looked at Michelle. She was cute and tough at the same time. And those curves. God! It was hard to believe she was only15. "You ever think there might be life out there somewhere?"

"Yeah, I do. There's got to be millions of planets out there that could support life."

"I wonder if we'll ever meet them."

Michelle smiled. "The little green men? Chuck thinks—and I guess I agree—that we would have already discovered aliens if they lived close enough to visit."

"So, we're not some alien's science project?"

"No. I think we just happened. Life's like that. It just happens."

The two continued to talk softly. The rest of the world seemed quiet and far away.

"Tell me more about your family. You do have a family, don't you?" Michelle's eyes glistened.

Connor hesitated, then answered. "No. I mean, yes, I do. I have a mom and dad, but no brothers or sisters. My folks divorced. I remember terrible fights they had when I was a kid. I split right after my mom and dad divorced when I was 16. I really didn't want to have to choose between them." Changing the subject, Connor gave Michelle a good-natured poke. "Let's get some sleep. Tomorrow's the floor vote. It'll be a big day."

                    * * * * * * * * * * * * * *

August 28th dawned warm and humid. At first light, Connor drove Annie to the bus station. Michelle had long disappeared leaving only a goodbye note to Annie on Renny's windshield wiper and arrangements to meet Connor later.

Police and National Guard barricades snaked everywhere making for a circuitous trip to the bus station. Connor realized the level of activity meant there'd probably be a clash that night, maybe even a big one. They arrived, parked next to the curb, and strolled into the terminal.

"Maybe you have the right idea," he told Annie as the two sat on a bench. "Still, I've got to see this thing through."

"Maybe you are right, Connor," Annie said. "Just keep an eye on Mickie. I'd feel a lot better if she was coming back with me. Like I've been saying, people are going to get hurt. Most of them won't really

know why, except maybe you. It's not too late to change your mind."
Annie said this with a resigned tenderness.

"Afraid my mind's made up. Look, I'll see you in a few weeks, and I
will keep an eye on Michelle."

"I know you will." Annie smiled.

"What do you mean by that?"

"What do you think I mean?"

Connor looked down at his feet.

Annie continued. "Connor, our relationship is changing. I'm not as
sure of you and me as I thought I was. Maybe I just miss John. I don't
know. Let's think about things while we're apart. Maybe we both just
needed a change and stumbled upon each other at the right time.
Anyway, let's talk when you get back."

Connor paused. "Okay."

A last call crackled out over the terminal.

Connor pulled her close. "Take care. I'll see you in a week or so." She
kissed him gently on the lips and pulled away. He watched the sway of
her hips as she moved away, realizing his instincts had been right on.
He'd been a diversion for a young woman—not a "chick"—who had
plans and was going places, probably with her soldier boyfriend. *John
Cole has to be special to keep someone like Annie interested.* Also, though
he couldn't put his finger on "why," Connor thought he might meet
John Cole one day. And that he would like him.

Michelle met Connor at Lincoln Park at noon. She approached him
excitedly, "Connor, we've got to split right away. The staging area for
tonight is at Grant Park."

"Cool," he said. "Think I'll leave Renny here. Get back here if we
separate and hide in the van if you have to. For now, let's stay on foot."

By mid-afternoon, a crowd of 10,000 had gathered by a band shell
across the street from the convention site in Grant Park. Following days
of clashes and rising tension, demonstrators taunted without respite.
The police clubbed and gassed in response. As the afternoon wore on

and a series of speakers droned, anger and fear spread through the crowd like ground fog.

A fire kindled when an overzealous demonstrator or an agent provocateur—no one ever knew which, for sure—tried to remove an American flag from a pole next to the rally. A squad of police in riot gear charged the crowd by the flagpole. One of the leaders went down hard further inflaming the crowd. An ambulance arrived, siren screaming, as though on cue and carted away his limp form. The rally resumed in starts and stops as the demonstration's other leaders scuffled for control.

Tom Hayden, still angered by the police charge, seized the microphone and exhorted the crowd to fight police brutality. A more moderate leader, David Dellinger, called for a nonviolent march through Grant Park and across the street to the convention site.

Connor and Michelle listened from a vantage point on a grassy rise in the middle of the crowd. Long hair and picket signs, garish clothing and the reds, greens, and yellows of flower power and revolution mixed with the sweet smell of marijuana that wafted on the breeze. Connor agreed with Dellinger who spoke first about peace and nonviolent protest. But Tom Hayden's words, words barely heard over the thumping of police helicopters overhead, chilled him. Hayden cried out for the flowing of blood across the city.

As dusk feel, the mob moved out through the park toward the convention site. Rally organizers tried, but failed, to keep the demonstrators together. The charging clumps became one as groups merged onto Michigan Avenue. Flashing blue and red police strobes mixed with harsh lighting for the television cameras in the parking lot of the Conrad Hilton Hotel across the street. Triple ranks of riot-helmeted, gas-masked, shielded Illinois National Guardsmen and Chicago police waited at the ready, blocking the mob's progress toward the convention site. Nightfall smothered combatants in a surreal inky swamp of shadow and strobe of flashing lights.

The crowd broke into raucous chants. Busloads of police and National Guard reinforcements poured in. Rolls of toilet paper, rocks and bottles spewed across onto the ranks of cops and National Guardsmen from demonstrators in front and from the upper-story windows of the Conrad Hilton behind them. The demonstrators answered the first loudspeaker order to disperse with profanity punctuated with middle fingers.

Without warning, a wedge of police smashed into the crowd hacking, prodding, and pounding where, as luck would have it, Connor and Michelle stood.

Connor and Michelle's cries were smothered by the shrill screams of other demonstrators. The two were pulled apart as the battle swirled across the street to the front of the Conrad Hilton, and into the glare of television cameras.

Michelle was cornered against an outside wall of the hotel by two Chicago police officers. She fell to the ground screaming; she just happened to be in the wrong place at the wrong time. It wasn't personal. Michelle covered her head with her arms.

"*Help!*"

Connor followed the sound of Michelle's screams. He pushed through and fell across her body. The two clutched and squirmed in each other's arms on the ground as the baton blows rained down. One blow reopened the wound on Connor's forehead. The cops gathered them up roughly and tossed them into a police bus standing by at the curb.

Both were bruised and cut but Connor's head wound was particularly bad. Blood poured down into his eyes. He couldn't wipe away the flow fast enough. They huddled in the bus, in shock.

"Should've listened to Annie," Connor mumbled, as he picked himself up off the floor of the bus and wiped his forehead flinging droplets of blood against the inside of the bus.

"You say something?" Michelle responded slowly.

"Nothing important."

"You okay?"

"Not really. How 'bout you?"

"I don't know. My ribs hurt."

The intersection of Michigan and Balboa was soon cleared of demonstrators, testament to the overwhelming strength and tenacity of the cops and guardsmen. Fighting continued, however, on sidewalks and in parking lots. Even bystanders were drawn in. Chicago cops charged Conrad Hilton guests who had been watching the carnage from behind a wooden barricade. The men, women and children fell backward into the hotel lobby through a facing plate glass window.

Television network cameras fed the violence from the Battle of Chicago directly into TV screens homes across the planet. Realizing the cameras were rolling, the crowd chanted, "The whole world is watching. The whole world is watching!"

Two days later, by the convention's close, more than 800 civilians and 150 police and National Guard had been injured; 668 demonstrators, including Connor and Michelle, landed in jail—Connor in the Cook County Jail by virtue of just turning 18; Michelle in a juvenile facility. One demonstrator had died.

During the same week, 408 Americans died in Vietnam along with a much larger, but uncounted, number of Vietnamese.

* * * * * * * * * * * * *

More than the whole world could have watched the Battle of Chicago. More than the whole world could have watched—and studied—the tragedy of Vietnam, including Hiroshi Akai's account of the My Lai massacre on NHK TV in Japan.

More than the whole world could have listened, along with Shirley Cole, to the fiery late-night KRRO broadcasts of the Reverend Isaiah Stringer, pastor of the First Church of Jesus Christ Washed in the Blood of the Lamb. More than the whole world has had the opportunity to study trillions of bits of information escaping the gravity well of Earth in the radio/light wave spectrum every minute of every day. But having the opportunity to listen is not the same thing as actually listening. Information educates and informs only if intelligent beings are present. The chances of a listener happening upon Earth's transmissions are remote. One must be very close to clearly observe transmissions in the light spectrum. And radio waves from Earth had been traveling outward only since the time radio technology became widespread on the planet—about 60 years. Sixty light-years are insignificant within a Milky Way galaxy 100,000 light years across. Natural wave emissions from Earth, though they would tell of a beautiful water planet, would be too insignificant to be noticed.

But what if a wandering Arkadian starship with appropriate receiving technology happened to ford a stream of Earth radio waves from the Earth-year, 1968? And turned toward Earth to hear more?

The Hive's passengers would follow the Battle of Chicago and tune in to follow the Days of Rage, an October 1969 hiatus when a militant faction of the Students for a Democratic Society returned to Chicago—wearing helmets and armed with baseball bats—to gain revenge by committing atrocities of their own.

By now, the Arkadians would be hooked by the drama streaming to them from the blue planet. They would observe Neil Armstrong's stirring first steps on the moon. News reports of the 1970 U.S. invasion of Cambodia and accounts of the shooting deaths of students at Kent State and Jackson State Universities would follow. They would note the 1971 court martial of Lt. William "Rusty" Calley for atrocities at My Lai and see him walk free three years later—despite an original sentence of life imprisonment.

The Arkadians would learn about a world where more supposedly sentient beings are hungry than not, where nation-states spend more on weapons than on education and social services combined. They would be alarmed by the destructive potential of thousands of nuclear weapons and the rampant despoliation of a glorious ecosystem as the Hive continued its long glide toward Earth.

* * * * * * * * * * * * * *

Peacemakers of all types were imprisoned as August, 1968 came to a close. John Cole would soon arrive at his new home in the Leavenworth military stockade. Connor and Michelle paced in separate jail cells in Chicago. The Peacemaker and other white-robed wawrens mediated behind electrobars in the Hive.

In the evening of the last day of August, Shirley Cole turned to Reverend Stringer for support at the news her rebellious daughter, as well as beloved eldest son, were both jailbirds. Chuck Cole stretched across the recliner in the Cole living room reading *Starship Troopers*, a sci-fi classic about interplanetary war. Ralph napped and replayed his nightmare of Korea.

Across town, Annie Simpson arrived home after a long, tiring bus trip. She hadn't yet seen the Associated Press photos of Connor Alexander and Michelle Cole as they huddled beneath police blows. Halfway across the country, Michelle lay awake on her back on a hard army issue- folding cot in her jail cell. She fingered the crystal amulet around her neck, the good luck charm she found as a child during a horror-show 1950s family automobile vacation to the Grand Canyon. "What good are you to me, anyhow," she complained out loud." She thought about Connor and hoped her parents wouldn't interfere with her trip home. Going back with Connor would be fun.

Eldon Moss was Connor's only visitor in jail. He slipped into Connor's cell the second night.

"Jeezus, son. That was a peace demonstration? You're kidding me." He looked down at the prisoner with a half grin. "Why cain't you folks ever git along?"

"What? What're you talking about? What folks?"
But he was gone.

* * * * * * * * * * * * * *

Ethnographer's report (continued)
More than a billion years passed before the first bacteria and microscopic plant life developed in the oceans of the new planet. Plants developed the ability to photosynthesize during subsequent millions of years, taking in CO2 and giving off oxygen and thereby returning precious water to the ecosystem. Plants became more sophisticated and spread to land. The time of fishes and reptiles followed. Dinosaurs were masters of the reptile period for more than 100 million years before they disappeared. Mammals began 65 million years ago after an asteroid impact destroyed the dinosaurs. The human evolutionary line began about 10 million years ago.

Contrary to popular opinion among human anthropologists, the evolutionary path of Homo Sapiens did not originate on the grassy savannas of what humans referred to as the late Miocene and Pliocene Periods. After great droughts had destroyed jungle and woodland that provided food and safety, human ancestors instead fled to the shores of great fresh water lakes, to estuaries, and to rivers. Those who did not migrate to the shoreline became food for better-equipped, ferocious carnivores that lived on the savannas and guarded the water holes. Their evolutionary line ended.

Retreat to water provided respite from the heat and protection from carnivores—particularly the great cats—that didn't like to swim. The seashore provided an abundance of food—shellfish, algaes, and fish—that didn't bite back and was relatively easy to catch. Eclectic dietary habits evolved in humans in response to the wide availability of varied food.

The Pliocene drought went on for thousands of centuries and encouraged evolutionary development in, and near, water. Aquatic life selected for characteristics such as webbing between digits for swimming and bipedalism to keep heads above waters in the shallows. Life in and near water made thick fur a liability, so hairlessness developed as another useful adaptation. Skull hair took the place of shade trees and vegetation as protection from the overhead sun. Rudimentary language developed as an effective way to communicate to others while wading in deep water.

Later versions of humans retained these basic physical characteristics as their brain pans grew in size, and skill as tool users continued to improve. The hominids that emerged from the Pliocene drought and shorelines were bipedal, socially organized, tool-using animals capable of traveling inland and adapting to a wide variety of conditions.

The planet had come a long way. Original stardust had evolved into oceans, mountains, rocks, trees, and into modern humans, including Annie Simpson, Connor Alexander, and the Cole family; into toys, automobiles, computers, and software; into rice, potatoes, and curry; into rich and poor countries, birth control pills, and TV dinners; into pollution, swords, and plowshares. And into the thermonuclear weapons that mimic the power of Earth's star, the Lifegiver.

1974: THE PRIESTS OF WA

CHAPTER 11

Arkadians had to cooperate to leave the planet before their home star took back its gift of life. As generations evolved from the time of fighting to a time of peace, a new caste emerged: the *wawrens*, high priests of Wa.

Wawrens mastered every Arkadian dialect and every contingency related to conflict. Wawren empathy, superb telepathic ability, and the pacifist framework of Wa enabled the white-robed peacemakers to mediate all significant disputes on the planet. From the three Tenets of Wa—that actions for peace speak louder than words, that actions for peace must be peaceful, and that in any dispute there must be found a superordinate goal or goals: a civilization steeped in violence made a peace that lasted 1500 years.

Wawrens supervised the building of the Temples of Wa and placed the raindrums outside each temple. Soon all Arkadians swayed in inward contemplation to the cadence of the drums save for a paltry few ravans who snarled impotently behind the fences of widely scattered, but secure, compounds. Arkadia's moon, Tirlol, became the totem of Wa. This totem adorned banners and buildings everywhere. A world government evolved faster than any Arkadian would have expected.

Peace allowed planet-wide resources to be shifted from endings—military applications and death: to beginnings—study of the universe and star travel. Marvelous discoveries followed. Straddletravel and hypertravel, discovered in 1115 P.W. (Post Wa) and 1119 P.W respectively, provided the long-sought roadway to the stars and escape from Arkadia's angry star.

Passing through the event horizon of a black hole, a straddlepoint, moved a traveler instantaneously hundreds—sometimes even thousands—of light years across the galaxy. Wizard theorists initially thought this passage literally involved straddling into a parallel universe. This notion was eventually discredited, but the idea of "straddling" stuck. Developing antimatter engines and antigravity technologies made it possible to pass unscathed through the crushing gravity of a black hole's event horizon.

Instantaneously zipping thousands of light years still didn't solve the problem of moving from star system to star system after straddling however. This problem was solved with the development of hypertravel, a technology that allowed for efficient travel across the vast reaches of normal, three-dimensional space. Hypertravel, as applied in the geometries of hyperspace, made half-light speed transit possible: a trip of 15 light years could be completed in 30 years. Wave transmissions of all types could still be plucked from three-dimensional space during transit. Relativistic effects that slow time for travelers approaching light speed did not occur in hyperspace. All of this was good news. The Arkadians would be able to track events on a destination blue planet as they approached it.

Straddletravel and hypertravel were elegant solutions, but there remained the challenge of tranversing space within an individual star system. Also, it wouldn't do to overshoot a planet in hypertravel and inadvertently come out in the middle of a star or planet. Arkadian wizards perfected proton-proton engine technology as a solution for short intrasystem hops.

Regardless of the mechanics of travel, there loomed the question of destination. Hundreds of systems within the home galaxy might possess a blue planet, but finding one of those systems in the vastness of space could be likened to sifting all the beaches of Arkadia to find a single, special grain of sand. The wizards solved this problem with searcher technology.

Hundreds of robotic searchers would be launched to roam the galaxy. They would locate and pass through straddlepoints. They would scan and find candidates for colonization; go into hyperdrive for the trip to the system; "gear down" for an intrasystem hop to the candidate planet; then seed it from orbit with a sending maser, a manufactured crystal calibrated to receivers to be placed in the Hive. (The Tirlol-sized starship to follow the searchers was referred to early on as "the Hive" because it would enclose colonists much like a hive encloses a colony of Arkadian bees.)

Technicians planned to activate maser receivers in the Hive after each straddle. Finding a maser signal meant a potential home had been seeded and existed within 100 light years of the Hive. If a maser signal couldn't be found, the Hive's standard receivers—the same receivers used by robotic searchers—would be engaged. Besides capability to read gravitons and x-ray waves necessary for locating straddlepoints, the Hive's standard receivers could read waves in the radio and light spectrums ranging from short-wave gamma rays to x-rays and ultraviolet light and long-range infrared waves.

Though the searchers might seed dozens of planets, only four or five candidates might be found during the Hive's life. A habitable world had to be colonized before the Hive's ecosystem stagnated to the point where its regenerating systems decayed. Cryonic storage and clever systematic recycling of waste would extend the Hive's life. These steps, however, would only postpone the eventual demise of the Hive's technical systems and ecology. It was widely hoped, indeed even expected, that the first blue planet found would suffice.

Searcher construction finished in the year 1330 P.W. Hundreds of searchers ripple-launched the next year. Construction of the Hive outside Arkadia's atmosphere began in 1355 P.W. and concluded in 1522 P.W.

The great starship's shape was modeled after Tirlol as a reminder of this totem of Wa, as a tribute to the moon's minerals that, along with asteroidal materials, made construction of the Hive possible and because the physics of construction made a globe possible. The interior ecosystem mimicked the climate of a nice day on Arkadia's equator. Twice a day, computer-driven climate controls induced a pleasing, tropical rain shower throughout the Hive's interior. Designers even built the raindrums into the Hive's superstructure as a tribute to, and reminder of, the Tenets of Wa.

The Hive's slow rotation provided centrifugal force necessary to maintain one G of Arkadian gravity. Living quarters ringed the outer edge of the ship; the next ring contained hydrophonic farms and holding pens for food fishes; the next, syntheofactories for production of necessities and warehouses; the inner circle contained administrative offices and the seat of Hive government. Mating pools were located throughout the Hive for convenient access by all.

The entire complex nestled in the Hive Sea, its waters colored gray by reflected light from the roof that arched above from horizon-to-horizon. Ceiling lamps illuminated atmosphere; glow globes provided lighting for transfer pods and for free-form travel in the Hive Sea and in buildings.

No great hue and cry arose when the time came to select colonists. Arkadia's death was long in the future. Besides, the majority preferred to take a gamble on known, if doomed, ground. The mediation skill of the wawrens further eased the selection process. The soft light of Tirlol and, alternately, harsher light from the disloyal Arkadian star illuminated a steady stream that shuttled to the Hive around the clock. The Tirlol-sized starship filled with 519,000 colonists, a number deemed necessary for colonizing a blue planet.

All castes had a place in the Hive, even the ravan caste. This depleted and thoroughly discredited caste had little use after 1500 years of peace. A small number of ravans selected in the replacement allotment and trained to be warriors within secure compounds were carefully monitored on Arkadia. Ravans served as a protection of last resort if Arkadia itself was ever invaded by extraterrestrial life. Ravans, in full battle armor, with bladed forehorns, bolos, cybernetic fighting talons, and guidance monocles for high-explosive homing spears also reminded Arkadians of the horror of military solutions. Including ravans in the Hive seemed sensible. The wyruls couldn't be too sure what might be encountered "out there."

The Hive orbited Arkadia for two years as the colonists settled in and as wizards and technicians debugged systems. Life rhythms in the Hive soon matched those on Arkadia. Each of the castes lived in a separate community in the outer ring of the Hive. It was only during the workday or in the mating pools that castes mingled. At night (commonly referred to in the Hive as a "dimming"), Arkadians returned to their homes via transport pods or conveyor tubes submersed in the Hive Sea. An Arkadian fortunate enough to live in a housing compound close to work might simply swim home.

All systems, social as well as technological, checked out and, in 1523 P.W., the Hive blasted out of Arkadia's system to begin the long journey to the first straddlepoint. The Wandering had begun.

Back on Arkadia, a sad and prophetic postscript could have been written. Another superordinate goal, equal to the one that had led Arkadia to the stars, never evolved. Ecological concerns might have been a candidate but with the end of the planet in sight, albeit far in the future, few Arkadians worried about the environment.

A charismatic wyrul filled the vacuum. She released the ravans of her tribe from their prison compounds and actively propagated them. She gained power in the planet's Council of Wyruls and established a local dictatorship based on her widely expressed belief in the genetic superiority of the ravans and wyruls of her tribe. A pogrom on her home island drove the wawrens out of their lush compounds, out of the Temples of Wa into underwater ghettos. Discrimination against wawrens soon infected all corners of Arkadia as the charismatic wyrul consolidated her power and eventually seized control of the entire planet.

The raindrums were silenced and Temples of Wa razed. A new totem replaced gentle Tirlol in all Arkadian temples, the unstable Arkadian star that adorned the charismatic wyrul's banners. Instead of soft glow and incense, instead of the soothing pounding of the raindrums, a visitor to the temples on Arkadia was now met with strobe lights and synthoscreaming.

Arkadia's final solution began. Crematoriums on every island continent belched smoke into the polluted, blood-red sky as wawrens, by millions, swam peacefully from their ghettos to mustering points and from there into the ovens. The wawren caste, a caste that had blessed Arkadia with selfless contributions to beauty, to peace, and to understanding for hundreds of years was soon no more.

The charismatic leader died of old age, pleased with the life she had lived and the future she had wrought for her tribe. No successor was named. Even if a successor had been named, conflict was inevitable. Differences among factions had simmered a long time, and the high priests of Wa were gone. A new arms race began using weapons of unimaginable potency, weapons built on a foundation of 1500 years of unimpeded scientific discovery. A final, unrestrained holocaust soon turned all of Arkadia into a crematorium.

Travelers in the Hive might have learned from this quick return to savagery. But it had been decreed that records of life on Arkadia be eradicated from the Hive's data banks so that the colonists would never look back. The colonists carried only their technology, memories of life on Arkadia that grew fainter as generations passed, and the culture of

Wa. The Hive wyruls thought their actions wise. After all, a culture suitable to Hive life and to the life beyond had to be developed.

But the star travelers never learned that the dying Arkadian sun destroyed an already long-dead planet.

* * * * * * * * * * * * * *

The tad dove downward into the tepid, cloudy-green water of the Hive. A worker nanny chased her.

It is time for food, not play

But the tad loved to play. She blasted through a clump of seaweed and was momentarily obscured from the pursuing adult. She called out telepathically for her brood-mates to join her. None would. Instead, the worker nanny's telepathy intruded. *Return to me immediately or you will be punished.*

The tad shot through the water past the tube entrance to an intruder screen that separated the waters of the nursery from the Hive Sea. The mild electric current that pulsed through the screen kept out unwanted visitors. The tad sensed a malevolent presence buried in a kelp bed on the other side of the fence. She shied away from the screen as though burned, rapidly executed a loop and passed right over the top of the frustrated worker nanny who grabbed, but missed.

Come to me now or the ravans will get you.

The tad stopped. She didn't know about the thing hiding in the kelp bed, but she knew about ravans. She flipped over on her back, looped under, and wiggled back to the worker nanny.

* * * * * * * * * * * * * *

Ralph Cole died of a heart attack while having the dream about Korea. But he didn't exactly slip away in his sleep, as Shirley later liked to say.

He was minding his own business, lying in the freezing gunk of the Chosin Reservoir foxhole covered by the same headless buddy who, this time, for the first time, turned to him and bubbled out somehow, "They're going to get you this time, Cole. Just like they got me. It's time, pal. Time to take your medicine. Time to take it like a man."

Ralph Cole stood. The rocky, moonlit landscape was littered with bodies obscenely sprawled in death. The bugles of the enemy bleated behind the whistling of the freezing wind. Darkened shapes crawled up the slope in moon shadows. He saw the flash of their burp guns. A jackhammer slammed into his chest, a suffocating blow that burned down through his left arm.

Ralph Cole might have thought about his family, his life; he might have thought of what might have been. Instead, Ralph Cole's last thought was one of relief.

CHAPTER 12

October 14, 1974

Dear John,

I was sorry to hear about your dad. I really liked him. Remember when he drove us to the freshman prom and the car got a flat? You were in a tux and didn't want to get dirty, so your dad changed the tire in a rainstorm all by himself.

I know you wanted to go to the funeral. As I'm sure you guessed, the Reverend Stringer officiated. What a blowhard! I'm sure he hardly knew your dad, but he still talked for over an hour. You didn't miss much. Believe me, memories are more important than any funeral service, this one in particular.

There were a bunch of guys there wearing VFW hats. Did you know your dad was a war hero? I sure didn't. Anyway, these guys stood up unannounced and saluted your dad's coffin as it passed by. You should have seen the look on Reverend Stringer's face!

Work is going great. I just finished management training at the bank. It's a good move, though I'm always pooped. I'm working six days a week. Right now, Seafirst Bank needs to come first.

I've been thinking about us a lot. Reading your letters has really helped me get perspective. Though we've had our ups and downs, I don't feel our relationship ever really died. In a lot of ways being apart has helped us to grow. As you know, I've gone out with other guys. But they've never measured up to you. (Including Connor!) I think that's one reason I never got married. I've been waiting for you, John, as hokey and old-fashioned as that might sound. On the other hand, maybe I'm just been too busy to hook up with someone! (Kidding!)

By the way, Connor and Michelle are doing okay. They fight a lot, but I guess that's just natural (though I sure hope it never becomes as natural between you and me). They probably shouldn't have got married. Time will tell.

Connor finished student teaching and landed a job at Queen Anne High. He's doing great. Guess the acid trips and blows to the head during his revolutionary days didn't kill too many brain cells. I still can't believe how stupid I was to go with him to Chicago. Seems like yesterday we were running from the cops. Has Mickie told you she's going to graduate magna cum laude from the university as a 20-year old? What a brain! She and Chuck should both be rocket scientists, but I think Mickie wants to be a newspaper reporter. I can just see her getting in people's faces to get a story! Wish she would quit smoking.

I know we agreed to be platonic for now (it's been tough to be anything but!), and then decide what to do, but I'd sure like to try living together when you get out. Reading between the lines of your last letter, I figured that'll be okay with you. Let's talk about it. I'll call at the usual time this Sunday.

Got to go or I'll be late.

Bye, sweetie.

Love,

Annie

October 19, 1974

Dear John-san,

It is always a refreshment to read your letters. You are very Japanese in the way you maintain a friendship. Perhaps we Japanese should give you gaijin more credit for longevity in the knowing of another person.

I decided to take the position at Mitsuibishi. My uncle works in finance for them. I am not deciding to stay with them forever although my family believes I will. I am glad to be done with school at Waseda University. I want to begin my life's work, to make money, and to be my own person.

Alan and Fumiko, as forever, send warm regards. I have included photographs. You can see that my sister is as beautiful as always she has been. Alan grew a long beard and creates quite a stir when in Tokyo. He travels wearing his blue jeans and bright Hawaiian shirts. The Blue Dot is very popular. They serve whiskey there now, along with sake and beer. The Beheiren trouble we had never hurt them.

I have a new girl friend. Her photograph is included also. What do you think?

The time of your prison stay is becoming shorter. Just two more years! You are a brave man. I will always respect you and be your friend.

Very truly yours,
Hiroshi Akai

* * * * * * * * * * * * * *

John Cole finished reading, folded the letters, and packed them back in his locker, getting ready for lights out at 2200 hours. He was alone. Each of the 1300 inmates in the only maximum-security military penitentiary in the United States lived alone. The cellblock was quiet. All inmates were required to jack in with headphones whenever they turned on a radio.

Each day, after being roused at 530 hours, Cole showered, got dressed in brown slacks and shirt, and reported to work at the 18-hole golf course maintained for military retirees and officers on the military reservation at Ft. Leavenworth. Cole earned his keep as a groundskeeper. He kept the grass green, the flowers colorful, and the sand traps smooth for the generals.

Cole ended up in Leavenworth only because his sentence was greater than five years and a day. He had been judged a hard case by the military justice system. The discipline imposed at Leavenworth included a strip search and shakedown every 90 days. Each inmate had to be totally dedicated to serving his time quietly and escaping, legally, when his time was up. No other escape was possible. The stone walls of the facility, built in 1875, were not only thick, but the military guards shot to kill.

Cole thought about the phone call from Michelle last week. His sister didn't like to write but never failed to call. He thought about his dad's heart attack and tried to remember Ralph's face. *Sorry, pop. I know you were proud of me. Like when I got perfect grades in eighth grade, like when I lettered in football as a freshman. I know you didn't want me to join the military. I'm sorry I didn't listen. Hope you forgive me and that you're in a better place. I hope you think well of me wherever you might be.*

Cole dumped his sadness into the same pit where he buried other psychic garbage, garbage that always burned in him just on the edge of his consciousness like an old tire fire at the city dump. Other inmates sensed Cole's rage and let him be, seemingly in fear of what might happen if they pushed him even just a little bit too far.

He closed his eyes to leave one nightmare, hoping he wouldn't drift into another. But he did.

* * * * * * * * * * * * * *

Ethnographer's report (continued)
Homo Sapiens had built a great civilization as the end of the 20th century approached. Still, a fundamental imbalance existed. Advances in medicine, telecommunications, industrial productivity, computers, transportation, and even recreation were more than offset by advances in military technology.

No social institution or philosophy existed to counter the death culture of the planet

As the 21st century approached, religious philosophies, obvious balm for conflict, contributed instead to planetary strife. While the Pope issued messages of peace and reconciliation from Rome, Catholic members of the Irish Republic Army killed Protestants in Dublin and were killed in kind. Jewish, Muslim, and Christian factions killed each other in the Middle East. It was the Middle East—the birthplace for major religions—that boasted the planet's highest per capita military spending as the millennium approached

Economic instability—a primary contributor to war—had been accelerated by massive arms sales to underdeveloped countries. Over $500 billion worth of weapons were sold by arms merchants to countries of the Third World between 1988-1998. The United States accounted for well over half this figure selling weapons to all takers while also spending billions to protect itself from the weapons it had sold. Yet, during 1998 alone, 135,000 Earth children breathed their last each day from malnutrition and disease

Military expenditures did not keep the peace. Over 170 conflicts occurred between 1945—the end of World War II—and 1998. More than 47 million human beings, more civilians than soldiers and more children than adults, died in these wars. 170 million human beings were murdered in separate acts of government genocide between 1900 and 1998.

These figures from war and from genocide do not include the dislocated, the stabbed, the strafed, the impoverished, the gassed and the raped survivors. These figures cannot include the uncounted.

By 1998, the stage was set for holocaust

1978: A CHILD IS BORN

CHAPTER 13

Shortly into the "me decade" of the 1970s, the U.S. declared peace with honor in Vietnam, plucked beleaguered troops off embassy rooftops in front of the advancing North Vietnamese Army and got out of Dodge. But the legacy of Vietnam could not be plucked off a rooftop.

During the 1970s, the U.S. was rocked by presidential crimes that came to be known as "Watergate." Oil turned tiny sheikdoms into world powers. Japan forged ahead in a worldwide economic war that no one except the Japanese had known was being waged. A murderous regime in Cambodia sent two million citizens to the killing fields by the close of 1978. An Algerian terrorist detonated a five-kiloton atomic bomb in downtown Paris.

The Earth's ecosystem suffered as its rain forests fell to developers and its beaches became oil-drenched wastebaskets. The "greenhouse effect" caused by hydrocarbon pollution was documented with little fanfare or concern. In 1978, a new dictator in Ecuador promised democracy. The Chinese government started to tax families with more than one child. The Prague Spring, crushed under the tracks of Soviet tanks ten years previously, experienced a rebirth as "Solidarity" in Poland. And, during 1978, Tom Hayden—the revolutionary who had called for "blood in the streets" in Chicago—won election to the California State Assembly.

Tom Hayden's defection to the establishment he once condemned shouldn't have come as a surprise. The evolution from hippie to yuppie and from flower power to middle-class values transformed baby boomers everywhere, though boomers in the U.S. and Europe did experience problems scraping up the cash to buy the dream. A pot of brown rice, a shared joint, and love and sunshine to the sounds of Crosby, Stills, and Nash just didn't cut it with a mortgage banker. The boomers now had career tracks and investment portfolios to think about.

Disco music had its moment, soon to be overwhelmed by a new generation sporting Mohawk haircuts, black leather jackets, nipple rings, and a fascination for body slamming to heavy metal rock, music that venerated an ethic of punker nihilism and hopelessness.

✻ ✻ ✻ ✻ ✻ ✻ ✻ ✻ ✻ ✻ ✻ ✻ ✻ ✻

If truth be told, Shirley hardly noticed Ralph's death four years previously. She still talked about her day in the direction of her dead husband's easy chair while fixing dinner. Only his occasional grunts and the rustling of the protective evening paper went missing. Now she ate for two.

Shirley Cole lived in a spiritual cocoon of her pastor's design. The charismatic Reverend Stringer's apocalyptic message and emphasis on the Second Coming reassured Shirley. It provided the order she craved. The evil will be cast into the lake of fire. The good will prosper. Neat and clean.

Shirley sat in her assigned pew the first Sunday in September 1978 as the organ music died and the congregation rustled. Stringer's faithful prepared for the final scripture reading. Because of growing popularity, the First Church of Jesus Christ Washed in the Blood of the Lamb offered three services each Sunday. Stringer's broadcast ministry in the Pacific Northwest region of the U.S dwarfed this congregation. His future, and the future of his church, lay far outside the tiny congregation he met three times each Sunday.

On this particular Sunday, Shirley took note of Stringer's appearance as he strode purposefully from a side door to the pulpit. The Reverend Isaiah Stringer wore a blue silk suit, alligator-skin cowboy boots, and flashed a one-carat diamond pinky ring. His tall, skinny frame was capped with an oily pompadour of red hair. Shirley did not think his appearance bizarre in the least.

Stringer reached the lectern. He glared at his flock, then began with a dramatic whisper.

"There shall come an Antichrist. He shall be male, born in our time, and innocent until touched by the Evil One. Perhaps one close to him, perhaps a mother or father, will know he is special, but his unholy mission will be unknown to all others. This messenger of hell shall bear a birthmark, the Mark of the Beast. He shall be either in a position of influence or one of innocence. He could be a child. He might be a fallen pastor. He could be a teacher of our children.

"Satan shall visit the Antichrist in the guise of a beautiful temptress, a favorite nanny or perhaps even a little old man. The devil can take many forms. Satan will befuddle, confuse, and misdirect his messenger, perhaps over the course of many years, or perhaps just for a moment. He may urge the Antichrist to take action for peace. He may compel his messenger to warn of a great threat. There is much we do not, and cannot, know about Satan's special messenger, the Antichrist. But we can know, we do know, the face of the real threat. *Who* is the *real* threat?"

As one, the congregation chanted "Satan, Satan, Satan."

"And *what* is he?"

"He is evil, evil, *evil.*"

"And *who* is Satan's special messenger?"

"The Antichrist. The Antichrist! The *Antichrist!*"

Stringer paused, then continued. "In time, the Antichrist shall sway a great host. But our Lord and Savior, Jesus Christ, *shall* emerge to uncover the evil. Jesus Christ *shall* battle this evil. Good *shall* prevail. The Antichrist and his evil counselor, the Fallen One, *shall* be cast out. A thousand years of peace *shall* then descend upon the Earth!"

Stringer took a gulp of air and again mopped his brow before finishing,

"The time of the Antichrist is approaching. We see it now in signs: the earthquakes, floods, and fires. There will be others. Look to the heavens! There will soon appear a portent of the Antichrist, a bright light like the star that led Mary and Joseph to Bethlehem. This time, the light shall signal danger! You must be vigilant. You must not allow the subtle, lecherous hand of Satan to cleave unto you. Rail against the forces of the night, the forces of Satan and the Antichrist, the forces of *evil*. Stand as a soldier with Jesus at the final battle, at Armageddon. "Hearken to Isaiah 24:18:

'The sluice gates will open and the foundations of the Earth will rock. The Earth will split into fragments. The Earth will be riven and rent. The Earth will stagger like a drunkard.'

"You shall be sorely tested. You shall go through a great trial and tribulation. But, our Lord and Savior shall prevail. The Evil One, and his messenger the Antichrist, *shall* be cast out. Forever!"

Shirley squeezed out of the front pew at the service's conclusion stopping only to clasp Stringer's hand in wordless tribute before starting on the dozens of administrative tasks that defined her work for the ministry. It was well after one o'clock before she finally left the church and waddled out to her sedan.

Muffin yipped a happy puppy greeting when Shirley opened the car door. She let the little dog out and commanded, "Do your business." The poodle whined, then skipped over to the church's front lawn, efficiently peed, and hopped back in for the drive home.

Shirley drove slowly. She was alone now except for the church and for Muffin. At least, that's how it felt. It was too bad Mickie married Connor back in 1971. At 18, she had been too young to marry but married that hippie boy anyway over Shirley's shrill protests. Still, the kids remained married, a miracle of sorts in a society with a divorce rate approaching fifty percent.

And Mickie actually completed college! Shirley smiled at the thought of her rebellious daughter and Connor attending high school together at Edmonds Community College with Michelle getting permission from the high school administration—no doubt glad to see her go—to finish at a community college. The girl actually finished a full year ahead of her high school class! Mickie had brains. Shirley was absolutely flabbergasted when she later earned a Bachelor's Degree in English at the University of Washington at the tender age of 20 and was hired as a *Seattle Times* reporter the following year, the youngest reporter ever hired by the Seattle daily.

Still, the girl had not come to the Lord. Shirley blamed Connor. Connor Alexander presented a formidable barrier because he hated the First Church of Jesus Christ Washed in the Blood of the Lamb and all it stood for. Connor particularly and intensely disliked the Reverend Stringer.

"That boy should not be teaching the young," Shirley muttered to Muffin. Something evil about Connor unsettled her. He had teased her about secular humanism the last time the two talked. Shirley didn't know what secular humanism was, but she knew it had to be evil. The Antichrist was coming. It could even be Connor. "Why not?" Shirley said out loud to the poodle. "After all, the boy teaches the young; he is male and has that funny birthmark on his forehead. For all I know the Horned One has been visiting him and whispering nonsense into his ear. The Reverend does say it could be anyone."

Shirley complained often to the poodle that squirmed next to her. Muffin went everywhere her mistress went. The weepy-eyed dog waited patiently in the car only during church services and when her mistress visited people who didn't understand that little dogs like Muffin are special. "God knows Mickie can skitter all over town after stories for that newspaper job of hers, but she'd be better off by a mile to quit that silly reporter business and settle down, as the Good Lord intended." Muffin wagged his tail in agreement.

Shirley's thoughts rotated pleasantly to Chuck. She respected Chuckie. He had just completed a Ph.D in astrophysics at the University of Washington and had taken a job in Socorro, New Mexico working on the construction of the Very Large Array, a bank of radio telescopes that would be strung across the desert floor. He hoped one day to conduct advanced research in very long base line interferometry. He had started to lose the last of what his mother called his baby fat. His fat was now of the mature variety. *Takes after me,* she thought turning a corner into her home neighborhood.

Still intensely curious and still a bachelor, Chuck lived for his research on gravitational tides associated with black hole accretion disk interaction with binary star system companions. Discovery of X-ray emissions from the Cygnus binary in 1970 by the NASA satellite Uhuru had told Chuck of the potential of radio telescopes and binary star systems. He hadn't entirely stopped using the optical telescopes that had defined astronomy since the days of Galileo, but he definitely wanted in on the ground floor of radio astronomy.

His mother understood only that Chuckie's work had something to do with the stars created by the Lord at the beginning of time. Chuck called home every Sunday evening, knowing he would be rewarded with a lecture about working on the Lord's day.

Shirley's estrangement from her eldest was complete.

John Cole was still behind bars in Leavenworth when Ralph died in 1974. It was not as if Shirley blamed John, but Lord knows if a father can't count on his oldest son to be a comfort, no wonder he decided to lie down and die. John's military medals, the medals he earned before disgracing himself, lay moldering in a box with his father's medals next to copies of stories Michelle had written for the University of Washington student newspaper. Shirley had seen John only once after he was released from Leavenworth early in 1976. The visit went badly. *Johnny needs to get some gumption and pull himself together,* she told herself then. Unfortunately, she had also shared this view with John.

Shirley kept track of John through her occasional talks with Annie Simpson. She was glad for John's sake that he and Annie had reconciled. That girl had some gumption. Annie had risen rapidly through the ranks of Seattle First National Bank and now toiled as a branch manager in Tacoma. She and John shared a condominium. A few months back, Annie had called to say the couple was expecting a child.

Shirley was hard put to see what Annie saw in John. *God only knows it's good someone can talk to the boy,* she thought. *But he can't hold a steady job and he drinks too much. It's just a matter of time before the girl grows weary of his problems and moves on, or before Johnny gets in trouble again.* John Cole's problems and the man he had become confused her. She never understood why he got mixed up with those sinister elements in Japan, or why he left a promising military career in the first place. *The military certainly was good for my Ralph. I sure don't know what went wrong with Johnny.*

She prayed every day for her eldest son to lay his troubles down at the feet of the Lord, get a decent job, and become the boy she had once loved dearly. She prayed he and Annie would stop living in sin, beg forgiveness from the Lord, and become man and wife in the eyes of the church. "Otherwise," Shirley muttered to Muffin, turning off the engine in her driveway, "their child will be born a bastard."

Muffin yipped enthusiastically and wagged his tail.

✳ ✳ ✳ ✳ ✳ ✳ ✳ ✳ ✳ ✳ ✳ ✳ ✳ ✳

Connor rolled out of bed, literally. He and Michelle had yet to set up the bed frame after moving into the new house. Connor preferred sleeping at floor-level, residue from much less pressured hippie days. He didn't wake Michelle. He knew she could use the sleep.

Connor showered, then stood in front of the bathroom mirror in after-shower steam. He wiped the steam off the mirror impatiently, and studied the oddly shaped strawberry-colored birthmark that intersected the scar from Chicago. *Birthmark's not really getting bigger. It's just that my hair's disappearing. Oh well. Mom always said the birthmark was part of what made me special.* His dad had gone totally bald. He figured he'd share the same fate. He thought fleetingly about his dad, then about his mom. He wondered what had ever become of them.

Connor turned on the hot water, lathered his neck and cheekbones, and started to trim his closely cropped beard. *Got to get my notes together for first period.* He jiggled the razor in the hot water and watched soap and bits of beard, like iron shavings, swirl down the drain. Connor prided himself on being organized and always ready for his students. He looked back up into the mirror.

Eldon Moss leered back.

"*God!*"

Connor crashed back against the wall, head down. He peeked at the mirror quickly, and glimpsed a vague shadow disappearing in steam from the tap. He stepped forward, wiped the steam off again, and really looked. Only his face looked back.

But a voice whispered behind the running water, "Why do you call on a deity, Connor?"

He slammed off the tap.

Silence.

* * * * * * * * * * * * * *

First the rains came. Wawrens still meditated to the raindrums, as had the two hundred generations of wawrens in the Hive before them. They had no way of knowing that the drums on Arkadia had long since been silenced. As it was, the drums had long lost all meaning to the other Hive dwellers. Lately, the twice-daily drumming lasted longer, testimony to decay of climate control systems within the Hive.

After each raindrumming, the electrobars always powered down throughout the prison compound. The wawrens did not know why this brief respite occurred, but were grateful for the opportunity to leave their cells and travel within the prison compound. Of course, access to the waters outside the wawren complex was always carefully guarded. In truth, the practice of systematically spelling the power grid conserved energy.

*Peacekeeper, Peacekeeper…*A student telepathically signaled her assigned teacher using the traditional honorific given to each wawren fullmaster.

Time for a lesson, the first for this particular zeromaster. Imprisonment didn't stop communication among wawrens with the Hive. They had long since broken the prohibitions against telepathic communication in atmosphere. The fullmaster could telepathically address all members of the caste simultaneously, and they him, though community meetings were seldom necessary.

The Peacekeeper signaled back. *Come. Let the lesson begin.*

Wawrens preferred personal contact, not telepathy, when involved in the serious business of teaching. The zeromaster soon signaled her approach. The outside guard passed her through into the fullmaster's chambers. The fullmaster was the only wawren with a personal bodyguard.

She approached the caste fullmaster ritualistically, bowing to the floor, forehorn just touching the waters that sloshed throughout the cell. It was this youngster's good fortune to be assigned the Peacekeeper as a teacher.

"Float comfortably, young one. We will have much time together during respites from the electrobars. You might as well be comfortable." The Peacekeeper chuckled in the Arkadian way as he spoke. Arkadians often floated side-by-side on their backs in the shallow water of a living space when communicating informally.

Cells in the prison compound each had a resting area, small living room, toilet, and small altar where burned the blue flame of Wa. The sound of dripping, running water was ever present. To a human, each Arkadian living compound within the outer ring of the Hive would look like a great gray anthill ringed with windows. The cells within each caste compound were arranged in circles five stories high with zeromaster quarters ringing the outside, than quartermaster, then halfmaster cells. The living quarters of the caste fullmaster occupied the tip of the anthill—the top center cell of each compound with a portal facing the center of the Hive. Caste administrative and support offices tiered through the center of the anthill below to sea level.

The Peacekeeper could view the Hive Sea and, were it not for electrobars between the portal and the outside, he could even conceivably dive five stories into the sea from his balcony though such an act would be beneath the dignity of a wawren fullmaster. Some wawren zeromasters used to fling themselves down to the sea just for fun. But that had been generations ago, before imprisonment and before the things had invaded the Hive Sea. Of late, few Arkadians would have wanted to swim outside the safety of intruder screens. Something evil lurked in the organic soup that the Hive Sea had become. Still, the quarter and halfmaster wawrens who lived deep within the compound and who could not often view the Hive Sea sensed the waters and longed for them.

The Peacemaker settled beside his student and said, "Ask the first question, novice, so the lesson may begin."

Since their last incarceration, dwindling numbers of zeromaster wawrens began their formal education by asking a prescribed question.

"Peacemaker, why are we imprisoned?"

With this cue, the Peacemaker began the story of the Hive. "I will tell you the story of our imprisonment, but first you must learn of the Wandering.

"Arkadia was threatened by its unstable star. All of Arkadia had to join together to find a solution for our survival. The Wawrens were established in the year 1 P.W. to mediate differences. Our caste was once the greatest in all of Arkadia. With wawren help Arkadia established great technologies that led to building of the Hive. As you know the year is now 7523 P.W. The ancestors embarked from Arkadia 6,000 years ago to find a new home. It was more difficult than had been anticipated to find straddlepoints. We have experienced straddletravel only five times in the life of the Hive, though not in your lifetime or mine. The window of opportunity to penetrate a straddlepoint is a fleeting thing. The Hive was once parked for 1300 years outside a singularity for conditions to be right. In this, as well as all things, the Hive's sensors guide us. Without automation we would have been lost long ago…" The Peacemaker's beginning was uncharacteristically disjointed.

"Peacemaker, I am sorry," the zeromaster interrupted. "I am sure it is my lowly ability, but I do not understand. I respectfully ask that you simplify your presentation so I may better absorb your words. I do not understand what you mean by 'singularity.' May we return to the original question?" The youngster did a poor job of masking the frustration she felt at the fullmaster's meandering.

The Peacemaker chuckled again in the Arkadian way. Tads learned rudimentary facts about the universe from worker nannies during basic skills training. The training was still insufficient. The wawren leader considered that, save for himself, halfmasters of his caste and a small group of wizards, few Arkadians had any conception of the vast universe outside the musty, dripping, polluted habitat they all shared.

"Well, young zeromaster, a singularity is the point of infinite gravity at the center of a black hole. But your request to return to the subject of our incarceration is reasonable.

"The Wandering weakened the Tenets of Wa early on. Despite best efforts of the wyruls and wawrens, factions developed soon after launch from Arkadia. Some wyruls began to ignore the Tenets of Wa. Their actions became aggressive and, in time, obtaining power in the Hive became more important than the goal of finding a home, a goal all Arkadians had once shared. "Once factions formed, conflict was inevitable. The first Hive War followed in 1619 P.W., less than a hundred years after launch from Arkadia. That was the first time wawrens were imprisoned."

"Peacemaker, was this war the reason some of the Hive housing compounds have been burnt, and is this why many of the transport tubes are corrupted?"

"Well, no, damage done in the first Hive Wars was repaired though, in later times, our technicians lost the ability to make other than routine repairs and, consequently, you now observe more recent damage. The bolts of warring ravans did some of this damage; other damage has been caused by the passage of time. This damage will not be repaired unless we have planetfall…May I continue?"

"Yes, Peacemaker. I apologize for interrupting."

The wawren fullmaster signaled amusement in the Arkadian way, collected his thoughts and continued. "Only straddletravel followed by a maser signal from a potential home ended the first Hive War and brought wawrens out of imprisonment. As a people, we have a remarkable capacity to pull together when we need to, but only wawrens have the innate ability and training to make sense of alien cultures, and to communicate with other sentient life. That is why, despite our inability to mediate conflict within the Hive, our caste is still replenished during each replacement allotment. The others need us if we are ever to find a blue planet."

The Peacemaker stopped and rose to a standing position. He fiddled with a hair braid, then tossed it behind his back. He smoothed his often-patched, white wawren robe with a carefully manicured claw. The syntheofactory allotment of wawren robes had fallen off. His personal servant, a halfmaster worker, kept busy simply trying to keep the wawren fullmaster appropriately clothed for his office. He rippled through the water around the floating student.

"In all, maser signals have been received from three planets during the Hive's 6,000 year transit. Wawrens failed to convince creatures from the first planet to share their home. The creatures fully mobilized, and threatened use of nuclear weapons when ravans tried to take the planet during 1700 P.W. We could not conquer them without a war that would have destroyed the ecosystem we require. For reasons not well understood by our wizards, nuclear weapons technology—and the weapons themselves—were not included in the Hive's data banks or armory. This puts our ravan zeromaster cohorts at a distinct disadvantage when doing battle with an adversary that possesses these weapons.

"In her anger at this defeat, the ravan fullmaster convinced the Council of Wyruls to approve destruction of the planet with backwash from the Hive's proton-proton engines. After the planet's incineration, wawrens were returned to prison as punishment for their failure to negotiate a home."

"Nuclear weapons, Peacemaker? What are they?"

"Well, young one, these weapons possess the power of the stars and spread death long after their use. Now, may I continue?"

This time, the zeromaster looked sheepish in the Arkadian way. "Yes, I am sorry. There is just so much I wish to understand."

"Twice more we came across potential homes, but the same events occurred. Different planets, different times, but identical outcomes. Blue planets were found by maser signal during 5222 and 6437 P.W. Wawrens studied intelligent life and designed negotiation strategies during transit to the planet. Each time, wawrens failed to negotiate planetfall. Each time, the zeromaster cohorts went in to take the planet by force. Each time, the ravans failed when nuclear weapons were deployed.

"The last battle was gruesome. The zeromaster cohorts refused to retreat and were almost destroyed. The Hive itself was attacked in orbit around the planet. The Hive's proton-proton engines had been aligned toward the surface, ready for a fast departure. This alignment saved us. As it blasted away, chased by hundreds of nuclear rockets, the enemy rockets as well as the entire planet, were incinerated.

"Wawrens went back to prison, escorted by the few remaining ravans. Respite from ravan dominance was short-lived. Within a generation, the zeromaster cohorts had been replenished."

"Peacemaker, destroying whole worlds never served our purpose. Why was this done?"

"Failure and hatred, young zeromaster, are corrosive. Wa teaches us to step outside the perceived humiliation of defeat to search for peaceful, mutually beneficial answers. Wa teaches us that hate is poisonous. But Wa lies dormant in the Hive."

"Peacemaker, why were not the ravans also imprisoned? Did not they also fail?"

"Good question, zeromaster. As I said, our efforts forewarned inhabitants on each occasion. The ravans claim that without this warning, they could have gained victory before the inhabitants deployed nuclear weapons, or otherwise mobilized to overwhelm the zeromaster cohorts. This argument is logical. But there is another reason as well. The ravans kill all who thwart them. They are the jailers, not the jailed."

"What will the future bring, my teacher?"

"The future. The future...A difficult question, young one. The Hive's ecosystem degenerates. The antimatter and proton-proton engines have little remaining life. It is said that we can straddle but one more time.

Moreover, our science is poor. The wizards are now few in number and most are assigned to military research. The tyranny and apathy of the present reign degrades all learning; technicians operate systems by rote; machines cannot be repaired or replaced; computers cannot be reprogrammed. We have lost the ability to develop new technologies from the information stored in the Hive's data banks.

"We are lost, young zeromaster. We are adrift without the capacity to renew our science, or to develop our culture. The Tenets of Wa no longer guide us. The ingenuity and vitality that created the Hive are lost. On top of this, another Hive War is brewing. Third Wyrul Harn controls the ravans. She is at odds with First Wyrul Tok and Second Wyrul Toltek. This is the first time in Hive history that a wyrul, such as Harn, has had the allegiance of most of the ravans."

"So, the Wandering will cease?"

"Yes. We will either be destroyed through a final Hive War or by the decaying ecosystem. A blue planet must be located after the next, final straddle. That is our best hope. Still, if a blue planet is found, it is unlikely wawrens will negotiate. We have failed three times. This time, our approach will be stealthy. The outcome will be violent. Millions may be slaughtered. The next blue planet may be conquered in the end, but our new home will have been born in blood. A cycle of hatred, death, and destruction will flourish on the soil and in the seas of the new world."

"Is there anything we can do?" The zeromaster's concentration had flickered during the early part of the Hive's history, but her flame burned blue now, her attention riveted to the Peacekeeper's words.

"There is an old Arkadian saying: 'the longest swim begins with the first stroke.' We must pray to Wa we find a blue planet and that it is uninhabited by intelligent life. If such life does exist, we must pray it is docile and that it follows the Tenets of Wa."

The lesson ended. The zeromaster rose, thanked the wawren fullmaster and splashed back to her cell arriving just before the electrobars hummed back to life. She sought the blessing of the flame of Wa and prepared for devotions before final dimming.

Suddenly, the electrobars of the zeromaster's cell powered down and her chamber door opened. In the dim light of the outside passage the wawren fledgling glimpsed two cloaked figures framed in the doorway. She scanned. Death, blood, and hunger flashed back.

Ravans. Why?

A bright flash crackled.

    ✶ ✶ ✶ ✶ ✶ ✶ ✶ ✶ ✶ ✶ ✶ ✶ ✶ ✶

"Let the wawrens suffer," hissed Third Wyrul Harn. The meeting of the Council of Wyruls dragged on. Time was short. Straddletravel loomed.

As the Hive's technicians prepared for the coming straddle, the Council debated the familiar dilemma posed by potential or actual contact with intelligent life. Only anticipation of the next straddle and remnants of Council protocol prevented bloodshed. Council debates blistered; they did not yet kill.

"We must ignore wawren prattlings based on outmoded religious myths. The zeromaster cohorts must be sent in!" Harn exploded with anger. The blue flame danced up her back, framing her head in a fiery glow as she faced the other wyruls.

Toltek, Second Wyrul, took the bejeweled speaker's wand from Harn and replied. "We have been unsuccessful. Three planets located; three failures. Thousands of years lost. The technicians say little life is left in the Hive and that at reduced capacity. We have one straddle left. As it is, climate controllers are unreliable. The rain periods have increased. I hear the raindrums in my sleep. Algae and molds are everywhere. Most of Arkadians will die in cryonic storage. The ravans not only eat Arkadian flesh, they prefer it. I am told they have been hunting wawren zeromasters for food."

"That accusation is unfounded, Toltek." Harn interrupted. "As to the rest, why blather on about the obvious?"

"I have not finished, Harn," Toltek continued. "I hold the speaker's wand and will be heard. We must have planetfall. Yet, I am unwilling to commit genocide. A peaceful home is not built on a foundation of offal. We must negotiate."

Rollit, Eighteenth Wyrul, requested and received the speaker's wand. "Why continue to meet?" she asked. "The technicians must first locate a blue planet. On this point, the past failure of wawrens is moot. Release them from incarceration! Our decision to approach the next planet with wawrens or ravans has no bearing unless a blue planet is found."

Harn grabbed back the wand and whistled incredulously, "You would have us convene this meeting *after* locating a target? Would you have Arkadians die while we argue? Remember stories told of the last great debate? Wawrens or ravans? Wawrens or ravans? Twenty circlings of a blue planet's system. Two years wasted. Time the enemy spent preparing for battle. More time wasted with negotiation. All was lost by the time the ravans attacked. What of the last debacle? We almost lost the Hive on that occasion. Let us settle the issue now. Use the wawrens to learn about the target's defenses, assuming one is found, *then* send in the zeromaster cohorts. We must have a home."

✷ ✷ ✷ ✷ ✷ ✷ ✷ ✷ ✷ ✷ ✷ ✷ ✷ ✷ ✷

The Hive reached straddlepoint 6500 light years from Earth at a location known to human optical astronomers as HDE 226868; and to radio astronomers like Chuck Cole as Cygnus X-1. To every one else, this location was just another star in the constellation Cygnus, also commonly known as "the Swan" or the "Northern Cross."

The binary system's blue giant whirled around the accretion disk of a black hole, tied to the event horizon by stellar particles that flowed from the massive star into the oblivion of infinite gravity. To a human, the scene would have looked like an immense blue yo-yo, fifteen times larger than the sun, being twirled on a great raging particle string held by a deep space whirlpool.

The technician pilots in the Hive couldn't see any of this because there were no portals to outside space anywhere in the Hive and, besides, the pilots' frame of reference would have been Arkadian, not human. The few simple toys used by tads most definitely did not include anything that resembled a yo-yo. The final approach to a straddlepoint was always an abstraction handled entirely by the Hive's automated systems.

The autopilot whipped the Hive around the blue giant to gain momentum. Centrifugal force, automated acceleration from the antimatter engines at exactly the right moment together with stellar-wind speed brought the Hive—now a dot bobbing in the raging, hot particle current of the "cosmic yo-yo's" string—to light speed, through the event horizon, and into the singularity. Only the Hive's shields and antigravity field kept it from vaporizing from either the heat of the particle current, bombardment from quantum particles inside the accretion disk, or from the infinite gravity of the singularity. Passage through the straddlepoint occurred instantaneously without sensation on the part of the travelers. Antimatter engines cut off automatically. Proton-proton thrust boosters reversed and slowed acceleration to one-fortieth light speed.

Then, the waiting began. An enormous amount of energy—a blast equivalent to 100 solar masses—always preceded the Hive at the exit point of a straddle. Travel through a straddlepoint rippled energy forward, the energy generated from infinite gravity acting on the mass of the moon-sized starship as it moved through a singularity. The residue had to dissipate in the vacuum and vastness of space before maser and wave receivers in the Hive could operate. The waiting was long. Ninety dimmings passed before the static waned and the search could begin.

The maser search was inconclusive. A sending maser might be within range, but the technicians could not be sure. Arkadians faced the bleak prospect of certain extinction. Whether the next Hive War or the relentless decline in the starship's systems, the end of the Wandering beckoned. First Wyrul Tok desperately ordered a search using standard wave receivers.

A rich radio wave stream immediately overwhelmed the sensors. It was the first time a candidate for colonization had been found using standard receivers and, better yet, it was the closest planet yet found after a straddle. A world of unimaginable richness appeared a scant ten light years away—twenty years away in hyperdrive.

Tok contacted the Peacemaker and ordered the wawrens to begin study of the planet's life. She ordered pilot technicians to set a new course.

The Hive turned toward its final destination.

CHAPTER 14

The vocational rehabilitation counselor at the American Lake Hospital in Tacoma yawned as he looked at the vet before him. John Cole's flannel shirt and work jeans hung on a skeleton frame. To the counselor, Cole resembled Ichabod Crane, although with white hair and a blond straggly beard, he looked distinctly more Nordic than the character from American folklore. Like Ichabod, 29 year-old John Cole was haunted.

Scenes from My Lai festered in Cole, untouched by years of antidepressants and counselors, not unlike the sanctimonious jerk smirking in front of him. Many war survivors found ways to put their pain to rest after returning to the world. But eight years of regimented life behind the stone walls of the Leavenworth military compound, layered onto memories of My Lai, had affected Cole in ways he could not understand or release. Since the massacre, there had been few days when the bleakness of his surroundings had not been eclipsed by the grayness of his thoughts. Cole carried with him always the pink mist and the stench of death.

"John," the counselor said, his voice distant as it cut through John's haze. "John."

Cole looked up. He sat in the counselor's chair for Annie and their unborn child. It mattered little to him where he was. But the terror buried inside occasionally erupted with a force that scared them both. He had promised Annie he would give counseling one last try.

"John," the counselor said. "Did you think about what you want to do? Are you looking for work? I see here that you worked as a groundskeeper at Leavenworth. There are golf courses in the area that might hire you." The counselor brushed lint off the sleeve of his J.C. Penny's polyester wash and wear suit.

"No."

"Still taking the medicine? Is it working okay? It's not making you sleepy, is it?"

Cole grimaced. He didn't know how much of his haze was him and how much was the daily regime of 200 milligrams of the tricyclic Tofranil prescribed to counter clinical depression. Some days he didn't care. Occasionally, he cared a lot. He shrugged.

The counselor took a deep breath. A tough case. Still, he had received high marks in his counseling practicum. A freshly minted Master's Degree hung on the wall behind his desk. The counselor looked at John with clinical compassion, nervously straightened his desk calendar, and lined up three pens in a row on his desk as he considered his next attempt to get through.

"Perhaps we'd feel better if we found work…" The counselor stopped in mid-sentence, shocked by the intensity with which his client suddenly glared at his desk. Cole's eyes rested on the photograph of the counselor's pretty wife and young son who laughed out from a silver and gold frame on the desk.

"What do you mean 'we?'" John snarled, gaze never leaving the photo of a young boy in his mother's embrace. "We are not out of work. Look's like you got a great job."

"You're right, John," the counselor replied. "What I meant to say…"

Cole cut him off, his eyes riveting from the photo to the counselor. "Do you realize the guy who ordered the My Lai massacre served less time than I did?"

"What massacre? Is that what you dream of?"

"Forget it. You wouldn't understand."

"Well, I don't know, John, what a massacre means here. I mean in the context of what you and I have been talking about…"

"Finally I get out of Leavenworth and I'm told, 'Okay, John, you're free. Go home now, John. You've done your time, John. But how can I do that? How in the hell am I supposed to do that?" Cole abruptly switched gears. "You're a veterans' counselor. Where'd you serve?"

"Huh? Where did I serve? Uh… I was in a motor pool in West Germany. I, ah…"

Cole leaped from the chair. He grabbed the framed photograph and hurled it against the wall. Glass showered the counselor as the frame boomeranged back to Cole. Remnants of the smiling mother and son smiled up at the heel of his boot as he crunched down and stomped with rage-filled steps out the office and down the hall. He was well down the corridor before the counselor caught him, coming up from behind at a fast trot.

Michelle, waiting in a visitor's lounge at the other end of the building, heard the commotion and started to walk in the direction of breaking glass.

"John?" Michelle whispered. "John?" Louder this time. She walked faster. Sighting Cole in the hallway, she started to run.

"John, let's rap…" The counselor reached up from behind and laid his hand on Cole's shoulder. He knew from school that a reassuring touch could facilitate a client relationship characterized by warmth and trust. This particular situation sure seemed to call for a comforting touch.

Cole whirled around, no longer in a veteran's hospital in Tacoma. With a fluid forward motion, he violently met the counselor's forehead with his own. A loud crack split the stale medicinal air of the corridor and reverberated off the pale green walls. The counselor collapsed like a sack of stones. As Cole prepared to deliver the *coup de grace*, he heard a voice through the fog.

"John. Stop it. You're home! John...*John!*"

Cole stopped and faced his sister. Her face, framed by the institutional green walls of the veteran's hospital, came into focus. He reached for her, unafraid. Michelle and Annie were his strongest links. He would never hurt them. He held his sister as they both trembled.

Michelle looked down at the counselor when he moaned and began to revive. Approaching footsteps echoed down the hall.

"Let's get out of here," Michelle said. Taking Cole by the hand, she led him, like a child, quickly out to the parking lot.

Michelle doubted the counselor would blame John. He probably figured he was a tough case and had a lot to work out. That came with the turf when counseling vets. She didn't expect retribution from the counselor. But she also realized John wasn't going back.

* * * * * * * * * * * * * *

"Marx, in his critique of Hegel, said that religion is the opiate of the people. What do you guys think? George, what did Marx mean? Was he saying that religion is an addictive drug?"

Connor walked casually across the classroom and leaned on a windowsill. He absentmindedly rubbed the scar on his forehead, a badge, not of honor, but of the unrealized hope of an earlier era. His students knew the story of Michelle and Connor at the Chicago convention. Even 10 years later, the Pulitzer prize-winning photo of the couple being pounded during the police riots invariably made its way into every classroom.

Unlike many of his colleagues, Connor had made the transition to adulthood gracefully. He gained only ten pounds. He liked to tease Michelle that he had finally reached his fighting weight. His remaining hair was short and styled. Emerging crow's feet around his eyes looked more like a twinkle in the eye than a harbinger of middle age. The beard he had neatly trimmed that morning, despite Eldon Moss's disquieting visit, was a good companion to the professorial tweeds he liked to wear. He didn't smoke or carry a pipe. That would have been a bit much.

Connor enjoyed teaching history. He buckled down after Chicago. After finishing an education degree and student teaching in 1973, he landed a job at Queen Anne High in Seattle. He had been on the faculty for five years. Students liked him. After all the years spent sitting in class on the other side of the podium, Connor now laughed when he found himself taking issue with the current generation, particularly with regard to their naivete and horrible music. He'd never been like that... had he?

George had slumped in the back of Connor's history class all semester. A large young man, he liked to think of himself as a trendsetter. He had been the first in his crowd to listen to the sounds of The Clash and one of the first to slam dance. On this day, he wore an over-large black cape over dark clothing. The spike of his Mohawk was dyed green and purple, a safety pin hung from a puncture in his left ear lobe. He had a black eye. George fancied himself a poet and was always scribbling.

"George?" Connor crossed the room to pin George down with direct eye contact. The lad roused from his wordsmithing and responded in a nasally, irritating ramble.

"Well, uh, I guess Marx was, you know, saying that people like religion and, you know, it makes 'em dead in the head." George relished the laughter that erupted from the class. He went back to writing his poem.

The first bell rang.

George looked around defiantly, then handed Connor a scrap of paper. "Here, saved by the bell. Enjoy." With that, he stomped out the classroom door just a few paces away.

Connor walked back to his desk at the front of the room and sat down. He waited for the room to empty before reading George's poem:

> *The Man is coming, coming for you.*
> *Might be here now. What will you do?*
> *Do you feel the heat? Do you sense His goal?*
> *Do you feel the tugging, the pushing at your soul?*
> *You know He's coming; you know He's near.*
> *The Man is coming. Can you feel the fear?*

The early September sun went behind a cloud. The room darkened. Connor glanced up. George hadn't left after all. The poet grinned at him from the half-light of the doorway, transformed into Eldon Moss, then back again into George.

The last bell shrilled.

*   *   *   *   *   *   *   *   *   *   *   *   *   *

That evening, Michelle and Connor sat at a card table on folding lawn chairs because they couldn't afford a real dining room set. They hadn't even finished unpacking yet, but they'd signed away their future for a tiny cracker box in the Wallingford District on the north side of Seattle, compliments of an obscene purchase price and usurious interest on a 30-year mortgage. Credit cards strained to their limits. The bills arrived faithfully all month like thunderbolts from hungry gods.

Chandelier light flickered off brand new walls and unpacked boxes still built towers to the ceiling. The Bee Gees warbled about night fever on the recently unpacked stereo.

Michelle whispered. "I don't know what to do. I can't believe how John reacted. You should have seen what he did to that counselor. You can tell when it's going to happen. He gets this glazed look on his face, then goes berserk. I don't think the pills are doing any good. I kind of wonder if they're making it worse." Her voice trailed off, as though someone might hear if she spoke any louder.

Michelle remained petite but was still as buxom as ever. Her blond hair had darkened, but it finally had some curl in it, to Shirley's relief. Work was going well, though it was tough being the youngest reporter on the staff of the *Seattle Times.*

"We all were hurt by Vietnam, John worse than most," Connor said, rubbing the scar that cut across his birthmark for the hundredth time that day. I was thinking about your brother today and about Chicago."

Connor pushed his plate away, got up from the table, and took vanilla ice cream out of the freezer section of their new refrigerator. He almost stepped on Binky. The cat liked to snooze almost as much as it liked to eat and preferred to nap right where people tended to step. Binky looked like a big, fluffy black and white potato with toothpicks stuck in its sides for legs. The animal and Connor had a history. Binky was one of the few reminders of the unhappy home life Connor had fled. They had both been kittens when Connor had traveled down a road that eventually took him through Chicago and to Michelle. His mom had surrendered Binky to him shortly after Chicago. The two had been together since.

"I hadn't thought of Chicago in a long time," he said on returning to the table. "But John's problems are a reminder that things are worse now than ever." Connor told Michelle about George then handed her the poem.

He concluded, "That kid usually says more than he thinks. Still, that whole punker thing he's into is so antisocial and evil."

Michelle looked up from her reading and replied, "Looks like the kid was saying that *you're* the one who's evil."

"Yeah, I know. It's creepy. Speaking of which, did I ever tell you about Eldon? Eldon Moss?"

Michelle smiled. "Wasn't he the ghost, or whatever, that used to appear to visit when you were tripping back in the 60s? The one who used to make you feel guilty?"

"Yeah. Anyway, I haven't seen him since." Connor got up, put the ice cream back in the freezer, and returned to the table. "I saw him today. Twice."

"Saw who?"

"Eldon Moss. Aren't you listening?"

"Don't get snotty, Connor. We were talking about John, then George. Now, Eldon Moss. I'm just trying to keep up…what did he want with you this time?" Michelle smiled again.

"I don't know."

"Do you think Eldon Moss has anything to do with the special purpose you used to talk about? What was that about?"

"Yeah. Well, in between beers, my mom used to say that I was destined for something special. I've just never figured out what it was. It sure as hell wasn't being a peace activist. I'm not sure it was being a teacher, either."

"Oh, Connor, why can't you ever make up your mind about things?"

"Hey, that wasn't a nice thing to say. I usually know what I think."

"I don't mean thinking. I'm talking about believing. They're different."

"There you go again. Why are we fighting? Why do we always have to fight? Can't we ever have a serious conversation?"

"We're not fighting."

"Yeah, we are." Connor was starting to get angry, but stifled the impulse.

"I disagree," Michelle replied softly.

"You disagree and we're not fighting? That's rich! Will you at least answer my question?" Connor's reply was of the get in the last word variety.

"Don't raise your voice. I still didn't hear a question. What are you talking about?"

"Eldon Moss," Connor replied quietly, "Is he haunting me? Am I nuts?"

Michelle paused, lit a cigarette, then replied. "You might be nuts or just susceptible. Maybe you *have* been singled out for something like your mom used to say. Maybe it's Eldon Moss who's special. Maybe he isn't who he seems. Could be the light was bad and you have an active imagination. I'm not sure. You might not ever figure it out. It's probably not a big deal. On the other hand, you're being visited by a supernatural being, you've got a rather distinctive birthmark on your forehead…"

"What's my birthmark got to do with it?"

"Maybe it's the Mark of the Beast." Michelle laughed.

"What?"

"Let me finish… You're male and in a position to influence the young. Your mom—and and mom's have great intuition—said you have a special purpose in life. Let's see…you're an atheist; a punker weirdo wrote a satanic poem about you. I don't know, Connor. I sure wouldn't tell Shirley any of these things."

"Why?"

"You don't know? You know Shirley and you don't know? Why, Connor, she'd peg you as the Antichrist! And if you're the Antichrist, then Eldon Moss must be the devil." Michelle laughed out loud at the serious expression on Connor's face.

"Can't you ever be serious, Michelle?"

"Why can't you ever figure out what you believe in?"

"I don't know. Maybe Eldon Moss has the answer." Connor smiled grimly.

* * * * * * * * * * * * * *

Tok directed the Hive's Council of Wyruls as the caste fullmaster. The other nineteen members of the Council comprised the only halfmasters in the ruling caste. There were no quarter or zeromaster ranks among wyruls. As with other castes, the halfmasters elected their leader, promoting her to fullmaster. Otherwise, wyruls were ranked two through twenty based on seniority. Females from the bureaucrat caste filled vacancies in the ranks caused by old age, disease or, in bad times, by assassination.

Each member of the Council was given a ceremonial name at ascension, a tradition that purportedly went back to the days of life on Arkadia. Among Arkadians, a telepathic intuition—not normal Arkadian telepathy exactly, but more a comparable ever-present "sensing"—combined with highly developed nonverbal communication skills made personal names irrelevant. To have and to hold a formal wyrul name, however, was a great honor.

Maintaining power wasn't a problem in the Hive as long as the wyruls provided privileges to the ravan caste in general and to their personal bodyguards in particular. The ravans received priority in the allotment of tads. Moreover, most remaining wizards were assigned to military research and development at the behest of the ravans. The ravans planned to never lose a battle again.

The Hive's ecosystem provided the phytoplanktons, zooplanktons, algaes, leafy plants, and insect life necessary for a regenerating food chain with the Arkadians at the top, though most Arkadians now depended for sustenance on foul-tasting algaes skimmed from the Hive Sea and crude insect pastes. These foodstuffs were harvested, processed, and distributed by members of the worker caste.

Zeromaster members of the ravan caste harvested another type of food. Fish, a staple on Arkadia, had died out as the ecosystem in the Hive failed. Ravans compensated for this loss by eating fellow Arkadians, a practice never publicized and usually spoke of in the thoughts and whispers of other caste members. It was simply understood that some Arkadians occasionally "disappeared," not to be recycled as fertilizer, but to be used in another, nefarious way.

Ancient, automated syntheofactories generated clothing and other necessities of life from their place in the Hive's second ring. Only about a third of the factories still functioned in the Hive and, with each generation, decreasing numbers of technicians could accommodate requests for unusual clothing and sometimes even for necessities. Arkadians increasingly made do with standard patterns for clothing and utensils. Simple barter-driven markets required little regulation. There was no petty crime. Where would a criminal go to with ill-gotten gains? Bureaucrats investigated the occasional crime, the Council of Wyruls rendered a judgment, and the guilty party always went into cryonic storage or became food for the ravan table. Ravans administered all punishment, so only they knew for sure what *really* happened to perpetrators.

An ongoing lottery meant innocent tads and grown Arkadians went into cryonic storage as well. Erosion of the Hive's ecosystem made this lottery necessary and two-thirds of the Hive's population now slumbered in storage. An Arkadian could be stored for 90 years before thawing became necessary. Of late, thousands of Arkadians were never thawed when this time passed, so these unfortunate beings died without ever recalling having once lived. Only ravans, wyruls, some wawrens, and necessary workers, technicians, bureaucrats, and wizards now could be assured of living a normal life span in the Hive.

Cryonic storage was necessary to maintain a population large enough to colonize a planet, even though the odds of doing so declined steadily with each passing generation. In the meantime, tads were still raised in the Hive and allotments to castes still continued as a means of maintaining continuity. It wouldn't do to achieve planetfall only to have forgotten, through disuse, the rituals associated with the care, training, and assimilation of tads into caste life and the continuation of Arkadia on foreign soil and in foreign seas.

＊ ＊ ＊ ＊ ＊ ＊ ＊ ＊ ＊ ＊ ＊ ＊ ＊ ＊

The wawren community hummed after discovery of the blue planet. Wawren zeromasters worked with technicians to collect and organize data plucked from space by Hive receivers. Quartermasters developed decoding protocols and translated communications. Halfmasters interpreted translations and worked to master languages. The Peacemaker, as the caste fullmaster, supervised all activity.

Most of the sometimes garbled transmissions were in English, a tribute to advanced communications technology in English-speaking countries in 1968, particularly the United States. The most powerful transmissions received were from U.S. networks and the British Broadcasting Corporation, though Japan's NHK was also received. English became the first language decoded for a variety of reasons. It was prevalent in broadcast waves spinning off into space and intercepted by the Hive and, at first glance, because the United States appeared to be the ruling entity on the planet. In 1968, the U.S. with less than five percent of the world's population controlled more than half of all planetary income and wealth. Also, the U.S. children's program, Sesame Street, provided decoding protocols.

The wawrens learned that quicksand wasn't quick, a boxing ring was square, and hamburgers were made with beef, not ham. They marveled at the different uses of the word "fly" and the notion that Americans had noses that could run, and feet that could smell.

Some halfmasters quickly learned Russian, French, German, and Japanese. The Peacemaker mastered these languages as well as English. Decoding experience gained by past generations of wawrens as well as the primitive level of Earth language made this learning easy for the Peacemaker and other wawrens. The Arkadian palate, tongue and lip structures allowed for Earth languages to be spoken. For the first time, wawrens actually spoke an alien language.

A description of Earth's sentient life, with emphasis placed on the United States, soon was ready for the Council of Wyruls.

* * * * * * * * * * * * * *

First Wyrul Tok switched off the holodisc projector and adjusted the blue robes of leadership. She leaned back, drifting in the water of her living chamber, and contemplated the challenges ahead. *How do we control the ravans? What if this blue planet is not the one? How long will the Hive hold together?*

A gentle telepathic signal interrupted her thoughts. The Peacemaker and his ravan guard had arrived.

Only the Peacemaker entered. The wawren fullmaster wore the white robes of peace. Though patched, the robes were immaculate. His forehorn crystal glittered with a soft yellow from a recent polishing. Wawrens had their natural forehorn modified at transition. The horn was shortened and implanted with a highly polished facsimile of a maser crystal—signifying the wawren commitment to communication and healing reconciliation. On Arkadia, this modification had been made under anesthesia in a Temple of Wa accompanied by incense burning and wawrens chanting in hypnotic cadence to the raindrums. In the Hive, physician technicians still performed this minor surgery under the supervision of the Peacekeeper or that of a halfmaster designee.

The Peacemaker settled next to Tok and the two Arkadians floated on their backs side-by-side. Tok began, "Tell me more about humans. The holodisc does not tell all. How do these creatures really appear?"

To a human, spoken Arkadian would have sounded like variations of creaking doors intermeshed with pops and clicks.

The Peacemaker replied, "as you have seen from viewing the holodisc, human skin is many different colors. It is also thinner than our skin, and does not require continuous moisture. They have hair on their heads as we do, though they have more of it on their bodies. Human hair has many colors. Humans do not have forehorns or sidehorns as do we. They are bipedal, but their appendages are not webbed nor are they clawed.

"Humans are shorter than Arkadians. They are terrestrial, not aquatic as we are though they can swim. They lack our capacity to take oxygen from both atmosphere and the sea. There is a male and female gender, but the human drive to join is based on pleasure, not on relief from pain."

"Wa! I do not understand. Humans do not receive the call? They do not experience the cramps and the need for relief?"

"No, Tok. They mate for recreation, as well as for procreation. This drive dominates the thinking, behavior, and customs of all human societies. You should also know that unlike Arkadians, their leaders are predominantly male. Under healthy circumstances, they live about as long we do."

"Innate abilities? Do they have telepathy? Can they bolt? How do they compare in terms of intelligence? The latter is particularly unclear." Tok splashed impatiently.

"No telepathy. At least not telepathic abilities Arkadians would understand. There may be some humans who possess extrasensory perception that might allow for rudimentary telepathy, but our information on this point is incomplete. We believe, though cannot confirm, there are aquatic creatures on the planet called eels that store an electrical charge, but humans are not among them, hence, humans cannot bolt. Our ravans could easily defeat humans in combat though I hope to Wa it does not come to that. I can not speak with authority as to human intelligence. There is dynamism to them difficult to define. They may possess a type of intelligence we have not yet encountered."

Tok glanced intently at the Peacemaker. She flipped a switch at her side. A holographic projection of a crowd scene in Paris, France floated on the ceiling of the chamber. "What is that? The little creature walking alongside the human female."

The Peacemaker studied the three-dimensional image that floated in front of him, and said, "That is a pet, Tok. A pet dog. Humans often make friends with little animals, primarily mammals. Though they sometimes make friends with fish and reptiles as well. Humans in the United States spend more resources on their pets than they do educating their young."

Tok shook her head in a distinctly Arkadian manner that indicated disbelief. "Peacemaker, what is your dominant impression of these creatures?"

"Their culture is incredibly varied. We have counted more than 300 different languages and dialects; we know there are many more."

"Do humans have weapons of mass destruction?" Tok inquired gently.

"Yes. We estimate there are approximately 50,000 thermonuclear devices on the planet's surface."

"*Wa!*" The First Wyrul knew well the problems encountered by ravans when battling adversaries armed with nuclear weapons. "Have they used these weapons?"

"Yes, there have been three detonations over human populations, two in a nation-state called Japan, the other in the major city of a nation-stated called France."

"This is discouraging. What else?"

"Humans also possess enormous quantities of virulent chemical and biological weapons. A single drop of one of these agents—a nerve gas called VX—can kill a human within seconds. Biological weapons can spread deadly microbes through human populations."

"Do these chemical or biological agents affect Arkadians?"

"We do not know."

"It appears humans are more warlike than Arkadians. They do not know Wa." Tok clicked her claws together in contemplation.

Arkadians continued to affirm the Tenets of Wa even though their actions for thousands of years of Hive life said otherwise. Tok turned off the projector and looked up at condensation that had formed on the ceiling. She glanced again at the Peacemaker. This unspoken request for more information was as well understood by the wawren fullmaster as if the First Wyrul had actually spoken.

"Humans are warlike are they not?"

"Yes, I am afraid so. There have been only a few times in human history, for brief periods, when peace reigned on the planet. On two occasions, conflagrations covered the entire globe. During the second of these wars, one nation-state systematically captured, killed and cremated six million humans beings."

"*Wa!* A very large number to kill. Arkadians would never commit so grievous an atrocity."

The Peacemaker paused as though to reply, then appeared to reconsider. He continued, "We expect to find other examples of genocide. In their year 1968, the time we now receive, a war is being fought in a nation-state called Vietnam. We have discovered much brutality committed on the part of both sides. There has been much civil disobedience related to this conflict, particularly in the United States. Humans periodically march in the streets in protest.

"Private citizens in the United States are allowed to purchase antipersonnel weapons called handguns which they use on each other frequently. Citizens across the planet hunt animals for sport, including creatures of the sea. They drag them from their homes with hooks and nets and eat them. One form of mammalian sea life called whales may possess intelligence not yet appreciated or understood by humans. This sentient life is being systematically eradicated."

Tok shuddered. "You mentioned that humans make pets of sea creatures. Yet, they also eat them? I do not understand. Do humans usually eat their friends?"

"Humans may eat the same type of animal they have as a friend. However, they usually do not eat the same animal that serves as a friend. It is difficult to explain, First Wyrul."

"Are humans cannibals?"

"No. They do not practice cannibalism, at least not in the societies we have studied." The Peacemaker continued. "Humans have also been unkind to their environment. Spectral analysis confirms planetary pollution is high, unrestrained, and increasing. Enormous quantities of hydrocarbons have been burned in the atmosphere. Global warming will severely disrupt planetary climate in the near future, perhaps more so than supposedly intelligent life on the planet realizes."

Tok started to speak, paused and then finally spoke. "Hydrocarbons. *Wa!*" The First Wyrul wasn't sure exactly what hydrocarbons were, but pollution in the Hive had sensitized all Arkadians to environmental degeneration.

Tok looked at an alien artifact hanging on the wall, testament to an earlier failure. "Peacemaker, it will take the Hive twenty years in hyperdrive to reach the planet. We will arrive in their year 1998. Will there be a world left to colonize?"

"I do not know. But I urge you to travel the way of Wa, the way of peace if the planet is habitable."

Tok affected the Arkadian equivalent of a grimace. "Do you actually believe peace can be negotiated with these creatures?"

* * * * * * * * * * * * * * *

Annie Simpson looked up from her desk through the window of her office. A few paces away loan officers labored on the platform, a term from the old days when aspiring debtors literally had to pass through a railing to step up to the bankers. Across the lobby she watched the teller line. Her bank, a Tacoma branch of Seafirst, clicked like a finely oiled, well-calibrated machine. She noticed a slender, well-dressed, older man walk with a cocky bounce toward her office. Her stomach fluttered.

"Hey, good looking, how's it cooking?" Paul poked his head through the door and then walked in. Paul Forester's job as Regional Vice-President made him Annie's boss.

"I'm fine, Paul. How are you?"

"Deposits are up. The troops are happy. Even the carpet's clean." Paul shrugged in the direction of the mint green carpet that covered the lobby floor. "You're doing a great job, Annie."

"Thanks."

The executive sat down across from Annie. He noticed the neat, well ordered desk that showed a ten-key, telephone, a copy of *The American Banker*, and a photo of Annie with a gaunt-looking guy with white hair who looked older than Annie, but probably wasn't.

"I'm your supervisor. I know it's important to keep business and pleasure separate. Work is work and play is play. Still, I was wondering if you'd like to have dinner with me this Saturday. How does the Space Needle sound? Say, I meet you there about eight?"

"Why meet there? Why not come by my place?"

"Well, uh, you live with a guy, don't you? I don't think…"

"No you don't."

"Don't what?"

"Don't think. Paul, you don't think. I'm not available. What's going through your mind? You know I'm pregnant. You know I've been with John for years. You've got the sensitivity of a toad."

"Hey, don't get mad. You can't blame me for trying."

"Yes, I can and will. Now, do we have work to discuss, or were you just out trolling?"

* * * * * * * * * * * * * *

The conversation between the First Wyrul and the Peacemaker continued.

"Humans have no understanding of Wa. How can we possibly negotiate with them? Also, with whom would you negotiate? Would it be leaders of this United States or with someone else? What is your opinion, Peacemaker?"

"It is very difficult to identify a clear center of power, Tok. As I said, their culture is varied. At first we thought this question answered when we discovered the United Nations. But this body, it turns out, is not united. The United Nations purportedly represents all countries on the planet, but is physically located in the United States. It purportedly represents all humans but excludes the most populous nation-state, the People's Republic of China.

"We have identified entities called multi-national corporations that hold promise. These corporations are located in dozens of nation-states. Consequently, they better match the heterogeneity of the planet's population. They have financial resources and power in excess of most nation-states, save the very large ones. The control of these corporations is centralized; we need only deal with one chief executive officer or perhaps a 'chairman of the board.' Unaccountably, multinational corporations do not have membership in the United Nations, but this is an ineffective body anyway. Perhaps we should attempt to negotiate with the leader of a corporation like General Motors, IBM, or Dutch Shell."

"Interesting."

The Arkadians floated quietly as the meeting wound down. A final question needed asking.

"First Wyrul?"

"Yes, Peacemaker."

"Will wawrens be given the opportunity to negotiate, or will the Council instead send in the zeromaster cohorts?"

"I am not sure. But I do know the Council must take the action with the highest probability of success. This time, we must not fail."

✳ ✳ ✳ ✳ ✳ ✳ ✳ ✳ ✳ ✳ ✳ ✳ ✳ ✳

John's counselor didn't press charges nor did Cole return to therapy. Counseling and everything else went nowhere for him as September began to fade.

On this particular evening, Cole and Annie had enjoyed good food and company at Michelle and Connor's house in Wallingford. The barbecue and cards went uneventfully. As night fell, the two couples pushed back plates that had held grilled chicken, potato salad, and watermelon and moved to lawn chairs around a card table. It was chilly out, but still bearable. Cole produced a beat-up pack of bicycle poker cards and began to shuffle while Michelle counted out chips.

Two hours passed as the couples played. Night had rolled in, so Annie turned on the backyard lights. Connor, Michelle, and Cole drank beer; Annie enjoyed iced tea. It was the last hand of the evening. Connor had been the big winner at low-stakes poker all evening, but Cole threatened to overtake him on the last pot. It was huge pot that had been built up by successive rounds of progressive draw poker. Michelle and Annie dropped out leaving the two men face-to-face across the table. Annie went back in the house to get a sweater and Michelle sat down next to her big brother. Connor called Cole and smiled at the three deuces John put down on the table. He smiled again and laid down three sixes.

"Read 'em and weep, Cole! Triple sixes. Think you were playing with kids?"

"You got me. Man, I haven't seen luck like that in years! I played a lot of cards in the service and the joint. Best player I ever ran into was Hiroshi Akai, but even he couldn't have touched you tonight."

"Hey, I enjoyed giving you a lesson," Connor chortled. "I did luck out on that last hand. I pulled the sixes right out the deck on my last discard."

"Well, I was the dealer, so you couldn't have cheated. Fate."

Given their unusual history, the ease of communication among John, Annie, Michelle, and Connor might have surprised an observer. There was the occasional joke. John, in particular, liked to tease Annie about her long-ago affair with Connor. Annie had long since given up trying to stop John's friendly jealousy.

It really helped when Connor fell in love with me right after Annie dumped him and went back to John. Michelle giggled at the thought as she looked over at Connor from where she sat at John's side.

Connor swallowed a swig of beer before looking at Michelle and replying, "What're you laughing at?"

"Oh, nothing," Michelle replied. "It's your turn to do the dishes." *Connor and I sure don't talk much anymore.* She looked at her husband.

He smirked back and said, "I'll get around to it. The stars are out. You don't want me to miss that, do you? It's a pretty night." Connor looked up at the explosion of stars sprinkled across the sky. Air pollution was nil and the heavenly vista before Connor was about as clear as it ever could be. He thought about how much he took the stars for granted. *I first noticed Michelle on a night like this. Sure wish I could get those nights and days back. Maybe the stars have an answer.* Connor briefly waited, but the stars didn't answer. He began to pack up the chips.

Michelle leaned back in her lawn chair while absentmindedly fingering the amulet she wore on the thin gold chain around her neck. She glanced to her side. "John…"

"Yeah, Mickie."

"Don't call me, Mickie," Michelle replied softly with a smile. "You're probably going to think this dumb. But I don't care. Sisters get to be dumb sometimes." She lifted the amulet from her neck. "Here," she said. "I want you to have this."

Cole took the crystal from Michelle and looked down at it in his hand. It seemed to glow ever so faintly in the waning light.

"Michelle, you've worn that thing for years. You don't want to give it away."

"I don't know why for sure, but I want you to have it. It's for luck. I've believed that ever since I found it when I was little when we went to the Grand Canyon. I wore it when I met Connor and when I finished school. I wore it while surviving Mom and the loss of Dad. I want you to have it. I want you to wear it and remember you're not alone, and that I love you."

Cole looked away, avoiding his sister's eyes. The amulet hung from his fingers. He shivered in the cool of the night.

* * * * * * * * * * * * * *

A week later, Connor endured chaperon duty at a Queen Anne High School dance.

"*Stop it!* Back off, George." Connor, broke up the fight between George and a John Travolta-styled disco dancer before it started. George had spent the afternoon listening to the sounds of Johnny Rotten, Sid Vicious, and the rest of the Sex Pistols and was acting out their message. Disco dancers and punker body slammers really needed to get together, and what better way to do that than with a bit of slamming?

Connor sighed. These kids either gyrated to Saturday Night Fever-like synchronized mannequins or slammed each other silly at an age when he, Annie, and Michelle had traveled to Chicago to change the world. Where are those lofty ideals now, Connor? Is making a difference in the world—working for peace and justice—really something that should have been put on hold? No excuses. Maybe he shouldn't be so hard on these kids after all. *Eldon Moss must be rolling over in his grave,* Connor thought.

Then he wondered if the old boy was in a grave.

CHAPTER 15

The First Wyrul didn't have to wait long for her next appointment. Instead of a gentle telepathic signal, a loud pounding on the chamber door heralded her next appointment.

"Enter."

Third Wyrul Harn rushed into the chamber accompanied by the ravan fullmaster. The ravan wore the scarlet robes of killing. Her recently sharpened sidehorns and bladed forehorn shimmered in the softened light. The forehorn was functional. Ravans could kill by thrusting the blade that jutted from their forehead downward. Implanted without anesthesia during transition, the blade replaced an Arkadian's natural forehorn. Ravans could also slash with cybernetic fighting talons, also implanted at transition without anesthesia. These blades were of a unique alloy forged before the Hive's launching and stored in ravan armories. Ravans could also bolt. A healthy ravan could sear an adversary with 10,000 volts at fifty paces and be fully charged within seconds. The ravan bristled.

What a difference existed between the wawren and ravan fullmasters, Tok thought. The wawren caste had fully developed innate Arkadian telepathic powers; the ravan caste, the Arkadian capacity to store and discharge static electricity. Wawrens used their ability to mediate, to make the blue flame dance; ravans used theirs to kill.

The visitors stood impatiently in front of a floating Tok. Harn finally said, "Come with us, Tok."

"Why? I am content to remain in my chambers." The First Wyrul reclined lazily, drifting a talon in the pool that lapped around her.

"Your presence is requested at a zeromaster garrison. It will be good for ravan morale to know the Hive's First Wyrul supports war preparations and training."

"Is my presence requested or mandated?" Tok said this as she stood.

"Do not make this difficult, Tok," Harn said testily.

"Difficult? Where lies the difficulty?" Tok glared at her adversary. "I did not ask to attend military exercises, nor did I request your presence. Your mandate is nothing more than the imposition of your will. You have never shown this disrespect to my office before. Why now? Do you crave the Scepter of the First Wyrul?"

"I do not need that symbol, Tok. The ravans are committed to me, not you, and they are the power in the Hive."

Tok glanced at Harn and wondered if she truly had the commitment of the ravans. She subtly scanned just on the boundary of bad manners, but the Third Wyrul did not give up any secrets. Tok finally said, "You do not control all ravans, Harn. My personal bodyguard will convince you of that point."

The ravan fullmaster stepped forward imposing herself between Tok and Harn. While powering up her body shield, she intoned, "Your ravan bodyguard might choose to follow their caste leader if presented with a choice between life with me, or death with you."

"My bodyguard will defend me to the death. Theirs *and* yours." Tok replied with false bravado.

"Times change, Tok," the ravan hissed.

"Come now, there is no reason to quarrel." Harn gently interrupted. "Do come with us, Tok. You will be back in your chambers by the dimming."

Raindrops rattled the chamber's portal. A deep booming from the raindrums began to reverberate throughout the Hive.

"Wa. I wish we could turn those cursed things off," the ravan snarled. Because the builders had shaped the raindrums into the Hive's superstructure, the drums couldn't be destroyed without breaching the Hive's hull.

"Listening to the drums might do you some good, ravan fullmaster," Tok said.

"Not likely."

Harn again interceded. "Let us go. Do not signal your bodyguard, Tok. You have nothing to fear."

The Arkadians waded outside Tok's first floor chambers. The wyrul compound in the outer ring stretched above and around them, a gray slab with identical portals that spiraled in neat columns into the grayness of the Hive sky. Tok noticed the mottling on the building's metal exterior. The rust seemed to grow with each dimming. The group dove into the facing pool and swam underwater toward a transfer pod docked above water in an adjacent parking area. Swimming was as natural to Arkadians as walking is to humans. Underwater, telepathic messages naturally replaced spoken communication.

Why do you insult me so, Harn? I have behaved reasonably toward you. We are so close to our goal, to planetfall. Why do you agitate so?

I have plans far beyond our miserable existence in the Hive, Tok. You must learn that true power among Arkadians belongs to me.

Then take my scepter. It is yours.

I cannot waste precious time with administrative matters. I have more pressing business at present with the ravans.

Oblivious to their shielded communication, the ravan swimming ahead reached the docking area and leaped out of the water. She spun rapidly and ritualistically to dry, then stepped into the driver's seat of the transfer pod. The wyruls followed, spun, and sat in the back seat. Doors slammed shut. The ravan navigated into the main channel that flowed through the calm waters of the wyrul compound. The pod streamed above the water toward the intruder screen and exit.

"What is our destination? There are many ravan garrisons."

Harn ignored the question.

The ravan compound had long since been distributed throughout the Hive into garrisons. In the past, different garrisons professed loyalty to different wyruls. At present, the wyruls, with the exception of personal bodyguards, were united in loyalty to Harn and the ravan fullmaster. Tok suspected this loyalty to Harn could dissipate like the mist of first light.

The travelers passed through half-submerged gates and the intruder screen that marked the boundary of the wyrul compound. Members of Tok's personal bodyguard rippled by within quick striking distance of the entrance. No ravans, except the loyal bodyguard and the ravan fullmaster, ever entered the wyrul compound. Tok's bodyguard had been on alert because an attack was expected soon.

An assault by assassination squad against a wyrul's living quarters and those of her allies usually signaled the beginning of the next Hive War. Bodyguards would battle the assassins until the waters of the wyrul compound tinged red around floating corpses. From there, the war would soon spread to all rings in the Hive except the inner ring. By tacit agreement and long custom, wars never started nor were they fought in the seat of Hive government and administration. This prohibition allowed the Hive's systems to be maintained even during the bloodiest of wars. It also provided a sanctuary for the treaty negotiations that invariably occurred when the war had run its course.

"What do you want from me?"

Harn hissed, "You mean other than your morale-boosting presence to review the troops? We need better information. Have you been briefed on life on the target?"

"The target? The blue planet is not yet a target, Harn. Yes, I have been briefed. You know that. You have access to the same holodiscs I do."

"The information is inadequate. It tells the ravans little about human troop dispositions or military technology. Do humans command antigravity and antimatter? It is difficult to believe their cities and individual warriors are unshielded. The ravans must know how well humans fight in order to defeat them quickly before they resort to nuclear weapons, weapons that all cursed creatures in the universe seem to possess except for us!"

"Harn, the Council of Wyruls has not yet decided on the best method of colonizing the planet. We may still send in the Peacemaker rather than ravans. Your request for information is preposterous and premature. Why waste my time? Return me to my chambers immediately."

Harn studied Tok briefly then gazed up at the rain now pouring down in a torrent, streaming down the sides of the bubble compartment of the transfer pod. The raindrums boomed. She motioned to the ravan who nodded and steered the pod down into the sea. Even here, the vibration of the raindrums could be felt. Outside, the green, murky water was filled with the flitting of oddly-shaped things. Several glow globes along the route they traveled had burned out causing a strobe-light effect as the travelers moved through eerie darkness and light. The Hive Sea seemed foreign to Tok. Not like the sea she remembered as a tad, or remembered even a few short years ago.

Harn finally said, "No. You will review a zeromaster cohort before your return. As far as war preparations are concerned, keep up the pretense of negotiation if that helps motivate the wawrens. But you and I both know that the zeromaster cohorts will be sent in. There is no other option."

"That remains to be seen, Third Wyrul. Even the ravans will accept negotiation by the Peacekeeper if it is necessary. They fear defeat, particularly by nuclear fire, more than any of us. And they want planetfall as much as any of us."

Tok's assessment did not sway Harn. "The ravans have nothing to worry about. They will overwhelm the target before humans can react with their filthy weapons."

Wham! The pod shuddered. Another thump shivered the small craft.

"What was that?" Harn was more puzzled than alarmed.

"We are under attack, Harn." The ravan fullmaster gunned the engine. Something skittered off the side of the pod and fell behind.

Tok understood what had happened. Evil had many faces in the Hive.

The pod slowed as the group approached an intruder screen. The screens kept whatever now crawled and swam malevolently in the Hive Sea out of Arkadian compounds. The pod passed through a gate and surfaced in the midst of a ravan garrison. The rain shower had stopped and the raindrums with it. Mist rose from the waters.

Tok followed the ravan fullmaster and Harn into a great gray circular-shaped compound, a training arena and target range for ravans. She spent the remainder of Hive light—the time before the lamps dimmed—watching in silent reticence from a reviewing stand.

She nodded dully as waves of ravan zeromasters practiced military maneuvers; she observed streams of ravans attack from fighting machines that hummed overhead, their simulated particle beams spitting with perfect effect at targets. She followed the tactics of individual ravans who had dismounted for squad-level maneuvers. She observed the close coordination between machine and warrior, a grand choreography, a dance of death.

Later, Tok observed individual combat drills. Though muted, fighting talons and bladed forehorns still drew blood that clouded the pools and flowed on the red mats of the practice arena. Tok was appalled at the brutality and figured it would escalate out of control as it eventually did.

An over-zealous zeromaster, probably pumped up by the presence of the First Wyrul, fired an illegal bolt at her sparring partner. The crackling flash missed its target and burned another. Angered by the attack, the injured ravan powered up his shield and leaped across the training mat at the over-zealous zeromaster who responded by powering up her shield. The ravans unsheathed fighting talons and circled, looking for an opening. Their shields buzzed when they briefly brushed.

A halfmaster moved to break up the fight, but was telegraphically waved off by the ravan fullmaster sitting alongside Tok who intoned, "Observe, First Wyrul. Observe and remember."

Long ago, wizards, co-opted by the ravan caste had perfected individual body shields, and programmed a syntheofactory for their production. These shields used the same technology that allowed the Hive to withstand the infinite gravity of black holes and quantum particle bombardment during straddletravel. Shields had to be dropped to bolt, so a long-range attack became a guessing game as shields flickered on and off and bolts crackled.

The alternative, moving in close to force a talon or forehorn through an opponent's shield, would have sounded and looked like a buzzsaw to a human. Forehorn strikes, fighting talons, and projectiles moving at somewhat less than light speed could make it through a shield and body armor. Knocking an opponent off his feet with a bolo toss and frying him before he could recover was a particularly elegant way to kill an adversary. The shield only protected a ravan's front. Hitting an opponent in the back though it killed was less elegant.

The fight intensified. Shields and bolts flickered on and off. With feral screams, the enraged ravans closed. Tok winced at the hate that telepathically washed the arena. The rank smell of burning ozone signaled the buzzing passage of fighting talons through a shield. The loser screamed as talons slashed his face and stumbled away blind, only to be felled by whirling bolos and knocked to the mat with a splash.

The winner powered down his shield, extended his right arm, and grunted as thousands of angry volts blasted from his claw tips into the writhing form. The body twitched momentarily and stopped moving. A smell a human could have only recognized only as roasting pork pervaded the dank steaming air.

"Zeromaster, approach." The ravan fullmaster rose from her place in the reviewing stand.

Tok suddenly felt vulnerable.

The ravan stepped from the practice mat and splashed through shallows to face his fullmaster, who sat several rows up in the reviewing stand. A burned flap hung from his cheek.

"Receive this field promotion to quartermaster. You will command a squad within the fifty-first zeromaster cohort. Report immediately to the cohort commander on my authority."

The satisfied ravan saluted his fullmaster and resolutely sloshed away. Tok then, as before, always felt—even with the precise battle maneuvers and high-tech weapons—that the average ravan preferred hand-to-hand tearing, slashing, and ripping.

Eventually, she was escorted back to her housing compound in the outer ring where she spent a restless dimming.

* * * * * * * * * * * * * *

Chuck Cole loved his work. That love had grown, from scanning the night sky as a youth with his twin sister Michelle to his present job as a post-doctoral research associate at the Very Long Base-Line Interferometry (VLBI) station in Socorro, New Mexico. The radio telescope array, now under construction, would soon probe objects millions of light years away.

Chuck looked forward to viewing the heavens while seated at a computer terminal rather than peering through a telescope. Others prescribed Chuck's job description. As a research associate, it would be a long time before he had the authority to pursue his specialized interests in binary star systems and black holes. Still, he could think of no other place he'd rather be.

To most of his colleagues, Chuck's life appeared boring. He had no romantic interests. He read nonfiction with an occasional science-fiction novel thrown in for variety. He didn't exercise because he didn't like to sweat. Besides, 300-plus pounds made working out too difficult, maybe even dangerous. Chuck wasn't a voracious eater. Like his mother, he just had a tendency to pack it on. He never watched TV. He wasn't trying to make a statement. He just preferred classical music and reading to alpha waving before the tube.

He kept his blonde hair short and his face clean-shaven. His clothing was quaint, even old-fashioned. He lived in a trailer adjoining the telescope array administrative offices still under construction. The only apparent color in his life was the red flush on his rounded cheeks that appeared whenever he had to exert himself. He was exerting himself now as he shuffled through a hallway of the facility. Sawdust, the smell of new paint, and construction signs were ever present.

A more insightful observer might conclude that Chuck Cole lived an adventure of the highest order. Shooting rapids, traveling around the world in a balloon, or a torrid love affair paled in comparison to Chuck's primary activity—exploring the boundless soul of the universe.

"Hey Chuck! Where're you going?" Mary Moore, also a research associate, yelled. Mary had been leaving after a long day when she had spotted her friend's hulking shadow in the corridor.

"To the library. How come you're still around?"

"Working late like you. Chuck, don't you ever do anything just for fun? Cosmology's great, but there *is* more to life." Chuck knew Mary's reputation. She was a gorgeous woman he could never hope to attract. Mary's flame had been a senior associate Ph.D who looked like the lead character from a surfing movie.

"Cosmology is life, Mary. Everything that ever was or ever will be is out there. Past, present and future," Chuck returned with a smile.

"Really, why aren't you back at that double-wide trailer of yours watching Johnny Carson?"

"We were having trouble calibrating the array for the Orion simulation. We should get good test data tomorrow. Looks like we're finally getting ready to go online. How's your life? Still interested in the Cygnus binary?" Chuck Cole's interest in black holes was as well known by all staff, as was Mary's penchant for flirtation.

"Yeah, I've been looking at secondary sources. The Uhuru data's pretty good, but I'd sure like to have a chance on the array some day."

"What'd you think's going on with the Cygnus binary, Chuck? A blue giant circling a black hole sounds exotic."

"Shouldn't call it a black hole, Dr. Moore. It's a Kerr Singularity. Geez, I can't believe you went to college!" Chuck's eyes twinkled, the trip to the library forgotten for the moment. "I'm interested in the properties of the thing. There's definitely new physics happening. There's a lot we don't understand."

"Thing? What thing, Dr. Cole? Oh! You mean the Kerr Singularity." Mary chuckled as she slipped through the exit. "Night, night, cutie. See you tomorrow."

Cutie? Stunned, Chuck stood for a moment before shaking his head and walking away.

* * * * * * * * * * * * * *

"Watch out!" The bartender screamed.

John Cole looked at the bartender, then turned into the full fury of a barstool that crashed into his chest and face. He turned to the attackers: the logger who had thrown the stool and his even drunker buddy whom Cole had insulted with a caustic remark.

Cole casually flipped the first logger over the bar. He thought about really hurting the other guy. He didn't notice flashing red and blue lights from the squad cars that had just pulled up front, and he hadn't heard the sirens.

Cole circled the logger who appeared to be a bit worried, having just seen the ease with which his buddy had been dispatched. The logger stumbled forward to meet a lunge from Cole that didn't happen and fell prey to a hip throw. He knocked over the bartender who had come around the bar to break up the fight. Both men lay on the floor, unmoving. The logger wasn't hurt all that badly but decided not to get up. He wasn't sure about the bartender. How did this skinny guy with the long white hair move so well?

Cole turned to the sound of cops rushing through the door. But seeing the uniforms, he dropped his arms. Another night in the drunk tank. Maybe even criminal charges if someone had broken something.

Wait...these guys aren't cops. They look like cops. They talk like cops. But they're not cops. Got to get my arms up. They won't move! Come on arms. Move. Got to protect myself. Damn

But the cops didn't hurt Cole. They were real cops after all. They cuffed him, and read him his rights. They led Cole out front and gently sat him down in the back seat of a government-green Ford Sedan. Suddenly, and unaccountably, he was nestled up against the side of a ditch. It was blistering hot. Sweat ran off him. Where did the cuffs go? Where was he?

Cole stood up in the ditch. He smelled the copper stink of fresh blood, the reek of voided bowels, and urine. In horror, Cole turned away from groaning bodies stacked before him like twitching cordwood, and clambered out of the ditch slipping on warm, blood-wet, loose soil. Shirley beckoned to him several steps away. What was his mom doing here? He ran to her with clumsy, halting little steps. Shirley's big fleshy arms enveloped him. Suddenly, he was catapulted back toward the ditch. He passed through a cloud of pink mist and landed in the middle of the warm, wet, twitching cordwood. He rolled off the stack into a hot pool of blood.

Cole opened his eyes. The first thing he saw in the bad light and shadows was Annie's worried face. She peered at him from her side of the queen-sized bed the couple had shared the past two years.

"Wake up, honey. Let it go. Let it go."

Cole stopped flailing. He whispered, "Another bad one."

As was their custom on nights plagued by "bad ones," they got up to drink a cup of tea. John put water on to boil. Over a cup of peppermint tea he talked with Annie about the dream, and the jitters died. The two would soon return to bed to whatever remained of the night.

"Sounds like the same dream."

"Yeah, it was, but my mom was in it this time."

"Wonder what a counselor would say?" Annie never stopped trying to get Cole back into therapy.

"Well, a counselor would probably wonder why my mom was there. My counselor might have said I was seeking emotional support, but I don't know why I'd look for that from my mom. You and Mickie prop me up these days."

"Well, I'm here, and always will be," Annie replied. Then, an afterthought, "I'm amazed that last counselor forgave you for punching him out."

"He has to be used to that working with trip-wire vets. Anyway, the counselor's just part of the furniture as far as I'm concerned. But you're not. I'm glad you're with me, Annie, though I know I'm not much good for you."

"Let me be the judge of that. I love you, John."

"What about Connor? Love him too?" John said with a smile. No response. A worn-out, tiresome joke, that had never been funny.

"Sorry."

Not really, Annie thought.

"You know, nothing's working for me. You're not to blame. I know it's me."

"Why not quit drinking? You've been in the drunk-tank twice in the last year. I don't mean to nag, but you could lose your driver's license. You'd sleep better too."

"It's drinking that puts me to sleep, honey."

"Why not go to college?"

"Nah."

"Go back to Japan then. You've kept in touch with Hiroshi. He's working for a big company, isn't he? Maybe he could help you find something."

Hiroshi Akai continued to climb the corporate ladder at Mitsubishi. He went to the right school, had the right contacts, and came from the right family. His work with the Beheiren hadn't hurt him because his actions expressed what most Japanese citizens had believed to be right.

"You really want me to leave you and the baby?"

"John, we're not married. Besides, you've got a lot to work out. You won't go to counseling, so you're going to have to do it on your own. Maybe a change of scene would help. Like I said, I love you. I want you to be here. But if you left, I'd sure understand." She patted her stomach as though to reassure the unborn child.

"Well, maybe I will and maybe even soon. But I've got to figure out where to go, and why."

"I don't understand why you don't go to school."

"I'm too old for school."

"God, John, you're only 29. That's nothing."

"Doesn't seem like nothing to me."

* * * * * * * * * * * * * *

The late summer rolled into September, then October. Rock and sand don't change colors in the desert, but there still was an autumn feel.

Chuck Cole stood on the outside edge of the parking lot away from the lights of the VLBI facility. The 27 new radio telescopes, each 94 feet high with dishes 82 feet in diameter never stopped scanning.

Daylight savings time had just ended, making the early evening even darker. The stars were on their way. Chuck could just now see Polaris—the northern star that had guided man since he first looked up at the night sky—making its appearance. He watched a car turn down the entrance road and into the parking lot.

"Who'd come by at this hour?" Cole muttered from his place on the edge of the desert.

The car stopped some 20 paces from where he stood. High squeaking voices could be heard. Three creatures crawled out of the car that clearly weren't human. Braided hair snaked down a blood-red cape. He could see horns. A human driver followed them to the main entrance as though a puppet on a string. The three creatures pounded wildly on the door. Chuck could just make out Mary Moore opening the glass double door. She faced the demons, alone.

"Trick or treat!"

Chuck smiled. He had almost forgotten about Halloween. He was getting jumpy. Too many hours spent working. He wondered if Mary was prepared. She was. Each of the kids had something slipped into their bag.

"Wonder why they came all the way out here?" Cole said out loud, then realized the desolation of the desert made for slim pickings on this all-important night in the life of an American child. Perhaps the children belonged to a staff member.

Seeing the kids made him think of Annie.

✳ ✳ ✳ ✳ ✳ ✳ ✳ ✳ ✳ ✳ ✳ ✳ ✳ ✳

"Come on, Annie. Focal point. Focal point. Breathe!"

She gasped, then relaxed. "How much longer?"

"Not much longer, honey. The nurse said you're fully dilated. Baby's on the way." John Cole wiped sweat off Annie's brow. He grabbed ice chips from a bowl on the bedside stand and gently placed them in her mouth.

"Oh, God…*John!*" Annie tensed. The ice chips sputtered out. She grunted.

Doctor Paulson walked in. "Okay. Time to move." An attendant followed. Annie moaned. The doctor and attendant rolled her onto a gurney while Cole watched helplessly.

"Stay with me."

"I'm right here, honey. Don't worry. Keep breathing."

Thirty minutes later, at precisely the witching hour on Halloween eve, Dylan Ralph Simpson-Cole screamed his way into the world. Little Dylan fixed onto his mother's breast without a moment's hesitation. John left the recovery room at Annie's urging to call Shirley from a pay phone in the hall.

Shirley picked up the phone on the first ring.

"Hi Mom. It's me, John."

"Johnny? Oh, I haven't heard from you in so long. I'll bet you're calling me about the baby? It's about time. Quiet, Muffin!"

Cole could barely hear his mother over the incessant yapping of a little dog.

"Uh, mom. Why don't you put the mutt in another room so we can talk?"

"Hush. Oh, not you, Johnny. Hush, Muffin. Bad doggie. Be quiet for your mommy-wommy, ookums. That's a good doggie. Muffin! Bad, bad doggie. Mutt? Johnny, did you just call my Muffin a mutt?"

"Hey, Mom. You've got a grandson!"

"Have you married that girl yet? Bad Muffin! Naughty, naughty doggie. I declare I don't know what's got into my baby waby." The yapping escalated.

"Mom, we just had the baby. Annie's fine and…"

"Yes. I know. You told me. Muffin! Bad doggie." Cole heard a doorbell ring in the background. "Johnny, I've got to go. Tell Annie to call me when she's up to it. Poor girl." The receiver clicked.

"Bye, Mom." Cole replaced the receiver and tried Michelle at home. No answer. He hung up.

It had all happened so fast. Just a few hours ago he and Annie had been talking at the dinner table.

"Honey, I've found something. I've looked into it and it sure looks good. Didn't want to talk to you until I was more sure."

"What's that, John?" Annie seemed distracted as she picked at a taco salad.

"You know I got to get out, even out of the country. I need to do simple work, get away from booze, and get into doing something good. There's a place... it's actually on the island of Crete." He took a swallow of table wine. "I got to get away from the dreams."

"Crete? Why Crete?"

"There's an institute there. They want me."

"They want you? Want you for what? I know you need to do take on something different, but going to Crete is *really* different. What type of an institute? What will you be doing?"

"It'll take some explaining. Let's put on some tunes and pour some wine. I'll tell you all about it."

"We don't need to drink to talk, John... wait... oh... what's that?"

"What's what?"

"Just a second," Annie gasped. A few long seconds later she said, "I've been having pains all evening. I wasn't sure if they were real or not. But that last one sure was."

* * * * * * * * * * * * * *

The yearly allocation had begun in the Hive.

A talent for bolting or telepathic ability might mean assignment to the ravan or wawren caste respectively. High intelligence might mean allocation to the wizards; leadership ability and social grace could mean assignment to the bureaucrats. A mediocre assessment might lead to assignment as a worker; mechanical aptitude, to placement as a technician.

For thousands of years, the goal had been simply to replace the numbers who had died during the past year either in the Hive or in cryonic storage. The ravans also claimed increasing numbers—half to be trained in the ravan arts; the other half as food for the ravan table.

CHAPTER 16

"Sit!" First Wyrul Tok's command lashed Harn into silence. Memory of the forced trip to the garrison and the recent allocation of most tads to the ravan caste festered in the First Wyrul's mind. She slowly lowered herself into the ornate cushions at the head of the table. Tok had balanced factions and problems since her ascension ten years ago. But emotions now roiled out of control. Another Hive War loomed. This one would be short. The ravans now all pledged allegiance to their unusually charismatic fullmaster. Tok was not even sure she still had a bodyguard.

Tok's furious gaze met Third Wyrul Harn's. "Our situation is grave," Tok said. "No one knows that better than I. But no matter how serious or urgent the decision, decorum must be maintained. Outbursts will not be permitted. You will conduct yourself with the propriety expected of a wyrul." Her gaze never wavered. Neither did Harn's. Blue sparks of anger crackled down the Third Wyrul's arms dissipating at her claw tips.

"Of course, Tok," Harn finally said with silky evenness as she looked away. "Decorum will be maintained."

"Fifth Wyrul Pire, you may continue. You have the speaker's wand," Tok said. She leaned back, every motion conveying authority. "Pass the wand to Harn when you are finished."

Pire looked at Harn, then at the others. "Our life in the Hive has been a gift of Wa, a most sacred opportunity. Scorn my words if you will, but that will not change reality. The Hive was sent forth in harmony; it is in harmony that we must approach the blue planet even if the trip itself has not been harmonious."

Several Council members joined Harn in clicking, rumbling disagreement at Pire's words.

"I know my message is difficult for many at this table!" Pire said determinedly above the discontent. "But Arkadians violated the Tenets of Wa each time worlds were destroyed after each of our failures. We continue to violate the Tenets of Wa by imprisoning the wawrens. We must recommit to Wa. Wawrens, not ravans, are the key to survival both in the Hive and in our new home."

Discord, albeit subdued, continued. So did Pire. "Wawrens must be freed to work unabated by the threat of blood. Only then can they successfully negotiate and gain for us the home for which we have searched. The wawrens are not at fault for past failures to colonize a blue planet. It is the ravans who have failed Arkadia, who have bludgeoned the spirit of Wa." With a flourish, Pire released the speaker's wand to Harn.

Tok's warning lay heavy on the Council and although members continued to tangle, hiss, and click among themselves in response to Pire's eloquence, their displeasure was muted.

Harn raised the speaker's wand. The Council braced. But in contrast to her earlier outburst, Harn spoke in even, abeit razor-edged, tones. "The facts are clear. Three times Arkadia has negotiated. Three times the wawrens and their Peacemaker fullmaster have failed. We teeter on the brink of extinction. The problem is not one of belief. We all believe in Wa. The problem is one of power. Wawren negotiation is less convincing, less certain, less reliable than the might of the zeromaster cohorts. We cannot rely on half measures. Use wawren skill to gather information to help the zeromaster cohorts gain final victory. Would not this cooperation among Arkadians be commendable? Is not establishment of a superordinate goal one of the Tenets of Wa?"

"Yes. But that is not the point." Pire interrupted. Toltek added, "The Tenets of Wa say that actions must be peaceful!"

"Order!" Tok trilled. "Harn has the speaker's wand."

Harn again lifted the wand.

Silence. Only background dripping from condensation and the rattle of an atmosphere recycler could be heard in the chamber.

Harn intoned, "Wyruls, you know I am right. The upcoming battle must be the last. Let it be the battle to end all battles."

After a pause, agreement clicked back from several Council members. Harn returned the speaker's wand to Tok and settled back.

The First Wyrul sighed. The upcoming Council vote would be close.

* * * * * * * * * * * * * * *

Harn sat on cushions in her quarters and stared at an unappetizing evening meal of algae and insect pastes. She had been spoiled by occasional, splendid meals of fresh Arkadian flesh provided by her ravan friends.

The Council session—and Tok's admonition—grated more than Harn had shown. "This has gone far enough," she sputtered aloud. "I have suffered her pomposity long enough. How *dare* she!"

A worker zeromaster interrupted her thoughts. The servant's head hung low in subservience as he spoke, "Third Wyrul, the ravan fullmaster has arrived and requests an audience."

"Very well," Harn said, pushing away the food. "Admit the visitor."

The ravan fullmaster strode in and filled Harn's chamber with her presence. She did not ask for permission to speak nor did she begin with a ritual bow acknowledging Harn's position as a wyrul. She began instead with a quick, rude dip of the head. "I am disturbed by accounts of the Council's last meeting. I was appalled by reports I received. Tok may contest our authority." The ravan paused and then went on, "There are some among the Council who say she humiliated you." The ravan stared down at Harn.

"Feeble attempts by pathetic weaklings do not concern me," Harn spat.

The ravan nodded approval. "We continue then?"

"On schedule. Time presses. The Council will act soon. Pire, Toltek, and Tok are respected—and dangerous. Their calls to Wa will sway romantic fools. If the Council vote goes against us, on my signal you will assassinate those three. The others will fall in line or meet the same fate. The vote *will* go our way, even if some new members of the Council are required afterward to fill vacancies."

The ravan nodded, unsheathing fighting talons from under her webbed claws. The cybernetic implants sparkled in the soft light of the chamber. "We will violate tradition against bloodshed in the first ring. A bold move they will not expect. I like it. It will be a pleasure to tear into those weaklings."

Harn replied, "The road to power has been long, fullmaster. Soon, a blue planet, all of it, will be ours to plunder. The rewards will be plentiful."

The ravan inclined her head, this time with respect.

✶ ✶ ✶ ✶ ✶ ✶ ✶ ✶ ✶ ✶ ✶ ✶ ✶ ✶

"Hi, Mom."

Shirley jumped. She turned and stared at the apparition standing in the driveway. She had just returned from the grocery store.

"What? Johnny?" She stopped. "I am surprised to see you. What are you doing here?"

"I'm here to say goodbye," Cole replied.

"Goodbye? What you mean? We hardly say hello to each other and now you're saying goodbye?" Shirley stood her ground, not sure why. "Well, you're here, you might as well help out. Here, carry these."

Cole took a bag of groceries and followed Shirley through the garage. Muffin brought up the rear, yapping at his heels. Cole noticed his tricycle still hung high on a hook from a garage rafter. The family's camping paraphernalia was piled in the far corner next to Chuck and Michelle's old telescope. Cole unaccountably thought of the family vacation to the Grand Canyon when Mickie found the crystal he now wore. Through the garage door and inside the kitchen, a ceramic chicken and rooster salt-and-pepper set propped up a handful of paper napkins in the middle of the kitchen table, just as they did in Cole's earliest memories. He stood in the kitchen holding the groceries, transfixed by memories. *Nothing's changed.*

"I, ah, I don't have long, Johnny," Shirley began. "The Reverend Stringer will be here shortly to discuss fund-raising. I'm sure you understand. You're all right aren't you? Muffin! Hush!"

"Yeah, I understand Mom. Fund-raising's real important. Thanks for your concern. I'm fine, thank you. And you?" *I'd like to dropkick that frigging rat dog through the wall.* Muffin began to tug on the cuff of Cole's jeans, snarling ferociously.

Shirley put down a sack, picked up the wiggling animal, and dropped it outside the back door. She shut the door and sat down at her usual place at the table.

"You treat that dog better than you do me."

"Johnny, please. I don't want to fight. *My, his hair is so white. Must've gotten that from Ralph's side of the family. He certainly could use a haircut.*

"We don't have to fight," Cole said, setting the groceries down on the kitchen's orange counter. He threw his windbreaker over the back of a kitchen chair and sat down in his old spot at the kitchen table. "I came to talk to you about two things. First, I want you to accept Dylan. I know you don't approve of me, but the kid's blameless. Second thing, I wanted to tell you I'm leaving."

Shirley snapped. "What do you mean, `leaving'? You're not planning to abandon poor Annie in her time of need? It's bad enough the child isn't sanctified in the eyes of the Lord. But to desert the mother? I can't believe I raised you. That child was born just a few weeks ago."

"I'm not sure Annie's in need, Mom," Cole grimaced. So far, things had gone as expected. "Annie and I agree on my leaving. I'm no good to her or Dylan the way I am. She's been supporting me, not the other way around. I've got to get myself together. I've found a place in Greece. An academy dedicated to peace. I've been offered a job and a home there. It is the first thing I've felt like doing since getting out of Leavenworth. I don't know why, but I think it'll help, not just me, but others too. Annie agrees. She's lending me money to get there and Michelle's helping out too. I didn't come here expecting you to approve. I don't need or want your permission. I just thought you might want to know I'm leaving and that everything's okay with Annie and Dylan."

Shirley got up to stack canned goods in a cupboard, her back to Cole. She paused then, without looking at her eldest son, moved to the stove to turn up the heat under the teakettle.

"Greece? You're going to Greece? That's absurd," she finally said. "You're not going anywhere until you marry that poor girl. You don't want baby Dylan to stay a bastard, do you? A bastard has no standing in Heaven, Johnny. No. You've got to make things right with the Lord. You could get married right here. We can talk with the Reverend Stringer when he arrives. He'll be here any minute. The Lord will heal you if you open your heart. He will bestow the gift of true salvation on you, Annie, and the child. Johnny, this child could be a sign from God. I'm sure if you just asked the Lord to forgive your sins, he would lift the burdens from your heart and you could…" Shirley started to raise her arms.

"Don't start!"

Shirley turned to face him. "Johnny, I don't know what is wrong with you," she said. "I don't understand why you do the things you do. I don't feel I even know you. Now this. A bastard in our own family!

"Your father was so proud of you; we all were proud of you. You got good grades in high school. You played football and even could have had a college scholarship. You made a success of yourself in the military. Then you threw it all away. You won't talk about why. That's fine. But with the Lord's help you could put the past behind you and get on with having a responsible life. Your poor father would be so ashamed."

"This isn't about Dad. I told you. I'm going away. I don't know why I'm even here talking with you. I should have known this wouldn't work."

Cole grabbed his jacket off the back of the chair and started for the door back through the garage. He stopped and faced Shirley.

"Don't ever talk to me about my father," Cole said with a bitterness he couldn't contain. "You've been cutting me with that since I got out. I didn't kill Dad. *You* killed him. He couldn't do anything right. He couldn't say anything right. He didn't dare do anything but sit in front of that damn TV and molder. None of us did. You had to do it all with nothing for us but ridicule and rules. *You* didn't have time for us. We were just mortal. Dad was the lucky one. He died."

"John Michael, that is enough," Shirley sputtered. She reached for her heart and massaged. "I do not know why..."

"Where was your beloved God when I was rotting in prison? When I was watching young mothers, a lot younger than Annie, and babies— babies like Dylan—get shot and dumped in a pit. Ever see a mother try to shield her baby from a bullet? I didn't see God there, Mom. You weren't there either. Don't ever talk to me again about God. And don't ever talk to me again about my father." Cole turned to leave.

"Son, wait," Shirley said in the pause. "Please don't go."

Cole stopped. She hadn't said "please" or called him "son" in years.

"I can see there are great forces at work inside you," Shirley said, beginning again to move about in the kitchen. Had she ever addressed her family without being in the middle of preparing food? Cole scanned his memory while he sat back down. He couldn't recall.

"I know the things you say do not come from you. I don't hold them against you. They are to be expected. They are the work of the Evil One who tries to unsettle our minds and our lives."

Cole shook his head. Just when he thought she was going to say something meaningful.

"I know you don't agree with me, Johnny. That's fine. I don't expect to be appreciated. Whether or not you believe it, I've still only had the good of this family in mind. Your father understood. He didn't always agree with me—I pray to God every day he now sees the truth and that he is at rest—but your father knew I devoted my life to saving this family's soul. I tried in every conceivable way to protect you, even in the face of your disapproval. My work was not for myself because I will be saved when the time comes. My work has been for those threatened by Satan. People like you, Johnny."

"There is no God or Satan, Mom. There's only human stupidity. Only the things we do to each other," Cole said in a quiet, resigned voice. "If there was a God, he would have given up on us long ago."

"That's where you're wrong. God's plan unfolds according to His own schedule. The atrocities you have seen foretell the Times of Tribulation. The prophecies are being fulfilled. We don't have much time. The good book is clear. The third chapter of II Timothy says," Shirley looked away trance-like and recited from memory: " … in the last days difficult times will come. For men will be lovers of self, lovers of money, boastful, arrogant, revilers, disobedient to parents, ungrateful, unholy, unloving, irreconcilable, malicious gossips, without self-control, brutal, haters of good, treacherous, reckless, conceited, lovers of pleasure rather than lovers of God."

She turned back to her son. "Now, Johnny, doesn't that sound like now? Like the times we now live in?"

His mom definitely needed to have her pencils sharpened. Same old crap and same old defense against inadequacy and intimacy—whether talking in her own kitchen or the few times they talked since Leavenworth, her message was always the same. Still, who can blame a woman for trying to do what's right for her family. For trying to get her act together. After all, I'm leaving Annie and Dylan to do the same thing. For just a moment, Cole felt empathy.

Shirley was heartened by her son's thoughtful expression. This was the longest the boy had let her talk to him about salvation. Perhaps this was a sign. She pounced on the possibility.

"Johnny, the Antichrist will come to us as a savior. He will come with warnings of evil and will actively work for peace. He will be hailed as a prophet. But he will not be holy. The devout will recognize him as the beast. He must be cast out. We must prepare the soil for the Second Coming of Jesus Christ, our Lord and Savior."

Cole again turned to rush out the kitchen door.

"Why, my dear, an excellent synopsis," the Reverend Isaiah Marcus Stringer's oily voice floated through the room as he stepped into the kitchen from the living room. "I must make greater use of your speaking ability. Forgive me for eavesdropping. The front door was open, so I let myself in. You must be John. Your mother has spoken to me often of your needs. I trust Sister Cole's counsel has eased your burdened heart."

Muffin skittered in through the Reverend's legs and launched himself at Cole's ankle with bared teeth, missed, and crashed into the wall. The little dog tottered away in a daze.

Cole looked at the intruder. He was immaculately dressed and perfectly groomed. His double-breasted suit and puffed-up pompadour were distracting.

"Why, Reverend Stringer," Shirley fluttered, lifting up from her place at the table. "My, how time has flown. I am so sorry we didn't hear you. Yes, this is Johnny. He stopped by for a visit, isn't that lovely?"

Cole cringed. "Mom, I have to…"

"Yes, dear. Reverend Stringer, may I offer you some tea? I believe the water's still hot. Now Johnny dear, why don't you move to the other chair so we can offer the Reverend a proper seat?

"Mom, I'm leaving. I'm going. I don't know when, or if, I'll ever be coming back."

"Yes, yes, dear. Drive carefully. I hope our talk has helped. Please think about what I've said. Reverend Stringer, would you care to sit in the living room? My late husband, Ralph, used to prefer the chair by the window."

Cole stepped out the kitchen door. Shirley didn't hear the door slam as she settled comfortably into place with the Reverend Stringer by her side in the living room.

* * * * * * * * * * * * * *

"The vote is tabulated," First Wyrul Tok began.

A silver overlay caught the chamber's lights and showered her blue robes with mirrored rainbows. She pulled herself to full standing height, her posture revealing no outward sign of the turmoil within. She wondered why the ravan guards had stepped forward from their positions on the wall.

"The necessary majority of the Council of Wyruls has spoken. Ravans are authorized to begin war planning. The zeromaster cohorts will be sent in. The wawrens will pay particular attention to planetary defenses as they study humans. Until further notice, all new allotments of tads will go to the ravan caste. Harn, you will serve as the Council's liaison to the military."

Harn bowed her head in acknowledgement. The ravan fullmaster who had moved to her side, agitated just a moment ago, visibly relaxed. Other ravans settled back.

"The will of the Council of Wyruls will prevail, esteemed First Wyrul," Harn said.

* * * * * * * * * * * * * *

Energy snapped as the Peacekeeper floated in heavy meditation. Bolts of blue popped between his claws and skittered along his arms. His head drooped in anguish. Even the normally soothing thump of the raindrums was of little solace.

"Peacemaker, may I enter?" The call came through the chamber's door both verbally and telepathically. Disruption during meditation was unheard of. There was not a shred of respect left for the rites of peacemaking! The Peacemaker rose, seated himself on a cushion, and prepared to chide the visitor but hesitated when the chamber door opened and he saw Tok. The hum of the electrobars silenced as the First Wyrul stepped into the chamber.

"It is done, then?" the Peacemaker asked.

"It is done. There will be no conditions or restraints placed on ravan war preparations or on their ultimate attack."

"Then the Wandering comes to a disgraceful end?"

"Yes."

"Tok, all will be lost if the zeromaster cohorts are sent in. I am not willing to give up. Perhaps the wawrens can still find the path to a peaceful solution."

"A way to a peaceful solution? I do not know how, Peacekeeper. I only know peace is subtle; force is certain. A majority of the Council felt we need certainty in uncertain times."

"Why should wawrens help plan the killing?"

"We must work together, Peacemaker. I realize these circumstances sully the Tenets of Wa. But we have no choice. There is still a thin thread of hope. Wawren information will gain a quick and certain victory for Arkadia—one that may save human as well as Arkadian lives."

"And after we have assisted the ravans? What then? How will wawrens serve an Arkadian civilization spawned in blood? We will never swim in the seas of a new world. In the seas of blood."

"Peacemaker, do not assume I disagree with you. Much can happen during the long journey to a blue planet. Besides, we still have to find one. If we do not, then whether we have decided to attack or not does not matter."

The Peacemaker gazed closely at Tok. "You still hold hope for negotiation? Will the Council reconsider?"

"I doubt it, but I do not know for sure. As I said, much can happen. For now, you and the other wawrens must do your work while imprisoned." Tok stood abruptly and waded out of the room.

The buzz of the electrobars resumed.

✶ ✶ ✶ ✶ ✶ ✶ ✶ ✶ ✶ ✶ ✶ ✶ ✶ ✶

"Goodbye Annie. Goodbye little Dylan. I love you guys more than you'll ever know." The airporter honked again like an impatient goose as the driver idled the van's engine at the entrance of the condominium complex. Cole drained a beer and put the can on the porch railing. He took Dylan from Annie. It was a cool, wispy late November morning.

John Cole wanted Annie to stay with Dylan at the condo. He didn't like to say goodbye at the airport. "Dylan," Cole murmured to the son as he nuzzled the baby smell of a blond wisp-covered head.

He handed the child back as the two stood on the porch. Annie cradled Dylan lovingly in her arms while Cole reached in his pocket for something. "Here, little guy, I've something for you. It's helped your

Aunt Michelle and, though I've only had it since last summer, I think it's helped me. It's for luck."

With that, Cole circled his son's neck three times with the crystal amulet's leather strap. The crystal caught the sun and glittered against Dylan's white swaddling blanket.

"Annie, honey, can you find a kid-sized chain for the crystal? We don't want our son to choke. Never take it off the little guy. Like I said, it's for luck," Cole whispered.

Dylan cooed.

* * * * * * * * * * * * * *

It was Christmas 1978 at the Cole homestead. Shirley's house was immaculate. The living room flickered with light from a roaring fire, and shadows swayed softly to the flickering of Christmas tree lights. "Holy Night" played softly on the living room stereo.

"Look, Dylan, look. Smile for Uncle Chuck." Annie babbled into the baby carrier.

Baby Dylan yawned and stretched. His eyes were still sleepy. He looked up at his uncle and mother.

Chuck said, "I can't believe it. What a beautiful kid. He sure is tiny."

"He's not so little any more," Annie replied, picking up the dozing tot. "I can't believe how fast he's growing. It's good you got to see him before he got much bigger. Pictures just aren't the same."

"Chuckie, Annie, bring baby Dylan and come in here. We're all ready for the Christmas portrait." Shirley's giddy order cut through the holiday babble.

Muffin pranced at her feet. The reindeer antlers Shirley had attached to the little dog with a velcro strap made it look ridiculous, but no one had the heart or courage to say anything to Shirley.

Chuck and Annie exchanged a knowing glance and shook their heads.

"Yes, mother, we're coming," Chuck called with a touch of the old insolence. Only he got away with it in the Cole household. "She'll still be calling me Chuckie when I'm accepting my third Nobel Prize," he muttered to Annie as the two joined Shirley at the other end of the living room. Annie had perched Dylan on her hip.

"Okay, Annie dear, you sit here on the chair with the baby next to the tree. Connor, you trigger the camera. Chuckie, honey, stand here behind Michelle. Leave room for Mama. Oops. Catch that, will you? Move over just a little, dear. It's kind of tight back here. Let's get Muffin in the picture. Okay, Connor, we're ready. Isn't it wonderful to have everyone home for Christmas?"

"Not everyone's here," reminded Michelle. "John's not here."

"Yes, of course, dear. I just meant… Okay, everyone, smile for the camera. Connor, let's get the tree in the middle of the picture, shall we? I do want to send a copy to Cousin Edna."

"And to John too." Michelle insisted.

"Yes, yes. Of course, dear."

"Okay, everyone smile on the count of ten," Connor said, tuning out his mother-in-law. He clicked the camera's timer and moved next to Michelle. He circled her shoulder and gave it a squeeze. She tensely smiled back.

Michelle thought about her luck. Then thought about John's. *If only he could be here. I still can't believe what happened.*

The airporter had dropped Cole off at the Seattle-Tacoma Airport for the first leg of the trip to Athens on that November morning. The airport was fogged in, delaying the American Airlines flight. Cole went to a bar by the gate to have a few beers. He only wanted to kill time and ended up killing a human being instead. An obnoxious salesman who had been at the bar too long took a swing at him. Cole's conditioned response tumbled the drunk backward into the bar where he cracked his head, hemorrhaged, and died.

Cole's dishonorable military discharge, poor employment record, history of alcohol-related arrests, and his role in starting the fight—according to the guy's travel partner—would eventually lead to a fresh eight-year term for assault and manslaughter, this time in a civilian penitentiary. On this Christmas Eve, John Cole sat alone on a cot in the King County Jail. A judge would eventually have him transferred after his trial to the Monroe Reformatory outside of Everett, thirty miles north of Seattle.

Annie smiled at Michelle and Connor. It was odd how things had worked out. Michelle and Connor. She and John. Once again, she and John were apart because John had been in the wrong place at the wrong time. *I wish you could be here, Sweetie. Wish the trip to that academy in Greece had worked out. Wish you could have found peace.* Still, Dylan bound them together forever. They were a family. She didn't plan to end the relationship, particularly with a "Dear John" letter like that time so long ago when John had been in Vietnam. She didn't like being single only because she didn't relish the idea of being hit on by every jerk who sniffed her out. But she knew her future happiness didn't depend on a man, except maybe for her son, Dylan. She had high hopes for the boy.

Shirley saw the look between Michelle and Annie. *Brave girl.* She thought. *Left to raise a child alone. Dylan truly needs the Lord's help.*

Chuck stood next to his mother and smiled the required Christmas portrait smile. Even though it had been a long time since he'd been with his family, he could hardly wait to get back to the desert and to his work.

"Okay, smile." Connor hoped everyone followed directions. He didn't want to do it over. Wasn't it about time to get home to a fire and a football game? Maybe Chuck would come over. He liked his quiet, obese, intelligent brother-in-law and glanced at him after the shutter clicked and the group began to disperse.

In the darkened flashing Christmas tree light, a perplexed miniature Eldon Moss, baseball cap, bow-tie, blue jeans, tennis shoes and all, perched on Chuck's shoulder pointing at a Christmas decoration extolling "Peace on Earth." He shook his finger at Connor and frowned. In a voice only Connor could hear, he shouted, "You ain't done with me yet!"

Connor blinked. The apparition was gone.

✱ ✱ ✱ ✱ ✱ ✱ ✱ ✱ ✱ ✱ ✱ ✱ ✱ ✱

Ethnographer's report (continued)

A desperate attempt to end another conflict in the Middle East went awry in late-August, 1998. Paratroopers of the U.S. 82nd Airborne tried but failed to capture the Iraqi leader, Saddam Hussein, while he was reviewing his troops at a desert command post. In a fit of pique, Hussein ordered the launching of scud missiles tipped with VX nerve gas at the civilian population of Tel Aviv.

The Americans immediately delivered chemical weapons by B-2 stealth bombers and cruise missiles to military and civilian targets in Baghdad. The Israelis publicly accepted this quid pro quo, but secretly made other plans. The Americans learned of the double-cross when Israeli tank columns smashed into Jordan on their way to Iraq. All Arab countries soon joined in Jihad against the Israelis and Americans.

It became necessary to transfer all U.S. armored and mechanized divisions from Europe into the conflict. Hundreds of thousands of troops and their machines slugged it out in the desert by early September 1998

The American people held their collective breath, including John, Annie, Chuck, Connor, and Michelle. Dylan was indifferent. The whole thing seemed like a video game to the troubled 19-year old. Shirley rejoiced. Earlier that month, the First Church of Jesus Christ Washed in the Blood of the Lamb had completed its most successful revival ever, "Times of Tribulation," an entire week spent exhorting the faithful in Seattle's Kingdome. The revival had been carried on CBS and had been watched by tens of millions in the United States and around the world.

Though the Antichrist had yet to appear, events in the Middle East and elsewhere in the world matched biblical prophecy perfectly. There was strife in the Middle East accompanied by an uncommonly high number of natural disasters, earthquakes in California and Kobe, Japan; fires, floods, and hurricanes. There was civil war in Russia and elsewhere and the AIDS epidemic exploded out of control—all signs that foretold the coming of the Antichrist and the second coming of the Messiah.

Holocaust could have been averted except the political and economic experiment in democracy in Russia finally failed, and the country collapsed into anarchy. A fascist dictator took power and unleashed the frustrated Russian war machine. Unrestrained by NATO forces tied down in the Middle East, three Russian tank armies led by the elite 5th Guards Army smashed through neutral Ukraine and Poland into a hopelessly outgunned Germany.

Within a week of the invasion, Russian tankers sighted the Rhine. NATO command authorized use of tactical nuclear weapons to stop the enemy tank columns. The Russians retaliated by detonating a hydrogen bomb over NATO headquarters in Brussels and by using tactical nukes to punch holes in NATO lines for their armored columns to exploit. Electromagnetic pulse from nuclear air bursts in the European Theater disrupted communications and NATO field commanders, unable to request clarification or to receive orders from superiors, unilaterally fired tactical nuclear salvos in reply.

The North Koreans picked this time to launch Rodong-1 missiles each tipped with a 50-kiloton nuclear warhead at Seoul and other targets in South Korea. A million North Korean soldiers poured across the 38th parallel to continue Ralph Cole's war begun some fifty years before.

Even then, holocaust could have been averted except a crazed commander of a Russian Typhoon class missile sub, reacting to the death of his wife and five children in a NATO air raid over St. Petersburg, fired all SS-20 missiles under his command at cities in the United States, 180 hydrogen bombs in all. The United States and its allies responded in kind.

And that was just the beginning.

1988: CHUCK'S FOLLY

CHAPTER 17

The cold war ended in 1988. On December 15th of that year Soviet Premier Mikhail Gorbachev, shortly before his death in an automobile accident, announced massive military reductions and said in a speech to the United Nations General Assembly that "...we face a different world for which we must seek a different road to the future." On another December 15th, forty-seven years previously, the Japanese had decimated the American Pacific fleet at Pearl Harbor. And so it goes.

The U.S. military teased its foes—real and imaginary—with the first photos of the new B-2 Stealth bomber, a bomber that cost American taxpayers $2 billion per copy. The American destroyer, Vincennes, shot a commercial airliner that might have benefited from stealth technology out of the sky. Hundreds died, but this loss of innocent life paled in comparison to the million people who died during the ongoing war between Iran and Iraq. The Middle East remained an unsettled place. Saddam Hussein continued his war with Iran, supported by Western "allies" who hoped to use Iraq as a foil, not realizing the full extent of Hussein's ambition.

In Nicaragua, the Sandinista government signed a cease-fire with the contra rebels. Starvation racked Ethiopia; developers continued to develop the Amazon rain forest; apartheid smothered South Africa; and Jimmy Swaggart, who had called fellow evangelist Jim Bakker "a cancer on the body of Christ" for his sexual indiscretions, got caught with a whore named Jessica Hahn. The AIDS epidemic raged on—global projections called for forty million carriers by the turn of the century.

And the Hive was halfway to its destination.

✳   ✳   ✳   ✳   ✳   ✳   ✳   ✳   ✳   ✳   ✳   ✳   ✳   ✳

Moonlight floated across a plateau in the distance in the New Mexico desert. The stars, unencumbered by city lights, flickered brightly. It was a warm July night.

"Why me?" Chuck Cole questioned the empty night. He had only himself to question because he had kept the bad news a secret.

In 1988, two million Americans carried the HIV virus, the forerunner of AIDS. This number included Chuck Cole. Active symptoms had not yet affected his work as an Associate Director of the same Socorro, New Mexico radio telescope array where he started as a research associate. And where he had met Mary Moore.

"Chuck, I'm sorry. It shouldn't have happened to you." Between sobs, Mary whispered, "I didn't know. You have to believe me. I didn't know. How could this have happened?"

Chuck replayed Mary's deathbed apology every hour of every day. He skipped a stone with his foot. The night sky spread in front of him. Even a full moon couldn't dilute the spectacle of the stars.

Ironically, his infection started with an attempt to be healthy. Diets had always failed him. He'd lose weight, then somehow the lost fat either managed to find him or he found it. Imprisoned by this body, he only dreamed of the things that others experienced. Mary changed all that. She encouraged him not to be skinnier but to be healthier. He soon was both. She already loved his mind and, now, became attracted to all of Chuck. A short courtship ended in a spring marriage.

Mary came down with a mononucleosis-type bug that October, developed severe diarrhea, and then lost thirty pounds without trying by December. A fungus-like growth that had been crawling across her face was diagnosed as Kaposi's sarcoma, a harbinger of AIDS. She had been with several lovers before meeting Chuck but had always been more spontaneous than promiscuous. She loved life, and loving men was part of life. But her infection hadn't come from a weekend fling. Instead, in 1980, Mary had needed a blood transfusion after an auto accident.

Mary Cole had liked dolls and sunshine and wore her hair in pigtails as a little girl. She had discovered math in the fifth grade and earned a Cal Tech Ph.D. She had looked forward to children and a career. Now she died a death made both lonely and horrible—lonely because she could no longer hear, see, or talk; horrible because she had only excruciating pain, her memories, and thoughts of what might have been to keep her company. In the end, Mary had only excruciating pain.

Chuck often wondered about his own health whenever he took the time to think about it, as he did this night walking in the desert. He felt more tired than usual. It could be the virus or it could be exhaustion caused by the hubbub of "Cole's Folly."

Four months before, on a night similar in splendor to the present night, Chuck Cole had spotted an interstellar explosion in the direction of his old friend the Cygnus binary. He and his colleagues at the facility hurriedly confirmed the discovery. Chuck experienced a once-in-a-lifetime thrill of reporting a major astronomical discovery, every astronomer's dream. Even amateur astronomers and soon people everywhere, marveled at the blaze in the sky. Then, the energy blasting out of deep space with the force of 100 exploding suns inexplicably faded over a period of ninety days and disappeared.

Measurement of parallax motion indicated the blast was impossibly close to Earth, only ten light years away. A red giant had never been plotted where the explosion occurred. How could there have been a supernova without the presence of a dying star? Where were the gamma rays and X-ray emissions from the explosion? No one was sad the radiation never showed up; it would have severely disrupted life on

Earth and caused the deaths of millions, but still where did it go? Why didn't the explosion leave a neutron star or a black hole? Where was the nebula?

The promise of a major discovery faded just like the photons from the deep space explosion that had washed harmlessly over Earth. Chuck Cole's discovery was fated to become, at best, a minor footnote in astronomy textbooks. A massive amount of energy had been released in deep space. It had been released only ten light years away during the year 1978. Light from the blast had appeared in the night sky in 1988. But from what source?

"Mom's probably right. God *is* signaling us." Chuck spoke out loud as he tossed a rock into the sagebrush.

* * * * * * * * * * * * * *

The Reverend Isaiah Marcus Stringer made his preparations a thousand miles from where Chuck walked in the desert. Studio audiences love to skewer guests. However, it didn't happen this night. Town Meeting, a talk show in the Seattle area, had seldom hosted such a convincing visitor. Even the unbelievers listened carefully. The Reverend Stringer of the First Church of Jesus Christ Washed in the Blood of the Lamb had constructed a compelling case.

"Scientists cannot explain that light in the sky. Where did it come from? Only Holy Scripture has the answer. Hearken to Isaiah 9:1 'The people who were in darkness have seen a great light.' Isaiah 8:18 and Revelations 12:1 speak of 'a portent in the sky.' Matthew 24:29: 'Then will appear the sign of the Son of Man in heaven.'

"You *know* mankind has been undergoing bad times: plagues, earthquakes, crime, floods, and war. This is the tribulation! After the tribulation comes the sign; after the sign, the Antichrist and the Second Coming of Jesus Christ. The time of tribulation is here! The sign, the great light in the sky, has come. Next will come Satan's messenger, the Antichrist and then his nemesis—and our savior—the Prince of Peace."

"Is it any surprise the sign comes from the constellation known as the Northern Cross? The Northern Cross. Where did Jesus die? On a cross! What more proof do you want? What more proof do you *need*?"

✳ ✳ ✳ ✳ ✳ ✳ ✳ ✳ ✳ ✳ ✳ ✳ ✳ ✳

The Hive traveled Earthward in hyperspace ten years behind the fiery sign of its arrival.

The Peacemaker took a last appeal to the Council of Wyruls. He had forsaken the robes of office during a series of presentations aimed at helping the Council to identify with the vibrancy and worth of human cultures—a mosaic to be reduced to ashes by the ravan caste and its zeromaster cohorts. Alternately, during past presentations, the Peacemaker wore a Scottish kilt; a Japanese kimono; and the baggy shirt, trousers, boots, and fur cap of a Cossack. For the current presentation, the Peacemaker wore a Disneyland T-shirt and a facsimile of Levis 501 jeans. The technicians had replicated the Peacemaker's clothing requests in a syntheofactory with quite some difficulty.

To a human, the vision of a seven foot alien, with forehorn and sidehorns, gray rough skin, claws, and long blond braids dressed as though to visit the Magic Kingdom and sit on Mickey's lap might have seemed hilarious, outside anything even Hollywood could have imagined. The Council of Wyruls didn't think it was funny. Neither did the Peacemaker. He was trying to make a point.

"Wyruls, you have heard me. Surely, you see the logic of negotiation and peace. If you can not be persuaded on the basis of Wa, then consider that Arkadians need human help and human guidance…"

"Why?" Though the Peacemaker held the speaker's wand, protocol for this occasion allowed Tok to interrupt or to change the subject.

"First Wyrul, we need their dynamism, their spirit of adventure, their capacity to explore." The Peacemaker waved the speaker's wand in agitation. "Our culture—the environment we create and can control—has stagnated beyond its previous glory and health. Without new ideas we will become like that which now swims in the Hive Sea."

"Why should humans be willing to share? Why should humans be any different than those who turned us away with nuclear weapons in the past?" Tok did not speak with hostility. But she no longer tried to change the Council's present course. The recent loss of Second Wyrul Toltek to a wasting disease sapped her resolve. Harn, newly promoted to Toltek's position, now sat by Tok's side, ruler of the Hive but in name only.

"Humans will share. Particularly when they gain the knowledge of the ancestors stored in the Hive's data banks and useless to our society. Our data banks will help humans develop the technology to solve their problems. Besides, they are primarily terrestrial. We are primarily aquatic. Three-quarters of the blue planet is covered by water. There is ample room for all."

Tok replied, "Do they know Wa? Do they have the spiritual capacity to keep the peace once it has been established?"

"Do we?"

Tok ignored the Peacemaker's question. "The Council has other work to complete, Peacemaker. Do you have anything to add?"

The Peacemaker paused. He faced the Council in the tepid, knee-deep water among the shadows the Council Chambers had become. Half the chamber's glow globes had burned out and not been replaced. The wyruls faced him in a row seated on frayed, soggy cushions.

"Yes, Tok. I do have more to say. Wawrens have studied humans for ten years. We are convinced Arkadia needs more than their world. We need *them*. The Council should learn from the history of Native Americans in one of the great landmasses on the blue planet. These people lived and prospered in cooperation with natural forces on land that was eventually taken from them by an invading, spiritually-depleted, militarily-advanced culture from far away."

Some Council members rustled at the inference that spiritually depleted Arkadians planned to overrun humans for their land.

"Arkadia will die if it is reborn in death. It matters not if we find a home and make a temporary peace among ourselves or with humans if we lack the capacity to *live* in peace. Arkadians must return to the Tenets of Wa. We must return to the lessons of our ancestors."

"Very dramatic. Still, your pathetic words change nothing." Harn ripped at her old adversary.

"Harn, you and other members of the Council of Wyruls cannot escape the responsibility you have to the blue planet and to its inhabitants, your responsibility to peace, your responsibility to Wa, and your responsibility to Arkadia. Those who live by the sword will perish by the sword."

Harn smirked in the Arkadian way and asked, "What is a sword, Peacemaker?"

She received no response. The Peacemaker had abruptly turned and was already sloshing away in the direction of the chamber door.

"Your testimony changes nothing!" Harn shouted at the retreating figure.

CHAPTER 18

"It is good to see you, Peacemaker, even if in a mating pool. What a pleasant coincidence." Through obvious physical discomfort, Tok effected the Arkadian equivalent of a smile.

"It is a coincidence, but hardly a surprise, First Wyrul. There are few thousands of us left awake; you are female and I am male so we both still need to answer the call, though at our ages that inconvenience shall soon be a memory." Use of the formal honorific of "First Wyrul" conveyed the Peacemaker's displeasure with Tok.

The mating pool was the size of a backyard swimming pool. Warm water lapped against metal sides. Quartermaster workers languidly splashed in the corners of the pool. The nearest worker would move to pick up fertilized eggs as soon as each couple had evacuated their gametes. The Peacemaker's ravan bodyguard watched the waters closely for any threat. Tok's bodyguards stood farther back near the entrance to the pool.

"Why did you desert me and my caste, First Wyrul? Surely, you understand an invasion of the blue planet means the end of Arkadia. We may escape the Hive, but death always begets death. You have seen this in our history of Hive Wars. We must break the cycle."

"I am powerless, Peacemaker. We cling to a tenuous peace, even now. Be patient. Time's passage often brings a solution to the most vexing of problems."

The Peacemaker began to reply, then stopped, groaned, and grunted loudly. As though on cue, Tok quivered and responded in kind. The water clouded around the Arkadians. Both ritualistically backed out of the pool.

"Perhaps your anger will abate now that you have answered the call, Peacemaker."

"I will be displeased as long as the wawrens are imprisoned and unless we return to the tenets of Wa. Now, excuse me. I must return to my cell."

* * * * * * * * * * * * * *

"I'm sorry, Michelle, but I just had to have it. I drove Renny for years, then the old Volvo. I saw the little doggy in the window and just had to have it."

"A thirty-thousand dollar doggy? I just can't picture you in a Corvette. Why'd you do it? Why didn't you talk to me first?" Michelle inhaled deeply on her cigarette and stubbed it out.

"I don't know. I guess I was bored. We don't have kids, our bills are paid…"

"Look, Connor, it's not money. Money's just money. That's not the thing. I'm more worried about your boredom. We used to spend time together. We used to talk. Now, you run off and buy an expensive sports car. What's next? Sport sex with bimbos?"

"Hey, I'll take it back. The dealership won't hassle me."

"That's not the point."

"I love you, Mickie."

"Don't call me Mickie. Creep." Michelle smiled grimly. "You can't keep trading on cute. It's unbecoming to a 37 year-old man." She paused. "There has to be more to our life together."

"Why does there have to be *more*? I don't get it. Women say they want more but get confused. They want a strong man but get upset when he's aggressive. They want a man who is sensitive but don't want him to be a wimp. How much 'more' do you want?"

"Who are you talking about? I'm talking about you and me. You're talking nonsense about women in general."

"Let me finish. Women want men who are financially secure but get upset if a man works too much. Want a guy who's an experienced lover but get jealous if he's experienced. Women are attracted to spontaneity but get upset when a guy like me buys a sports car. There! I made my nonsense relate. You think I'm cute, huh?"

"Connor, I'm not just any woman. I'm your wife. We used to talk things out. Yes, you are cute but why can't you also be serious?"

"I can be serious. We still talk, Michelle. Aren't we talking right now?"

"Yes, yes, we are. But it's a stupid conversation. Back to my point. Where's it all going? Has life for you boiled down to a red Corvette? What happened to that special purpose?"

"It's still there. Look, I'm sorry. Sometimes, I work and sometimes I just play…"

"I don't know what you stand for anymore. I don't know what we stand for any more." She gathered up her purse, grabbed her coat and cigarettes, and made for the door.

"Where're you going?"

"Out."

*   *   *   *   *   *   *   *   *   *   *   *   *   *

Much later Connor sat in the living room of the Wallingford District home he shared with Michelle. The house payments that strangled them in 1978 were now nicely manageable. It was late. Michelle was still out. The clock chimed midnight. Connor put down the book he'd been reading and looked at the grandfather clock Michelle picked up at an antique store for a song. She had a real eye for a bargain. *Where in the hell is she?*

He got up from the sofa, used the bathroom putting the seat down the way Michelle liked, and stopped to look in the mirror.

The oddly shaped birthmark with the crescent moon of a scar running through it reminded him of Gorbachev's. Before his death, the Soviet leader had had more important things to worry about than a birthmark. "*So do I*" thought Connor. The rest of him looked okay. Older by the day, but still not *old*. "Where's the time going?" he said to the reflection.

He settled back on the sofa, this time lying down with pillows behind his head. He thought about his job. God, teaching made him tired. He didn't like the classroom much anymore. A buddy made it into administration at a local community college and said there might be a place for Connor. Michelle still seemed to like journalism. *At least she likes something*, Connor thought bitterly.

Binky creaked over and with considerable effort managed to drag herself across his stomach. *What an old, fat kitty.* Connor did some calculating while Binky snored. "You're twenty-one years old. Old enough to drink and about a million years old in dog years," Connor said aloud. He wondered if Binky might be approaching some kind of age record for cats.

He picked up the remote and flicked on the television. Boring. He channel surfed until he hit the film, *Blade Runner*, an absolute favorite. He easily fell under the film's spell and dozed.

"Good movie, ain't it. I like the part where the big android talks about living and dying as the rain comes down."

Half asleep, Connor replied automatically. "They're not androids, Mickie. They're replicants. Don't you know the movie?" He sat up and turned in the direction of Michelle's chair.

Eldon Moss wore the same funky clothes he'd worn through the years, and the same devilish grin.

"How'd you get in here?"

Moss didn't respond. He just kept grinning.

"How long have you been sitting there?"

No reply.

"Where've you been? Why are you here?"

"Thought you'd never ask. Been watching' you, Connor. Watching you git older but not wiser. Just 'cause you and I don't talk much don't mean I ain't been tracking you. I have a keen interest in your life, son. I've a keen interest in the lives of all humans."

"'Humans'? Aren't you a human?"

Instead of replying, his tormentor asked a question. "Why do you and that smart wife of yours always fight? Seems you been scrapping at each other for years. Can't you be peaceful? Do men and women always fight?"

"What do you want from me?" Fully awake now, Connor leaped off the couch and grabbed for Moss. To his surprise, Moss was solid; he wasn't a spirit. The little man easily wiggled out of Connor's grasp and faced him angrily.

"What'd you do that for, son? Geez Louise, you might'a hurt me. I'm just wanting information. Why don't you answer my question?"

"You answer my question first. Who or what are you?"

"Well, may be that I'll tell you, son. Eventually. But I asked furst. Why you and Michelle always fighting? Looks to me like oil and water. See that kind of behavior evertime I see men and women get together."

"Maybe you could answer that. You tell me. Was there ever a Mrs. Moss? Ever have a girlfriend, Eldon?"

"You're clever, son. Still grasping at straws, though. Afraid to answer my question?"

"I forgot what it was. Why don't you answer mine?" He thought about grabbing for the old man again.

The front door opened.

Huh? Connor yawned and looked down at the television. He was standing in the middle of the living room. The dying replicant, Roy, was telling the blade runner about what it felt to be alive.

Michelle called out from the doorway "You didn't have to wait up." She walked upstairs to the bedroom, seemingly unconcerned whether Connor joined her or not.

✶ ✶ ✶ ✶ ✶ ✶ ✶ ✶ ✶ ✶ ✶ ✶ ✶ ✶

Dylan slammed down the Nintendo controller. He'd beat Mario Brothers if he could just get through the eighth level.

Dylan was tall for a 10-year old. He had Annie's red hair and green eyes and his dad's lanky frame. He wore blue jeans, a black and red D.A.R.E. T-shirt from a drug resistance program at school, and designer tennis shoes that cost more than most family vacations. He wore the crystal given to him by his dad outside his T-shirt. He did that sometimes to impress his friends. The crystal was rad.

"Crap! This ain't getting it. Let's go get dilly bars at Dairy Queen."

Ronny replied, "I can't. I got to get home. It's almost dinnertime. Is your mom working late again?"

"Yeah. She won't be home until late. She'll be a zombie again when she gets home."

Annie worked on special assignment for Seafirst and spent three hours commuting to and from corporate headquarters each day. She and Dylan now shared a condo in Monroe, a small town 40 miles northeast of Seattle and location of the Monroe Reformatory that was John's home until 1986. Between work, Dylan, and Sunday afternoons spent with John, Annie had had few spare moments. Promotions at work more than swallowed up the time freed up by Cole's departure to Greece upon his release two years ago. Annie's Sunday afternoons now were taken up with balance sheets and strategic plans.

Dylan grew up watched by daycare center and Montessori school minders, helpful neighbors and, occasionally, by his grandmother Cole.

"Where's the babysitter?"

"My grandma? I don't know. She probably forgot me. That happens. Grandma's old and kinda loony. My mom says I can be by myself when I'm 12."

"Cool… hey, Dylan, I really gotta go."

"Yeah. I'll see you later." Dylan turned back to the Nintendo while Ronny let himself out. Dylan's stomach growled. He turned off the machine and went to the kitchen. He opened a can of minestrone soup, slopped it into a bowl, zapped it in the microwave for two minutes, and ate the lukewarm soup. Still dissatisfied, he wiped out a bag of potato chips while watching MTV. He didn't feel like doing homework.

CHAPTER 19

John Cole sat in reverie. The Aegean Sea sparkled before him. He leaned against a boulder on a cliff high above sea and sighed. Cole vowed never to become complacent about the beauty of this part of the world. He had found this spot during the first month he spent at the Institute in Crete, his home now for the past two years.

If only the dream would stop.

The eight years at the Monroe Reformatory had been a breeze compared to the same stretch he had served in the military maximum-security lockup at Leavenworth. He had attended school earning a college degree in education and had become one of the first inmates to do student teaching while on work release. A human-interest story written by Michelle and featured in a Sunday *Seattle Times* had really helped him out. The fact that remedial English students tended to be adults, not children, also helped to allay public fears about an inmate doing student teaching, as did Cole's increasingly gentle demeanor.

Cole had continued to write to Hiroshi Akai. Though his Beheiren days were well behind him, his friendship with Hiroshi never wavered. He had also written Nicholas Papaderos, a priest in the Greek Orthodox Church and John's future mentor at the Greek Orthodox Academy of Crete. Cole's real work as a teacher began at the Academy after he left the Monroe Reformatory and arrived in Crete in 1986. Two peaceful, productive but lonely years had passed since his arrival.

The Greek Orthodox Church founded the Academy after World War II to promote peace and healing. The Church's thinking was that if the Greeks could forgive the Germans their atrocities, any conflict could be reconciled. The good work of the Academy had continued unabated for more than forty years.

Cole taught English to Greeks and conducted public relations work in the U.S. on behalf of the Academy. He traveled extensively through the states, a circumstance that allowed him to slip into the Seattle area from time-to-time for visits with Annie, Dylan, Connor, and Michelle. He avoided Shirley.

Dylan and Annie had visited the Academy the previous spring. Cole smiled at the memory from his place in the sun. Dylan had slipped away when they'd gone into Kolympari, the little fishing village on the outskirts of the Academy. Annie had been frantic. They found their son an hour later visiting with a group of kind elders. Dylan hadn't understood a word of Greek: the elders not a word of English but communication with kids, particularly with kids like Dylan, involves a language all its own.

Annie enjoyed the sight of white washed, simple, elegant stone houses stacked against a hill, and gorging on spicy *souvlakia* and *moussaka* later in the cafe where Cole had been warmly greeted by the proprietor. John's decision to stay in Crete rested better with her after that afternoon.

"John."

Cole jumped. "Oh, Father, I did not hear you coming up the trail." He replied in Greek, a language he had quickly mastered to the delight of the church and village community.

Nicholas Papaderos, the elderly priest with whom Cole corresponded while incarcerated, smiled warmly in greeting. A strong, roughly-hewn man with a bushy, white beard, he looked as rugged as the scrabble rock Cretan fields and foothills that had nurtured his ancestors.

"It is good to see you in a meditative mood. It is good to see you relax. How are you, my friend?"

"I am better in the day than the night, Father Nicholas. After all this time, I still have the dream."

"I am sorry to hear that, son."

The priest settled comfortably next to Cole. He stretched out. The light cassock he wore scarcely cushioned his back, but the priest gave no notice of discomfort. Despite the kilometer hike up the trail, his advanced age, and the heat of the day, the priest breathed easily.

"But you know, John, I have dreams of my own. Did I ever tell you why I joined the priesthood?"

"You mentioned only a personal tragedy. I am afraid you have been a better listener over the years than I. You never told me what happened, though I believe it had to do with the war."

"I do not wish to darken this beautiful day and your contemplative mood, but I will tell the story if you wish to hear it." The priest's deeply personal gift of trust was not given lightly.

"I would like to know you better," John said.

"Then, I will tell you."

Nicholas Papaderos paused, as though bringing his thoughts up from a deep well. "Another lifetime ago, I was ten years old. I was big for my age and mature, but still just ten years old. I was the baby of my family…"

"My son, Dylan, is ten."

"He is? You must be proud of him."

"I am. But, I interrupted, Father. Please continue."

"My father, two brothers, sister, and mother lived outside Modhion, a village just a few kilometers from where we sit. We farmed, harvested olives in the groves, and milked goats. We lived a simple, farming life. We were happy. We did not know any better."

John nodded. The priest, with a faraway look in his eyes, wise eyes surrounded by crinkles of age and time, continued with somewhat more vigor.

"It was a beautiful morning, much like this morning. My father and I had finished our chores. Walking back with the house in sight, I saw my family sitting on the porch enjoying the day, as you and I are doing now. My father turned to me with a smile, but before the words could leave his mouth, his head exploded. It was as if a gourd had been hit with a mallet. A burning pain grazed my neck. I frantically looked around but saw nothing. To this day, I do not recall hearing the gunfire that killed my father and wounded me. It all happened so fast.

"I looked up and saw parachutes, many parachutes. The sky was full of the whispering color of black, pink, green chutes. A German paratrooper, drifting no more than five meters away, fired a machine pistol at me. It had been his pistol that ended my father's life. The soldier had to lower his weapon to land. That probably saved my life. Paratroopers dropped out of the sky all around me.

"My brothers, Alexander and Nikos, foolishly tried to fight, one with an axe, the other with a stave. They were shot down right in front of my mother, my sister, and me. Then, I saw my mother fall. I never learned what happened to my sister, Alexandra. I hope she died quickly.

"I ran for the olive grove and felt bullets whizzing by me. I was grazed again, this time in the shoulder, but made it to safety. From a distance I watched soldiers in gray uniforms burn my home and, with it, my childhood. I retreated into the countryside. My wounds were not serious. I joined others, remained vigilant, and soon learned how to kill…"

"Father Nicholas, I did not know. I am sorry. "

The priest did not seem to hear.

"Germany had attacked Crete with their *Fallschirmjager*, the hunters from the sky. The paratroopers were fearsome in their skull-shaped helmets and futuristic uniforms. Anyway, I was taken in by a group of villagers led by a British officer. We fought the Germans for ten days. I dodged strafing runs by Messerschmitts and Stukas and used weapons stripped from the bodies of German soldiers. Even a child can learn to load a weapon and to press a trigger, John. It took Germany longer to conquer Crete than it did all of France, but still we lost.

"During the Battle of Crete, thousands of German soldiers were killed by villagers armed with captured weapons, rocks, sickles, and knives. We were, and still are, common people who killed out of love for their country and King George. In reprisal, the Germans burned our villages to the ground.

"I did not give up. I remained with a resistance group. I wore blood-soaked rags, ate scraps; endured for weeks, months, and then years, and never stopped killing Germans. I passed into manhood in these hills, John.

"I came to the Academy not to forget the tragedies of war, but to remember, and to honor the sacrifices of its victims, German as well as Greek." The priest sat up. He gazed at Cole with a steady eye born of experience, pain, and the passing of years.

Cole did not reply. The men looked down on the beautiful waters and the green of surrounding hills.

"John, I heard you compare my memories—my burden—to yours. It is not right to make such a comparison. We have both sought solace to heal wounds languishing long after infliction."

"Yes, Father."

"Perhaps you should join us more formally. Have you thought of the priesthood? Annie could still be your wife and Dylan your son. We are not like the Catholics, our priests take wives who often bear many children." Nicholas chuckled.

"Thank you, Father. I am not sure what I will do. I am attracted to a spiritual life but not right now. I have much to think about…"

Shortly thereafter, the priest stood and held out his hand. John took it and was hoisted to his feet. The men walked down the rocky path to the Academy, and to sanctuary.

★　★　★　★　★　★　★　★　★　★　★　★　★　★

Ethnographer's report (continued)
Six hydrogen bombs exploded over the greater Seattle area on a lazy, early September afternoon in 1998. The bombs vaporized Shirley, Annie, Dylan, Michelle, and Connor.

Targets included the Bremerton shipyards, the Navy base in Everett, the Trident submarine base at Bangor, and various Boeing plants in the area. The power of the Seattle-area detonations alone was five hundred times greater than the power of all the bombs dropped in all the wars of human history.

Over one thousand thermonuclear detonations shook North America within a two-hour period on that quiet September afternoon. A comparable number erupted over and into the Russian landmass.

Chuck and John Cole, shielded in the New Mexico desert and on the isle of Crete respectively, died of radiation poisoning within a day of each other soon after the spasm ended. Chuck had been dying of AIDS anyway; John had been preparing to come back to Annie and Dylan for good.

The burning of the Northern Hemisphere suffocated the earth in a great cloud. Nuclear winter set in. The cold would have ushered in a new ice age were it not for the destruction of the ozone layer by thermonuclear blasts. Intense solar ultraviolet radiation scorched the Earth once the cloud and dust cover dissipated.

Almost everything died.

Human predictions of Armageddon had come to pass.

Revelations 6:12:

"I looked, and behold, there was a great earthquake; and the sun became black as sackcloth, the full moon became like blood, and the stars

of the sky fell to the earth as the fig tree sheds its winter fruit when shaken by a gale; the sky vanished like a scroll that is rolled up, and every mountain and island was removed from its place."

Humans started over. Like their Pliocene ancestors who had struggled against millennia-long drought, the surviving humans retreated to the safe harbor of estuaries and coastal areas. Life was hard, but shorelines provided food, respites from heat pouring through a badly damaged ozone layer and protection from hungry predators.

Thousands of years passed. Humans recovered, moved out from the waters and built a great civilization.

Then, the bombs fell again.

Late Summer, 1998:
The Antichrist

CHAPTER 20

By late summer 1998, Saddam Hussein had rebuilt the Iraqi war machine and was ready to strike again. The U.S. planned to kidnap Hussein and to charge him for war crimes. Israel prepared to defend its sovereignty. Quality of life in the Russian Republic deteriorated as the country's fledging market economy moved in starts and mostly stops and a charismatic, fascist politician gained followers. North Korea started a nuclear arms race in Asia. Full-blown revolution and civil war ripped at forty countries during the 1990s.

War planning went on in the Hive as well.

The worst natural disasters in human history occurred across the planet during the decade between 1988 and 1998. The state of California—a favorite target of apocalyptic charismatic preachers because of the peculiar excesses of many of its citizens—bore witness to one calamity after another as the millennium approached. The list was long: the Northridge and Loma Prieta earthquakes, a six-year drought in northern California that ended with devastating rains and floods, wildfires in the Oakland Hills and Malibu, and the ongoing devastation caused by AIDS in the gay enclave of San Francisco. California Governor Tom Hayden quipped that California had been visited by every biblical misfortune except a plague of locusts. Religious fundamentalism of all flavors fed off the chaos in California and elsewhere in the world.

The AIDS epidemic kept killing. It destroyed countries in Central Africa and in Southeast Asia and decimated urban areas in the U.S. and Europe. In 1998, tens of thousands of Americans either died or were infected with the HIV virus. Included in this number were hundreds of high school kids who would never finish high school.

Economic recession gripped the United States and Japan. Financial resources that might have staved off war in the former Soviet Empire now barely kept the free democracies alive. Gang wars and the quick triggers of frightened citizens turned American city centers and suburbs into free fire zones. In 1998 alone, 54,622 Americans died in firefights in streets, schools, shopping malls, and homes—a figure comparable to American combat deaths during the 10,000-day Vietnam War.

The Internet and World Wide Web connected tens of millions across the globe. But more communication didn't necessarily mean better communication.

Americans suffered through the Bill Clinton and Monica Johnson story.

And in the late summer of 1998 the Hive arrived in Earth's solar system, slipping into orbit around Jupiter between the Jovian moons Ganymede and Callisto.

✳   ✳   ✳   ✳   ✳   ✳   ✳   ✳   ✳   ✳   ✳   ✳   ✳   ✳

"The zeromaster cohorts are ready."

The ravan fullmaster occasionally failed to use an honorific when addressing Second Wyrul Harn. Ascendance of the ravans was complete.

"So you say. Let me hear more." Harn replied gruffly.

The two Arkadian leaders sat in a docking bay far above the Hive Sea. Seldom-used elevators creaked and groaned up the walls of the Hive as the invasion force assembled supplies and war material. Water roaring down the sides of the Hive—pent-up condensation with nowhere to go—blasted the top of the elevators and sprayed worker zeromasters scurrying frantically to complete tasks assigned them by worker halfmasters and their ravan overlords. Harn had traveled to the docking bay with the ravan fullmaster to check war preparations. The Arkadians looked down at the Hive Sea below.

Diatom blooms mottled its surface. The colorful blotches could just be seen through steaming fog in the dim light provided by the ceiling lamps and still functioning glow globes. The Arkadian leaders knew something horrible lived beneath the waters. The wizard fullmaster recently reported to the Council of Wyruls that this predatory insect, a creature carried by accident to the starship during the first planetary campaign, had evolved rapidly in the isolation and organic soup of the Hive Sea. The aliens had killed off aquatic life that had survived suffocation. Now, they ate each other.

Arkadians no longer traveled by transfer pod through the Hive Sea. Only the original tube and conveyor belt network provided safe passage among buildings and compounds though its safety had recently been compromised. Swimming in the Hive Sea meant a quick and sure death.

"We salvaged fifteen transports. Each transport carries ten fighters. Each fighter carries a zeromaster cohort of forty ravans. Particle beam cannons are operational on most of the fighters. Launch will occur within the dimming."

Harn thought for a moment and said, "Only six thousand ravans? Will this force be sufficient?"

"Yes. We can and must defeat the United States with this number. The United States is the military and economic center of the planet. Once it falls, the other nation-states will surrender. We cannot attack with more cohorts because most of the transports no longer operate. Do not fear. The ravans will be victorious. Most of United States' military strength is either dispersed across the globe or is aligned toward a place called the Middle East. A major war in this place is imminent.

"Besides, Harn, United States military technology is primitive. Their ravans and fighting machines are unshielded. A single zeromaster could destroy an American carrier task force without benefit of a fighter. Homing spears and bolts at close-range will destroy all the military equipment they possess."

"They cannot hurt you…?"

"That is correct, Harn. Their missile technology cannot penetrate our personal shields much less the shields that protect the fighters. Our transports are unshielded, but they will be safe in orbit. Humans will be too concerned with repulsing our first wave to attack the transports. The transports should be safe."

"*Should* be safe? You are reticent, fullmaster. What are you hiding?"

"Harn," the ravan fullmaster straightened at her place at the table, "We again face nuclear weapons. This time, we face a species that has them everywhere. Humans have them aboard their ships above and below their seas, in their military transports, in their command headquarters. They have nuclear mines, shells, torpedoes, and missiles. These weapons are powerful enough to overwhelm our shields and could destroy the transports and us.

Harn understood the problem of radioactive pollution. The ravans had been defeated on two previous occasions by civilizations willing and able to use nuclear weapons. In all cases, like humans, their foes had not known the self-defeating effects of the weapons. Regardless of who appeared to win, the widespread detonation of the bombs always rendered a planet uninhabitable.

Harn replied, "We must have a quick victory. In any event, you must make sure the transports are safe. We must have transports to colonize the planet. We can lose ravans by the thousands if necessary, but we must not lose transports."

"Yes, Harn. But there is more. Military forces in the United States have chemical and biological weapons. Their citizens have the right to carry antipersonnel weapons called handguns. Even if they do not go nuclear, it will be difficult to subdue them unless we strike with total surprise and win quickly."

"How will you do that?"

"We will put the transports in geosynchronous orbit and drop the fighters down through the atmosphere. If victory lags and the transports are targeted, we will be in trouble. There is the possibility they possess weapons that can reach the transports though the wawrens do not know specifics. If the battle goes badly, if nuclear weapons are used, the zeromaster cohorts will escape first to the sea and then to the transports. We will return and blow the planet to stardust with the Hive's engines. It will be our world or it will cease to exist."

Harn ignored the ravan's bravado. "How will you assure a quick victory?"

"We will close with them quickly."

"You have not answered my question."

"We will attack coastal cities facing their Pacific Ocean—Seattle, San Francisco, Los Angeles, San Diego, and Portland. The wawrens will offer unconditional terms of surrender to the rulers of the United States at the same time. Humans across the planet will sue for peace shortly after the United States surrenders. We will orbit the Hive around the planet and bring Arkadians out of cryonic storage. Transports will move our people to the surface. We will settle in their oceans and coastal areas. Humans will be disarmed and brought into Arkadia."

"As a new caste? Creative thinking. I laud you for looking ahead. The Council of Wyruls has not yet discussed what to do with humans. *As though the Council is making the decisions.* Where would this new caste stand in Arkadian society?"

"Not as a new caste, Harn. Humans will become slaves without rank or they will become food."

* * * * * * * * * * * * * *

The ravan fullmaster looked out a viewing portal as her transport left the Jovian system. Second Wyrul Harn stood by her, sharing in the view. The gas giant filled space. An angry storm the size of fifty Earths swirled over the planet's surface. A moon of Jupiter winked in the distance.

The Arkadian armada moved through a gossamer ring of Jupiter with the ravan fullmaster's transport in the lead. Fourteen other transports spread out behind in a V formation like a flock of gigantic, robotic geese.

The arrowhead pointed at Earth.

CHAPTER 21

The Peacemaker watched condensation roll down the walls from the resting-place in his cell. He knew about the torrents also pouring down the interior sides in other parts of the Hive. Most atmospheric dryers and climate controllers had broken down. An oddly shaped insect buzzed outside the cell's portal. Green algae floated in the blood-warm water of the wawren fullmaster's chamber. The same scum covered his robe, hair, and thrived in between his claws. The Hive's interior dripped with 100% humidity.

Time to rise. *Wa! It is difficult to grow old. My time will soon be over.* The Peacemaker had led his caste longer than any other wawren in the Hive's history.

Tok had also been a survivor. No Arkadian had held the Scepter of the First Wyrul for as long probably because discovery of the blue planet 20 years previously had focused Arkadian attention outward.

Clarity of signals from Earth borne on waves in the radio/light spectrum had increased steadily as the Hive approached. Now located scant light minutes from the blue planet, the Peacemaker and other wawrens read an open book of human life.

The Peacemaker wanted to save these strange, dynamic creatures more than ever, but was not sure how to accomplish this feat. He considered human fate.

The zeromaster cohorts have launched. Within ten dimmings, the transports will be orbiting over targets on the West Coast of the United States. A terrible cargo will then be disgorged.

What will humans think of the falling lights? The Peacemaker thought of the Blazes—entry burns of fighters dropping to the surface—that humans would see as the first sign that their lives had changed forever.

After coming into clear view, the hovering fighters will systematically destroy, by particle beam, all targets of opportunity. Skyscrapers, factories, freeway overpasses, the Golden Gate Bridge, the Space Needle, commercial aircraft in the air, whole neighborhoods. There will be urban terrorism on a massive scale. The U.S. military will respond with jet fighters possessing crude missile technology.

The Peacemaker considered the technological advantage possessed by the zeromaster cohorts. Humans would be unprepared for Arkadian anti-gravity technology customized for use as shielding. *Their fighter missiles will be easily deflected and their jet fighters will be destroyed.*

The Peacemaker thought about the next stage in Earth's defeat, knowing that ravans would not be content to ravage from the protection of fighters. *The ravans will leave their fighters to go hunting.* The Peacemaker considered the first sighting of Arkadians by humans. *What will they do? What will they think?* But already he knew. *Panic, terror, wonder, and more terror will commingle.*

Arkadian casualties might occur at this stage of the invasion. Fighting hand-to-hand with police officers and armed civilians could result in Arkadian deaths. National Guard units and even light infantry might have time to engage. *Human snipers will use their animal hunting skills to hit unwary ravans from behind, away from the frontal protection of personal shields.* Arkadia had never experienced such independent and militant creatures. *There are more handguns in the United States than people. Still, handguns will be of little use against a fully charged ravan.* The Peacemaker shrugged and began to pace within his cell.

Water splashed against the walls, matching the agitation of the Peacemaker's mood.

Ravan discipline and efficiency will prevail. The battle will end in a few days with the American humans quickly learning the futility of fighting the zeromaster cohorts. That struggle would only lead to the devastation of other population centers such as New York, Philadelphia, Boston, and Washington D.C. *Surrender to Arkadia is inevitable, first by the United States, then by the rest of the world.*

After that, all wawrens will die and humans will be enslaved. The Peacemaker knew this to be a certainty. What would possibly compel the wyruls to recall the transports? And the ravans to obey?

*   *   *   *   *   *   *   *   *   *   *   *   *   *

In the antechamber of the Peacemaker's cell, groups of wawren halfmasters amused themselves, while waiting for an audience with the Peacemaker, by watching a Simpson's re-run on a monitor. This cartoon was as popular among the wawren caste as it was among television watchers of the Fox Broadcasting Network in the United States.

By now, most Arkadians spoke English. The language was commonly used throughout the Hive. Television programs beamed through each compound and information picked up from satellite communications had profoundly influenced Hive life. Television viewing interests depended on caste: technicians enjoyed home improvement shows; wardens liked dramas, police shows, and mysteries; wizards were particularly fascinated by PBS's Nova and the Discovery channel; workers liked Mexican and Japanese soap operas; the ravans studied war documentaries.

The wyruls now allowed wawrens more freedom of movement within their compound. The group watching the Simpson's cartoon wanted to meet personally with the Peacemaker, so had traveled from their quarters in the lower ring of the wawren compound to the Peacemaker's cell at the top.

The Peacemaker felt uneasy. Tok had not stopped the ravan plans. The lengthy meeting of ten years ago when he had appeared before the council dressed to attend Disneyland had been the Peacemaker's last conversation with the Council of Wyruls. Nothing had helped. Tok continued to avoid the Peacemaker. Studies of human life and capabilities were routed from the wawren prison compound, to the Council and ravans through warden and worker intermediaries.

"Wa," the Peacemaker signed, sinking easily into the solace of meditation. The constant pounding of the raindrums from steady rainfall helped with mediation, though some wawrens now swayed to the drums in a constant stupor. The Hive had developed its own perverse, totally unpredictable weather patterns. The rain, condensation, and rising temperature though daunting were still livable for an Arkadian.

The Peacemaker offered prayer, not to a god, but to the idea of reconciliation. He spoke out loud:

"We face a final travail. Illuminate us with an answer as we traverse this dangerous time. Instead of healing emissaries of Wa's eternal truths, Arkadia has chosen to arrive as combatants. Let hope and peace be revealed now. Wa seeks a solution."

Slowly, as set forth by the Peacemakers before him, he willed the blue flame to dance. He traveled inward as he settled backward onto the water, staring at the flame dancing in front of his eyes. The waiting halfmasters, sensing the Peacemaker's meditation, respectfully splashed away through the scum, stink, and humidity to return another time.

Hive day dimmed into Hive evening. Still, the Peacemaker floated and meditated. Dimming brought darkness. Still, the Peacemaker made the blue flame dance. Through the time of sleeping, he floated on his back and stared into the flame that cavorted between his clawtips. At first light, he stretched his arms straight out from his body in exhaustion. The blue flame now rippled up and down his entire body. In the dimness of his cell, the outstretched Peacemaker would have appeared to a human to be a floating, glowing cross.

A worker zeromaster, assigned to bring an algae paste to the Peacemaker, appeared in the doorway. She called the ravan bodyguard over to observe.

Bolts crackled an angry cobalt blue from the Peacemaker. Spikes of power rippled off his body, creating a humming aura. An acrid, ozone smell assailed them.

"Hurry," the ravan hissed. "Go for aid. Summon another wawren, preferably a halfmaster. I have never seen this before. Hurry."

Before the worker could leave, the Peacemaker shuddered and emitted a loud groan. He shuddered again, mumbled something, then shook himself as though to waken. The ravan and worker entered the cell. The worker reached over as though to assist. "No, do not touch him." A just-arrived wawren quartermaster implored from the doorway. He waded into the cell to restrain the worker.

"What did he say, what did he say? Did you hear him?" The quartermaster inquired.

"We did not hear his exact words." The wawren confirmed this with a quick, crude telepathic scan of the worker. "But it sounded like, 'It is done.'"

"I return," the Peacemaker uttered as he opened his eyes and wobbled to standing position. He signaled the wawren in the group.

"Quartermaster, it is good to see you. Signal the wawrens." He paused. "We have much to do."

✶ ✶ ✶ ✶ ✶ ✶ ✶ ✶ ✶ ✶ ✶ ✶ ✶ ✶

Each wawren floated in meditative position within the dripping confines of his individual cell. They linked telepathically. No other

Arkadians knew or would have cared about the wawren assembly. War preparations dominated the attention of all others.

I have an answer the Peacemaker addressed his receiving castemates. *Wa has spoken. There is a way out of the darkness. It is risky, but the way is clear. We must warn humans. We must tell them of the invasion armada carrying the zeromaster cohorts.*

The thoughts of the wawrens washed across the fullmaster like waves on a stormy beach. *That cannot be... We have never interceded... We have never interfered before...Wa must be accepted peacefully. Deceit is unacceptable...*

But the dominant impression lashing the Peacemaker was *how?*

The Peacemaker responded. *We have endured long years of imprisonment, as have the wawrens before us. Wawrens have never interfered with war preparations whether a Hive war or battle for a planet. This time we must interfere. The transports have been launched. The zeromaster cohorts soon will attack. We must find a way to warn humans. Do you agree?*

A psychic babble ensued. It coalesced finally with *We agree in principle, but we do not know how humans can be warned. We are here and they are there. We wonder if a warning will do any good.*

The Peacemaker replied. *There may be a way to communicate. But first I will explain why we must.*

The wawrens bobbed silently, their quiet meditative posture in contrast to intense mental activity.

Human history is rich with examples of quick resort to aggression when humans are threatened in the slightest. Defensive preparedness and a human willingness to die for the greater good will stop the ravans. The Peacemaker flashed images of the valiant Jewish defense of the Warsaw ghetto during World War II, the death of the Texans at the Alamo, and the battle between David and Goliath.

Ravan history is also rich with tradition, but it is a tradition of defeat after being confronted by an adversary with nuclear weapons. The

Peacemaker conveyed images of ravans on alien worlds fleeing from mushroom clouds.

Humans are warlike, far more warlike than any other life we have encountered, even more warlike than Arkadians. If humans threaten the use of nuclear weapons the ravans will be dissuaded. The use of these weapons to destroy Arkadian transports or fighting machines will make the planet uninhabitable for Arkadians as well as for humans. The ravans know this. By warning humans, we may rouse them to a defense that will turn away the zeromaster cohorts, and win for us a final opportunity to negotiate.

The wawren community signaled understanding and consensus.

A quartermaster then transmitted. *Humans are unruly and cynical. Their societies are fragmented. Their cultures are noisy and quarrelsome. Peacemaker, you say there may be a way to make contact, but even if we succeed, why would humans be willing to listen?*

The Peacemaker telepathically replied. *Your point is well taken, quartermaster. Humans have been dulled by words. As you know, American society in particular is assailed by persuasive words and implorations called advertising. Americans hear thousands of messages of warning and other information constantly. Consequently, there will be much competition for the message we transmit. But if the words were accompanied by what humans term a miracle, and if the communication takes place in a public place, the message most assuredly will be believed.*

Fullmaster, how will we communicate through an intermediary? How will we arrange for a miracle? interrupted a cynical halfmaster. *Working together, our telepathy may breach great distances in space, but we must have a clear target for our message, one that can be accessed continuously.*

The Peacemaker replied. *That is a difficult challenge. I have considered this question carefully. I have a possible solution. There is some risk.*

The wawren community waited.

You recall the masers seeded by the robotic Searchers?

All wawrens knew this history of the time before the Wandering, a history first learned during their lessons as wawren zeromasters.

The Peacemaker continued. *We know the blue planet was seeded because it has been confirmed that a weak signal was obtained after the last straddle. Technicians assumed the maser had been damaged. They were correct. During the last dimming, I telepathically located a maser particle on the planet surface, coincidentally, in the United States...*

WA! Shock vibrated through the wawren community.

The polished piece of maser crystal we carry in place of our natural forehorn—symbolic of our role as communicators—is a facsimile. It only approximates the raw crystal discovered and modified by the ancestors. The unadulterated maser crystal is very different. It is the most powerful transmitter ever developed. Maser receivers in the Hive can pick out and clearly separate a maser signal from a distance of 150 light years. I found a real piece. It took great effort, but since we are virtually on top of the planet, it is discernable to me.

The maser is being carried continuously on the person of an immature male human who lives in the United States. By linking our wawren community telepathically we can speak through this human. We might even manipulate him.

A halfmaster interjected. *What of the human? Might our communication be damaging?*

That is a possibility, the Peacemaker replied. *Once we start we can not stop. We must be convincing. Humans must believe a separate, miraculous power is speaking through the child and is warning them of great danger.*

Is that the miracle to which you refer? Another question from the halfmaster.

Only in part. We must also conduct telekinetic manipulation of the young male.

Telekinetic manipulation? The wawrens were unprepared for this contingency. A quartermaster responded. *Fullmaster, there are strict rules in the Hive that inveigh against telekinesis. For good cause. Objects could otherwise be dropped on adversaries at a distance. Assassination would be rampant. This prohibition means our skill at mentally manipulating objects is unpracticed. The young male could be harmed. Surely, the potency of this human's words will suffice.*

The Peacemaker reply was unequivocal. *As I mentioned before, humans have been dulled by words, by advertising. More than words are needed to convince them.*

The wawrens understood this logic, and after some debate, concurred with the use of telekinesis.

The Peacemaker continued. *Our message—besides being continuous—must provide a warning to which humans can identify, not a description of who we are, or from where we come. We must avoid specific references to aliens from outer space.*

The Peacemaker transmitted an image of a grocery store tabloid with a bold headline announcing an invasion of little green men from the planet, Zeon. *This sort of warning constantly occurs and is not believed by humans, for good cause. It is more unbelievable even than their advertising.* The Peacemaker chuckled mentally in the Arkadian way.

He continued. *We do not have time to convince humans of the reality of extraterrestrial life. We may even hurt our cause should humans initially believe extraterrestrial life is addressing them. We must instead create a convincing puzzle. In the process, we will communicate the presence of the Hive in orbit around a planet humans call Jupiter. If they know where to search, the Hive will be found. They need not know what it is, but their science is good enough to know it represents a threat. They will go on the defense. The ravans will see this and will back down. The Council of Wyruls will then allow us to negotiate. The Council will forgive our manipulation—should it be discovered because our negotiation skill will truly be the last hope. We can...*

Peacemaker? The inquisitive halfmaster again.

Yes?

Why not have the human simply go to an influential leader in this United States and tell of the ravans in convincing terms using information that an immature human could not possibly know. Would that not be effective?

A naive question. Still, the Peacemaker, as a master teacher, responded with patience. *We can communicate a specific message, but not in the context of a specific exchange. In human terms, The Hive in Jupiter orbit is thirty-five light minutes from Earth. We receive through the maser and transmit with the burden of this time lag. We cannot engage in a real-time conversation. Furthermore, a private conversation would be too inefficient. Time presses. A dramatic display to a wide audience better serves our purpose.*

The Peacemaker returned his attention to the caste. *Are we agreed?*

Fullmaster, if I may…I have not a question, but a concern. The communication pulsed from the same halfmaster.

Go ahead, halfmaster. Communicate your concern. The Peacemaker was patient. This wawren showed leadership traits uncharacteristic in one so young. He might one day become a future fullmaster, a leader of all the wawrens.

What if our 'miracle' coincides with a real supernatural occurrence? I have been assigned to the study of human religions. Many in the United States believe in a story about a messiah who will confront an evil spirit who is called the Antichrist. What if this devil appears? Might we not create inefficient confusion, particularly if humans are confronted by two supernatural threats? By two miracles?

The Peacemaker pondered before replying. *An interesting question, halfmaster. I am familiar with your research. I can only assert that the devil humans will know if the zeromaster cohorts attack is real. We can do nothing about the other devil if it appears.*

The Peacemaker concluded his presentation. *I will monitor the human and let you know when he is in the presence of a large number of*

other humans. We will work in shifts after the link is established.
Transmission must be continuous. Wawrens, what say you?
    Agreed, fullmaster, the wawrens signaled as one.
    Excellent. I have been in touch with the young male. He has felt my
influence, though he knows not what it means. His name is Dylan.

✶ ✶ ✶ ✶ ✶ ✶ ✶ ✶ ✶ ✶ ✶ ✶ ✶ ✶

The horned alien reached for him, but Dylan scampered away. Pulling the gun out, he pointed, but the alien wasn't there. He saw movement out of the corner of his eye, whirled, and fired. A miss. A flowered tree exploded in flame where the alien had been. The purple, red, green haze of the planet's surface shimmered. Suddenly, a squad of the aliens appeared over a ridge in the distance, advancing rapidly. Dylan fired and smeared one of them out of existence. He fired again and missed. Something grabbed his shoulder from behind.

Dylan turned away from the Sony Playstation II game on the screen and looked up into the angry face of his grandmother.

"Dylan Ralph Simpson-Cole! Young man, you get yourself downstairs right this minute! Put away that video game nonsense."

Shirley Cole had stopped by to pick the boy up from the condo in Monroe where Dylan and Annie still lived. There had been no answer to her knocking at the door, so she had let herself in. Shirley was a spry 67 years of age. An amazing state of affairs given her bulk as well as age.

"We're going to be late. Now finish getting dressed and get down to the car this very minute."

"Whatever."

The Reverend Stringer's crusade, Times of Tribulation, had arrived in Seattle. A large audience had attended each stop on the worldwide August, 1998 tour. Unrest in the Middle East and Russia, the AIDS epidemic, and natural catastrophes throughout the 1990s, particularly in the Sodom and Gomorrah of California, helped the Reverend to promote the idea of the Second Coming and the apocalypse. Events unfolded just like the Bible and Reverend Stringer had predicted.

Dylan stomped down the stairs to where Shirley stood. "God, Grandma, I don't see why I got to go." A killer headache and ravages of testosterone fed his bad attitude.

At 19, Dylan was just about finished growing. Despite his gangly height, a shade over six feet, he looked young for his age. He shaved once a week and could easily pass for a 16-year old. He wore his red hair in a bowl cut with shaven sides. His pasty complexion had erupted with pimples. He wore a gold stud in his right ear lobe and the crystal around his neck.

The headache and weird dreams had nagged him for several days. It added to the normal grouchiness of late teenage years. Annie babied him, a factor that further contributed to his immaturity.

Glad Mom got me a doctor's appointment for tomorrow, Dylan thought as he stood defiantly at the front door in front of his grandmother. Maybe the doctor would give him some painkillers. The prospect of zoning out with a video game while wrecked on codeine appealed to him.

"God, Grandma. I don't see why I got to go," Dylan repeated.

Shirley started to tell Dylan not to use the Lord's name in vain, then stopped. What good would it do anyway? The boy was clearly caught up in the demonic elements that had affected youth everywhere. The Final Days had truly arrived. The Antichrist would soon crawl out from hiding and make his presence known.

She replied instead, "I'd say you, young man, have to go more than just about anyone I know. The message of the Lord is the only path toward salvation you young people have. And take that earring out of your ear. If you think I'm taking you to the altar of the Lord with jewelry stuck in your ear like some kind of pagan, you're mistaken."

"Can't, Grandma. It's stuck there. Look, I got a great idea. I'll drive you down and drop you off at the Kingdome. You can do your gig. I'll go over to Connor and Michelle's and watch you on TV. I'll pick you up when it's over."

"Very funny, young man. You don't have a car yet and you are not insured to drive mine." Shirley said as they walked out the door. "Don't you have a tie? Honestly, I don't know what Annie was thinking about. She knew we were going to the revival this afternoon."

Shirley stopped, turned back to Dylan and said, "Now, honey, when we get to the Kingdome you'll have to sit by yourself. Grandma's got a lot of details to take care of. I declare, sometimes I wonder if the Lord forgot to give me the strength that I need with the ministry growing this fast. You should be thrilled by this opportunity. The Reverend's message is the Lord's miracle for sure. Now, get in the car. I am quite tired of your foolishness."

Sit by myself? Dylan bit back a smile. "Not a problem, Grandma."

The two reclined in the luxury of Shirley's late model deep purple Cadillac, a gift from the First Church of Jesus Christ Washed in the Blood of the Lamb. Shirley backed down the driveway with Dylan slouched beside her.

"Now dear, pay attention during the service. I'll get back to you as soon as I can. But you never know when the camera will be on you. You'll be sitting in the front row just a few feet from Reverend Stringer and his security people. There's going to be dozens of cameras, can you believe it?"

"Whatever."

Shirley loved the boy. Truly she did. But occasional visits with family members were still a poor substitute for the company of her dearly departed Muffin.

Dylan brightened. The ache in his head had eased. Wham! Back it came. *This is getting old, just like Grandma.*

"Hey, righteous," Dylan interrupted. Then forgot what he wanted to say.

"Righteous? Why did you say that? You must be excited about today. Yes, honey that's what the revival is all about. Being righteous. Say, dear, look in the glove compartment. See if there's any of that candy left. That lunch just didn't fill me up at all. Go ahead and have a piece, and pass one on to Grandma. It might be a while before we eat a decent meal."

* * * * * * * * * * * * * * *

It is time.
The wawren community concentrated as one.

* * * * * * * * * * * * * * *

"Precious, sacred scenes unfold, precious, sacred scenes unfold, precious memories."

A chorus of one hundred voices wavered in harmony over the public address system of Seattle's Kingdome.

The choir sat down. The announcer went to the podium. Sixty-four thousand people rustled expectantly. Millions more watched "Times of Tribulation" on CBS. As his grandmother had promised, Dylan sat in the front row less than twenty feet from the speaker's podium.

"A beautiful hymn. Thank you to the Stringer Singers for the delightful hymn, 'Precious Memories.' It is now time for what you came for. I present to you the deliverer of the Word, God's appointed and anointed, the holy Reverend Isaiah Marcus Stringer!"

The Reverend bounced up to the podium to the roar of swelling applause. The ten-city tour had gone well. Hundreds of thousands had flocked to the First Church of Jesus Christ Washed in the Blood of the Lamb. Trouble in the Middle East had spurred the frenzy. Financial offerings swamping the Ministry's coffers meant that more branches of the Stringer Institute of Praise could be opened. The Institute offered an expensive Christian education from locations throughout the United States. It was unaccredited by all but the Lord.

Stringer looked down from the high reaches of the elevated pulpit. For those seated at the top of the Kingdome balcony, he appeared to be little more than an ant, but his amplified voice compensated, booming out throughout the massive indoor stadium.

"The hour of the Lord is at hand!" he bellowed. "Already, the forces of darkness gather. Forces that have plunged this world into pandemonium."

Cameras zoomed. On the screen, Stringer's nostrils flared and his eyes blazed, as he shouted out each word with long-practiced clarity and precision. In the control booth, a technician modulated the strength of the transmission to compensate for the preacher's vigor.

"Long ago, the plot was written. It is unfolding now and cannot be changed. A great battle in the home of Jesus will soon be joined. As I speak, armies gather in the Middle East. Dark days of hate have descended upon us. The signs are everywhere: the portent in the sky, the earthquakes, fires, floods, conflict, and AIDS plague that represent the riding of the four horsemen of the Apocalypse. The Antichrist, now cloaked, awaits his opportunity. He could be someone you know. Someone you love. He will come in peace and will warn of evil. But we know the identity of evil. Lovers of the Lamb of God, who is the *real* threat?"

As one, the crowd chanted "Satan, Satan, Satan."

"And *what* is he?"

"He is evil, evil, evil." The chant grew in power.

"And *who* is his messenger?"

"The Antichrist. The Antichrist! The *Antichrist!*"

* * * * * * * * * * * * * *

The Peacemaker signaled, *Begin.*

* * * * * * * * * * * * * *

The Reverend ranted for the next half-hour. He alternated his warnings with suggestions for living the good life and for enriching the coffers of the One True Church.

"Only then, in the deepest days of Earth's pain will the Lord Jesus Christ himself come to us as a savior," Stringer's voice boomed above the crowd's exclamations. His voice then dropped to a whisper that floated over the sound system in a soothing hiss. "Jesus will defeat the pretender in a final battle between good and evil. The Lord will prevail and bring a thousand years of peace. True believers will dwell in the house of the Lord forever!"

The crowd erupted. Dylan yawned. After all, he'd listened to Stringer all his life. His head hurt.

"How magnificent, dear." His grandmother squeezed into the seat next to Dylan she had staked out earlier. Shirley leaned over to shout in his ear. "Isn't this wonderful? Isn't he magnificent today? This is truly the best service of the tour." Shirley leaned as far back in her seat as her bulk would allow. "What a gift," she muttered. "Too bad Ralph isn't here in the flesh to see it."

The Reverend raised his arms high and the crowd quieted. Even Dylan felt compelled to look.

"To be accepted, to be delivered to His grace, you must accept the Lord Jesus Christ as your personal savior. Come forward and be saved. Protect yourself. Protect your families. Join me now at the altar of the Lord. Move into the safety of His arms. Come forward and be saved!"

The organ thundered over the Kingdome's amplifiers. Members of the audience trickled forward, then became a pulsing deluge. Stewards maintained order.

"Come, Dylan, go forward. Kneel before the Reverend Stringer. Join the multitude." Shirley whispered urgently in her grandson's ear.

"What?" Dylan turned toward her. "You said you wouldn't do this to me. No way! Get outta here."

"Dylan, you must hurry. Please, dear, it would mean so much to me. I'm sure you will be touched by the Lord's message if you just submit." Shirley stood, trying to pull Dylan to his feet.

"No way, man! Grandma, are you nuts! I'm not going down there." He turned to jerk his arm away just as a television camera honed in on the crowd moving behind him up the aisle. His thoughts cycled. *Crap, they're going to see me fight with Grandma on TV.* Dylan gave up for the moment and let Shirley pull him gently but firmly toward the Reverend Stringer. The stream of humanity coming up from behind blocked his escape. His headache amplified.

My head! Dylan then screamed as pain axed him to his knees. Just as suddenly he stood upright. He had moved so abruptly, so purposefully, that the crowd around him gave way.

"Beware!" Dylan boomed suddenly, in a voice much deeper and more resonant than his own. He exhorted the crowd around him in an amazing voice that commanded instant attention. "All who hear this message, beware!"

Shirley stopped her pulling. "What…"

"The battle for survival begins!" Dylan shouted. His eyes glazed with fright. He looked frantically around. He fought for breath, but the voice continued.

"Be warned. *Evil* is coming!"

"Dylan?" Shirley gasped. She turned frantically from side to side. "What are you doing? Hush, now. Dylan…Dylan, are you all right? Honey, shush!" She was mortified.

Dylan looked at his grandmother through terrified eyes a universe away. He mutely appealed for help as new words of warning rushed in a nonstop flood from his mouth.

"Disaster lies ahead. Earth is in horrible danger. Look to Jupiter. The answer lies with *Jupiter!*" The crowd began to scatter away from Dylan pushing into those coming up the aisle.

"Dylan!" Shirley screeched.

Television cameras turned and targeted the commotion. What was happening? Was this part of the show?

"Reverend. Reverend!" Shirley called frantically to Stringer standing twenty-five feet away. Stringer stopped giving dispensation to a group at his feet and now looked in the direction of Dylan's shouts that boomed above the crowd noise. Shirley hung on to her grandson's flailing arms as he fought to release himself from the grip of the unknown force.

"Help me!" Shirley shouted in panic when she realized Dylan had started to levitate. She released her grip. Screaming a warning of impeding doom the teenager abruptly shot fifty feet in the air.

Nearby observers could see that no wires propped the boy up. Those farther away in stadium seats weren't so sure, but the suddenness and odd timing of the levitation took them by surprise. Then Dylan's exposed skin began to crackle with a blue flame. In the darkness of the Kingdome, he flickered and glowed with a brightness all could see. Television cameras captured his every action and word.

Those waiting for Stringer's blessing backed away. "Death lies ahead!" Dylan screamed. "Look to Jupiter! Look to Jupiter! Look to Jupiter!" He twirled and spun out slowly over the mass packed in seats on the floor of the Kingdome. Then suddenly he repeated over and over, "*Alea jacta est. Alea jacta est. Alea jacta est!*"

At first, Stringer couldn't spot the commotion that had interrupted his work. There would be hell to pay when the perpetrator was found, he silently vowed. Then he looked up and saw Dylan. At about that time, Shirley finished fighting her way to his side.

"I was bringing him to you!" Shirley cried above roar. "At first he didn't want to come, then he stopped complaining. All of a sudden he started shouting and he won't stop. He can't stop. My God, why is Dylan floating? Why is he glowing? What is that blue fire? What is he saying?"

Stringer looked up at the boy, the blood drained from his face. "Good Lord," he muttered as he studied the boy. "He calls to Jupiter, the king of ancient Roman Gods, the king of pagans. The god that Jesus Christ turned out of the temple. Jupiter, the false god of thunder, lightening, rain, and destiny. He's babbling in Latin!" Stringer knew a smattering of ancient languages, knowledge that came in handy when swaying the masses. "Latin is the Roman pagan language. He's saying the die is cast. His call is not to Jupiter, but to Satan, his father! He is saying that his father is coming! So this is how it begins…"

"What? Dylan doesn't know Latin. His father is Johnny…"

Suddenly, using the full power of the stadium's speakers, the Reverend Stringer ranted. "Deceiver. Liiar! *Antichrist!*"

"*Danger!* Look to Jupiter!" Dylan's extraordinary voice could be heard over the crowd.

The cameras alternated between Stringer and the boy, tracking a rally at a perverse and supernatural tennis match.

"Fear not. The Lord will protect you. We will not be harmed! Do not listen. The deceiver is among us, cloaked in the innocence of a child. Do not heed his calls! They are calls to the *Devil!*" Sweat poured down Stringer's forehead. His pompadour was askew as he shouted himself hoarse.

People backed off in horror from the spinning, shouting apparition above and the screaming reverend before them. Panic ensued. The crowd broke for the exits, pushing to get out. Hysteria swept through the main floor of the stadium like water from a burst dam that threatened all who stood in front of it. The panic became a rout. Screams drowned out both Dylan's unceasing cries and Stringer's amplified ones.

People fell crushed to the ground trampled under the feet of the believers above them. The balconies and upper reaches of the stadium emptied as people fled an unknown terror. Television cameras on the main floor crashed to the ground as the cameramen lost their balance in the panic. Other cameras still rolled.

"No. Wait!" Shirley cried, as she was flung against the corner of the stage, "Dylaaaan! Come back!"

✶ ✶ ✶ ✶ ✶ ✶ ✶ ✶ ✶ ✶ ✶ ✶ ✶

Cole took his turn weeding the vegetable gardens and tending sheep. His training as a groundskeeper at Leavenworth and exercise regime at the Monroe Reformatory later had prepared him well for the physical labor at the Greek Orthodox Academy of Crete. Cole's appearance remained unchanged. His long skinny body, gaunt face, and streaming white hair fit in well with the pastoral setting. He looked like the recluse he had become. His life had evolved into an incongruous set of experiences that, from Cole's perspective, felt like traveling back in time as well as space. On returning from Academy business, after deplaning from thirty thousand feet, he'd traveled first by van, then by cab, by boat, and occasionally by donkey-drawn cart to the Academy where he might pull weeds until his evening meal.

His work as an English teacher reminded him of his brief stint with the Beheiren. He hoped to see Hiroshi Akai again some day. Though the two had continued to correspond, Cole had not seen his Japanese friend in thirty years.

Twelve years had passed since his release from the Monroe Reformatory and departure for Crete. He marvelled at the swift passage of time. It couldn't have been that long.

Annie. One of the very few who understood his escape and the life he had lived since leaving the States. She loved him enough to allow a peculiar, long-range relationship. She never complained though Cole knew she suffered particularly when Dylan had been tiny, and particularly of late as their son failed in school, got in constant trouble, and seemed to lack direction. Cole made it home for a one-week visit every three months. He knew that wasn't enough.

Annie's a wonderful mom, Cole thought, as he yanked another weed. It was early evening. He'd finish up soon, take a shower, get some food, and go to bed. The pit of his stomach clenched over the thought of motherhood, the memory of his mother, and the memory of her abuse. *Breathe deep. You know where you are. You know who you are.* Cole deepened his breathing, concentrated on the quiet vision of a blue sea and felt a now-familiar wave of peace wash over him.

Cole thought back to the morning's conversation with Nicholas Papaderos, now a bishop and still assigned to the Academy. The two men met every morning on the hilltop, Cole's special place, for conversation and spiritual renewal, a practice begun many years before when Papaderos shared with Cole his story of death and suffering during World War II.

"You have grown," the Bishop had said. "Your inner spirit has been restored. It is time to make peace with those who caused your pain. It is time for you to leave us, John."

"Oh, man," Cole said out loud, recalling the conversation. "Papaderos is right. I know it's time."

Cole thought back to the first years on Crete. He'd never been introspective while incarcerated. Leavenworth only allowed for hard work and discipline. At Monroe, his studies had occupied him. Safe in Crete, he had traveled inward to horrific discoveries.

Over the months and years, the flashes of memory had solidified. A silent motion picture played of the events that had scarred his soul. Terrified, Cole sought solace in ritual, even prayer. In an atmosphere of acceptance, peace, and with the quiet urging of Papaderos, the genesis of his descent into hell finally unfolded.

As well as he could reconstruct it, his mother's abuse started well before he could talk. Cole's earliest memories were of her blows but, as a toddler, he lacked the coordination necessary to do anything more than just flail and scream. No one intervened, not even Ralph, his loving but hopelessly distracted and ineffectual dad. Sometimes, his mother clasped him to her bosom.

Cole recalled her hugging him one time and begging for his forgiveness. He was older in this memory. "Forgive me," he heard his mother cry. "I'm so sorry, Johnny. Mommy is sorry."

One time, when he had nabbed a brownie out of the oven, Shirley forced him to eat the whole pan in less than fifteen minutes. She even tracked him with a timer. He recalled choking and heaving up brownies on the kitchen floor as the timer dinged. When he was eight years old, he broke one of her prized China cups, and she hit him until he lost consciousness. It was the last memory he had of his mother's abuse.

Cole realized that beating must have jolted his mother into some type of action, some type of change. That must have been when she saw the light and discovered the Lord. Thereafter, Shirley treated him in a kindly, even cloying fashion. She overcompensated in the opposite direction, until he got busted in Yokosuka and thrown into Leavenworth. After that, she ignored him and he her.

Cole dumped weeds and yard waste into a compost pile, put away his tools, and walked back to the welcoming lights and warmth of the Academy's rectory.

Michelle and Chuck claimed their mother loved John most of all her children. They had never seen or experienced her physical abuse. Cole thought back to My Lai and to a long ago outburst in a counselor's office. The toddler at My Lai fighting in terror for her tiny life. The photo of a smiling family on the counselor's desk that he crushed under his boots. He understood his anger. It made sense. It all made sense.

He needed to talk to Shirley, to his mother. He planned to face her, and to go home to stay.

✳ ✳ ✳ ✳ ✳ ✳ ✳ ✳ ✳ ✳ ✳ ✳ ✳

"Forget it." Michelle laughed.

"I can't think of anything I would rather do, dear wife," Connor mugged with exaggeration as Michelle tried to hit him with the long braid of her prematurely gray, brownish hair.

The television flickered in the background as the two giggled and rolled around on the bed in an unfair fight.

Michelle was still tiny. Connor had gained another twenty pounds over the last decade. His thinning hair was cut short at Renee's for fifty bucks a pop, and the beard was long gone. Lasik eye surgery had replaced his eyeglasses.

Connor had also had plastic surgery to reduce the birthmark and scar. The work was completed prior to his 1990 separation from Michelle. Despite the surgery, the birthmark had made a comeback though Connor shrugged off its reemergence as simply the loss of more hair.

After birthmark and scar surgery, he lost weight and got contact lenses. Binky's death in the spring of 1990 and a particularly acrimonious argument with Michelle tipped him over. The cat's death must have reminded him of his own mortality. So, Connor had abruptly zoomed off into the sunset in his red corvette.

He dragged back to Michelle and the Wallingford house after three, at first exciting, then lonely years in an apartment that never quite recaptured the magic of his youth.

Michelle and Connor had been reunited for five years now. Connor regained the weight he had lost, and then some. Their relationship mellowed, though they never stopped fighting. Connor never stopped trying to discover his purpose but, at least, he now pursued the subject a bit more tentatively. He hadn't seen Eldon Moss in years.

"It is my life's dream to spend my paltry, meaningless day off in the bosom of the Cole clan and to feel again the warmth of its matriarch. To revel in the joy and acceptance that permeates Cole tribal rites."

"Knock it off, Connor." Michelle punched him in the gut. The blow actually rocked him, though he tried to pretend it hadn't.

"Knock what off?" Connor asked, gasping. "Ah, my dear. I can't stop extolling the virtues of the family from which you spring. The prospect of the opportunity to spend a beautiful summer day among them that I would otherwise be wasting fills me with a joy that…"

"Okay, okay… shut-up. We can come home early. It's no big deal. But we *have* to go over to Shirley's. John's in Greece and Chuck's in New Mexico. You and I are Annie and Dylan's only hope. I swear Shirley hasn't let up on Annie since the kid was born. I don't think she'll ever be satisfied until Dylan enters the ministry as an acolyte to the Reverend Stringer's crusade." Michelle lit a cigarette and took a drag.

"Fat chance of that. Dylan's just on this side of being a full-blown juvenile delinquent. Good thing he never joined a gang. At least not that we know of. That bit with him in a stolen car and a gun was really something."

"Cut him some slack. Dylan's getting it together. I seem to remember you had problems with authority when you were his age."

"That was different. We were fighting a revolution."

"Yeah, right," Michelle smirked. She hit again on the cigarette.

"Anyway, we'll go, be polite, eat the free food, and get back. Your mom does know how to cook."

Michelle abruptly shifted gears. "Do you have to go in early tomorrow?" She referred to Connor's administrative position at the community college. At first, he'd worked ungodly long hours determined to prove himself, but now.

"Nah, the Dean's meeting has been postponed. What about you?"

"Nothing special. I'm sick of being the only assistant editor that gets in at eight in the morning and works until midnight. I may be the new kid on the city desk, but I don't want to be worked into the ground before I hit fifty. Okay if I take the Beemer tomorrow?" The BMW sedan was Michelle's favorite.

Connor didn't know why she even asked. He always drove the Corvette. He figured in another five years or so, it'd be a classic. "Hate to change the subject," Connor grinned wickedly at the sight of Michelle reclining seductively across the bed, "but no one swoons like me at the sight of my mate."

"Don't get used to it," Michelle teased as she got up to click on the bedroom television. Her back to Connor blocked the view. "I want to check out the news. Copy off the wires didn't look good this afternoon. Looks like there's going to be another war in the Middle East. I heard the President is thinking about sending in troops and he's been negotiating with the Israelis. Russia's unsettled and even the North Koreans are lighting up. Times are scary. I wonder when the President…"

She stopped in mid-sentence.

"Michelle? What are you looking at?" Connor wasn't concerned, just curious.

Michelle moved.

People running and screaming danced across the screen. The Kingdome floor writhed with the bodies of people who had tumbled while trying to flee.

"Jesus. What happened?" The voice-over said the riot had occurred earlier that afternoon. No one had been killed, but several people were in intensive care at Harborview Hospital.

Then they saw Dylan—it was Dylan, the close-up left no doubt—floating wraithlike across the top of the crowd. His face glowed; electricity snapped and popped off his fingertips, nose, and ears. He was screaming something that was drowned out by the commentator's voice-over.

*   *   *   *   *   *   *   *   *   *   *   *   *   *

Annie sank into the sofa and kicked off her shoes. Her new job, the biggest leap yet on her fast track career exhausted her. She had made a good life for herself and Dylan. The condo was cozy. In two more years, it'd be paid for.

The phone rang. She sighed again and snuggled deeper into the soft leather. The machine could handle the call. She needed a few more minutes of quiet.

"Hey," squawked the machine in Dylan's voice. "Leave a message. We'll call you back. Maybe."

The caller hung up.

Annie grinned. With Dylan in charge of the answering machine, the message never stayed the same for long. He had grown up. Calls from teenage girls already outnumbered calls to her. Raising a kid alone had been tough. It showed. The boy had some rough edges. The capper came when he dropped out of high school and got picked up in a stolen car the previous year. Dylan swore he didn't know about the car or about the gun one of the kids had been packing. He'd worked odd jobs since then. Maybe he would finish high school at a community college just like his Uncle Connor. She hoped so.

Annie got up, a glass of white wine on her mind. Dylan had been good about going to the Kingdome. The kid didn't like being with Shirley, but Annie had insisted. The old lady really doted on him.

"Things will get better," she promised the empty room. "Dylan's getting it together, and John should be coming back for good. Maybe I'll get some breathing space." Cole's last letter had mentioned some kind of personal breakthrough.

The machine no sooner had shut off than the phone rang again. She let it go. This time, the party hung up as soon as the message machine kicked in. Annie walked into her Spartan kitchen and uncorked a bottle of Chablis. The phone started up again like an insistent pots and pans salesman who just wouldn't be ignored.

Better get it. Annie reached over and grabbed the receiver.

"Hello?"

"Annie!" Shirley's voice screeched in her ear. "It's Dylan. The Devil's got Dylan. They had to pull him down with ropes!"

"What? What are you talking about?"

"Something horrible happened. Dylan was called by Satan. He started to float in the air and glow…"

"Float? *Where* is he?"

"At the hospital! At Harborview. Come quickly. He won't stop! He's in the clutches of the Devil. We have to save him!" Shirley's plea echoed through a dangling receiver.

Annie was already out the door.

CHAPTER 22

"*Saigo no senso ga yattekuru!* The battle will soon be joined! Danger! Look to Jupiter. The time is at hand! *Bon Tonnere! Le monde meurt!*"

Dylan screamed a perplexing message of doom in different languages without pause for three days and nights. By the evening of the third day his eyes had glazed over with the exhaustion-induced pain that now racked his body. He didn't recognize Annie or anyone else. His vital signs became increasingly erratic. Annie, Connor, Michelle, and Shirley had been constant companions to Dylan's terror.

Al Jordan, Dylan's attending physician, entered the room and signaled Annie to join him. Jordan was part of the medical team at Seattle's Virginia Mason Hospital that got larger every day. Dylan had been transferred from Harborview when it became apparent that he needed more than emergency care. Annie left her son to join the doctor. Shirley, Connor, and Michelle left their vigil and joined her.

"I'm sorry. The test results are just not as clear as we had hoped," Dr. Jordan began as the group sat down in a conference room just off the nurse's station on the floor. Observing the strain etched on Annie's face, the doctor moved quickly to the point. Annie rose in alarm from her chair at his words.

Michelle put her arm around her sister-in-law. Connor leaned forward in his seat, his elbows on the oak table. Shirley sat strangely silent in the corner.

"We've not been able to find a physical cause for Dylan's condition," Dr. Jordan continued. The words stung Annie like hailstones.

"The scans show stress and unusual electrical activity but the results don't fit any recognizable disease pathology. From a physical perspective, we are at an impasse. We have performed a variety of tests without result."

"What can you rule out?" Connor asked.

"Well, he doesn't have a brain tumor."

A rapping at the door interrupted further questioning. Dr. Jordan invited Laura Andersen, staff psychiatrist assigned to study Dylan, into the room. "This is Dr. Andersen. I've asked her to brief us on the psychological data she has collected."

The small, dark-haired middle-aged woman acknowledged the doctor with a nod. "I wish I had more to tell you. As you know, it is difficult to work with Dylan. He cannot answer questions or control his body movements. Quite frankly, we have never seen a case like this. The physical agitation without respite is extremely rare but the use of several foreign languages he could not possibly know is highly unusual. It's a condition called 'xenoglossy.' This condition is rare. There's usually a logical explanation for it such as repressed memories from a childhood spent in a foreign culture. But Dylan could not possibly have learned Hebrew, German, French, Japanese, Greek, and Swahili. His ability to recite is also unprecedented. The boy and his mother, Annie, are not religious—yet he recited verbatim the entire book of Revelations from the New Testament in Latin! He keeps warning about Jupiter, though we don't know whether he's referring to the planet, or to the Roman God. The rarity of this case and the pressing need to find a solution before Dylan is… uh… physically compromised…"

Annie interrupted, her face scrunched in the effort to keep tears from erupting into sobs. "Dylan's going to die if we don't do something, isn't he? He can't take it any more. Isn't there a reason for all this? He can't…" Her voice broke. She looked at Michelle for support.

"What do you propose? Dr. Jordan, what do you think?" Michelle said, hugging Annie tighter.

Dr. Jordan touched Annie's shoulder before replying and looked at her. His ebony forehead glistened with sweat.

"You're right, Annie. Dylan can't go on like this. We must find a way to sedate him so his system can get relief from whatever is causing this hysteria. Perhaps then, after he has rested, we can solve the puzzle. We have no other alternatives."

"You've already tried that. Sleeping pills aren't doing a thing. He's as frantic now as he was the first night."

"I know, Annie. But we still have to try. I wish there were other options."

"What's next?" Connor asked.

Jordan replied. "As you know, a team from Johns Hopkins is on the way. They're on the red-eye from D.C. They arrive about midnight."

Michelle turned to Annie. "John will be here by then too. And Chuck should be here any minute. He called from the airport. I think you'd better let the doctors try again, Annie. Dylan has to sleep."

"One more thing, Annie," Dr. Jordan added. "I hate to bring this up now, but we need your cooperation. We're getting calls from news people all over the world. Millions saw Dylan float in the air at the Kingdome. The hospital is ringed with news crews and cameras. We have to deal with the media in an orderly manner so our other patients aren't disturbed any more than they have been already. The medical updates the hospital has been releasing have been inadequate. There is quite a bit of hysteria, much of it religious. Perhaps if a family member agreed to meet periodically with reporters…"

Annie pulled her hands through her hair and looked around.

"I'll take care of it, doctor," Michelle interjected. "I'm a journalist. I know what they want."

"Thank you, Michelle. I'll ask the hospital's public relations liaison to meet with you immediately. She'll be glad to make the necessary arrangements."

"Don't worry Annie," Michelle said, giving Annie another hug. "I'll take care of it. Go be with Dylan. Give him my love."

With a nod to the family, the doctors filed out of the room to issue a flurry of orders. Michelle followed. After they left, Annie sank into the chair and cradled her head in her arms. She sobbed.

"There's nothing you can do," Shirley pronounced stiffly from her chair in the corner.

"Shirley, please," Connor admonished in a tired voice.

"I have fought it for three days and nights," Shirley continued louder and faster. "I have thought of nothing else. My grandson is not the only one who has not slept. I cannot ignore this any longer. The doctors are wasting their time. I did not want to believe it, but Reverend Stringer is right. What is happening to Dylan is not of this world."

Annie looked up. She was numb. Connor groaned.

"Shirley continued. "You know, Connor, I once thought you might be the cursed one, but I now know that Dylan is the Deceiver, the One who has come to fool the world. Think about it. He keeps warning the world of a terrible danger just as the scripture said he would. People are calling from all over the world to follow him and are flocking to this hospital like he is a god or something. Just like scripture predicts. But he is *not* of God. He was born out of wedlock, on Halloween, the Devil's day. He is not baptized! He does not have a Christian name and has been in trouble with the law. He floated in mid-air and burned with the fires of hell. There have been portents in the sky. There has been war and the signs of war in the Middle East, floods, and plague. Signs of the tribulation are everywhere!"

"Shut up!" Annie scrambled to her feet to confront Shirley. "Stop it!"

"Shirley, I think it would be best if you…"

Annie cut off Connor's attempt to mediate. "Back off, Connor. You…" She pointed at Shirley. "How can you suggest such a thing? My son is dying. If God existed, he would help him. Dylan is sick, not possessed. He needs help. Do you think the Antichrist would be mortal and just die?"

"It's a ruse to draw the world to him, my dear. Just like when he floated."

"Annie? Connor? Mom?"

Chuck Cole stood in the doorway. He looked from Annie, to Shirley, to Connor. "How's Dylan?"

"Man, am I glad to see you," Connor said. "You're just in time." Connor shot his mother-in-law a silencing glare and gently took her arm helping to raise her bulk from the chair.

"Your mom and I are going down to the cafeteria for a cup of coffee. You and Annie come on down when you get a chance." Connor started to push Shirley from the room, then turned back to Chuck.

"Have you lost more weight? Man, you look awful. You okay?"

Chuck coughed and shook his head. "I'm fine," he said. "It's just a bad cold."

"No, Chuckie, honey," Shirley cajoled, as Connor steered her from the room. "Don't go in to see that boy. He *is* the devil."

Chuck winked at Connor as he left, then moved to Annie. "How is he?"

She despaired. "It doesn't stop. Chuck, I… I don't know what to do. It's bizarre. He just keeps shouting all those strange things and warnings in strange languages. The doctors don't know what it is. All the tests came back negative. He can't stop. I can see it in his eyes. He's scared." She stopped and gazed forlornly at Chuck. "He's going to die," she said, quietly. "The sedatives aren't working. I don't know what to do."

"There's still hope."

Annie nodded without conviction.

"Come on, let's go see him."

Annie gathered the stack of medical books and articles she had been carrying around, materials she had been studying nonstop since the ordeal had begun. They walked toward Dylan's room.

Hoarse shouts echoed down the hall. Dylan and his doctors had the floor to themselves now; all other patients had been moved to other floors to escape the chaos. Security guards patrolled the halls and exits to stop never ceasing attempts by news reporters and religious zealots to get at the boy. Chuck had been required to show two IDs with photos to get through the security screen.

"Excuse me, sir," the duty nurse left her station to stop Chuck as he approached Dylan's door. "One moment, sir. I'm afraid you can't go in there."

"It's okay, Joyce," Annie replied with a weary smile. "This is Chuck Cole, Dylan's uncle."

"I'm sorry, ma'am. The gentleman looks ill. Dr. Jordan's orders. No one is allowed in who may spread a communicable disease to the boy. We don't want to put any more strain on his system. I'm sure you understand."

"Look, nurse," Chuck said, drawing to his full height. "It's just a cold. There's no cause for alarm. I've come seventeen hundred miles to see my nephew." He turned and pushed past the nurse into Dylan's room, her protestations cut off. She turned abruptly and clip-clopped down the hall.

Dylan lay on the bed, his arms and legs straining against the restraints. "Repent! Danger approaches. *Endgueltige schlacht ist im kommen. Endgueltige schlacht ist im kommen!*"

Annie moved quickly to the far side of Dylan's bed and sat down. She stroked his arm and resumed her murmured comforts to her son. Chuck followed. He studied Dylan's every move as he moved to the boy's side.

"Dylan?" he said softly, with studied calm. "Hey, Bud. How you doing?"

Dylan's eyes stared transfixed at the ceiling in a far away world of panic and pain. His muscles pulled against the restraints; he gasped raggedly for breath in between the shouts that racked him.

Chuck stood, transfixed by the horrible sight, his mind whizzing as it assimilated and processed every bit of available data. He heard footsteps down the hall and knew he would soon be rousted. He moved in closer to study his nephew. Everything faded from Chuck's consciousness—even the approaching footsteps—as he quickly searched for a clue. Chuck Cole's training and years spent in science had ingrained in him the habit of careful observation and the need never to assume. He began to search Dylan's body.

"Chuck! What are you doing?" Annie was beside herself with grief and puzzlement.

Two blue-uniformed hospital security guards burst into the room followed by an indignant Joyce. They lunged at Dylan's emaciated uncle.

"That's got to be it." Chuck said as he began to yank at the chain around Dylan's neck.

"Jesus, Chuck. That's for good luck." Annie uttered with a look of surprise.

The security guards tried to pull Chuck off the boy, adding to the force applied to the chain. The crystal amulet ripped off with such force that the three men crashed into the far wall, knocking over a chair and nightstand. A water pitcher doused one of the guards. Annie screamed as she jumped out of the way.

"Are you all right? Chuck, what's got into you?"

"I'm okay," Chuck said as the men untangled and staggered to their feet. "I was just playing a hunch is all."

"You're in deep trouble, buddy. What's your name?" A guard said as he grabbed Chuck's elbow.

"I'm Chuck Cole, Dylan's uncle. What right…"

Annie gasped and shouted in a strangled whisper, "Look!"

The group turned toward the bed as one.

A physician responding to the sound of the thrashing in the room burst in. They all looked at the boy.

Dylan was asleep.

* * * * * * * * * * * * * *

The Peacemaker winced. The connection had been broken. Three dimmings of effort had exhausted him and the other wawrens. Was it enough? He hoped the young male was not harmed.

The invasion armada streaked past the fourth planet from the system's star, the target and its orbiting moon in sight.

* * * * * * * * * * * * * *

Chuck walked into the conference room that served the Metallurgy and Mineralogy Technology Center at the University of Washington. He had a meeting scheduled with Dr. Alice Rasmussen, the Center's Director.

The University's role as the premier research center of the Pacific Northwest with proximity to mineral riches of the Cascade Mountain Range contributed to the Center's international reputation in mineralogy and metallurgy. Chuck had called in chits with colleagues at the University. Two days had passed since Chuck brought the crystal into the Center. He looked forward to hearing a tentative analysis from the Director's lips.

Chuck's thoughts drifted as he found a chair. If anyone could figure out that damn crystal, it would be the professors and graduate students at the Center.

His reverie was interrupted by another round of wracking coughs. He intuitively knew the pneumonitis was developing into full-blown pneumocystic carinii pneumonia—a leading cause of death for AIDS victims.

Alice Rasmussen walked in the room. She stopped and stared. "Chuck. I wouldn't have recognized you. Looks like you've been on quite a diet." She sat down across from him, a look of concern on her face.

Chuck studied the crisp professorial appearance of his friend from graduate school days at the university. Dr. Rasmussen, a middle-aged, thin woman with prematurely gray hair and freckles, wore a tweed suit. The teal-blue bifocals perched on the end of her nose made her look like a worried owl.

"I meant no offense, Chuck. It's just I hadn't seen you in a while. Are you okay?"

"Yeah, I'm okay. Things have been rough. I'm getting over a bad cold. I've had better days. Look, Alice, I'm rather concerned about the crystal. I'm glad you guys got right on it. I'm dying to know what you found out."

Hmm…dying is right, she thought. *Wonder what's really going on with you?* Chuck, afraid I can't tell you much. You sure seem to get yourself connected to unsolvable puzzles in the physical universe; first that light in the sky and now, this." Alice had the good manners not to call the light by its well-known moniker, Cole's Folly. "The crystal doesn't match any mineral, gem, alloy, crystal or material we know of. Confirmation from other research facilities must be obtained, but their findings will corroborate ours. There's going to be a terrific paper in it for you and, I hope, for us here at the Center."

"Alice, I don't give a rat's ass about writing a paper. I'm not a crystallographer and, besides, right now I am much more concerned about my nephew and, as things turn out, my sister and brother too. My sister wore that thing for twenty years, then gave it to my brother; he wore it for about a year and then gave it to Dylan. My nephew has had it around his neck for almost nineteen years. Are they going to be okay?"

"I assume you're concerned about radiation. That's not a problem, Chuck. The amulet is benign to humans, by itself."

"That's a relief. What is it?"

"As best we can determine, the crystal is a piece of something larger, but not much larger. Probably something the size of the proverbial breadbox."

"Alice, don't dance around. Answer my question."

"I can't tell you exactly what it is. As I said, we have never analyzed a crystal of its composition or with its properties."

"Properties?"

"X-ray crystallography revealed an atomic pattern unlike anything we've ever seen. Nothing like this crystal appears in nature or can be manufactured using current technology."

"Come on Alice, what are you talking about?"

The Director peered at the sick man intently. "Chuck, do you remember what piezoelectricity is?"

"Sure, learned about it in freshman physics on this very campus. It's a current generated when pressure is applied to a crystal or when a crystal is placed in an alternating electrical field. It's what makes a quartz watch tick."

"What if I told you the Dylan Crystal radiates a potent, piezoelectric current detectable through lead without the necessity of pressure? We haven't figured out what electric field its tapping, but it's exotic whatever it is. The energy it generates has properties we've never seen. It shimmies around the frequencies of other waves in the radio spectrum; it is incredibly powerful but doesn't disturb other radiation. It is unique and would be particularly susceptible to sorting out with the right type of receiver. As a radio astronomer, you might actually do a better job of finding the right words to describe what we found."

"Where does it come from?' How and why did it effect Dylan the way it did?" He hacked again and fumbled for a handkerchief.

"The crystal was manufactured, Chuck. There's no doubt about that. Tool marks are discernible on the surface. It neither exists in nature nor did it develop there. We don't know how Dylan was affected, but from analyzing transcripts of his communications from the past three days the why part looks clear-cut. Appears someone is trying to warn us. About Jupiter. Dr. Mathis in cosmology…"

"That relic is still around?"

"Yeah, his grad students have been carrying him for years. Anyway, they scanned Jupiter through the glass on Cougar Mountain and found something."

"What?"

"A new moon."

"What? A new moon?"

Rasmussen shifted gears. "You said your kid sister found the artifact about forty years ago in the Grand Canyon. We don't think it was found very deep, but the Dylan Crystal has been on Earth at least hundreds of thousands of years. It was probably originally intended for use as a homing beacon. It's properties…"

"Been on Earth? Homing beacon? What in the hell are you talking about?"

"Chuck, we didn't make the Dylan Crystal. It doesn't exist in nature. It has to be an extraterrestrial artifact manufactured by an advanced civilization. The crystal's physical properties, its effect on Dylan, and its tie to Jupiter, together with the new moon that just materialized, can only lead to that conclusion. Looks like someone or something might be paying us a visit. It sounds crazy. Still, it's the only explanation. We're holding a press conference this evening. We'd like you to be there." She paused and studied Chuck. "Good God, man, you look terrible. Are you sure you're okay?"

* * * * * * * * * * * * * *

Within hours of the news conference, astronomers at the Keck Observatory atop Mauna Kea in Hawaii finished analyzing time lapse data and telemetry. A new moon had moved into orbit around Jupiter under its own power. Irrefutably, the new moon had to be a spaceship.

The news conference soon took on the role of a formality. The word got out long before Chuck Cole and scientists from the University of Washington faced the press. The Internet and World Wide Web hummed and television and radio shows everywhere interrupted broadcasting with the news.

The U.S. military quickly reacted. A message of doom and destruction conveyed through an alien artifact had been followed by discovery of a huge spaceship in the neighborhood. Either circumstance would have been alarming. The combination spurred an immediate response. The U.S. President, on advice from his National Security Advisor and the Joint Chiefs of Staff, placed all United States forces on full alert. NATO and Russian leaders followed his example.

The President changed the agenda of an upcoming emergency meeting scheduled with the Joint Chiefs of Staff. Rather than complete final planning for a bold plan to capture Saddam Hussein at a command post in the desert, the military leaders and President talked instead about the extraterrestrial threat. The crisis in the Middle East was put on hold. Russian and North Korean leaders also turned away from war planning.

The religious community's response was mixed. Traditional, mainline denominations withheld comment. Church scholars needed time to figure out ramifications of Other Life In The Universe. The events devastated charismatic, fundamentalist leaders like the Reverend Isaiah Marcus Stringer. Stringer had been riding the tide of the Second Coming. Dylan the Antichrist was a big disappointment. The balloon popped for all but a few diehards.

Stringer's words led off Michelle's front-page feature in the *Seattle Times*, an exclusive gained through the influence of Shirley Cole:

"No. I do not accept the conclusions of the so-called scientific community. The Antichrist is coming. He may have already arrived. He *may* be Dylan Cole. If not Dylan Cole, then another. These confusing circumstances are part of the tribulation. We will not reduce our vigilance. We will *not* be the pawns of Satan." Stringer said much the same thing at a sparsely attended press conference.

The rest of humankind waited. Some waited eagerly, others with trepidation, for what would come next.

✳ ✳ ✳ ✳ ✳ ✳ ✳ ✳ ✳ ✳ ✳ ✳ ✳ ✳

"Quartermaster, communicate with Tok and other Council members at once. Tell them I have important news from the blue planet."

The Peacemaker looked up from data that spilled from his communications screen and frowned at the fetid scum coating the water and walls in the dripping heat of the cubicle. *The algae we eat will soon begin to eat us.* A guard soon escorted him to the First Wyrul's dwelling. The route seemed circuitous to the wawren fullmaster.

"Guard, why do we travel through these tubes? Why not take the usual route?"

"Some of the passageways are no longer safe. Vermin have broken through. Some compounds have been overrun, including ravan compounds."

"I have heard that there is trouble. Are you referring to the alien presence in the Hive Sea?"

"Yes, fullmaster. But it appears the aliens are no longer satisfied with the sea. They have been attacking the living compounds of the outer ring."

A quorum of the Council, headed by Tok, waited impatiently to hear the Peacemaker. The wawren fullmaster stood before the group in much the same way as he had ten years prior when dressed to visit Disneyland but this time he stood confidently.

"What is it?" Taln, the Seventh Wyrul and an ally of Harn, began. "Why do you interrupt war preparations?"

First Wyrul Tok glanced at Taln, mildly surprised by the wyrul's preempting of her planned welcome to the Peacemaker. "Seventh Wyrul, you should have allowed me to speak first. We have not had the pleasure of a visit from the Peacemaker in some time. Show respect." Tok held up the speaker's wand and conveyed it to the Peacemaker.

"Humans have detected our approach, Taln," the Peacemaker replied smoothly. "I thought the Council should know at once. Military forces across the planet have been placed on full alert. We expect humans to communicate with us shortly."

"*WA!* How can this be? You assured us their communications technology was primitive." The Seventh Wyrul exploded. "Even if their telescopes found us, they would have needed more time to determine our intentions."

"How humans found us is unclear." The Peacemaker held up the speaker's wand. He wasn't exactly telling the truth, nor was he telling an outright lie. "Humans stumbled across a sending maser seeded by a Searcher long ago and deduced it was of alien origin. They also found the Hive and, as some humans like to say, 'put two and two together.'"

"That does not explain the high level of their military preparations. They could not have found the maser or discerned our true purpose unless they were somehow warned. How did you do that?" Another of Harn's supporters quizzed the Peacemaker.

The wawren stood silently.

Tok examined the Peacemaker. Perhaps all was not lost.

Like the Peacemaker, Tok had grown old. She felt the grip of a wasting disease in her bowels, as well as the ravages of age. The toxicity of the Hive was a perfect breeding ground for tumors. Despite her illness, Tok held on to power in the hope that Harn's ascendancy would never be completed.

She requested and received the speaker's wand from the Peacemaker. She then held the wand in a position of command. In perfect English she told angry Council members not to cry over spilled milk. It was a good saying, taught to her by the Peacemaker before they had stopped communicating. Tok looked forward to renewing her relationship with the Peacemaker. She felt gratified that not all Council members appeared to be angry by the turn of events.

Another Council member beckoned for the speaker's wand and then spoke. "The ravans must be recalled immediately. We must prepare to negotiate."

"Not so fast." Taln exclaimed ripping the wand out of the wyrul's grasp telekinetically. The Council gasped collectively at Toln's display of poor manners.

A short debate raged. In the end, a worried Council of Wyruls decided to recall the zeromaster cohorts.

After this decision was made, Tok delivered the final blow to ravan aspirations.

"Release the wawrens from their compound. We must have better access to them. They can better help us to plan for negotiations if their movement is unrestricted throughout the Hive."

The Council agreed. Wawrens were further ordered to prepare transmissions of peace and conciliation. Tok told the wawrens to tell the story of the Wandering as well. She hoped humans had empathy. She hoped humans would understand.

The Council of Wyruls shifted its discussions from war to peace. Many questions remained. With whom would they negotiate? How would they negotiate? What terms would be asked?

At the meeting's conclusion, Tok went to the communications center of the Council chambers and ordered the invasion armada to return to the Hive without delay.

* * * * * * * * * * * * * *

Upon his arrival back in New Mexico, Chuck Cole used his authority as the Associate Director of the radiotelescope array to suspend projects and to redirect the array in the direction of the Cygnus binary. He wasn't sure of the mechanism but suspected the galactic flare from the direction of Cygnus in 1988 had marked the arrival of the aliens. The visitors couldn't have just appeared overnight in Jovian space. True enough, shortly after his return, Socorro researchers tracked the starship's arrival from the direction of Cygnus. Though the physics behind "Chuck's Folly" were not yet understood, the blast from deep space now merited much more than a footnote in future textbooks.

Chuck Cole also got in touch with colleagues at Cornell University associated with SETI, the search for extraterrestrial intelligence. SETI had already begun transmitting a greeting in the direction of Jupiter at 1500 megahertz. Their effort was joined by the communication efforts of other academic, government, and military institutions. Even radio disk jockeys joined the fray, a source of continuing, albeit nervous, amusement for fans.

"It's KJR in Seattle, and its raining, so what? Hey, KJR listeners, before I send more moldy golden oldies your way let's give a great big KJR hello to the little green men and women from beyond the galaxy who have a camping permit next to Jupiter. A big Pacific Northwest hello from KJR Seattle!"

Messages continued to pour into space in the direction of Jupiter. Even ham radio operators got into the act. Cornell made first contact. Three days after the discovery and analysis of the Dylan Crystal and the discovery of a new and artificial moon of Jupiter, a reply in perfect English arrived at 1420 megahertz.

"Hello, we are Arkadia. We come in peace." The same message soon cycled across the planet in twenty languages. The message changed as the Arkadians told of the Wandering.

The Hive's orbit around Jupiter was carefully tracked. The Hubble Space Telescope added to data streaming in from observatories around the globe.

The Arkadians activated the Hive's faltering proton-proton engines for the short jaunt to Earth. Earth astronomers recorded the approaching glow of the Hive.

✳ ✳ ✳ ✳ ✳ ✳ ✳ ✳ ✳ ✳ ✳ ✳ ✳ ✳

"They're on their way!" The shout startled Associate Director Chuck Cole.

Phones throughout the facility rang in a cacophony of confusion.

Chuck looked up at his colleague standing in the doorway He grunted sardonically. "Ask and ye shall receive. Well, we invited them to talk. Are they coming to meet the neighbors or to massacre them? What do you think, Robert?" He didn't wait for his answer. "Think they really want to negotiate? Maybe they'll just snuff us. Talk about the ultimate gamble. But what choice do we have? They made it pretty clear we need to negotiate." He groaned. Then coughed.

"Hope your walking pneumonia gets better, Chuck."

"Yeah. Thanks. Anyway, wait till the politicians get done with this one. And why didn't the aliens ask to negotiate with the United Nations? Why the interest in Mitsubishi?"

CHAPTER 23

"*Wa!*" The ravan fullmaster looked up from the communications screen facing her command chair on the transport.

"What is it, fullmaster?" The ravan's exclamation had interrupted Harn's daydream of the slaughter ahead. And then the days of power. She swiveled in her chair and studied the ravan with a quizzical look.

"The invasion is canceled. The zeromaster cohorts are ordered back to the Hive."

"*Wa!* How can that be?" Harn looked out the viewing portal at the blue and white haze of the target less than two dimmings away.

"We have been betrayed. Humans know of our presence and are preparing a military response as we speak. Tok indicates that the target dominion of the United States is now in a high level of military readiness."

"We have discussed risk to the transports before. What is your assessment of that risk if we attack under present circumstances?"

"I cannot guarantee the safety of the transports. The United States may possess weapons that can destroy the transports in orbit. We do not know the composition or location of these weapons. We pay the price for depending on wawrens for information. We should have butchered and eaten the older ones, beginning with that wawren fullmaster."

"Enough." Harn stood and began to pace. "We cannot risk the transports. Without them, Arkadians have no way to get to the blue planet's surface. We must comply with Tok's order."

The ravan fullmaster heard Harn's words and realized, finally, that her ally was a consummate politician to the end. "How can you give up so easily? You never were truly committed to invasion, only to advancing your own cause, whatever that might be!"

"Now, fullmaster, you must relax…"

"You would rely on the wawrens to negotiate planetfall? They have failed miserably with life forms much less militaristic than these humans."

"We have no choice, fullmaster." Harn returned to her seat.

"I have a choice."

"I do not understand. Surely, you cannot be speaking of continuing the full invasion. You cannot count on the zeromaster cohorts following you rather than Tok if they are confronted by humans with nuclear weapons."

"All cohorts except my personal bodyguard will transfer to the other transports. My bodyguard and I will continue to the target in this transport. One vessel has a much better chance of going unnoticed than does an entire fleet. With my forty ravans and a single fighter I will descend to the surface and destroy one of their cities. The Peacemaker can then negotiate from a position of strength."

Harn stared at the ravan in disbelief. "That tactic will fail. The zeromaster cohorts will be sent back to destroy you."

The fullmaster looked smug. "By the time they return I will be killing humans. Besides, Tok knows that some of the ravans sent to stop my rebellion might still join me instead, particularly when they witness my success. She will not risk civil war with the goal of 6,000 years now in sight. She will be satisfied to have the other transports return to the Hive. Besides, we will not risk a nuclear response from humans with one cohort. They will be damaged just enough so that favorable terms can be negotiated."

"Your impulsive plan will never work, fullmaster. Humans will kill our negotiators, or take them hostage if Arkadians attack them now without provocation."

The ravan stood and turned toward Harn. In the twilight glow of the transport's command center her blood-red cape swirled around her. She raised up to her full height, swept her braid back and tossed her head. The bladed forehorn glittered. Her fighting talons gently rippled into the air. She whispered to Harn, "I do not care. There is no life for me back in the Hive or on a world influenced by wawrens. I will not be subdued. I will not submit." The fullmaster moved slowly toward, and then behind, Harn.

Harn sat back heavily in her chair. She had sowed the seeds of her own demise. It had been an error to underestimate the wawrens. They should have been more closely watched. She realized the power of the zeromaster cohorts was broken forever. Desire for a home unpolluted by nuclear fallout and fear of facing a prepared enemy ended all hope of full-scale military action. The ravans, save this edgy fullmaster and her bodyguard, would know that. She knew the suicide mission of the ravan fullmaster would be counterproductive. The attack might end any hope of negotiating a lasting peace. But how would it be stopped. What would become of her?

Harn never felt the fighting talons slice through her neck. She sensed a sudden movement behind her and then was drowning. The room spun. She had a sense of falling, then felt nothing.

✳ ✳ ✳ ✳ ✳ ✳ ✳ ✳ ✳ ✳ ✳ ✳ ✳ ✳

The wawren community rejoiced.

Fullmaster! We are free! This sentiment engulfed the Peacemaker as he sat in his cell. The wawrens could now travel the length of the deteriorating Hive, but the Peacemaker felt reticent to do so. He worried. The sea bloomed uncontrollably with algae. It crawled with alien killers. Arkadian gill covers no longer worked in the deoxygenated, murky waters of the Hive compounds, and breathing the humid, reeking atmosphere was like sucking on a straw.

Condensation steamed and dripped everywhere. A dank mist permeated the Hive. The raindrums never stopped now because the rain never stopped. The hypnotic mantra of the drums boomed unceasingly. The temperature had risen far beyond a "nice day on Arkadia" and now approximated what must have been a typical day in an Arkadian desert, except for the 100% humidity which gave new meaning to "desert." The Hive was a moon-sized sauna badly in need of disinfectant. Power shutdowns to conserve strained generators disrupted Arkadian life continuously. Uncontrolled blackouts killed Arkadians in cryonic storage by the thousands.

The electrobars would soon have failed anyway. Negotiations must succeed. Only a short time is left to us. The Peacemaker thought of a Hive devoid of all power. Total darkness, slithering killers coming through impotent intruder screens, psychic screams, slow cooling, and suffocation in the bad air. He pushed away these thoughts along with the rancid tea that he had been drinking.

A gentle telepathic signal—conveyed by a worker messenger—interrupted the Peacemaker's agitation. Tok had requested an immediate meeting.

✳ ✳ ✳ ✳ ✳ ✳ ✳ ✳ ✳ ✳ ✳ ✳ ✳ ✳

"It's good to have you back, Dylan." Annie smiled as she sat down on the edge of his bed. "Dr. Jordan says you should be up and about by tomorrow."

"Hey, Dylan." Cole came bounding into the bedroom, slamming the door behind him. "Annie. I've got an idea."

"What?" Dylan beat his mom to the punch.

"Let's go camping."

"You got to be kidding, John. Dylan's still in bed. And we've never done that. We don't have the gear. There isn't a sleeping bag in the place." When together, the Simpson-Cole household tended to stay at home with an occasional night out for pizza. Dylan had been camping only a few times in his life and then only with his Uncle Connor. A couple of summers ago, they had spent a week at a spot Connor knew on the Yellowstone River in Montana.

Cole insisted, "Let's do it. We'll only be gone for a few days. We can borrow Connor's equipment. Dylan, you can even bring along a powerbook, your mom's cell phone and laptop so you won't be completely disconnected while we're gone. It'll be just be the trees and the three of us. We can go out to the Olympic Peninsula."

Neither Annie nor Dylan answered at first. Dylan finally said, in sharp contrast to his father's animation, "Dad, if we go on this trip, will you stay when we get back?"

"I'm not sure, Dylan."

"John, if we do what you want, will you do what *we* want?"

Cole walked over to the bed and put his arms around Annie. With his shoulder-length white hair tied back in a ponytail, his flannel shirt, dockers, and loafers, he contrasted sharply with Annie, the elegant, captain-of-industry executive she was, even when she was hanging around the house in sweats. "You mean, come home to stay?"

"Yes."

"Let's talk about it in the woods, honey."

Dylan smiled, rolled over, and immediately fell asleep. His parents walked quietly out.

* * * * * * * * * * * * * *

The technician fullmaster straightened the folds of her green robes and settled her cape over the back of the cushion. She splashed in the knee deep, blood-warm water that lapped at her seat. She had just delivered a report to First Wyrul Tok. The Peacemaker joined them in the First Wyrul's personal chamber.

Tok seethed. "You are positive a single transport is still on an attack intercept?"

"Yes, Tok." The technician fullmaster didn't like delivering bad news, but the facts were the facts.

Tok started to reply then pointed at a ripple moving through the tepid water of the chamber. "What is that?" A V-shaped wave closed in on her. She rolled into the water away from the approaching ripple. The three huddled in the corner of the chamber and watched.

Something a human would have described as a three-foot long scorpion with large pulsating gill covers leaped onto the just-vacated cushion. Its exoskeleton rippled with a fluorescent pink and green shimmer. Its tail, tipped with an oversized stinger the size of small dagger, waggled malevolently back and forth, as though searching.

Without thinking, Tok fired as much of a bolt as a wyrul could muster into the insect. It thrashed. The technician did the same. A ravan bodyguard splashed through the chamber doorway and bolted the insect to ashes without hesitation.

"Have you been harmed, First Wyrul?"

"No, ravan. My guests and I are fine. Where did this thing come from?"

"The intruder screens are not always fully charged. It must have crawled through during the last blackout."

"Thank you, ravan. You are dismissed."

The group resettled. "I am...am unaccustomed to killing. This is most distressing." The Peacemaker uttered in a quiet, stilted way.

"Sometimes, it is necessary to kill or to be killed." Tok's reply did little to comfort the wawren fullmaster.

"Where were we? Ah, yes." Tok continued. "Technician, you reported a transport on an attack intercept? With only Harn, the ravan fullmaster, and her bodyguard cohort on board?"

The Arkadians did not know Harn was now being digested by the ravan fullmaster and her bodyguard.

"Yes."

"What are their plans? There is no strategic value to a suicide mission." Tok thought out loud.

The technician shrugged in the Arkadian way. "They have cut off all communication with the Hive."

"Peacemaker, what do you advise?" Tok appeared to be desperate, for good cause. Arkadians could not return to a full-scale attack without the threat of nuclear retaliation by humans. Conversely, death and destruction from the attack even of a single zeromaster cohort would be devastating to humans with a high probability of ending any hope of negotiation.

"First Wyrul, technician fullmaster, I believe we must communicate the problem of the wayward transport to the government of the United States. Harn and the ravan fullmaster will most certainly follow the attack profile programmed by the technician. We can communicate the plan to humans. Perhaps this information will help them to defend themselves. At the very least, our warning will communicate our good intentions."

"What about returning the invasion armada to the blue planet? With orders to attack the rebels?" Tok asked while scratching her chin with a single closely trimmed claw.

The Peacemaker thought for a moment, and replied, "No, Tok." The transports cannot return to the blue planet in time. Also, the possibility that some or all of the zeromaster cohorts may join the rebels is too great."

Tok nodded in agreement. "Technician, open communication with the appropriate military command in the United States. Peacemaker, convey the transport's attack profile to humans. With any luck, the transport will end up like that thing." Tok gestured to the ashes that floated a few steps away.

✶ ✶ ✶ ✶ ✶ ✶ ✶ ✶ ✶ ✶ ✶ ✶ ✶ ✶

"Jesus H. Christ! You've got to be kidding. This is too much. Seattle will be under attack within a day? By aliens possessing advanced technology that we can't stop? And you say, you learned this from the aliens themselves?" The President of the United States glared at the chairman of the Joint Chiefs, the National Security Advisor, and the Secretary of Defense.

The Situation Room in the basement of the White House flickered with computer screens and consoles. Blue smoke wafted through the air as three of the men chain-smoked and gulped coffee at four a.m. The President was a tall, dapper, silver-haired politician. He looked great in the power suits the First Lady favored, but at present he appeared decidedly disheveled and pissed off.

"These things claim they come in peace and then *this?* Why can't they be stopped? Your briefing mentioned only forty troops in the attack force. Why can't a few rounds from an Abrams main battle tank take care of the problem?" The President frowned in the direction of the National Security Advisor. "If they're attacking, why did this 'Peacemaker' warn us? And why don't these things have proper names?"

The advisor grimaced. "Sir, most of them don't have names. Apparently, these creatures can telepathically signal the individual with whom they wish to speak. They don't call out a name. Anyway, conventional weapons won't stop them. Their attack craft is fully shielded and individual troops have a personal shield that's highly effective.

"On top of that, their troops each have an organic capability to discharge electrical energy sufficient to kill a troop carrier or tank. They recharge within seconds. Each alien carries a sheath of what they call homing spears. As well as we can determine these explosives pack a one-kiloton wallop. They operate on the same principle as our wire-guided antitank weapons but are much more powerful.

"In summary, sir, one of these so-called zeromasters could decimate an armored company or a carrier screen. But that's not the worst of it. Their attack craft possess a fully operational particle beam accelerator capable of chopping down an entire skyscraper. It's hard to imagine what these things will do to Seattle…"

"You're sure Seattle's the target?"

"Yes, sir."

The men at the table looked at one another, then at the President.

"Well, any ideas? Solutions? I need a solution. It needs to be a dandy. Its got to be now, not next month and not after a prolonged, expensive study. I pay you to think. So, think." The President drummed his fingers on the briefing table.

No response.

"Sir," the Chairman of the Joint Chiefs finally said. All heads turned toward him. "My staff and I put something together that might work. It's not a sure thing, but it may be the only thing we've got." The craggy, broad-shouldered ex-marine looked quietly confident.

The President snuffed out his cigarette, folded nervous hands together, and waited.

"The plan uses Brilliant Pebbles."

* * * * * * * * * * * * * *

"Connor, what's eating you?" Michelle lit another cigarette and looked out the window of their BMW. The automobile said a lot about their lifestyle. Connor's job change into management and Michelle's promotion at the newspaper meant much more income. With two incomes, and no children, the cash flowed in. Their new home on Lake

Washington in the middle of Seattle, membership in a racquetball and tennis club, and a swimming pool should feel right, shouldn't it?

"What's the problem now, Connor? God, don't you ever stop with the angst?"

The rain streamed down. Connor had the BMW's wipers on high. He remembered the trouble Renny had had with a hard rain. He thought about the red Corvette. It was good to have those days behind him.

"Nothing's wrong. I just feel like I'm still missing something that is really important, something that's just around the corner. We've come a long way. Looks like you and I will stay together, small miracle in this day and age. But don't you ever wonder or worry about the future?" He eased off the freeway. They were minutes from home. It was late afternoon.

The car phone buzzed. Michelle picked it up. "Oh, hi Frank. Connor's with me. We're heading home. Yeah… it's been a long day. Yeah… yeah, I understand. Okay, how about a good medium growth fund? Something like CGM or Voyager? They're both no-loads… Yeah, I see. Look, we've got to go somewhere with the cash. I'm not comfortable rolling it over. Look into CGM and get back to me tomorrow. Okay. Thanks."

Michelle placed the receiver back and took a drag on her cigarette. "Frank thinks the market's heading south. Wants us to stay liquid. I disagree. I'm going with another mutual fund. Sound okay?"

"Sure, fine. Now, you were saying?"

"You were whining about the future. Again."

"I just feel like there's got to be more to life. Michelle…" Connor glanced over at her. "What do you think about having a kid?"

"A kid? I thought you didn't want children. You had a horrible childhood."

"You said the same thing, Mickie. And I didn't say children; I said a *child*."

"Don't call me Mickie."

Connor laughed and ducked when Michelle pretended to slug him. The heavy roadster slewed ever so slightly.

"Connor, I know we've agreed in the past about not having kids. Neither of us liked being kids. We also agreed the world doesn't need more people. I mean, look at all the fighting that's going on in the world. Crime and poverty are incredible. School kids go through metal detectors to get into concerts and even to go to school. Then, there's this alien thing. Why bring a kid into all of that?"

"How about hope? Simple hope for a better future?"

"Fat chance of that. I mean aliens are visiting us! There's no telling what that's going to mean. We could become slaves to extraterrestrial things that like eating human flesh."

"Yeah, right. Come on. I'm being serious."

"I'm way too old to have a baby, Connor."

"It's not too late. You come from good breeding stock." This time, Michelle whacked his arm for real, and the BMW skittered onto the shoulder of the road. Connor easily swung it back.

Connor turned into the driveway, punched the garage door opener, and disengaged the security system by remote after the door creaked shut. The two walked in. A dinner of broiled swordfish, spinach salad, pasta, Brie cheese with apple slices, and a good white wine awaited them.

It was Connor's turn to cook.

* * * * * * * * * * * * *

"... Target acquisition. Probability is high. We have target acquisition. Probability is high." The audio from the U.S. Space Command at Peterson Air Force Base in Colorado hissed into the White House Situation Room. The President watched as a blip materialized on a wall screen, and began to move west across Ohio in a straight line.

The technician caste operated by rote. None of their caste had made creative, quick changes for thousands of years. The technician pilot on the rebel transport could be counted on to follow the flight plan. The Peacemaker had communicated this inflexibility to the military planners attached to the Joint Chiefs of Staff.

"General," the President looked toward the Chairman of the Joint Chiefs, "give the green light."

The Chairman reached for a red phone. He spoke softly into the receiver. "'Knockout' is a go. I repeat, 'Knockout' is a go. Initiate."

* * * * * * * * * * * * * * *

"Fullmaster, your zeromaster cohort awaits you in the fighter bay." The halfmaster bowed.

"Very good."

The ravan fullmaster looked out at the blue-white, hazy heartland that filled the portal as the transport passed over Chicago.

* * * * * * * * * * * * * * *

Connor switched on the broiler and placed the swordfish under the heat. Michelle set the table and uncorked the wine. She turned on the CD. The Bose speakers softly pumped Roberta Flack's "Killing Me Softly" into the room.

* * * * * * * * * * * * * * *

Five hundred miles above the Earth a cluster of bullet-shaped objects orbited together at 19,500 miles per hour.

Termed "Brilliant Pebbles," the interceptors had been developed as an alternative to the technologically hopeless, multilayered "star wars" antimissile system envisioned by President Ronald Reagan in 1983.

The primary mission of Brilliant Pebbles was to protect the continental United States from a limited nuclear attack. Three Brilliant

Pebbles clusters circled the globe. Fifty of the interceptors in each cluster destroyed missiles or enemy satellites by impact. Ten of the interceptors were "specials." Specials were two feet longer—the extra length necessary to accommodate a five-kiloton nuclear warhead.

On a cue from ground-based control, three specials broke away from cluster Alpha and accelerated to 28,000 miles per hour toward the West Coast of the United States. Supercomputers on each interceptor engaged. The projectiles fanned out in a search pattern, seeking a specific target based on parameters uploaded by U.S. Space Command technicians during the previous hour.

* * * * * * * * * * * * * *

"It's almost over Seattle. Where in the hell are the interceptors?" The President's agitation infected the others. "How much time between when the transport arrives on station and when these things attack?"

"Their representative said they will attack immediately." The Chairman of the Joint Chiefs couldn't hide sweat stains blossoming under the armpits of his usually impeccable uniform. "We only have a window of about five minutes. It's going to be close."

* * * * * * * * * * * * * *

Suddenly, first one, and then another of the interceptors darted toward a target framed against the blue-white glow of Earth. The target lumbered along slowly by comparison. A third interceptor followed right behind. The target errupted in a fireball. Then, another. And another.

* * * * * * * * * * * * * *

What happened to the CD? Connor thought to himself. Roberta Flack had stopped in mid-note. He tried a light switch. No luck. He checked out the broiler rack and complained out loud, "Broiler's out. Oven light's off. No power. Fish should still be okay, though."

"What's happening?" Michelle stumbled in blindly from the living room. "Is it a fuse?"

He gazed out the window.

"Nah. Something's zapped the whole area."

"We've got candles. Let's have a candle-light dinner." Michelle suggested in a mischievous voice. "Then, we can make our own music."

Connor smiled back. "It's been awhile. Hope I still remember how."

* * * * * * * * * * * * * *

A cheer roared through the Situation Room. Individuals hugged and pounded each other on the back. Even aides joined in on the celebration.

The Chairman of the Joint Chiefs ignored the commotion. He moved to a communications board and picked up a phone. He listened and then asked, "Any collateral damage?" Again he listened. "Yes…very good. Thank you." He hung up. "Mr. President."

"General?" The President smiled broadly at the head of the briefing table. The cheering quickly stopped. All eyes were on the Chairman.

"Good news, sir. As you know, a nuclear blast causes electromagnetic pulse that destroys unshielded electronic circuitry. EMP was minimal. The power grid in the Pacific Northwest will be out for 24 hours. Some isolated data loss but nothing significant. Detonations occurred over heavy cloud cover at four hundred miles above sea level so were invisible to the naked eye."

"Radiation?"

"Not a problem. Dissipated in the atmosphere. No need for spin control. I'd say the operation was an unqualified success."

"Congratulations, General."

"Thank you, sir."

CHAPTER 24

"Do humans understand the attack was not sanctioned? That we did not intend harm?" Tok glanced sideways at the Peacemaker. The two floated on their backs side-by-side in Tok's chambers.

"Yes, Tok. The President of the United States and other world leaders are convinced our intentions are peaceful. As some humans would say, we are back to square one."

"Do not speak in riddles. Though I now speak English, I still have much to learn. What do you mean by 'square one?'"

"Nothing had been lost, Tok."

"What is the chance of successful negotiations?"

Technicians had set up fans to create a breeze in Tok's private chambers, but all that did was blow the fetid, steaming air about.

"Three times in our history we have negotiated and failed." The Peacemaker reminded the First Wyrul. "I cannot say this time will be different."

"You must succeed. We have nowhere else to go. Our survival is a heavy burden to lay on your shoulders my old friend, but, still, that is where the burden rests."

"The burden is on Wa," the Peacemaker replied.

"Why did you decide to negotiate with a corporation? Why not with a nation-state or with this United Nations?"

"We meditated on that question at length…"

"Meditated? The Council decided to send in the ravans. Why meditate at all?"

"Tok, just as the ravans develop plans to wage war, wawrens develop plans to wage peace. It is our way."

"Yes. But tell me, why a corporation?"

"On other occasions, wawrens first learned to communicate with sentient life and then approached the planet's leader. That was not possible this time because the planet has no world leader or organization. The United Nations is not really united. That is why we plan to approach a large corporation. You and I discussed this idea a long time ago after the blue planet had first been discovered. A large corporation has a chief executive officer with whom we can negotiate. Many of these officers are more powerful than rulers of individual nation-states. These corporations also have powerful ruling boards."

"Ruling boards? Like our Council of Wyruls?"

"Yes." The Peacemaker nodded. "It was difficult to find the right corporation. We eventually found a corporation chartered in the nation-state of Japan, a company called Mitsubishi. It is the largest of Japanese trading companies.

"Why pick a corporation in Japan? Why not one in this United States?

"There are two reasons we picked Japan. First, Japan is an economic center of power that rivals the United States. Second, the Japanese constitution—a collection of governmental policies—specifically renounces the use of force. Japan knows the pain of nuclear fire. Two of their cities were destroyed by atomic bombs during the last planetary conflagration. The Japanese are pacifists."

"Why did you choose Mitsubishi?"

"Mitsubishi has annual sales greater than the economic output of most nation-states. It is one of the ten largest economic entities on the blue planet and has a presence across the blue planet. As a trading company, its officers are used to negotiating with individuals from different cultures. Mitsubishi is well-suited to represent Earth."

Tok wasn't sure what the Peacemaker meant by 'sales' but the explanation sounded convincing. "Very well, then. How will you proceed?"

"We will contact Toshihiro Suzuki, Mitsubishi's chief executive. I will invite him to act as Earth's negotiator. I will seek neutral ground for the actual negotiations."

"Why not meet in Japan?"

"Earth people are jealous. We must avoid the pettiness associated with sovereign territory. Therefore, we will determine a secure meeting place after contacting Toshihiro Suzuki. At present, we are discussing different options for making first contact. We may use an old technology, holographic projection."

"I wish you the best, Peacemaker."

"I serve Wa to the best of my abilities."

✳ ✳ ✳ ✳ ✳ ✳ ✳ ✳ ✳ ✳ ✳ ✳ ✳ ✳

Word of the extraterrestrial visitation drove global financial markets into profit taking. The markets plunged in free fall. The New York, London, Tokyo, and Moscow stock exchanges were closed until more information about Arkadian intentions became available.

On a humid mid-August evening, Toshihiro Suzuki, chief executive officer of the Mitsubishi Trading Corporation strolled toward the elegant Mitsubishi Club. His personal secretary, Hiroshi Akai, John Cole's friend of 30 years, accompanied him. The plush Mitsubishi Club, open only to Board members and high-ranking Mitsubishi officials, was located atop the 11-story Mitsubishi Building in the Marunouchi District in Tokyo. The men entered the building, and Akai ordered the elevator operator to take them to the top floor.

"Akai-*san*."

"*Hai*, Suzuki-*san*."

"Please speak English. Do you think the aliens are really going to negotiate when they arrive?" Suzuki practiced English with Akai whenever possible.

"I do not know. I cannot say which is stranger, the arrival of the aliens or their request to talk with you."

The men left the elevator and entered the private club. They ordered yakitori, sake, and beer. The room glowed with the reflection of candlelight off hardwood paneling. White-coated waiters moved soundlessly over plush red carpet. A blue haze of cigarette smoke obscured the track lighting.

"Business is hurt, Akai-*san*. People wait to see what will happen. They stay close to their families."

"Yes, Suzuki-*san*." Hiroshi Akai replied tentatively. He felt guilty. His family waited for him in Chiba-City, a two-hour commute by train from where the men sat. A loyal Japanese employee, Hiroshi had stayed late to drink with the boss.

Suzuki switched to Japanese to talk about the Nagoya Dragons, his favorite professional baseball team. Talking about baseball when the future of Humankind might rest on his shoulders served as a distraction. The executive was clearly preoccupied.

Hiroshi listened, then became transfixed—first in disbelief, then in horror—at something odd happening just beyond Suzuki's shoulder. A table fell over as three older executives scrambled for the door.

"Suzuki-*san*!" Hiroshi cried and pointed.

A flicker of light fully materialized in the dimness of the club. The Peacemaker appeared just a few paces from the men. He bowed perfectly and, in flawless Japanese, greeted Toshihiro Suzuki and Hiroshi Akai by name in the traditional way. Suzuki and Akai stood and bowed. The men fumbled for their *meishi*, the business cards without which a correct introduction could not be completed in Japanese life.

They then stopped realizing the futility and silliness of this response. A holograph cannot accept a card.

The Peacemaker stood three heads taller than both men. He wore his white robes of office with a white cape. The yellow crystal forehorn complemented the natural yellow of his eyes. His sidehorns spiked upward on the side of his head. Golden hair trailed in three thick braids down his back to the floor.

"I am the Peacemaker. I apologize for this intrusion but must request an audience with Toshihiro Suzuki, Chief Executive Officer of the Mitsubishi Trading Company. The purpose of this meeting will be to conduct negotiations affecting the future of Arkadians and humans. Time is of the essence. I will arrive on the surface of the blue planet within fifteen of your days ready to begin negotiating and I need landing coordinates. I ask that the negotiation site be as neutral and secure as possible and that Dylan Simpson-Cole be present to greet me."

In a halting, shocked way, the men tried to reply then realized a holograph cannot hear or respond anymore than it can accept a business card.

The Peacemaker's image flickered and abruptly disappeared.

"I know about that boy," Hiroshi Akai uttered after the apparition vanished. "I know his father. John Cole and I worked with the Beheiren back in 1968. He and I are still friends. We have corresponded through the years. What an incredible coincidence." Thinking of John Cole, Akai had an inspiration.

"I know a perfect place to negotiate, Suzuki-*san*." He told his boss about the Greek Orthodox Academy of Crete.

Suzuki listened carefully and nodded in agreement. Later that afternoon, he secured permission from the Bishop in Kolympari, then held a press conference.

✶ ✶ ✶ ✶ ✶ ✶ ✶ ✶ ✶ ✶ ✶ ✶ ✶ ✶

The next day, Chuck Cole analyzed a plot of the Hive's last known position at his desk. The starship had just passed Mars. Chuck decided to leave immediately for Crete to join the scientific community that would assemble there. He wanted to witness extraterrestrial life first hand before he died.

Annie, Dylan, and Cole cut their camping trip short after hearing the news reports of the Peacemaker's holographic visitation on Dylan's transistor radio and the subsequent decision to hold negotiations at the Greek Orthodox Academy of Crete.

"What a great trip." John rustled his son's hair in the living room of Annie's condominium.

Instead of his customary snarl, Dylan smiled. The camping trip had been more fun than he had anticipated. Still quick to tire a week after his ordeal, Dylan excused himself and went to bed. Annie and Cole cuddled on the couch to watch Jay Leno tell alien jokes on late-night TV. The phone rang.

After a rapid-fire conversation in Greek, Cole returned to stand in front of Annie.

"John, who was that at this hour? Everything okay?"

"It was the Bishop. I've got to get back. They need English translators."

"Oh, John. Why can't those damn aliens leave us alone! I was hoping with Dylan well that all this was behind us."

"Sorry, honey, what can I say? It's not over. There's one more thing."

"What's that?"

"The alien negotiator wants Dylan there."

"No." Annie said firmly. "He's been through enough. There's no way he's going. For Christ's sake, he just left the hospital! We don't know what's going to happen over there. Dylan's done enough."

"We've no choice," John replied. "He's been requested. He has to be there. And I want you there too. We all need to stay together."

*   *   *   *   *   *   *   *   *   *   *   *   *   *

The approaching Hive now appeared as a pearl button glowing in the night sky. The invasion armada had rejoined the Hive as it approached Earth. One of the transports had re-launched, this time with the Peacemaker and a technician pilot as its sole passengers. The transport soon orbited the Earth.

Three more Brilliant Pebble interceptors split out from cluster Alpha to shadow the transport. U.S. Space Command technicians waited tensely at computer terminals.

Connor and Michelle met John, Annie, Dylan and Chuck at the Greek Orthodox Academy. Michelle was on the biggest story of her life. Connor took vacation leave from the college.

Not to be left out, Shirley also came to Crete officially to serve as the Reverend Stringer's assistant, unofficially to be close to her family. Stringer, along with several other representatives from the clergy, was allowed to attend in order to garner support from the religious community for whatever lay ahead.

Cole had barely settled his family into the guest quarters when the Mitsubishi delegation arrived.

"Hiroshi-*san*." John called out to his friend as the Japanese contingent moved through the Academy's modest receiving area.

"John-*san*," Hiroshi smiled in return. "Who would have thought we would meet again like this? Please allow me to introduce you to my employer, Mr. Toshihiro Suzuki."

The men exchanged a cursory and respectful greeting. After a polite interval, Cole turned to his old friend.

"We always had a penchant for trouble, Hiroshi-*san*," Cole said with a laugh. "All those years of writing, and now we finally meet once again. Come on, let's get you settled. We have a lot to talk about before tomorrow."

But neither Hiroshi nor John had time to visit that night. Delegations and advisors flooded island. Suzuki was oblivious to all attempts to brief him. That night and all the next day he meditated alone. He brooked no interference.

A tent city formed outside the Academy's boundaries. Leaders of the world's largest countries, denied by the Peacemaker a place in the negotiations for the future of the planet, formed an unofficial welcoming party. And they slept in tents.

As the night darkened, a crushing apprehension descended on the gathered community of scientists, diplomats, and journalists. Almost everyone drifted quietly to his or her own quarters. Suzuki slept. The next day would be the most important of his life and in the lives of all other humans, present and future.

Cole got away from the crush of his duties long enough to walk over to the Academy's guest quarters to look for Annie and Dylan. All members of Cole's family had received special consideration. Dylan slept in a bed while the presidents of the United States and the Russian Republic slept on cots. Cole had just made it to the path along the beach leading to the guest quarters when a voice called out.

"Johnny? Johnny, is that you? I was hoping I'd find you." Shirley Cole moved out of the shadows to intercept her eldest.

"Hi Mom," Cole replied simply, "Annie said you'd be coming."

"I know you're busy," Shirley stated without preamble. "But can we talk for a while? My, your hair is pretty."

"Huh? Yeah. Glad you like it. I was just heading to find Annie and Dylan. But, sure, we can talk. In fact, I've wanted to talk with you for a while now. Let's walk down to the water."

"This is a beautiful place, Johnny," Shirley said, waddling alongside her tall, thin son. "I can see why you like it here."

"The Academy saved my life," Cole said quietly, but without the edge that had characterized most of his past conversations with his mother. "If it wasn't for this place, I'd be dead."

"It's not what I wanted for you, you know that," she said.

"I had to give up a lot to stay here. Annie and Dylan gave up a lot too. I missed watching my boy grow up. I missed the life Annie and I could have had. But I didn't have a choice. I had to find a way out of what I was lost in." He cast a sideways glance at Shirley. "There's no way I could take the chance of doing to my child what you did to me."

John stopped as they reached the end of the path and looked at his mother. Waves crashed on the beach behind them. "It took me years to remember what you did to me, to dig down and find the source of my unhappiness. Here, at the Academy, it came back to me. At first, in flashes. Then, the whole thing." His voice started to break as tears welled uncontrollably. "A word here, a picture there. Terror I couldn't escape. The terror of a small child. A child beaten. By a large, angry woman, not a mother."

Shirley turned toward Cole, her face pale in the moonlight. She reached out to him. Reminded of the dream, he jerked away.

"I've prayed every night for forgiveness," she said, "You were so tiny. How could you remember? Satan is a powerful adversary. I have fought against him for years."

"Satan didn't make you beat me. Why did you? Was I so terrible? Why didn't you love me? Why didn't Dad stop you?"

"No, no." Shirley gasped. Tears streaking down her cheeks formed silver trails in the moonlight. "You were wonderful, such a beautiful, bright little boy. And your father didn't know. At least if he did, he didn't say anything. He was always so strangely quiet around unpleasantness. It was me. I just wanted you to be perfect. Sometimes I'd get so mad. At you, at the world, maybe at myself. I couldn't seem to stop. Sometimes you'd just start crying and I couldn't get you to stop. Oh, Johnny, I've prayed for forgiveness. I prayed you wouldn't remember."

Cole sank to his knees in the sand and heaved an exhausted sigh. Shirley did the same and then cradled him.

"What made you stop?" Cole asked finally.

"It was a nightmare," she said trying to catch her breath. "I was so scared. I was too afraid to tell anyone. One day, I thought I really hurt you. I hit you with…with my fist. You stopped crying. You just lay there. Your nose was bleeding. I just fell to my knees right there. I begged you to forgive me. I begged the Lord to help me, to take this curse away from me. I've walked in the way of the Lord ever since."

"That explains some things I've been wondering about."

After a moment of silence, the two stood and started to walk up the beach.

"Bishop Papaderos told me I couldn't heal until I confronted you. I never thought I'd never be able to, though. My sanity—my peace of mind—had become too important to me to risk. It's more important than anything. Well, just about anything." Cole stopped, turning to face her. "Still, if we get through this thing with the aliens, if we do have a future, I want to come home. I want to make a life with my family, with Annie and with Dylan. I want to be part of your life too. We can finish this together. I think we can do that if you don't hide behind Jesus."

Shirley paused, "I thought Connor was a devil; then I thought Dylan was a devil. I was wrong about Connor and wrong about Dylan. The Reverend Stringer disagrees with me about Dylan, of course. He is not a bad man, John, and he is right about many things. But not about Dylan. The Lord must love my grandson a lot. He gave him an important job to do. Dylan brought you back to me and I don't want to lose that. I want you home too, Johnny. I'll do whatever it takes."

Cole took a deep breath, leaned over, and kissed his mother's cheek.

* * * * * * * * * * * * * *

The Arkadian shuttle dropped down through the atmosphere in the early morning on September 2, 1998. Tracking radars followed the Peacemaker to 50,000 feet. From there, his passage received escort from a wing of F-15 fighters. The jets locked on radar-guided sparrow air-to-air missiles. Pilots couldn't find an infrared signature anywhere on the craft for their sidewinders.

The shuttle floated over the countryside of Greece as a rising sun bathed the fields in a golden glow. The Peacemaker looked out at a pastoral setting: farms, olive orchards, and open fields.

Two Apache gunships replaced the fighter jets, clattering up on both sides of the shuttle. Thirty-millimeter chain guns on the gunships tracked the small, unmarked, silver craft as it began to flutter down like an autumn leaf. The shuttle settled on the middle of the great lawn in front of the white washed main building of the Greek Orthodox Academy of Crete.

A crowd of political, religious, and business leaders huddled a respectful distance around the craft. The Bishop forbade any and all weapons on the Academy grounds. But a laser painted the shuttle from a hilltop, ready to guide in hellfire missiles from the Apaches. Thousands of miles away, U.S. Space Command technicians continued nervously to track the transport.

The shuttle shimmered in the light of early morning. Ten long minutes passed. A panel slid open and the Peacemaker stepped out. The crowd gasped at his demon-like appearance.

A string quartet started to play a national anthem selected by lottery. It was the *Marseillaise*.

Dylan Simpson-Cole stepped forward from the circling crowd. The Peacemaker had insisted that Dylan be the first human to greet him. The teenager walked alone to the shuttle. Cameras sent the image of the first exchange between a human and extraterrestrial to billions of viewers around the globe. After the first gasp, the several hundred diplomats, members of the media, and functionaries in the inner perimeter stood mute, anxiously waiting.

Watching, Connor thought of himself in Chicago, so long ago, when he was about Dylan's age.

Dylan did exactly as instructed. He stopped three paces in front of the Peacemaker. The alien loomed over him.

"*Abomination!*"

With that accusation, a figure dramatically emerged from the crowd, pointed at Dylan and howled: "Child come here. Move away from Satan unless you are his spawn. Move away from him, unless you are his *tool!*"

Dylan stared at the Peacemaker's sidehorns and yellow eyes.

Cameras rotated to the hysterical vision of the Reverend Isaiah Marcus Stringer resplendent in his gray tailored suit with a purple tie, matching handkerchief and cowboy boots, diamond studs and a tie pin.

No one moved.

Stringer turned to the crowd and boomed in his practiced voice, "What you see before you is evil! Pure, unbridled evil! Open your eyes. Open your souls before it is too late. Is that creature not Satan? Is that child not welcoming his father? Just look at it! Is that not a demon?" He pointed at Dylan, then at the Peacemaker.

Connor wanted to leap to his nephew's defense. He wanted to put an end to the sanctimonious monster that was the Reverend Stringer. He wanted to embarrass, humiliate, and to crush the cartoon preacher once and for all. But he didn't know what to say or what to do. *The alien does look demonic. Dylan was possessed, no question of it. What's happening? What's really going on here? Why is that creature really here?* Connor felt faint and out-of-body and, in a perverse way, as he felt as though he should be the center of attention rather than Stringer, Dylan, and the alien. Connor thought of his special purpose. Unaccountably, he thought of Eldon Moss. Who or what was Eldon Moss? Why was he thinking of him?

The crowd began to rustle. Panic began to build. Some people started to back away…

"*No!*"

The crowd recoiled at Shirley Cole's shout.

"Isaiah, you leave my grandson alone. You leave that creature alone. Our church is about love, forgiveness and acceptance, not about pride. Proverbs 16:18, "Pride goes before destruction and a haughty spirit before a fall." You have been prideful and wrong. Wrong about my grandson, wrong about that alien, wrong about a lot of things. You are also being very rude. This poor thing is our guest. Give it up and let it go."

Security guards arrived before Shirley could chide Stringer further. The guards gently but firmly led him away. The reverend appeared strangely shrunken.

Shirley called out to Dylan, who stood just a few steps away. "Go ahead, Dylan. Your Grandmother loves you. Make us all proud."

The Peacemaker never took his eyes off Dylan, never stopped gazing kindly at the teenager.

"Okay, Grandma." Dylan faced the alien, straightened his shoulders, craned his neck to look up at the Peacemaker and said, in a voice that sounded young and squeaky in the somber, clear morning air, "Hello... Welcome to Earth."

A bird chirped.

"Come closer, Dylan." The Peacemaker's soft, baritone voice sounded perfect to Dylan's ears even though his appearance was something else. *This guy's taller than a pro basketball player. It's got horns. What's that thing sticking out of his forehead? Are those claws? Looks like he's wearing a dirty white bathrobe with a cape. And what's he wearing over his face? And those gills, that blond hair. Wow.*

"Okay." Dylan shuffled a few steps closer. *Whew! Smells like mildew.*

The Peacemaker adjusted the crude filter a techician had fit over his mouth and nose. He doubted the device offered much protection and hoped no deadly bacteria lurked. The wizards had assured him the planet's atmosphere was breathable. He took his first truly deep breath, and promptly staggered collapsing forward into Dylan's arms.

Dylan fell backward as he supported the head and torso of the much larger alien. A gasp and a few screams exploded from the overwrought crowd. The wawren fullmaster kneeled on the grass, then slowly rose to standing position. He shook his head.

"You okay?"

The Peacemaker nodded. "Yes, Dylan. I am okay. I did not anticipate the richness of your atmosphere."

"Sure you're okay? There's gotta be a doctor here somewhere. Want me to get one?"

"I am truly okay. How are you? We wawrens did not mean to hurt you. Your life was not in danger, but we could not be sure of other damage. You helped us to communicate. Are you fully recovered?"

"Yeah. I mean, yes."

"Will you accept my apology on behalf of all wawrens? I hope you will."

"Yeah, sure. No problem. I don't really remember much of what happened. Though, my mom says it was pretty intense."

The Peacemaker looked down at the young man with kind eyes.

"Dylan, I brought you a gift." From the depths of his robe the Peacemaker retracted the bejeweled speaker's wand. "This is yours. The wyruls must learn new ways. Earth ways."

"Hey… Thanks." Dylan took the wand. Then, looked back up at the Peacemaker.

"Dylan, Suzuki-*san* and I will negotiate shortly. I want you to join us. We will speak Japanese, but I can do a simultaneous telepathic translation for you. I do not expect you to participate. Though I may ask you questions about humans from time to time."

Dylan thought, *What's he talking about?* then choked out, "Sure but why me?"

"Young people represent the future, Dylan. And it is about the future that we negotiate."

The two looked at each other. Not a sound could be heard from the crowd.

"Dylan?"

"Yeah...I mean, yes."

"I wish to meet the rest of your family. Would that be possible?" He nodded respectfully toward Shirley.

Annie, John, Chuck, and Connor were soon gathered up. Michelle trotted up breathlessly through the crowd from another direction.

The crowd waited, clustered around the shuttle on the great lawn. A few now whispered to one another.

The Peacemaker studied the Coles, Annie, and Connor. *An interesting assortment of humans. One of them appears ill. I wonder what has sickened him?* With those thoughts, he adjusted his filter and invited his guests into the shuttle.

The world waited an hour while Dylan's family visited with the wawren fullmaster. The spotter and gunship stood down. The U.S. Space Command continued to track the orbiting transport.

Negotiations began that afternoon. Toshihiro Suzuki wore the corporate uniform of Japan-a navy blue suit, white shirt, black wingtips, and a silk tie. He had wrapped a ceremonial scarf, blessed by a Shinto priest that morning, around his neck. Suzuki, his aide Hiroshi Akai, Dylan, and the Peacemaker disappeared into the shuttle.

The Peacemaker had politely spurned an offer to meet in a well-appointed conference room within the Academy indicating a need to have a part of Arkadia near him while he negotiated its future. Suzuki left the shuttle occasionally to consult with the Security Council of the United Nations.

Suzuki and the Peacemaker talked a long time. They reappeared shortly before midnight, Suzuki, Akai, and Dylan with weary smiles; the Peacemaker with the Shinto scarf draped about his neck.

CHAPTER 25

Connor walked the beach that night, much as John and Shirley had done the night before. Lost in thought and unsettled from the day's events, he hadn't noticed the approaching figure until he was almost upon him.

"Hey, Connor."

Connor looked up. Eldon Moss. The trickster grinned at him from just a few feet away. Connor uttered, "It's you. And you haven't aged a day. Wonder why I'm not surprised?"

"Not going to try and grab me again are ya?" Eldon Moss replied.

"Nah." Then it dawned on him. "I always figured you were just a dream or a hallucination. You always seemed to sneak up on me when I was waking up or falling asleep or sick from fever. You're real though, aren't you? I know I'm awake this time and I'm sure not sick."

"Yup. I'm real. Just as real as you."

"I don't understand. Who are you? Don't disappear this time without telling me."

"I won't, but you better listen close. I ain't going to repeat myself."

"I'm listening."

"I talked with you over the years for selfish reasons, Connor. You were picked as a fella to observe. Wanted to know how you'd react to conflict. I've been particularly trying to figger out why humans fight all the confound time. Been trying to see if humans could even change your ways."

"What do you mean by selfish reasons? Why do you say humans? What are you?"

Eldon Moss grinned. "You always had trouble with the long range of things. So, you want to know what I am, huh? I'll tell you, but first a question—how's now compare to getting your brains bashed in Chicago back in 1968?"

Connor didn't even have to pause to contemplate. "Looks like people are pulling together. We didn't do that too well back in 1968."

"Why are folks pulling together now, son?"

"It's happening because we're afraid of the consequences. We're afraid of being blown away by the aliens. The aliens have their own reason to avoid war."

"Phooey. Real peace is about *trust*, son. Not fear. There's trust now 'cause the Arkadians want the same things you do and could a had all along. These needs were communicated in an honest way, and you're both willing to take a chance. People need each other, whoever they are, where ever they be from."

Connor looked thoughtful.

"You've confused me over the years, and Lord, there's been a ton of 'em. You was so full of vinegar back in '68. I liked what happened in Chicago, son. You practiced what you were preaching. There was fire in your strut. You took good risks. Then you got boring. That mid-life crisis of yours might have been good if there had been some thought and work behind it. You always got to work for the good stuff. Got to take chances. It ain't enough to just go through a phase.

"Looks like you and other humans are coming around, though. Looks like you're finally ready for the Tenets of Wa. Hope it sticks though I don't know why it should. Your type sure do seem to enjoy fighting. So do them Arkadians. Still, I ain't going to recommend that you all be destroyed."

"Tenets of Wa? My type? Destroyed? What are you talking about? How do you know about the aliens? Why would the aliens destroy us? Are you one of them?"

"You don't understand. We would have destroyed them also." Eldon Moss no longer looked quite so old or folksy. A hint of a halo glowed around his entire body.

"You been an assignment of mine, son. My job's been to report to my bosses about you, your family, and your world in general since the beginning of your universe. By the way, your suspicions were correct. I am not human."

Eldon Moss continued to change. Globs of color flashed through his glowing body. "As a matter of fact, I'm ageless, formless, and from your three-dimensional perspective, omnipresent and omnipotent. I hope that is not too much to take in.

"What?"

The colors now overwhelmed the shape of Eldon Moss. A deeper voice, a rich bass, now emanated from a dazzling kaleidoscope of color with the moonlit ocean as its backdrop.

"No, Connor. I am not God nor am I an angel. That is what you were thinking, isn't it? Nor am I a devil or an Antichrist, a notion that may have played at the outer edges of your consciousness at times. I am intelligent life, like a human or an Arkadian."

"Where do you come from?" Connor was dazed.

"I exist in a higher dimension, a place you may refer to as hyperspace. I know your thoughts, your past, your future. You cannot know mine. That is the nature of relationships between higher and lower dimensional life forms."

"I don't understand… why would living in another dimension make you more powerful than humans?"

"Consider how two-dimensional creatures living in a flat universe called 'Flatland' might appear to you. A simple line that you, as a three-dimensional creature, could simply step over would stop them.

Connor nodded thoughtfully.

"Your world was selected for study. *You* were specifically chosen. I had to be careful about our conversations, though. I first met you in a dream when you were a child but we first talked when you helped me with my groceries. I had to set up all our meetings so only you saw me. That was difficult but necessary. It was also important that you attribute our talks to fever, bad lighting, to dreams, or even to steam from a faucet. Otherwise, who knows what might have happened? You could have been committed to one of your mental institutions. I certainly did not want that. A competent ethnographer—and I am one—does not unduly influence the culture or the lives of those being studied."

"I still don't understand where you're from."

"As I told you, I am not from a reality you can understand. I am from a higher dimension that transcends the three-dimensional existence that you know."

Connor appeared unconvinced.

"Think of yourself and other humans as intelligent gold fish in a small garden pond. You have a fair understanding of the watery environment of the small pond in which you swim—its flora, fauna, and other characteristics. Sunlight streams downward through the water, so you have an inkling of a greater reality outside your little pond. Are you with me so far?"

"Yeah…"

"But your understanding of that greater reality is limited by your technology and by your capabilities. You may suspect, but do not know for certain the characteristics of the garden in which your pond resides. You definitely have no conception of the surrounding neighborhood, the city, the state, the country, the planet, or of the greater universe outside your garden.

"Hyperdimensional beings are to humans what you would be to the gold fish I have described. Consider the control you have over the gold fish in your garden pond. You can understand them to a much greater degree than they can understand you. Your technology and powers would appear as magic to these intelligent gold fish just as my technology and powers appear magical to you."

Connor shook his head. "Okay. I can buy that you're from a higher dimension, and that you're powerful, but why study humans? And why choose me as a guinea pig? And what's this all about being destroyed?"

"Occasionally, the gold fish flop out of the pond. When that occurs we send an ethnographer to conduct a thorough risk assessment. We will gladly share our dimension. But it is still conceivable that a hostile, three-dimensional race might pose a threat to us. In your terms, it would be as though the gold fish developed teeth, left the pond, and began to attack you in your garden. We study any life, from any universe, that enters our domain. If we feel there is a risk to our dimension, we promptly destroy the gold fish without harming the other flora and fauna of the pond. Humans came close to destruction. But it appears that you are much more a threat to yourselves than you ever will be to us."

"How did you find out about us? Human beings have never visited a higher dimension."

"The Arkadians developed hyperdrive and used it extensively, first for their robotic searchers, then for their starship. They penetrated hyperspace, our dimension. They trespassed without understanding hyperspace and without understanding us."

"You would have destroyed Earth?"

"Not Earth, Connor. Just humans. Their past, present and, of course, future would have been erradicated within one universe. We are quite thorough."

"There is more than one universe?"

"Yes. Reality is more marvelous, more complex than you can imagine. There is an infinite number of universes within your dimensional plane, many almost identical to the one inhabited by you."

"How old are you?"

"Time does not have the same meaning for me as it does for you. I am as old as the beginning of your time and as young as a new born babe."

"Why are you telling me all this?"

"My work is almost finished. Soon I will finish my report and will return home. I thought you should know."

"Can you tell me…"

"Connor, I must go. Listen to your past, Connor. Make friends with your future. It is a bright one. Thank you for your help." With that, the colors faded from view.

"Wait! Don't go. I need to know. Are you the special purpose I've thought about all my life?"

The night air shimmered.

Connor waited briefly, slowly shook his head, and turned to walk back. Eldon Moss's smiling face floated less than five inches from his. Connor yelped and stumbled back.

"The answer to your question is 'no.' Interacting with me was not your special purpose. It just was. You have my best wishes, Connor. Goodbye."

The face dissolved into flashing red and green colors. The colors rose in the night air, expanded and coalesced into a circular disc while still flashing, exactly like many first-hand accounts of UFOs, and spun away in an iridescent flash.

* * * * * * * * * * * * * *

A lazy, early September afternoon passed uneventfully in the Pacific Northwest.

Three months after that uneventful day, the Hive orbited Earth by invitation, a vital part of human and Arkadian existence. With its reconditioning and repair under way, it circled the planet alongside Luna.

As a new moon of Earth, the Hive was christened "Tirlol," a name vaguely recalled in wawren lore as the moon of Arkadia. Tirlol became sovereign territory of a new nation-state populated by Arkadians and a few enterprising, curious humans. Arkadia joined Russia, China, the United States, France, and Great Britain as a sixth member of the permanent United Nations Security Council.

A strict quarantine would keep the vermin in the Hive Sea from Earth while Arkadian wizards and human scientists developed and carried out eradication schemes. Tirlol's perverse ecology would ultimately be restored and maintained with benign creatures. The presence of the new moon did not greatly affect Earth tides, because the hollowed sphere had only a fraction of Luna's mass.

The negotiated agreement gave Arkadians vast tracts of the Pacific Ocean. Arkadians and humans, working together, would learn to better use the aquatic gifts that give the blue planet its description. In time, a "blue revolution" using aquaculture technology would end all hunger on Earth.

Arkadian technology and knowledge gleaned from Tirlol and its data banks would soon lead humans to the stars. With access to a galaxy rich in resources, battling over scarce resources at home would soon become unnecessary.

The wawren success at negotiations, together with the deaths of the ravan fullmaster and Harn, broke the power of the ravan caste. Arkadian desire for a permanent home and interesting new duties for the ravans took priority and, in time, became a habit. The ravan caste would became known as the Peacekeepers and would assume responsibility for peacekeeping missions at the direction of the United Nations Security Council. This included stopping planetary drug traffic and disarming those who did not practice the Tenets of Wa. Their allocation would steadily drop as reasons for planetary strife—overcrowding, hunger, economic and social inequality—steadily lessened.

Information from the Hive's, now Tirlol's, data banks—combined with the creativity, curiosity, and vigor of an Earth scientific community weaned from military projects—would also end a host of Earth plagues, including all forms of cancer, diabetes, AIDS, and the common cold. Humans and Arkadians suprisingly had no difficulty adjusting to one another's bacteria and viruses.

Problems and squabbles continued. But the future held the promise of solutions, not the threat of holocaust.

"We can learn to live together. Wa is not easy. But it is just as easy, if not easier, to work for harmony than for discord," the Peacemaker said to Hiroshi Akai shortly after their first meeting at the Academy. "The Tenets of Wa are, after all, but a foundation upon which to build a lasting home."

In time, the negotiated agreement gave the Arkadians the new home for which they had searched, and a future different from the one they otherwise would have faced.

It did the same thing for humans.

＊　＊　＊　＊　＊　＊　＊　＊　＊　＊　＊　＊　＊　＊

On a warm November night, Cole sat once more in his spot, the alcove above the Aegean Sea. Annie and Dylan slept back in his sparse quarters in the Academy's rectory. He ran his hand through shoulder-length white hair and looked out at the sea with wonder. He thought back over the tumult of the past three months. It had been the best three months of his life.

Annie accepted his proposal of marriage. Dylan, as tall as his dad, stood as best man at an October wedding officiated by the Bishop. Cole's resignation from the Academy saddened the Bishop, but he knew his friend needed to move on. The Simpson-Coles planned to leave for the States in two weeks.

Dylan never tired of the tutoring he received in Crete in lieu of his first term of community college. The Peacemaker was an expert mentor with much experience in teaching young people. When not engaged in meetings with world leaders at the Academy or attending to myriad details befitting his role as the Arkadian ambassador, the Peacemaker enjoyed sharing his wisdom with the young human. The Peacemaker and Dylan Simpson-Cole would continue their special relationship until the Peacemaker's death from a wasting disease in the year 2002.

Cole's work continued. John Cole became the first human accepted into the wawren caste, the first to receive the honor of becoming a high priest of Wa. Dylan returned the maser crystal fragment found by Michelle forty years before in the Grand Canyon to his father. Cole wore the Dylan Crystal over his white robes with pride. He would help to fashion a future of abundance and joy for Arkadian tads and human children. Annie returned to banking and joined in the economic upturn that swelled into the foreseeable future.

Cole chuckled as he recalled the fax received just that morning. For the past couple months, Michelle had been experiencing "female problems." Was it menopause? Cancer? No, thankfully. Turned out Mickie was pregnant.

Michelle and Connor looked forward to the birth of a child conceived the night the lights went out. Connor returned to his job at the community college. Michelle's first-hand accounts of the Arkadian visitation gained her a worldwide readership and accelerated her already successful career as a journalist.

In time, the birth and rearing of a daughter with blonde hair and an iron will defined the sense of purpose and "special meaning" for which Connor had searched all his life. Michelle's financial acumen made them rich.

Things are going better with Mom…glad we finally started to communicate. Glad she's getting herself weaned from Stringer. Cole watched a shooting star sparkle into nothingness. *There's really nothing more I could wish for…*

Cole and Shirley would continue to talk. She would eventually open a small bookkeeping business from an office in her home. Her dependence on the Reverend Isaiah Marcus Stringer and her weight would moderate along with her life in general. She redirected some of her tithes from the First Church of Jesus Christ Washed in the Blood of the Lamb to a scholarship program at Connor's college.

Stringer returned to the original Seattle-area congregation where his work had begun. Shirley joined one hundred of the faithful to hear the Reverend Stringer's gentler, though still apocalyptic, message every Sunday.

He now held out for the millennium, the year 2000, as the time when Jesus would appear, emerge victorious at Armageddon, oversee a thousand years of peace on Earth, and lead true believers to heaven. Of course, he would again be frustrated.

Thousands of miles away from where Cole sat under the stars, Stringer and Shirley sipped tea in the living room of the Cole family homestead.

"I know I was fooled by Dylan. But, the events still fit prophesy. Remember, the Apostle Paul warned about deception in the last days. There have been times of tribulation and 'signs and lying wonders.' Dylan is a good example of this; so are these Arkadians. The good book speaks of the world worshipping an Antichrist. Could it be this Peacemaker? He certainly looks like a devil. Shirley, what if the true Antichrist lies in wait? Waiting for us to lower our guard?"

"Isaiah, you fret too much. Would you like another cup of tea?"

Cole considered the recent good news for AIDS sufferers. His brother, Chuck, and millions of others would soon be cured of the disease. Chuck now looked forward to a long and fruitful life. Thanks to Arkadian technology, there was a good chance his little brother would one day travel to the Cygnus binary and study the cosmic yo-yo first hand.

Cole stared into the depths of the clear night sky. Searching for another shooting star, not sure why. The thick grass felt good against his back. A warm breeze played chimes in the trees behind him.

Luna and Tirlol—the moons of Earth—hung full in the sky before him: one moon, a reminder of the folly of the past, the other representing hope for the future.

✶ ✶ ✶ ✶ ✶ ✶ ✶ ✶ ✶ ✶ ✶ ✶ ✶ ✶

Ethnographer's report (continued)

And so it went. Over hundreds of millions of years Homo Sapiens cycled. Time always healed the Earth; a remnant of the gene pool always survived and redeveloped a high level of technology. Then, the bombs would fall again. The survivors always found sanctuary near water. Eventually, humans stayed next to the water and in it.

Some civilizations had a better understanding of their ancestors and of the cycle than others. This understanding, however, changed nothing.

The human gene pool, buffeted by periodic doses of heavy radiation and ultraviolet rays from holocausts mutated drastically. A primarily aquatic existence selected for characteristics like telepathy to improve communication underwater and the capacity to store and to discharge an electrical charge to stun fish, important to survival during the early part of a cycle. Gill covers, sidehorns, and the forehorn developed. Physical anthropologists at the civilized stage of later cycles never figured out the survival value of the horns but acknowledged that horns sometimes develop in marine mammals.

Catastrophic events periodically occurred: asteroid impacts, massive quakes, and ice ages. A small comet even once hit the planet. Still, enough of the human gene pool survived to continue. Continental drift and slowed tectonic plate activity changed the global map significantly. The waters rose and reclaimed more landmass, accelerating the evolution of aquatic life.

Eventually this intelligent, mammalian life no longer resembled Homo Sapiens save for bipedalism, larger but still comparable stature, two arms and legs, and comparable brain size. The passage of hundreds of millions of years and periodic nuclear wars wiped out all evidence of human civilization. Arkadians did not, and could not, know their ancestors were human or that Arkadia had once been known as Earth and humans had no way of predicting their physical transformation into an aquatic, war-torn future.

By decree of the Council of Wyruls, records of Arkadia had been purged when the Hive left the home system; consequently, the blue planet's location in space was unknown to the star travelers. They had no way of knowing they had found their way home. The notion that "straddling" through hyperspace also involves travel through time simply would not have occurred to them.

Four billion years of evolution passed between the first global holocaust that killed the Coles, Annie, Dylan and Connor and the launching of the Arkadian Hive to escape a dying sun. Humans, then Arkadians, evolved through cycles of nuclear destruction and regeneration until the last time the bombs fell. That holocaust eradicated all life on the planet and the cycles with it.

But then new possibilities were born.

EPILOGUE: 2003

The millennium arrived without fanfare or miracles. No Antichrist, no Jesus Christ, no Armageddon. Soon thereafter, the Reverend Isaiah Marcus Stringer retired—fully convinced that God works in strange and mysterious ways with particular emphasis on the "mysterious."

✳ ✳ ✳ ✳ ✳ ✳ ✳ ✳ ✳ ✳ ✳ ✳ ✳ ✳ ✳

It was snake eyes on infinitely configured dice that led Arkadians back to their home world four billion years in the past to the time of humans. In a random sequence of straddles, Arkadians had returned to Earth, not unlike a weary traveler stumbling home after being lost in a blizzard. In an infinite cosmos improbable events can and do occur.

In the year 2001, human scientists and Arkadian wizards discovered that straddletravel in a relativistic universe involves travel back in time. They correlated this discovery with an amazing, improbable, but still conclusive set of other discoveries.

Autopsies and chemical analyses showed surprising similarities between humans and Arkadians. Arkadian musculature indicated their species evolved under the stress of one G of gravity. Arkadia had to have been the same size of Earth. Arkadian and human circadian rhythms were comparable and therefore derived from long evolution on a planet with the same rotation around its star; consequently, the similarities between Arkadian and Earth days and years could not be passed off as being an incredible coincidence. Wawren oral tradition spoke of Arkadia having only one moon as did Earth. The clincher, though, was mitochondrial DNA analysis. A team of researchers at the University of Hawaii determined there was a high probability that humans and Arkadians shared a common ancestor.

The time paradox remained. If Arkadians returned to alter circumstances in Earth's past that led to their development, how could they have evolved? How could they even exist? Chuck Cole led the group that solved this problem and validated Einstein's famous equation.

Matter is transformed but never destroyed at the infinite gravity of a black hole. Matter instead cycles through the singularity into a parallel universe. (Early Arkadian wizards had mistakenly discounted the existence of parallel universes.) The latticework of the infinite number of parallel universes created after the Big Bang is stable. The robotic Searchers and the Hive that followed moved through space/time to the same location in the same parallel universe after each straddle.

The bombs fell on a lazy, early September afternoon killing the Coles, Dylan, Connor, Annie, and billions of other humans beginning the cycles of destruction and the evolution toward Arkadia. But that was in another universe, or perhaps in countless others. In fact, an extention of Heisenberg's Uncertainty Principle applied to cosmology after the discovery of parallel universes indicated enough variation exists so that no two universes are ever *exactly* alike.

In at least one universe, whether by an accident of fate or through divine intervention, humans and Arkadians had the opportunity to build a satisfying, prosperous, and peaceful future together.

* * * * * * * * * * * * * *

Ethnographer's report (conclusion)
I recommend that we spare the humans and their descendants who reside in this particular universe and three-dimensional location. They are a contentious lot, but pose a much greater threat to themselves than they ever will to us.

It is unfortunate that conflict between and among parents and children, men and women, husbands and wives, and nation-states is a chronic condition for humans, their ancestors and descendants. When it doesn't have to be.

Respectfully submitted,
Eldon Moss
Ethnographer, Universe 7844491222333

NOTES

There really was a Beheiren that helped members of the United States armed forces during the Vietnam War. The Greek Orthodox Academy of Crete is also real as is the story of its founding. The leaders of these organizations depicted in this book are fictitious. I also took license with descriptions of Crete and the Academy e.g. I don't know if the Academy is on a beach.

The My Lai massacre happened as described though dates were changed slightly. My description possibly understated the atrocities. As far as I know, scouts did not witness the massacre.

Ralph and John Cole both experienced post-traumatic stress disorder (PTSD). This often misunderstood outcome of war claims many victims: the combat veteran who survives one hell only to live in another, and family, friends, and employer or employers who are affected by the veteran's PTSD. Referred to during the wars of the 20th century as "shell shock," "battle fatigue," and PTSD respectively, this condition continues to affect tens of thousands of American combat veterans as well as victims of domestic violence.

Arcadia (not "Arkadia") was once a real place populated by real Arcadians. Two separate Arcadias have existed in human history. The first was a warlike state that fought alongside Macedonia and Thebes about 235 BCE. After Arcadia fell to Rome in 146 BCE, its soldiers served in the armies that extended the Roman Empire. The second was a region in Nova Scotia populated by French colonists during the 18th century. The British and French Arcadians fought continuously. The British eventually deported large numbers of French Arcadians who were forced to wander in search of a new home and eventually ended up in Louisiana.

There is no Metallurgy and Mineralogy Technology Center at the University of Washington.

Human evolution is a controversial topic. The evolutionary pathway outlined in this story is possible, though it is not in the mainstream of anthropological thought. My description was inspired by Elaine Morgan's classic, *Descent of Woman* (Stein and Day, 1972).

Several references support the science part of my science fiction. Five that are particularly good are Herbert Friedman's book *The Astronomer's Universe* (W.W. Norton & Company, 1990); Issac Asimov's classic *The Collapsing Universe* (Walker and Company, 1977); Barry and David Zimmerman's *Why Nothing Can Travel Faster Than Light...* (Contemporary Books, 1993); and Michio Kaku's *Hyperspace* (Oxford University Press, 1994).

Finally, I can't take credit for the term "wa." It is Japanese and means "harmony."

Printed in the United States
20405LVS00004B/180

9 780595 193295